THE LADY TRAVELERS GUIDE TO

Scoundrels

& Other Gentlemen

VICTORIA ALEXANDER

THE LADY TRAVELERS GUIDE TO

Scoundrels
& Other Gentlemen

HQN™

Recycling programs for this product may not exist in your area.

ISBN-13: 978-0-373-80398-9

The Lady Travelers Guide to Scoundrels & Other Gentlemen

Copyright © 2017 by Cheryl Griffin

The publisher acknowledges the copyright holder of the additional work:

The Proper Way to Stop a Wedding (in Seven Days or Less)
Copyright © 2017 by Cheryl Griffin

All rights reserved. Except for use in any review, the reproduction or utilization of this work in whole or in part in any form by any electronic, mechanical or other means, now known or hereinafter invented, including xerography, photocopying and recording, or in any information storage or retrieval system, is forbidden without the written permission of the publisher, HQN Books, 225 Duncan Mill Road, Don Mills, Ontario M3B 3K9, Canada.

This is a work of fiction. Names, characters, places and incidents are either the product of the author's imagination or are used fictitiously, and any resemblance to actual persons, living or dead, business establishments, events or locales is entirely coincidental.

This edition published by arrangement with Harlequin Books S.A.

For questions and comments about the quality of this book, please contact us at CustomerService@Harlequin.com.

® and TM are trademarks of Harlequin Enterprises Limited or its corporate affiliates. Trademarks indicated with ® are registered in the United States Patent and Trademark Office, the Canadian Intellectual Property Office and in other countries.

www.HQNBooks.com

Printed in U.S.A.

CONTENTS

THE LADY TRAVELERS GUIDE TO

Scoundrels

& Other Gentlemen

This book and the Lady Travelers Society is dedicated to those friends and readers who know there is grand adventure to be found in picking up a suitcase and heading out the door or in opening a new book.

CHAPTER ONE

When deciding upon an agency to assist in one's travel preparations, always ask for references from at least three satisfied clients. Without this precautionary step, a lady traveler never knows what might happen and, worse, where it might happen.

—The Lady Travelers Society Guide

London 1889

IT CERTAINLY DID not look like the type of place where genteel, older ladies were bilked out of their life savings. Nonetheless—India Prendergast narrowed her eyes—it was.

India resisted the urge to tap her foot impatiently. She stood second in queue to reach a table set up near the door of one of the smaller lecture rooms in the grand mansion in Bloomsbury that housed the Explorers Club. A number of women chatted near a table bearing refreshments positioned along the wall. Several others had taken seats among the rows of chairs facing a lectern. The stout lady in front of her wore a tall beribboned hat entirely inappropriate for her age and did not seem inclined to hurry, even though a lecture on "What No Lady Traveler Should Leave Home Without" was scheduled to begin shortly. No, the lady ahead of her showed no consideration for the time constraints and chatted blithely with the woman sitting at the table as if there were no one waiting in line behind her.

India wouldn't be here at all if anyone had responded to her letters demanding information as to the whereabouts of her dear cousin, Lady Heloise Snuggs. In spite of the exotic nature of her name—a cross India had long ago learned to bear—she had no desire for travel and did not find the promise of adventure to be found in foreign lands the least bit enticing. She didn't understand why any otherwise sane and sensible woman would want to pursue such foolishness. No, the only thing that had brought her here today was concern verging perilously close to abject fear.

It had been nearly six weeks since India had received so much as a brief note from Heloise, and, even given the inefficiency of postal service outside the empire, it was not at all like her. Indeed, until then, India had received a letter at least twice a week, overflowing with her cousin's delight at the exploration of those places she'd only read about in books. It had long been Heloise's dream to travel the world. When she'd discovered the existence of the Lady Travelers Society and Assistance Agency—far less imposing than anything run by men—it had appeared that dream was now within reach.

The room filled slowly with other ladies, most of whom had obviously passed the age of fifty, just as Heloise had. And, exactly like Heloise, India suspected they all had dreams of exciting exploits in exotic places, no doubt with a handsome, virile stranger by their side. *What utter nonsense.*

While India had been uneasy about Heloise sallying forth three months ago to discover the world beyond England's shores, she couldn't bring herself to express her concerns and dampen her cousin's enthusiasm. She'd never seen Heloise quite that excited. Nonetheless, anything could happen to a lady traveling alone, even if Heloise was accompanied by her maid—the competent, no-nonsense Frenchwoman, Mademoiselle Marquette. Perhaps if India had expressed her concerns…

India firmly pushed the thought aside but failed to dismiss the dreadful apprehension that had weighed on her soul in the last few weeks. She was fairly certain Heloise would not have listened to her anyway. Regardless, she would never forgive herself if anything happened to the older woman. India was not one for frivolous emotion, but Heloise had claimed a place in India's heart from very nearly the moment they'd met.

Some twenty years older than India, Heloise was India's mother's cousin and the only family India had left in the world. She'd given her a home when India's parents had died—taking up the responsibilities of raising an eleven-year-old girl. Heloise had helped fund her continued schooling at the prestigious Miss Bicklesham's Academy for Accomplished Young Ladies, setting aside enough for a respectable dowry for India, should that become necessary. (It hadn't, which did seem for the best.) Very little of what India had observed about men inclined her at all toward chaining herself to one for the rest of her days.

Heloise had come to India's rescue when she was needed, and India would do no less for her now. Besides, the thought of losing her was entirely too much to bear.

At last, the lady in front of her moved off to take a seat, and India stepped forward.

"How may I help you, miss?" The blonde woman sitting at the table smiled up at her.

"I should like to join the Lady Travelers Society,"

India said firmly. It had been the suggestion of her employer, Sir Martin Luckthorne, that the best way to find out the whereabouts of Cousin Heloise might well be to join the society herself.

"How delightful." The blonde beamed. India's distrust wavered slightly in the wake of the woman's genuine smile, which did seem the best part of her. Oh, she was not unattractive, but neither was she especially pretty. Not a woman one would notice on the street one way or another. In that she and India were similar, and the tiniest pang of regret stabbed India at her deception. Still, it couldn't be helped. India returned her smile. The woman appeared close in age to India, as well, something else they had in common. At not quite thirty it was clear they were the youngest in the room. "Do you plan to travel then?"

India hesitated. "My plans are uncertain at the moment."

"Oh." The blonde drew her brows together. "Most of our members join precisely because they wish to plan their future travel."

"I do wish to *plan* my future travel," India lied. "I'm simply not sure exactly *when* the future might arrive."

"That's something else then, isn't it?" The blonde nodded in sympathy. "I understand completely. Some of us do not have the means to wander the world simply because we wish to do so." A determined note sounded in her voice. "However, making preparations for the future is exactly why the Lady Travelers Society was started."

"By experienced travelers I assume?" India asked although she knew full well who the alleged founders of the organization were.

"Oh my, yes." Pride glowed in the other woman's eyes. "Surely you've heard of Sir Charles Blodgett?"

"I'm not certain…"

"He was quite famous for his travels and expeditions and explorations. One of the premier members of the Explorers Club itself. Lady Blodgett lost him ten years ago now I think."

India nodded, not entirely sure if Sir Blodgett had died or had simply been lost in the jungles of some hot, horrid, uncivilized country.

"Let me think, where was I?" The woman's brow furrowed. "Oh yes, I was telling you about the founders of the society—Lady Guinevere Blodgett and her dearest friends, Mrs. Persephone Fitzhew-Wellmore and Mrs. Ophelia Higginbotham. Well, more like sisters really than friends. They were all married to men of adventure and travel, although Sir Charles was the most famous of the lot. The poor dears are all widows now, but they do indeed know a great deal about the rigors of travel and the adventures to be found on a tramp steamer traversing the globe or sailing the Nile in a felucca or—"

"So Lady Blodgett and her friends are the ones arranging tours and travel for members?" India interrupted, trying to hide her impatience.

"That would stand to reason, wouldn't it? They are all so knowledgeable." The woman paused. "Although I must confess, I'm not well versed in the running of the society, even though I did join shortly after it was formed. I only began to lend my assistance here last week—as a favor to Mrs. Higginbotham and the others—until someone is hired to manage the organization. The society has grown far faster than anyone ever expected."

"The society is relatively new, isn't it?" Yet another question India already had the answer to, but one never knew what further information one might uncover by pretending to be less informed than one was.

"It began about eight months ago and was sorely needed if you ask me." The woman's lips pressed together in a firm line. "In this day and age there is no reason why a woman cannot travel the world if she so desires."

"No reason except…finances." India studied the other woman closely.

"There is that, of course. And fear of the unknown I suppose." She shook her head. "It's rather sad when we don't pursue our heart's desire because we're afraid that it might not be as wonderful as we had hoped."

India tried not to stare, but it was obvious this woman was the worst sort of unrealistic dreamer. "About the charges? For membership?"

"Yes, of course. One pound for a month-to-month membership or ten for a full year membership."

"And that provides?"

"The lectures on travel—lectures are usually once a week—along with the meetings with like-minded women such as yourself. However, the majority of the monthly dues is set aside to provide future payment for arranging the details of a travel itinerary."

"So when I decide to actually travel—" India chose her words with care "—I have already paid for any charges for the arrangement of transportation, hotels, tour guides, that sort of thing?"

"For the most part, although I believe there is also another, relatively insignificant fee. To pay for additional expenses incurred in the arranging of itineraries. To be expected, of course." The woman picked up a printed form from a stack of papers. "Now then, if you would fill this out, you may bring it, along with payment, if you decide to return. There is no charge for your first lecture."

"How very generous." *Or clever.*

"Not at all," the blonde said, rising to her feet and handing India the paper. "You can't fail to delight in Lady Blodgett's tales and sage words. If you have even the tiniest flicker of yearning for the excitement of travel, Lady Blodgett will fan it to a full blaze." She smiled. "I should introduce myself. I'm Miss Honeywell and I have no doubt you'll be joining us."

"I am Miss Prendergast—" India nodded curtly "—and I suspect you're right." Again that annoying sense of guilt stabbed her. She simply wasn't used to deception. "How many members do you have?"

"We're up to more than ninety, I believe."

"That's most impressive."

"It is indeed. The society first met in Lady Blodgett's parlor, but now there are entirely too many of us for that. Because of the ladies' husbands' long association with the Explorers Club, the society was allocated an office here and permitted to use this room for meetings and lectures three days a week."

"How very generous."

The other woman scoffed. "They couldn't very well turn down the request of the widow of Sir Charles Blodgett."

"I would think not." India forced a note of indignation to her voice. Not at all difficult as indignant was the very least of her feelings. If the society had been more forthright and responsive to India's inquiries about Heloise in the first place, she never would have suspected the questionable nature of the organization. Nor would she have begun asking questions, the answers to which were less than satisfactory. "Do tell me about Lady Blodgett and the others. They sound lovely."

"Well, I have known Mrs. Higginbotham for a number of years. She and the others knew my…"

Either Miss Honeywell was the most sincere woman India had ever met or she was an accomplished actress. The more the blonde waxed on about the virtuous Lady Blodgett and her cohorts, the more India suspected Miss Honeywell was a total innocent. And India had always trusted her ability to assess character.

If the three ladies were as guiltless as they seemed to Miss Honeywell, perhaps there was indeed a man behind the scenes manipulating the old dears like a master puppeteer. That was the speculation of Inspector Cooper of Scotland Yard. He had spoken to India at the request of Sir Martin. But as dashing as he was with his slightly unkempt fair hair and his air of solid authority, he was most annoying in his refusal to understand that Heloise's disappearance was a matter of grave concern. The man pointed out that her cousin's lack of communication was no doubt due to the inferior mail services in other countries. He had added, in a vaguely chastising manner, that aside from all else, Heloise was an adult, accompanied by another adult, and was more than likely having such a grand time she'd simply forgotten about writing home. Nor would he acknowledge there was anything at all suspicious about the Lady Travelers Society. And, given there had been no complaints about the society, there was nothing the authorities could do. India had certainly complained quite loudly but apparently the complaints of one lone woman were insufficient. As he had made his pronouncements with such an amused, condescending gleam in his eye, it was all India could do not to smack the smirk from his face.

"I must introduce you to some of our members." Miss Honeywell directed India toward a group gathered by the refreshment table. "You will notice that most of them are substantially older than you or I, but you'll find we have a great deal in common."

A lifetime of savings, no doubt, and little resistance to the lure of far-off destinations. "I would imagine."

"Mrs. Vanderkellen." Miss Honeywell addressed the lady India had stood behind. "Do allow me to present..."

Miss Honeywell introduced her to several more ladies, all of whom were in the throes of anticipation about today's lecture. Without exception, those India met were either widows or spinsters. A few minutes later, India and Miss Honeywell took two of the few remaining seats left for the lecture. The room had filled nearly to capacity since India's arrival. Obviously, the society was doing quite well.

An elderly woman strode to the front of the room with a sprightly step. Two other equally enthusiastic older ladies trailed behind, pausing here and there to greet the women already seated in a charming and gracious manner, as if they were all the oldest and very best of friends and not shepherds leading unsuspecting sheep to a financial fleecing.

"Lady Blodgett is the speaker today," Miss Honeywell said in a quiet voice that nonetheless failed to hide her enthusiasm. "The other ladies are Mrs. Fitzhew-Wellmore and Mrs. Higginbotham. You'll like them, Miss Prendergast. They are all quite wonderful and extremely nice."

"I look forward to meeting them," India said with a touch of feigned eagerness.

Before her arrival, she hadn't been certain if the wisest course was to confront those in charge of the society and demand assistance in finding Heloise or to follow Sir Martin's advice to bide her time until she could determine where Heloise was. And determine, as well, if this was a legitimate endeavor or a fraudulent enterprise designed to siphon money from older women. Which had oddly become nearly as important as recovering her cousin.

Lady Blodgett took her place at the lectern; the other two seated themselves in chairs behind her and off to the right. Regardless of whether or not the ladies' endeavor was aboveboard they certainly weren't the least bit disciplined. Lady Blodgett continued to talk with a woman seated in the front row; the two others on the podium waved to another woman, then exchanged animated comments. Why, the entire room was still filled with feminine chatter. Clearly, with this sort of disorganization, it was entirely possible they weren't fleecing susceptible females but were simply too scattered to keep track of them.

"I suspect members are always going on trips abroad?"

"Not at all," Miss Honeywell said. "At least not yet. I'm not sure more than one member that I know of has actually traveled beyond England. It takes a great deal of time and preparation to arrange a trip to the Orient or the Grecian isles or the deserts of Egypt."

"A great deal of time and dues?"

"Well, one does want to be prepared." Miss Honeywell nodded. "And the ladies' lectures do precisely that."

"I see." And the longer a woman stayed in London paying monthly dues, the richer the coffers of the Lady Travelers Society became. And wasn't that an interesting thought?

India wasn't sure if it was Mrs. Fitzhew-Wellmore or Mrs. Higginbotham, but one of them abruptly stood, stepped to Lady Blodgett's side and spoke quietly in her ear. Lady Blodgett winced and glanced toward the back of the room, then sighed and smiled in a resigned manner. India's gaze followed hers.

A gentleman with a grim expression on his face and a leather satchel in his hand glared at the older lady. He was admittedly handsome with dark hair and broad shoulders, and appeared exceptionally tall. But then everyone seemed tall to India as she was somewhat shorter than she would have preferred.

"Who is that?" she asked Miss Honeywell.

"Lord Charming." Miss Honeywell fairly sighed the answer.

There was certainly something about the man, an air of confidence perhaps, or something in the assurance of his stride and the set of his chin that, in spite of his serious expression, did seem to scream *charming*. "His name is Charming?"

The other woman snapped her gaze away from the gentleman, her eyes wide. "I didn't…oh dear." A blush washed up her face. "Did I really say that aloud?"

"I'm afraid so." While India had little patience with women who mooned over men, no matter how attractive they may be, she couldn't help but feel a touch of sympathy. Gentlemen who looked like Lord Charming rarely preferred more ordinary creatures like Miss Honeywell, or, for that matter, India.

"I don't know what came over me," she said under her breath, "I should have said dashing." She grinned. "No, his name isn't Charming or Dashing, of course, and he isn't a lord, at least not yet. But he is the heir to

the Earl of Danby. That's Mr. Saunders. He's the son
of Lady Blodgett's niece."

"My apologies but it seems there will be a slight
delay," Lady Blodgett announced. "We should only be
a few minutes, but until we return please avail yourselves of the refreshment table. Oh, and—" her gaze
flitted over those seated "—where is Miss Honeywell?"

"Yes?" Miss Honeywell stood.

"Be a dear, Sidney, and hand out this week's pamphlets." Lady Blodgett smiled and followed her friends
to the back of the room. All three ladies kept smiling but
India would have wagered all three would have preferred
to be anywhere but here at the moment. Mr. Saunders
opened the door, and the three women filed through.

India rose to her feet. "Is he here often?"

"I really couldn't say." Miss Honeywell frowned. "He
was here last week. That was the first time I'd seen him,
but, as I said, I am new in this position."

"Lady Blodgett and the others don't seem especially
happy to see him." India's gaze lingered on the door.

"No, I'm afraid not." A thoughtful note sounded in
Miss Honeywell's voice. "Lady Blodgett seemed quite
pleased to see him at first. But no one appeared especially happy after Mr. Saunders and the ladies met
privately. They haven't been quite their usual, cheery
selves since."

"I see," India murmured. Still, while Mr. Saunders's
connection to the ladies did seem important, she wasn't
entirely sure of its significance.

Part of her hoped that this Lady Travelers Society was legitimate. But if so, why hadn't anyone here
responded to her concerns about Heloise? If the ladies who managed the society weren't simply taking
money for services they were not really providing, why

wouldn't they want to do everything possible to recover one of their own? No, there was something decidedly wrong here.

As much as she hated to admit it, Inspector Cooper might well be right. There might be a man behind it all.

And it was becoming fairly obvious exactly who that man was.

Still, at the moment, it was nothing more than speculation. Far better to face the inspector's smug, superior attitude when she had found Heloise and was, as well, able to present actual proof that someone had set up an organization for the sole purpose of taking money from those who could least afford it. Worse yet—stealing their long-held dreams of adventures on foreign shores.

India's resolve hardened. The overly attractive Mr. Saunders might well be able to fool three unsuspecting elderly ladies into being the face of his nefarious scheme, but India Prendergast was made of sterner stuff. She absolutely would not rest until Heloise was safely home. And if one hair on the dear woman's head was so much as ruffled, India would see to it Mr. Saunders spent the rest of his days in prison.

No matter how dashing and charming he might be.

CHAPTER TWO

"LADIES, IF YOU would be so good as to be seated," Derek Saunders said in his firmest, no-nonsense voice. Up until a few days ago, Derek had been unaware he had a firm, no-nonsense voice. But then, up until a few days ago, he hadn't needed one.

"I do hope you intend to be brief." Aunt Guinevere cast him a chastising look and seated herself in one of the surprisingly comfortable leather chairs at the far end of the unoccupied room the Lady Travelers Society had appropriated for its use. Derek still had no idea how his great-aunt and her cohorts had managed to convince the Explorers Club to give them the use of not only a room to serve as an office but a lecture hall, as well, for a fee that was little more than a token. He suspected the elderly ladies wielded their late husbands' prominence in the men-only club with the unflinching hand of an expert marksman.

"We have members eagerly anticipating Gwen's lecture, Mr. Saunders," Mrs. Fitzhew-Wellmore pointed out.

"And it's rude to keep them waiting." Mrs. Higginbotham pressed her lips together in a disapproving line. "Extremely rude."

"And we wouldn't want to be rude, would we?" Derek opened the satchel his uncle had given him in the hopes it would encourage the pursuit of something other than a good time, removed a stack of papers and placed it on the desk. He settled in the chair behind the desk and narrowed his eyes, which did seem to go along with a firm, no-nonsense voice. "Particularly not as you are taking their money under the falsest of pretenses."

All three ladies gasped. It struck him as both insincere and overly rehearsed. Since his first visit here last week they had no doubt decided exactly how to respond to what he had discovered. Obviously, their intention was to act as innocent and guileless as possible.

"My dear boy, we have no idea what you mean." Mrs. Fitzhew-Wellmore's eyes widened in feigned bewilderment.

"And I for one find your comment more than a little insulting." Mrs. Higginbotham sniffed. "False pretenses indeed."

"I'm certain, Derek, that this is no more than a bit of confusion on your part. Probably a simple misunderstanding." Aunt Guinevere favored him with the sort of placating smile one would give a small boy, as if he were still six years old. "I'm confident it's easily cleared up."

"I doubt that." He shuffled through the papers that detailed the workings of the Lady Travelers Society to give himself, and them, a moment to prepare. The impressive stack included the membership roster, membership applications, proposed itineraries for members, the agreement with the Explorers Club and several of the society's brochures. Not that he hadn't rehearsed exactly what he planned to say, but practice was one thing, coming face-to-face with these deceptively virtuous-looking creatures was something else altogether. Still, it couldn't be helped.

Before his mother had left to travel the continent with

his current stepfather—her third husband—more than a month ago, she had asked him to keep an eye on Great-Aunt Guinevere, her mother's sister, as the poor dear was getting on in years and, aside from her two lifelong friends, was quite alone in the world. Derek was one of Lady Guinevere's few living relations, and wasn't it his duty to make certain she was well? A duty, Mother had pointed out, that was not at all difficult and would go a long way toward showing he was at last accepting responsibility. And, at this particular juncture in his life, wouldn't he hate to appear irresponsible in any way? Given that Uncle Edward, the Earl of Danby, had taken the occasion of Derek's thirty-second birthday six months ago to threaten him with loss of his current income and much of his expected inheritance if he did not change his carefree, frivolous existence and begin acting a bit more like the next Earl of Danby should, appearing irresponsible was the last thing Derek needed.

Under other circumstances, it might well have been unfair for Mother to have played that particular card, but there was no denying she was right. Besides, how difficult could it be to make certain a sweet, elderly relative was well and comfortable? Derek rarely saw the older lady, and the depiction Mother had painted of a feeble, eccentric widow in failing health and mind had played on every sense of guilt he'd ever had.

Mother had lied.

When Derek had finally called on Aunt Guinevere, he'd been informed by her butler that she was not at home but could be found in her offices at the Explorers Club. That in itself struck him as odd, but he attributed it to some sort of benefit for widows of prominent members, which, in hindsight, was stupid of him. When he'd arrived at that hallowed shrine to adventure, he discovered Aunt Guinevere was anything but feeble, at least in mind and spirit. Indeed, the old lady and her equally aged companions were engaged in what, to him, appeared very much like some sort of scheme to extort funds from other older ladies.

He drew a deep breath. "I have studied in great detail all the paperwork you gave me last week. However, I do have some questions. Explain to me, if you will, exactly what is entailed in the operation of the Lady Travelers Society and Assistance Agency."

"In the operation?" Aunt Guinevere furrowed her brow. "Why, we operate right here at the Explorers Club. Three days a week."

"And we do have one hired staff member," Mrs. Fitzhew-Wellmore added.

"Although Sidney is more borrowed than hired," Mrs. Higginbotham said thoughtfully. "We're not actually paying her, after all. She is more in the manner of a volunteer."

"And a dear, dear girl." Aunt Guinevere studied him in an assessing manner. "You should meet her, Derek."

"You're not yet married—are you, Mr. Saunders?" Mrs. Fitzhew-Wellmore said with a calculating look in her eyes. Derek had seen that look before, although he wasn't sure if the ladies weren't more interested in distracting him than marrying him off.

"No, Mrs. Fitzhew-Wellmore, I am not. And I did meet her the last time I was here, Aunt Guinevere."

Miss Honeywell was one of those deceptive creatures that at first appeared entirely nondescript but was oddly engaging upon further inspection and might well be quite lovely with minimal effort and clothing designed to flatter the feminine form rather than disguise it. Not that his opinion of Miss Honeywell mattered one way or the other. Women—even those who appeared quite proper and eminently suitable for marriage—were among the pursuits he was currently avoiding in his efforts to convince his uncle of his reformation. In his experience, women in general tended to be a great deal of trouble. Often enjoyable trouble but trouble nonetheless. Still, he couldn't help but notice that Miss Honeywell, and a stern-looking woman sitting beside her with exceptionally rigid posture, were the only two in the lecture hall under the age of fifty.

Derek forced a pleasant note to his voice. "And while I am aware my marital status might be a topic of some interest, right now we are discussing the operation—"

"Derek," Aunt Guinevere began.

He held up his hand to quiet her. "Although *operation* may not be the appropriate term. So let's start from the beginning, shall we?"

"I suppose if we must." Mrs. Higginbotham plucked an invisible thread from her sleeve.

"The beginning is always an appropriate place to start, Effie, dear." Aunt Guinevere nodded in a gracious manner. "Do proceed, Derek."

"Thank you." He considered the ladies for a moment. He wasn't entirely sure of Aunt Guinevere's age, nearing her eighties he thought, but it was difficult to determine. She and her friends were certainly not decrepit in any apparent way. *Spry* was the word that came to mind. And, from the look in their overly innocent eyes, *crafty*, as well. It struck him that he would be wise not to underestimate this trio. "Now then, the three of you began this enterprise six months ago?"

"Closer to nine, I think," Mrs. Fitzhew-Wellmore said. "We met for the first two months in Gwen's parlor. But it soon became obvious that would not do."

"For the purposes of?"

"Why, acquainting women with the benefits of travel, of course." Aunt Guinevere beamed. "And providing expert assistance and guidance through lectures and brochures and touring services to fulfill their dreams of adventure through travel."

"And for this expert assistance—" He glanced down at the paper in front of him. "You charge your membership a full one pound sterling every month." He looked up at the ladies. "Is that correct?"

"It's really quite reasonable," Aunt Guinevere chided.

"And if you pay for an entire year at once, we give you a discount. A mere ten pounds." Mrs. Fitzhew-Wellmore smiled. "We are a bargain."

Mrs. Higginbotham nodded. "There is a great deal to take into account when one is traveling beyond England's shores, you know, Mr. Saunders."

"Yes, I can imagine," he said. "And for these alleged benefits—"

"I would dispute the word *alleged*," Mrs. Higginbotham said under her breath.

"You now have—" Derek sifted through the papers "—some ninety members. Is that right?"

"Actually, we're approaching one hundred." Pride curved Aunt Guinevere's lips. "We had no idea we'd grow so quickly."

"You can see why we could no longer meet in Gwen's parlor." Mrs. Fitzhew-Wellmore leaned forward in a confidential manner. "You'd be surprised at how many women are longing to throw off the shackles of everyday existence and live an adventurous life of travel. It's quite remarkable."

"No doubt." Derek's gaze shifted from one lady to the next. "So, the society brings in nearly one hundred pounds a month. And for their dues your members receive?"

The ladies exchanged resigned glances.

"Our expert advice on traveling the world," Aunt Guinevere said in a well-rehearsed manner.

"The companionship and camaraderie of like-minded women," Mrs. Fitzhew-Wellmore added.

"As well as knowledgeable guidance and, for a minor additional fee, the providing of arranged travel services," Mrs. Higginbotham finished with a flourish.

"And that, dear ladies, is where we have a problem." Derek folded his hands together on the stack of papers and studied the women. All three had adopted blameless expressions, and all three had nearly identical glints of cunning in their eyes. "I shall grant you that the society does indeed provide a convivial atmosphere for ladies with similar interests in travel."

"That was mine." Mrs. Fitzhew-Wellmore smirked.

"However." Derek's tone hardened.

Mrs. Higginbotham sighed. "I do so hate it when men use the word *however* in that forbidding tone. Nothing good ever came of a man starting a sentence with *however*."

Derek's jaw tightened. "Nonetheless—"

"*Nonetheless* is just as bad." Mrs. Higginbotham huffed.

He ignored her. "According to your membership brochure—"

"Isn't it lovely?" Aunt Guinevere said. "Poppy designed it herself. Don't you think it's fetching with her drawing of the pyramids in Egypt and the Colosseum in Rome and those charming American natives? Poppy is quite an accomplished artist."

"Goodness, I wouldn't say I was accomplished. I am scarcely more than an amateur." Mrs. Fitzhew-Wellmore blushed and waved off the comment in a modest manner. "I had hoped to be an artist when I was young, but that was one of those silly, girlish dreams and best forgotten."

"Nevertheless," Mrs. Higginbotham said staunchly. "You're very good."

"The brochure is indeed extremely well done." Derek struggled to keep the impatience from his voice. "However—"

Mrs. Higginbotham grimaced.

"Aunt Guinevere, it's my understanding that you rarely, if ever, traveled with Uncle Charles, which would seem to negate the claim of expert in regard to your knowledge of travel."

"I suppose…" Aunt Guinevere hedged. "If one goes strictly by personal travel…"

"I suspect as well—" his gaze shifted between his great-aunt's coconspirators "—neither Mrs. Fitzhew-Wellmore or Mrs. Higginbotham have substantially more travel experience than you do."

"On the contrary, Mr. Saunders." Mrs. Fitzhew-Wellmore sniffed. "I resided for nearly six weeks in Paris as a girl."

"And the late Colonel Higginbotham and myself spent several summers in the Lake District." Mrs. Higginbotham paused. "Admittedly, that does not equate to foreign travel but it is some distance from here."

"Domestic travel as it were," Aunt Guinevere said helpfully.

"And yet I imagine when your members speak of their *dreams of adventure through travel*, Lake Windermere is not the first destination that comes to mind."

"Lovely spot, though," Mrs. Higginbotham murmured.

"There is no need to raise your voice, dear." Aunt Guinevere cast him a disapproving frown.

"I did not raise my voice. In fact, I have been doing my very best not to raise my voice." He drew a steadying breath. "Correct me if I'm in error, ladies, but by no stretch of the most fertile imagination could any of you be considered experts in travel or the arrangement of travel."

Mrs. Fitzhew-Wellmore heaved a long-suffering sigh. "I suppose if one wanted to base judgment on actual experience alone, that might be considered inaccurate."

"Nonsense," Mrs. Higginbotham said. "I lived with the colonel for thirty-seven years, and he traveled continuously to the most interesting and exotic places. I would think the years spent in his company listening to his endless tales would negate the minor detail that I did not actually accompany him."

Mrs. Fitzhew-Wellmore nodded. "Nor did I accompany my dear Malcolm, but he did keep me apprised of his adventures and very often asked my opinion when he was planning one expedition or another."

"As did your uncle Charles," Aunt Guinevere added. "Why, he frequently said he could not step a foot off English shores without the benefit of my advice."

Derek stared in stunned disbelief.

"So you see…" Aunt Guinevere smiled pleasantly, but triumph glittered in her eyes. "Even though we have not traveled extensively, we do have extensive travel *knowledge*."

All three ladies shared equally smug looks.

"Let me put it this way." Derek struggled to keep his voice level. "While it could possibly be argued that you have a certain level of expertise as it relates to travel, most rational individuals would think your claim ridiculous. As would a magistrate or any court of law. What you are engaged in here, ladies, is fraud."

"Don't be absurd, Derek." Aunt Guinevere scoffed.

"I'm not being absurd, I only wish I were. At the very least, the consequences of your activities are scandal. At the worst—prison." He fixed them with a firm look. "You are falsely representing yourselves as being able to supply a service you are not qualified to provide. And for that you are taking money from women who trust you."

"Well, we had to do something," Mrs. Higginbotham snapped. "Minimal pensions and minor inheritances are simply not enough to survive on even with the most frugal manner of living."

Mrs. Fitzhew-Wellmore nodded. "It's not easy getting on in years. It would be one thing if our dear husbands were still with us, but as they are not, we have each found ourselves tottering precipitously on the very edge of financial despair."

"To be blunt, Derek," Aunt Guinevere said coolly, "we have outlived our financial resources. We were very nearly penniless."

"But you all have families," he said before he thought better of it. He tried to ignore a fresh wave of guilt. He'd had no idea of his great-aunt's circumstances, and he doubted his mother did, either. Aunt Guinevere had not seen fit to inform them, although, admittedly, they had not taken it upon themselves to inquire after her, either.

"Distant and disinterested." Mrs. Higginbotham sniffed.

"None of us were fortunate enough to have had children." Mrs. Fitzhew-Wellmore shrugged. "Nothing can be done about that now, although I suppose, in hindsight, breeding like rabbits would have provided some sort of insurance against being left alone in dismal financial circumstances. Still, I daresay poor Eleanor Dorsey has not found it so and she had nine children."

The other ladies murmured in agreement.

"Even so," Derek began.

"We have all lived relatively independent lives, Derek." Aunt Guinevere raised her chin a notch and met his gaze firmly. "We took care of ourselves and each other when our husbands were off doing all those things men so enjoy and do not for a moment think women would appreciate, as well. We do not, at this point in our lives, relish the thought of throwing ourselves on the mercy of relations who barely acknowledge our existence. Nor do we intend to."

Mrs. Fitzhew-Wellmore squared her shoulders. "I will not be relegated to the category of poor relation."

"And if it came to that, we would much prefer, all three of us…" Mrs. Higginbotham's eyes blazed with determination. "Prison."

"I doubt that," he said sharply, then drew a deep breath. "Forgive me, ladies. I do see your position. Truly I do, and I promise you I shall do everything I can to help alleviate your financial woes, but you must understand you cannot continue this endeavor."

"I don't see why not." Mrs. Higginbotham crossed her arms over her chest. "Our members flock to our meetings and lectures and are quite content with our services. Thus far, we have not had one resign her membership. Why, we've had no complaints whatsoever from our members."

"Not from members perhaps." He leaned forward in his chair. "But do you recall a Miss India Prendergast?"

"India Prendergast?" Mrs. Fitzhew-Wellmore's brow furrowed thoughtfully. "A lovely name but if I've heard it before I simply can't remember." She heaved a wistful sigh. "I fear my memory is not what it once was."

"She's written the society a number of times," Derek said. "Now do you remember?"

"Effie handles most of the correspondence," Aunt Guinevere offered.

Derek turned to the other woman. "Mrs. Higginbotham?"

"Prendergast you say?" Mrs. Higginbotham asked. Derek nodded.

"Let me think." She pursed her lips and considered the question then shrugged. "No, it doesn't sound the least bit familiar, but then my memory is no better than Poppy's." She cast him a helpless smile he didn't believe for a moment.

"That is odd." He laid his palm on the stack of papers on the desk. "As she has written you at least five letters demanding to know the whereabouts of her cousin."

Aunt Guinevere's eyes widened. "And who is her cousin, dear?"

Oh, they were good, this trio of septuagenarians. He would wager a considerable amount their minds and their memories were as sharp or sharper than his own. Still, he was not going to be outwitted by the pretense of elderly virtue or incompetence.

"Lady Heloise Snuggs."

"Of course." Aunt Guinevere beamed as if she was proud merely to have recognized the name. "Dear Heloise."

"Dear, dear Heloise," the other ladies murmured.

He resisted the urge to raise his voice. "Do you know where Lady Heloise is at the moment?"

Aunt Guinevere shrugged. "I haven't a clue."

"She could be anywhere, I would think," Mrs. Higginbotham said.

"Although I suspect she's somewhere between Paris and Constantinople." Mrs. Fitzhew-Wellmore thought for a minute. "Or perhaps Hamburg and Athens. It's impossible to say with any certainty."

Derek stared. "Did you or did you not arrange Lady Heloise's travel?"

The trio shifted uneasily in their chairs.

"An answer if you please, ladies."

"Certainly, we *arranged* Lady Heloise's travel." Mrs. Fitzhew-Wellmore chose her words with obvious care.

"There is a possibility," Mrs. Higginbotham said slowly, "that we did not arrange it as efficiently as one might hope."

"That is to say, while we did write to hotels and other establishments across the path Lady Heloise wished to take requesting accommodations…" Mrs. Higginbotham began.

"We didn't actually receive any definitive confirmations," Mrs. Fitzhew-Wellmore finished. "You see, once Lady Heloise decided to embark upon a life of travel, she was impatient to be off. She assured us our assistance had been invaluable."

"We did our best, Derek, to send her off with all the information she might possibly need, brochures, tourist guides, train and ship timetables. She couldn't possibly be more prepared," Aunt Guinevere said staunchly.

"Unless, of course, you had actually confirmed her travel and accommodations."

"There is that," one of the ladies conceded.

Derek pressed his fingers to his temples in hopes of forestalling the kind of headache he used to experience only after a night of drunken merriment. He hadn't the slightest doubt his great-aunt and her friends were well aware of Miss Prendergast's letters and her valid charge that their society had mislaid her cousin through incompetency and chicanery, as well as her threats to involve the police in the matter if something was not done to locate Lady Heloise and ensure her safety. Aside from the fact that he didn't want Aunt Guinevere incarcerated, his mother's request for Derek to keep an eye on her would certainly place the responsibility for any kind of scandal squarely on his shoulders. Especially in Uncle Edward's eyes. Besides, if he and his mother had paid more attention to the needs of an elderly relative, perhaps she wouldn't have turned to this scheme in the first place.

Now it was up to him to get Aunt Guinevere out of it. No, he amended the thought, it was up to him to extricate all three old friends from this mess. He suspected if one was drowning, the other two would do whatever was necessary to save her even if it meant they would all sink beneath the waves together.

He drew a steadying breath. "Well, it appears Lady Heloise has vanished. I do not want to think of the consequences if she is not found unharmed. In the letters you claim to be unaware of—" the ladies traded guilty looks "—Miss Prendergast threatens legal action." He met his aunt's gaze directly. "She has already contacted Scotland Yard."

Aunt Guinevere gasped.

"I made inquiries at a private investigation agency about efforts to locate Lady Heloise."

"How brilliant of you, Mr. Saunders." Mrs. Fitzhew-Wellmore beamed.

"I told you he was clever." Aunt Guinevere's smile matched her friend's. "I knew he would find a way to determine the whereabouts of Lady Heloise."

"I doubt that she's truly missing," Mrs. Higgin-botham said. "Why, I myself am quite awful at keep-ing up with correspondence."

"Although making certain she has come to no harm is probably a good idea," Aunt Guinevere pointed out. "We would hate for the membership to be concerned—"

"The membership is now closed," Derek said firmly. "You will accept no new members until the matter of Lady Heloise is resolved. Nor will you plan trips for any of your current members, and, for God's sake, should a trip already be in the works, do not let any of them embark upon it. Once Lady Heloise is located, we will then decide the future of your Lady Travelers Society and whether or not it can become something more legiti-mate than it now appears."

Mrs. Higginbotham sucked in a short breath, but Aunt Guinevere laid a hand on her arm and the other woman's mouth snapped shut.

"Unfortunately, the agency I contacted warned me it would take some time and considerable resources to locate a woman missing outside England. Given the in-creasing level of concern, as well as the growing out-rage in Miss Prendergast's correspondence, time is not on our side." He ran his hand through his hair. As much as he hated to admit it, his latest discussion with the agency that morning had left him with one inescapable conclusion. "I'm afraid at this juncture, leaving the trac-ing of Lady Heloise in the hands of even the best of pro-fessionals may not be enough."

"I couldn't agree with you more." A hard feminine voice sounded from the doorway. "That is not nearly enough."

CHAPTER THREE

While travel is the dream of many ladies, the first step in setting forth from one's native land should not be taken lightly. Without planning and preparation—the keys to successful travel—one might find oneself in unexpected difficulties far from home. Which is not at all the kind of adventure even the most intrepid among us seek.
—The Lady Travelers Society Guide

THE WOMAN HE'D noticed sitting beside Miss Honeywell stood in the now open doorway, a leather lady's traveling handbag on her arm, an umbrella in her hand. Derek could have sworn he had closed the door, but perhaps she had been listening on the other side. He wouldn't be surprised. There was an air of determination about her, from the top of her sensible hat perched firmly on nondescript brown hair to the tips of her sturdy, practical shoes. She was at least a head shorter than he, yet managed to convey an impression of towering indignation and barely suppressed ire. This was a woman who would let nothing stand in her path.

"Well, that's that, Derek." Aunt Guinevere rose to her feet, Derek a beat behind her. He could almost see the tiny gears and flywheels of her mind working. The woman was planning her escape. "As much as I would love to continue our discussion—" she cast a brilliant smile at the stranger "—it seems we have the needs of a member to attend to."

"The needs of the membership must come first," Mrs. Higginbotham said firmly and stood. Mrs. Fitzhew-Wellmore followed suit.

"I am most certainly not a member," the intruder said.

"Then you must be here to join." Enthusiasm rang in Mrs. Fitzhew-Wellmore's voice. "How delightful."

"I am not here—" the young woman began.

"I beg your pardon, miss, but you are intruding on a private meeting," Derek said in a harder tone than he might otherwise have taken, but she struck him as the kind of woman who would respond to nothing less than a firm, resolute manner. "However, as it's obvious you are not going to let a little thing like a closed door dissuade you, please do me the courtesy of allowing me a moment."

"My apologies for the interruption, but the door was not closed." She glared at him. "Do go on."

"Thank you." Derek breathed a bit easier. He had long prided himself on being an excellent judge of character—especially when it came to the fairer sex—although it did not take any particular skill to see this woman was both irate and indomitable. Nor was it especially far-fetched to assume this was Miss India Prendergast, as he was fairly certain Miss Prendergast's cousin was the only traveler the society had lost thus far. At least he had bought himself a minute, maybe two.

He turned to his great-aunt. "Sit down, Aunt Guinevere."

She opened her mouth as if she was about to refuse, then sighed and retook her seat.

He directed a hard gaze at her coconspirators. Both Mrs. Higginbotham and Mrs. Fitzhew-Wellmore looked as if they were about to sprint for the door. Under other circumstances, Derek would have paid a great deal to have seen that. "All of you."

The ladies sat, and Derek's attention shifted back to

the newcomer. He'd been expecting Miss Prendergast to make an appearance ever since he'd discovered her letters to the society and realized they'd been ignored. From her increasingly adamant correspondence, he did not think she was a woman who took well to being ignored. What he did not expect was the eyes flashing with suspicion and accusation to be so vividly green. Or that the lips now pressed together in disapproval would be so full and appealing—*ripe* was the word that came to mind. Nor did he expect the figure encased in eminently sensible, practical and unflattering clothing to be quite so provocative. And he did not anticipate she would be so young—no more than thirty he guessed. Derek had always had the knack of noticing a woman's good points well before her flaws. It was part of his nature, and he considered it a gift he employed well. Ladies did seem to appreciate it. Even so, it was obvious no amount of charm would endear him to Miss India Prendergast.

Still, nothing ventured, as they said. He adopted his most pleasant smile. "Thank you for your patience, Miss Prendergast?"

Her eyes narrowed. "Have we met?"

"I have not had that pleasure."

"I assure you, I do not intend for it to be a pleasure," she said in a curt manner.

No, charm would not work with Miss Prendergast. Regardless, it was all he had.

"Nor do I expect it to be, Miss Prendergast, as we have a situation of some difficulty to address. But first, I am Mr. Derek Saunders—"

"I know who you are."

"Then an introduction is not necessary." He gestured toward the older ladies. "But allow me to introduce my

great-aunt Guinevere, Lady Blodgett, and her friends—
Mrs. Fitzhew-Wellmore and Mrs. Higginbotham."

"It's a very great pleasure to meet you, Miss Prendergast," Aunt Guinevere began, "even under such trying
circumstances. I can assure you it was never our intention—"

"Not to respond to your letters of concern," Derek
cut in smoothly. God knows what Aunt Guinevere was
about to confess, but he was sure it would do more harm
than good. Far better to move on to finding Lady Heloise than acknowledge the incompetence of his aunt and
her friends. "We understand how difficult this must be.
I assure you, we are doing all in our power to locate
Lady Heloise."

"Are you?" Her brows rose. "It did not sound that
way to me."

"One never hears anything good when one is engaged in eavesdropping," Mrs. Higginbotham chided.

"I was not eavesdropping," Miss Prendergast said
coolly. "As I said, the door was open."

"And yet I could have sworn I had closed it." Derek
adopted a polite smile.

"Which is entirely beside the point." Miss Prendergast squared her shoulders. "What are you doing to
find my cousin?"

"Please, have a seat, Miss Prendergast, so that we
may discuss this in a civilized manner." Derek indicated another chair.

"Yes, indeed, Miss Prendergast," Aunt Guinevere
said. "It's most awkward with all of us seated and you
standing there like an avenging angel. Why, you've
quite frightened poor Poppy nearly to death."

"I am easily terrified." Mrs. Fitzhew-Wellmore widened her eyes. Derek wished she would look a little

more frightened and a little less like a stage actress in a bad play.

"I have no desire to sit, and I am unfailingly civilized," Miss Prendergast stated but sat in the empty chair nonetheless.

"Derek." Aunt Guinevere turned to him. "Perhaps you would be so good as to ask Sidney to bring us some tea." She glanced at the others. "I think a spot of tea would serve us all well right now."

"Brilliant idea, Gwen," Mrs. Higginbotham agreed. "I think tea is exactly what poor Poppy needs to calm her nerves."

"Oh, I do." Mrs. Fitzhew-Wellmore fanned her face with her hand. "I truly do."

Derek closed his eyes and prayed for patience.

"Come now, Derek." Aunt Guinevere sighed. "You needn't look quite so long-suffering. Even the most insurmountable problem can be worked out over a steaming cup of tea." She directed Miss Prendergast her most gracious smile. "Don't you agree, dear?"

"Well…" For a moment, the formidable Miss Prendergast looked somewhat taken aback. While Derek's charms would obviously get nowhere with the woman, perhaps his great-aunt's would. "Yes, thank you."

Oh no. The last thing he needed was to fortify Miss Prendergast with tea. Nor did it seem wise to leave the older ladies alone with her.

"I don't think tea is necessary right now," he said firmly. "Perhaps later." He turned to Miss Prendergast. "We have a great deal to discuss and a number of decisions to make."

"Indeed." She shook her head as if to clear whatever spell his aunt had cast on her, then sat up straighter if possible. Derek didn't think he'd ever seen posture quite so rigid.

"I demand to know what steps you are taking to find my cousin." The avenging angel was back.

"No tea then?" Mrs. Fitzhew-Wellmore said in an aside to Mrs. Higginbotham, who simply shrugged.

"As you no doubt heard, I have contacted a private agency in regard to locating the missing Lady Heloise."

"I also heard this agency said it would take time and considerable resources, which I take to mean funding." Miss Prendergast glared at him. "Am I correct?"

"I'm afraid so. Therefore, it seems to me there is only one thing to do." He braced himself. "I shall have to go after Lady Heloise myself."

"Excellent suggestion, dear boy. Now that we have that settled..." Aunt Guinevere started to rise, caught sight of the look on Derek's face, then sank back into her chair. "Although I am certain there is still much to discuss."

Her friends exchanged resigned looks.

"And what investigative skills do you have, Mr. Saunders?" Miss Prendergast crossed her arms over her chest. "What qualifies you for this kind of undertaking?"

"Admittedly, I have no investigative skills as such." Derek adopted a businesslike manner. "However, I am well educated, I have traveled extensively on the continent, I speak three languages and I am more than capable of following the trail of a woman who has somehow become misplaced."

"You are the one who misplaced her!"

"That, Miss Prendergast, is a question of some debate," he said sharply.

Her eyes widened in outrage. "Do you deny it then?"

"We do not escort our members on their journeys—we do not take them by the hand and accompany them. Therefore, we cannot be held responsible if they choose to wander off course." As much as his argument did have a nice, rational ring to it, given what he'd seen of the unconfirmed arrangements his great-aunt and the other ladies had made for Lady Heloise, he was fairly certain the authorities might see the situation differently.

"I daresay the police might disagree as to your responsibility for your members." Her eyes narrowed. "As would the newspapers."

"That would be awkward," Mrs. Fitzhew-Wellmore murmured.

"Scandal always is, dear." Aunt Guinevere grimaced.

"I contend that the legal responsibility for your missing cousin is uncertain." Derek chose his words with care. "But I will concede to a possible moral obligation."

"Possible?" She snorted in disdain.

"And I will not allow the reputation of this organization to be put at risk." He stood, braced his hands on the desk and leaned forward, his gaze locked on hers. "We do our best at the Lady Travelers Society and Assistance Agency to serve our members with expert aid and guidance in the planning and implementation of itineraries in their quest to fulfill their dreams of adventure through travel." He couldn't believe he had just said that, and without wincing.

Mrs. Higginbotham snickered, Mrs. Fitzhew-Wellmore choked and Aunt Guinevere stared.

"Be that as it may, Mr. Saunders." Miss Prendergast stood, her angry gaze never slipping from his. "My cousin is not the type of woman to fail in her correspondence when she knows such a failure would cause a great deal of alarm." Concern flashed through Miss Prendergast's eyes so quickly he might have been mistaken. Obviously this was not a woman who allowed her emotions to show. "Nor is she the type of woman to wander off her predetermined course. Therefore, something has happened to her." She leaned closer, her manner mirroring his. "I will not rest until I am assured of her safety. Failing that, I will make certain those responsible pay for shirking their obligations, moral or otherwise."

For a long moment he stared at her, a voice in the back of his head warning him not to be the first one to look away. Backing down from Miss India Prendergast would be a mistake that could never be corrected.

Aunt Guinevere cleared her throat. "When do you intend to leave, Derek?"

"As soon as possible. I will need a day to make certain my affairs are in order, but I anticipate leaving no later than the day after tomorrow."

"Excellent." Miss Prendergast's eyes flashed. "That will give me time to arrange for a leave of absence from my position."

Her position? Was she a governess? Or a teacher of some sort? *Surely not.* She didn't strike him as having the temperament needed to be patient with children. Although an unruly child would surely meet his match in Miss Prendergast.

"And what kind of position would that be, Miss Prendergast?" Mrs. Fitzhew-Wellmore asked brightly.

At last Miss Prendergast pulled her gaze from his, and the most ridiculous sense of triumph and relief washed through him.

"I hold the position of secretarial assistant to Sir Martin Luckthorne," she said, retaking her seat. "He understands my concern about my cousin and will grant me the time required to find her."

"The time required?" Derek stared. At once he realized her intentions. "Surely I misunderstand what you are saying."

"I wouldn't be at all surprised," she said coolly. "I daresay there are any number of things you misunderstand. You don't strike me as being particularly perceptive."

Mrs. Higginbotham snorted.

Any sense of triumph he might have had vanished under the specter of traveling with this epitome of outrage and indignation. "I have no intention of allowing you to accompany me."

"Allowing me?" Her brow arched upward in disdain. "I was not asking your permission. I will not be left behind."

"Regardless, I will not be taking you with me," he said firmly. The last thing he needed was this termagant dogging his every move.

"Very well then." She shrugged. "I shall simply follow you. Do not underestimate my resolve, Mr. Saunders. Everywhere you go, I will go, as well. I shall be no more than one step behind you until you find my cousin."

Bloody hell. This was a disaster in the making. If anything should happen to her, the blame would be laid squarely at his feet for not allowing her the protection of his company. Regardless, he had no desire to spend more time than was absolutely necessary with this woman. The moment she'd opened her mouth, he'd known the best thing about searching for Lady Heloise was that it would take him far away from her cousin.

"There is not one legitimate reason why I should permit you to come with me."

"I believe I just gave you one." She smirked. "However, I can give you another. I have her letters detailing where she has been as well as her plans."

"If I remember correctly, according to her itinerary, she could be in Switzerland by now. Unless she decided Switzerland was not to her liking," Mrs. Higginbotham said thoughtfully, "and set off for Greece."

"Oh, I think I would much prefer Greece to Switzerland." Mrs. Fitzhew-Wellmore nodded eagerly. "Greece sounds so warm and sunny, and Switzerland brings to mind snow and mountain goats. Although I imagine at this time of year Switzerland might be quite pleasant whereas Greece might be too warm. Perhaps you should start there?"

Derek stared in confusion. "Greece or Switzerland?"

"I think not." Miss Prendergast's look clearly said she thought he was an idiot. "Her last letter was from France."

"My inclination is to retrace her steps in an effort to determine where she might be now." Derek made no attempt to hide the resignation in his voice; it was obvious there would be no good way to rid himself of Miss Prendergast.

Miss Prendergast gave him a grudging glance of agreement. "I was thinking the same thing."

"Being of like minds is a superb way to begin," Aunt Guinevere said. "Now then, Miss Prendergast, did you have a chaperone in mind?"

"A chaperone?" The younger woman's eyes widened in surprise.

Derek groaned. Of course they would need a chaperone. A man and woman—even if they did not especially like each other—could not go running across the continent together if they were unmarried. Her reputation would be ruined, and while he'd never given his own any particular concern, with Uncle Edward's edict to straighten out his life hanging over his head, now was not the time to add to the long list of questionable behavior his uncle was keeping. Besides, this might be just what he needed to stop Miss Prendergast from accompanying him.

"A chaperone, Miss Prendergast, is essential," he said smoothly, resisting the urge to grin. "Propriety demands nothing less. As does your own reputation, which I assume is spotless—"

Miss Prendergast's jaw tightened. "I am willing to risk my reputation."

"Your decision, of course. However, the reputation of the Lady Travelers Society is also at stake. As is the reputation of my aunt and her friends." He shook his head in a regretful manner. "If it were to become known that the society, or these upstanding ladies, sanctioned an unmarried couple traveling alone together, well, surely you can understand the repercussions."

"Scandal, Miss Prendergast," Mrs. Higginbotham said darkly. "Nothing short of scandal."

"We will all be ruined." Mrs. Fitzhew-Wellmore sighed deeply. "And any chance you have for a good marriage, Miss Prendergast, will be destroyed."

Miss Prendergast paused, obviously to summon a measure of calm, although Derek could see it wasn't easy for her. "My concern right now is for the safety of Lady Heloise. My reputation is the very least of my worries. I am nearly thirty years of age, and the prospect of marriage is not a consideration."

"Oh, but my dear girl." Encouragement shone in Mrs. Fitzhew-Wellmore's eyes. "You must not give up hope.

I was in my thirty-first year when I met and married my dear Malcolm. One is never too old to find true love and lasting companionship."

"And one shouldn't throw away the possibility simply because one has reached an advanced age—"

Derek winced. No woman—regardless of excellent posture or unflattering attire—wished to be reminded of things like *advanced age*.

"And society says you are past your prime marriage-able years. Society, Miss Prendergast—" Mrs. Higgin-botham pressed her lips firmly together "—is made up of people who are unfailingly imperfect and very often have their heads—"

"Ophelia," Aunt Guinevere warned.

"Buried in the sand," Mrs. Higginbotham finished, then frowned at her friend. "What did you think I was going to say?"

"One never knows what you'll say," Mrs. Fitzhew-Wellmore murmured.

Aunt Guinevere shot both ladies a chastising look, then smiled apologetically. "You must forgive Effie. Her husband was a military man, and his language could sometimes be a bit salty. Effie forgets others are more easily offended than she is."

Mrs. Higginbotham shrugged, but a gleam of smug amusement twinkled in her eyes.

"So you see, Miss Prendergast," he began, "without a chaperone you cannot possibly—"

"Oh, we can arrange for a chaperone," Aunt Guine-vere said brightly. "In fact, I have a couple in mind who will do quite nicely."

"Aunt Guinevere." Derek aimed a pointed look at her. "There really isn't time—"

"Nonsense, Derek," Aunt Guinevere said. "Miss

Prendergast is extremely concerned about her cousin and will no doubt go quite mad if you leave her here to wonder what you are up to and whether or not you have located dear, dear Lady Heloise. In addition, she has already vowed to follow you if need be. We really can't have that. Why, we would certainly be to blame if something were to happen to her." She cast Miss Prendergast a sympathetic look. "I understand completely why you would wish to go with Derek. Indeed, I think it's quite courageous of you. If you can bear to put off departing on your quest for one additional day, the day following the day after tomorrow, I am certain the couple I have in mind will be eager to accompany you."

The look in Miss Prendergast's eyes softened, and for a moment, one could see how she might possibly, under certain circumstances, be considered almost attractive. "Thank you, Lady Blodgett." She drew a deep breath. "Three days from now is acceptable."

"Good." Aunt Guinevere nodded with satisfaction. "I shall speak with the couple I have in mind tomorrow, and, with any luck at all, you will have your chaperones. You and Derek will want to meet them, of course."

Mrs. Fitzhew-Wellmore leaned toward Miss Prendergast in a confidential manner. "It's always wise to meet one's traveling companions in advance. One would hate to be trapped on a journey with a companion one finds distasteful."

Miss Prendergast shot Derek a disgusted glance. "I suspect that would be…awkward."

"You shall join me for tea at my house to meet the couple the day after tomorrow." Aunt Guinevere announced with satisfaction. "Now that we have that settled—"

"We have settled nothing." Derek clenched his teeth.

This was quickly getting out of hand. If he didn't nip this in the bud right now, he'd have half of London following him around Europe. "I am not about to set off on a wild-goose chase—"

Miss Prendergast gasped. "I beg your pardon. This is my cousin. She is not a wild goose."

"Very well then." He struggled to keep his voice level. "A *missing*-goose chase—" Miss Prendergast's eyes narrowed "—dragging three people, their respective mounds of luggage and servants." He pinned her with a hard look. "How many lady's maids do you intend to bring with you, Miss Prendergast?"

Her chin rose. "I am more than capable of seeing to my own needs, Mr. Saunders. I can function perfectly well without a maid."

"Then you're the first woman I've met who can."

"Derek," Aunt Guinevere said sharply. "Your objections are pointless. Miss Prendergast strikes me as the kind of woman who will not be dissuaded simply to make your life less difficult."

"No doubt," he said under his breath.

"Then we are agreed." Aunt Guinevere's gaze met his, and a subtle but distinct look of victory shone in her eyes. *Of course.* In one fell swoop she would vanquish the woman who could shatter the unsteady house of cards she and her friends had built as well as the man who had put a damper on her plans.

"That matter perhaps," he said in a firm tone. "But there are still things we need to discuss before I leave."

"I was afraid there might be." Aunt Guinevere sighed, the gleam of victory changing to one of resignation.

Under other circumstances, Derek might feel badly about extinguishing the light in an elderly lady's eyes, but he had already learned Aunt Guinevere and her cronies were not nearly the sweet, doddering innocents he had initially assumed.

"Very well then." Miss Prendergast rose to her feet. "I shall be on my way." She turned toward the door.

Derek hurried around the desk to escort her out. He opened the door and nodded. "Rest assured, Miss Prendergast. We will find your cousin."

"Tell me, Mr. Saunders." Her assessing gaze searched his. "If I had not written expressing my concerns over the loss of my cousin and had not appeared here in person, would you still be venturing out to find her now?"

"Without question, Miss Prendergast," he said without hesitation. Admittedly, he hadn't known of the existence of the Lady Travelers Society or what his great-aunt and her friends had been up to until last week. But he had already realized he would have to take this matter in hand himself if he was to save the trio from the repercussions of their activities and save his own future, as well. "And you have my word that I shall do my very best to assure the success of our endeavor."

"How disheartening, Mr. Saunders. I was so hoping you could do better than that." She nodded, turned and took her leave.

"And a good day to you, too, Miss Prendergast," he called after her. Better to be at least nominally cordial than sound like an idiot. Unfortunately, all the brilliant responses that immediately came to mind would not have been nearly as clever when said aloud and would only have reinforced her opinion of him.

"Excellent retort, Mr. Saunders," one of the ladies said behind him, a distinct note of sarcasm in her voice.

A heavy weight settled in the pit of his stomach.

It was going to be a very long quest.

CHAPTER FOUR

"DARE I ASK if your visit to the Lady Travelers Society was successful?" Sir Martin Luckthorne studied India from behind the cluttered desk in his library. She made a mental note to tidy it up before she left for the day.

"It was…" She pressed her lips firmly together. "Adequate."

"And yet you seem in such a cordial mood," he said pleasantly.

Her gaze snapped to his. "Sarcasm, Sir Martin, is uncalled for."

"Sarcasm, Miss Prendergast, is the thinking man's defense against despair."

"Is that a legitimate saying, or did you make it up?"

"The fact that I made it up makes it no less legitimate."

"Now you're just trying to distract me by being amusing." She frowned. "I am not fond of your attempts to disarm me."

"And yet much of the rest of humanity is grateful for my efforts on their behalf." A wry smile quirked his lips.

"You know I never lose my temper." India prided herself on keeping her emotions firmly in hand, even on days like today when it was a distinct challenge.

"You, my dear, can say more with the look in your eyes than anyone I've ever met," he said mildly. "A look designed to strike terror into the hearts of even the most stalwart of men."

"Nonsense." She sniffed.

He raised a skeptical brow.

"I do nothing of the sort," she said, although her denial did not ring entirely true. And, unfortunately, Martin knew it. Aside from Heloise, he knew her better than anyone. And why not?

While it would be terribly improper to admit it aloud, she considered her employer a friend. Indeed, aside from Heloise, he was her only friend. It was inevitable really. When one spent almost every day with a man for eight years—taking care of very nearly everything in his life—some sort of cordial relationship would surely develop. Or one would have to move on. Although she hadn't expected the kind of affection one would feel for an impractical older brother to grow between them. But then neither had she expected to be in his employ for eight years.

In truth, she was fortunate to have found this position at all. While Heloise had a trust from her late father—who'd died long before she took in India—that was sufficient to meet their needs, it provided little beyond what Heloise considered the necessities in life. India had insisted on contributing to their unusual family's coffers and had sought work the moment she'd finished her education at Miss Bicklesham's Academy. Heloise knew her ward better than to encourage marriage, and, really, what was the point? Aside from the adequate dowry that Heloise had set aside for her, India had nothing to commend her as a suitable match. Her family was respectable but not noteworthy. She came from neither wealth nor power. As far as society was concerned, she did not exist. She'd had no debutante season nor had she ever

desired one. After all, the sole purpose of coming out
in society was to find a husband. Marriage was simply
not of interest to India. Heloise had never married and
she seemed quite content with her life.

Heloise had tried to persuade her to pursue higher
education, and they'd had an ongoing dispute about the
subject until India had reluctantly agreed to take evening classes at Queen's College. Classes she continued through her brief employment as a governess and
by correspondence during her mercifully short inter-
lude as a teacher at Miss Bicklesham's. India Prendergast was the first to admit she was not cut out to shape
young minds.

While in the throes of trying to determine what kind of
position to attempt next—she was fast running out of acceptable employment for a well-bred young lady of good
family—she happened across an advertisement for a person of sufficient education to assist a scholarly minded
gentleman with correspondence, the cataloguing and organization of various collections, and assorted tasks as
required. While India had no idea what "assorted tasks
as required" might be, she had nonetheless turned up on
Martin's doorstep that very day.

He had been younger than she'd expected, a scant
dozen years older than she. But, at the age of only thirty-
three, he had already settled into that category of bachelor that was referred to as *confirmed*. India suspected,
even as a youth, the man was probably set in his ways.
And his ways did not include hiring a woman.

Still, he had yet to meet India Prendergast. Within
a week she had his correspondence up-to-date. Within
a month she had his vast collection of ancient Roman
coins categorized by date and emperor. Within three
months, she had his financial records in order and his

incompetent servants replaced. By the end of her first year of employment, his household and his life were running as smoothly as clockwork. The only chink in India's fortress of organization was Martin himself, who spent much of his life immersed in whatever project happened to catch his fancy at the moment, be it of a scholarly nature, one of his numerous collections or tinkering with a convoluted—and yet oddly practical—invention of some kind. India considered him a modern renaissance man. Fortunately, he had a great deal of money and could support the quirks of his nature.

They got on quite well together. India thought of him as Martin, although they rarely called each other by their given names. It would be most inappropriate. India enjoyed managing his life and was secretly grateful there was no Lady Luckthorne as she couldn't imagine a man's wife being so liberal as to allow him to have a female assistant. Or a female friend.

"I do hope you are not going to keep details of your foray to yourself." Martin set his notes aside, rested his forearms on the desk and folded his hands together. "That wouldn't be at all fair as it was my idea."

"And an excellent one at that." India sank into her usual seat in the leather tufted wing chair positioned in front of his desk.

"I know." He grinned. "Better still, it kept you from descending upon the society like an irate mother hen."

"Avenging angel actually," she said. "I should have gone there weeks ago."

"It's been a scant six weeks since your last letter from Lady Heloise. You weren't overly concerned for a fortnight after that."

"I should have been."

"Rubbish. The unreliability of foreign postal service

could certainly account for a delay in the delivery of Lady Heloise's letters. No, Miss Prendergast, this is not in any way a failure on your part."

"Still, I..." She sighed. The man was right, which made her feel no less guilty. And no less helpless. "I should have done more sooner."

"You sent letters, you spoke to the police and you have confronted the people you deem responsible in person. Now—" he pinned her with a firm look "—tell me. Did you learn anything of substance?"

She thought for a moment. "What I discovered was not in the least surprising, even if most disheartening." She blew a frustrated breath. "If it had not been for my letters, I doubt that anyone there would have realized Heloise was missing. It strikes me as the most disorganized, haphazard enterprise I have ever encountered."

"Oh?"

"The three elderly ladies, the widows I told you about?"

He nodded.

"They are allegedly in charge of the society however—" she narrowed her eyes "—I fear your Inspector Cooper was right."

"He's not my Inspector Cooper," he said coolly. "In fact, I thought he was quite taken with *you*."

"Don't be ridiculous."

On occasion Martin had the most absurd idea that she was the kind of woman men considered attractive, but then he had a generous soul. Aside from various meetings and lectures, he did not often venture into society and, other than his housekeeping staff and his cook, India was the only woman in his life.

India was under no illusions as to her appearance. Her features were regular, her form average, tending toward full, her hair an unremarkable brown. Admittedly, her eyes were a lovely shade of green, but beyond that, there was nothing to commend her appearance one way or the other. She had accepted this fact of life as a child, and even Martin's overly generous nature did not change that. She was, however, intelligent and sensible and well organized, far more important attributes than mere appearance—especially if one was not wealthy and needed to make one's way in the world.

"I wasn't being ridiculous. I am nothing if not observant, and it is my observation that the man was definitely flirting with you. Or at least attempting to flirt with you."

"If that was Inspector Cooper's attempt at the art of flirtation, he obviously needs practice." Not that India had any practical experience to base her opinion on. Still, one would think flirtation would be more effective if it was at least noticeable. "I would imagine if a gentleman was taken with a woman he would not belittle her legitimate concerns by accusing her of making a mountain out of a molehill or suggesting female emotions had somehow addled her brain."

He chuckled. "Yes, well I can see where that would not serve his cause."

"Again, I do not believe he has a *cause* as you put it." As intelligent as Martin was, he truly did not understand the ways of the world. "Now, as I was saying, I think there is indeed a male mastermind hiding behind the facade of these widows."

"A *mastermind*?" His brow shot upward. "Have you been reading novels of mystery again?"

"I have no need for a fictional mystery when the question of Heloise's whereabouts is unanswered," she said, firmly evading the subject. Martin took a great deal of perverse pleasure in teasing her about her reading habits, which tended toward stories of mystery and detection. It was her one real vice, the one silly indulgence she allowed herself. She had devoured *A Study in Scarlet* and was hoping another book about Sherlock Holmes would soon be forthcoming. "And *mastermind* seems the most appropriate term. It was apparent to me that these ladies are no more than a false front to hide the machinations of a Mr. Derek Saunders."

"And you have jumped to this conclusion because?"

"I'm not jumping to anything. I have calmly and intelligently reached this decision based on my observations. The man is obviously a rogue and a scoundrel." Why, no true gentleman looked quite that devil-may-care. The spark in his blue eyes, the set of his chin—there was a definite air about the man that spoke of indiscretion and recklessness and...trouble. "While the ladies seem quite pleasant and very sweet, in spite of the experience of their late husbands, I don't think Lady Blodgett or her friends have so much as a vague idea what they're doing when it comes to the arrangement of foreign travel. They are, however, trusting and naive. You can tell that just by looking at them. I fear they are no more than blissfully unaware puppets being manipulated by a master puppeteer." She pressed her lips together. "Why, he wouldn't even allow them to say what they wished. No doubt for fear they would reveal everything."

Martin frowned. "You met him?"

"I most certainly did," she huffed. "He's the kind of man who thinks he can get whatever he wants through charm alone."

"So he was charming, was he?"

"In his eyes only." Although one could possibly see how a woman less susceptible than herself could be taken in by blue eyes set in a handsome face, dark unruly hair and broad shoulders. "I found him annoying."

"I see."

"However…" It was the only point in his favor. "Before I confronted him, I overheard him saying he had spoken to investigators about finding Heloise."

"Well, that's something."

"Very little. He only did that much because of the threat in my letters to further involve the authorities. Unfortunately, such an investigation will cost a great deal."

"I see." Martin paused. "Then he—they—were of no real help?"

"Well, not yet. He has decided to find Heloise himself, although I doubt he has the skills to do so."

"You must be pleased by that."

"Yes, well…" She wasn't quite sure how to tell him Mr. Saunders would not be traveling alone.

"You are being remarkably reticent to reveal anything of substance, which is not at all like you." Martin considered her thoughtfully. "It leads me to believe you have something you don't wish to tell me. As you have never been reluctant to confide in me in the past, I can only surmise this is significant."

"And you won't like it."

"Then perhaps you should tell me and get it over with."

"Probably." India braced herself. "When Mr. Saunders sets out from London to follow in Heloise's footsteps, I shall accompany him."

"You what?"

"I don't trust his abilities—or willingness—to find Heloise on his own. I intend to make sure he does whatever is necessary," she added. "In addition, by watching his every move I may be able to uncover proof of his wrongdoing and thereby save other women just like Heloise. The man belongs in prison. I am certain he is behind this Lady Travelers Society that I fear has no real substance and only exists to separate unsuspecting older women from their money."

Martin stared at her for a long, silent moment.

"There, now you know everything." Without thinking, she twisted her hands together in a nervous manner. "I do wish you would say something."

"How am I to get along without you?"

Any apprehension she'd had about revealing her plans vanished with his words. "Goodness, Martin, you're a grown man. I'm certain you can manage by yourself."

His eyes widened. "I don't know that I can manage at all if you abandon me."

"I am not abandoning you." This was not the response she'd expected although she probably should have. "You have a houseful of servants to see to your needs. Your cook will make certain you are fed, your housekeeper will attempt to keep your clutter confined to your library and your butler will keep the rest of the world at bay."

"But...but..." The man stared as if she were the worst sort of traitor. "Who will handle my correspondence and see to my schedule and organize my notes? You do realize I am trying to put together my reference of ancient Roman desert trade routes so that it may be published soon."

"Of course I realize that." What she hadn't realized was that he was quite so helpless. "You have been putting together that book since before I came to work for you."

"But I'm now closer to completion than ever," he said staunchly.

"And my absence will give you the opportunity to devote your attention fully to your work." Although she would wager her yearly salary that he would be no further along when she returned, whether that was in a week or ten years.

"But…" His brow furrowed; then his expression brightened. The tiniest hint of triumph shone in his eyes. "You accompanying this man—this mastermind—would be shockingly improper. I can't believe you're considering such a thing. And I don't imagine Lady Heloise would approve."

"As she is not here, that is a moot point. And I have already had this conversation. I'm not especially worried about my reputation."

"I am and concerned as well about your safety." He drummed his fingers on his desk. "I daresay I won't have a moment's rest knowing you are off with this… this *villain*."

"I'm not sure *villain* is entirely accurate—"

He ignored her. "Going off to Europe in the company of a man you know nothing about. A man you don't trust. A man you think is using a trio of elderly ladies to pilfer money from other elderly ladies. Why, you've already referred to him not only as a mastermind but as a scoundrel and a rogue, as well."

"Indeed I did, but—"

"Manipulation and deception are not qualities one usually looks for in a traveling companion." His jaw set in a determined manner. "I cannot in all good conscience allow you to go off alone with this man."

"We won't be alone," she said quickly, ignoring the fact that—even if he was her employer—Martin had no right to tell her what she could and could not do. "The ladies insisted on chaperones."

His eyes narrowed. "How do you know these chaperones are to be trusted?"

"I don't. Mr. Saunders was not pleased about my demand to go with him, nor was he happy about having chaperones accompany us. It was his great-aunt's idea."

"If she is his great-aunt," he said darkly.

"Given the way they behave around each other, there is no doubt in my mind as to their familial connection. And while I do think Mr. Saunders is clever enough to manipulate elderly ladies, I doubt that he can arrange diabolical chaperones on a moment's notice."

"Even so…" His fingers drummed faster, and she knew by the look in his eyes that he was struggling to come up with another reason why she shouldn't go. "I suspect if I forbid you to go, if I threaten that your position will not be here when you return," he said in a measured manner, "it will not be enough to dissuade you from this ill-advised course you've set."

"I do appreciate your concern, but no, it won't."

"Then there's nothing else to do. To ensure your safety and your honor—" he squared his shoulders "—I shall simply have to come with you."

For perhaps the first time in eight years, India had absolutely no idea how to respond. Martin had a brilliant—if unfocused—mind, but he was not the type of man one would turn to for protection. While not unattractive, he was a bit over average in height with fair, usually unkempt, hair, a boyish look about him—in spite of his age—and a build kept slender by regular exercise. Regardless, he exuded an absentminded air of scholarly endeavor not physical prowess. Why, India was probably more suited to be a rescuing knight than Martin. Beyond that, the poor dear did not take well to travel. Trains upset his stomach in the manner of mal de mer, and the mere thought of crossing the Channel usually turned his complexion green in anticipation.

"That's very kind of you, but it's not necessary."

"Oh, I think it is."

"Martin," she said gently, "if you are truly concerned as to my reputation, surely you can see that traveling with two single men—even with chaperones—would make this appear much more shocking." Indeed, it was a mark of her concern that she was willing to bend propriety this far in the first place. "But I am grateful for the offer."

"I am not happy about this, India."

"I'm not especially happy about it myself but…" She shrugged. "I do not trust Mr. Saunders."

"Perhaps," he said slowly. "If I paid for the investigation—"

"I cannot permit that, and you know it." She thought for a moment. "But there is something I will allow you to do for me."

"I am at your service. Always."

Usually, Martin's droll comments were nothing more than mildly amusing, but on occasion, she had wondered if there was more to them than he let on. This was one of those moments. Not that she had time for sentimental speculation.

"I will meet the chaperones on the day after tomorrow, and we leave the day after that. I believe it would be wise to have more information about Mr. Saunders than I currently have."

He nodded thoughtfully. "I will contact an investigator I know, very discreet and very efficient." He paused, a look of resignation on his face. "You will be careful?"

She nodded. "I will."

"I expect regular correspondence from you apprising me as to your progress."

She nodded. "I shall do my utmost."

"No, on further consideration..." He tapped his fingers on the desk thoughtfully. "I know you will not allow me to finance this endeavor—"

"I have savings as my salary is more than sufficient."

"Given all your responsibilities, that is debatable. Regardless, as mere correspondence will take entirely too long to reassure me as to your safety, I shall provide you with funds so that you may telegraph me as to your whereabouts and progress."

"Goodness, I really don't think that's—"

"Every third day will do." She started to protest, but he held up a hand to forestall her. "I will not take no for an answer on this, India."

"You don't think every three days is excessive?"

"Probably, but with any luck you will not be gone long." Resignation sounded in his voice. "I will expect you to telegraph me as well if there's anything you need—including funds."

"I doubt that will be necessary, but thank you." She paused. "And thank you for your friendship as well. I value it, Martin."

"As I value yours." He stared at her for a moment as if there was something more he wished to say. At last he nodded. "That's it then. We should get back to work. What is on our schedule for today?"

She picked up her notebook from its usual spot— precisely in the upper-right corner of his desk. "You wished to order supplies for the experiment you spoke of yesterday and we need to respond to the invitation from the Society of..."

While he could occasionally be somewhat perplexing, India was under no illusions about Martin. He was indeed her friend, and if he wished for more than friendship between them, well, he'd had eight years to do something about that. Not that she would welcome any overtures of a romantic nature. Certainly not from Martin. At this point in her life, India had no particular interest in romance. Any silly dreams she might have had as a girl were abandoned years ago when she'd realized dashing heroes were plentiful between the pages of books but rather lacking in real life. Besides, heroes did not ride to the rescue of heroines who were ordinary in appearance, sensible in nature and had little financial worth.

Without warning, flashing blue eyes and a wicked grin jumped to mind. She ignored it.

No, she had no interest in romance with Martin. Or anyone else.

CHAPTER FIVE

When choosing traveling companions, a lady traveler should be diligent in assessing compatibility in temperament, habit and nature. Nothing destroys the joy of a trip abroad faster than being in the company of a person one cannot abide. The rigors of travel have been known to turn mild annoyance into virulent loathing, even among the very best of friends.

—The Lady Travelers Society Guide

"I HAVE NO idea where Derek is." Lady Blodgett refilled India's teacup and smiled pleasantly. "But I'm certain he'll be here at any moment."

"No doubt," India murmured. She resisted the need to scream in frustration and instead forced a smile of her own.

Mr. Saunders was late by a quarter of an hour thus far. It was not an auspicious beginning. Not that she'd expected promptness from him. Why, one could tell from just looking at the man he was not the sort to pay attention to the rules that governed the lives of everyone else in the world. One would think when one's great-aunt invited one to her home promptly at four o'clock, one would arrive promptly at four o'clock. Aside from meeting the chaperones Lady Blodgett had promised, they had a great deal to discuss. Plans needed to be made.

"I would imagine he's making arrangements." Mrs. Greer piled a few more biscuits on her already-heaping plate. India wasn't sure if the woman couldn't make up her mind which of the delightful offerings to take or if she feared this was her last chance to ever have a biscuit again.

"As well he should," Professor Greer said under his breath, reaching for another biscuit, although he had already emptied and refilled his plate at least once.

Lady Blodgett had presented the retired professor and his wife to India with something of a satisfied flourish. The couple was old enough to be suitable as chaperones but not so old as to impede speedy progress. As much as India would have preferred not to have them at all, they were necessary to abide by the dictates of proper behavior.

The Greers were not particularly objectionable and did seem pleasant enough. The professor looked exactly as one would expect a former professor to look—a bit portly, with graying hair, full beard and kind brown eyes behind wire-rimmed spectacles. Clad in expected tweed, he had the slightest air of pomposity that declared his superior intelligence. Whereas the professor exuded solid, English stock, his wife struck India as a more exotic creature. Or perhaps a wren disguised as something more akin to a tropical bird. She was obviously enamored of bright colors. Her hair was a fading shade of red, her round figure clothed in a startling chartreuse gown bedecked with ruffles and ribbons, and her hat, well, there was much to observe in her hat, including an array of peach-tinted flowers and, of course, feathers. But her blue eyes were bright and inquisitive and friendly.

The couple was more than pleasant. They were very

nearly overwhelming in their eagerness over what Lady
Blodgett kept referring to as their *quest*. India wasn't
at all sure she liked the term *quest*—it brought to mind
grand adventures and legendary pursuits. She preferred
to think of this as a serious search, even a mission of
rescue. Although she did hope rescue would not be
necessary. She hoped—she prayed—nothing had happened to Heloise and she was simply unable to write
for whatever reason. A reason that might well turn out
to be completely insignificant. Heloise did tend to be a
bit scatterbrained and easily distracted. Still, as much
as India tried to convince herself of that, the horrible
weight of doubt still lodged in the pit of her stomach.

India glanced at the clock on the mantel in Lady
Blodgett's parlor and resisted the urge to shudder. The
clock was a dark bronze and perhaps the most ornate
thing she'd ever seen. Mythical figures cavorted about
its base, and fictitious beasts writhed around the sides,
climbing toward a goddess figure at the top. One could
barely see the clock face for the embellishments. Matching urns supporting candelabra flanked the timepiece,
the epitome of the current overindulgent style. But then
everything in Lady Blodgett's cluttered parlor—from
the small Egyptian mummy case—apparently for a
cat—in one corner to the Grecian statue centered between the front windows to the ancient Roman swords
hanging on the far wall—was at once unique and far-
fetched. And better suited to a museum than a home.
There wasn't so much as an inch of the ornately carved
tabletops in the parlor not covered with a Dresden figu-
rine, a knickknack of some sort or a souvenir from Sir
Charles's travels. Aside from the lack of poorly executed art on the walls, Heloise would have felt com-

pletely at home in this room. She would have described it as whimsical.

It was not the word India would have used. Even though India shared Heloise's London house, her private rooms were on the second floor, and she'd decorated them with an eye toward simplicity and function. Aside from her collection of novels of mystery and detection, little in India's quarters would have revealed much of herself to a casual observer. Whereas Heloise's friendly nature and delightful demeanor was evident in every nook and cranny of the rest of the house. The older woman had never met a knickknack or objet d'art she didn't love.

India would not have termed Lady Blodgett's filled to overflowing room as shabby, either, but it had obviously seen better days. Heloise would have felt at home with that, as well.

"Perhaps, while we wait for Derek, you would like to explain to Professor and Mrs. Greer exactly how you plan to find Lady Heloise." Lady Blodgett stared at her expectantly.

"You must have a plan, you know," the professor said firmly. "Can't go running about the world willy-nilly. Even the most intrepid adventurers have some sort of plan." While a longtime member of the Explorers Club, the professor had apparently rarely set foot out of England, which only heightened his enthusiasm for the *quest*.

"Our plans are not definitive as of yet. There are still some decisions to be made." India adopted a confidence she did not feel. "At our last meeting, Mr. Saunders suggested following my cousin's footsteps insofar as we know them. I do have the letters she wrote to me from various places and of course there is her itinerary. I assume the society has a copy of that?"

"I would think so." Lady Blodgett gestured absently.

"Fortunately, I made a copy before Lady Heloise left England, which I will share with Mr. Saunders." India tried and failed to keep the annoyance from her voice. "Should he ever arrive."

"Come now, Miss Prendergast," Professor Greer said in a chastising manner. "I have no doubt Mr. Saunders is engaged in preparations for our journey, as any good leader of an expedition would be."

Indignation surged through India. *Good leader, indeed!* "On the contrary, Professor, I would imagine Mr.—"

"Parkhurst!" Lady Blodgett interrupted, calling to her butler. "We seem to be running low on biscuits. I'm sure Mrs. Greer would care for some more. Wouldn't you, Estelle?"

Mrs. Greer glanced from the almost-empty serving platter to her still-full plate, then nodded. "Perhaps another one or two. They are delicious."

"Aren't they, though?" Lady Blodgett beamed. "My cook is really quite wonderful with biscuits, although you should try…"

Lady Blodgett continued rambling about scones and other baked goods in an obvious effort to avoid any discussion of her great-nephew's leadership abilities or anything else about him. India could certainly understand that. It had proven surprisingly easy for Martin's investigator to uncover a great deal of information about Mr. Saunders. Much of the man's life was an open book. A scandal-ridden digest of impropriety and excess. The kind of book that should be banned from respectable society.

Derek Saunders was indeed the heir of the Earl of Danby and, like so many young men of privilege, had spent most of his days enjoying the pleasures English life provided the offspring of society. A few years older than India, his reputation for spending, indulgence in gaming, women and drink were the stuff gossips dreamed of. His name had been linked to numerous indiscretions, and while admittedly they were not the kind that ruined lives or toppled empires, they were still notable. The latest rumor was that his uncle was no longer tolerating his irresponsible behavior and had cut him off. One did wonder if he had come up with the idea of siphoning money from susceptible older ladies in the form of dues and charges for travel services after the earl's edict or before.

"Now then, Miss Prendergast," Professor Greer began when Lady Blodgett had at last paused for breath. "You were saying that Mr. Saunders's plans for our endeavor were still undetermined."

"No, Professor," India said firmly. "I was saying *our* plans were—"

"Coming along nicely, I would say." Mr. Saunders strode into the room and straight to his great-aunt's side. "My apologies, Aunt Guinevere. Sorry I'm late." He bent and kissed her cheek, the faultless image of a perfect, doting nephew. One did hope he was fooling the Greers as he certainly wasn't fooling India. "It took longer than I expected to finalize a few details for our venture. I must say I'm pleased at how well all is working out." He nodded at India and settled into the chair beside Lady Blodgett. "Miss Prendergast, you're looking lovely today."

Such charming nonsense was not going to work on her. "Thank you, Mr. Saunders. You're looking well.

One was beginning to wonder if perhaps you had been hit by a bus."

He chuckled. "Or perhaps one was hoping."

She cast him an overly sweet smile. "Perhaps."

"Derek, you must meet some dear friends of mine who have agreed—at considerable personal sacrifice mind you—to act as chaperones for you and Miss Prendergast," Lady Blodgett began. "Estelle, allow me to introduce my nephew, Mr. Saunders. Derek, this is Mrs. Greer. Estelle and I have been friends for—oh, how long is it now?" She frowned at Mrs. Greer. "Can it possibly be nearly forty years?"

"Oh dear." Mrs. Greer winced. "That does seem like an awfully long time, but I'm afraid you're right."

"It's a pleasure to meet you, Mrs. Greer." Mr. Saunders stood, took her hand and raised it to his lips. His gaze never left the chaperone's in a manner too polished and obviously well rehearsed. Derek Saunders had no doubt kissed a fair number of hands. It was all India could do to keep from snorting in disdain. "But surely my great-aunt is mistaken, Mrs. Greer."

"In what way, Mr. Saunders?" The woman stared up at the younger man, admiration shining in her eyes.

"I cannot believe you have known each other for forty years, unless perhaps she first made your acquaintance when you were barely out of the nursery."

"Goodness, Mr. Saunders." A blush colored Mrs. Greer's cheeks. "You are a charming devil. Why, you will quite turn my head with such nonsense."

"I do hope so, Mrs. Greer." Mr. Saunders flashed her a smile that would have made even the most unyielding woman swoon. "And, as we are to be traveling companions, you must call me Derek."

"Very well, *Derek*." Mrs. Greer dimpled. "But only if you call me Estelle."

India wanted to choke.

A smug gleam showed in Lady Blodgett's eyes. "And this is Estelle's husband, Professor Greer."

"Professor." Mr. Saunders nodded and shook the other man's hand firmly.

"Professor Greer is an expert in medieval architecture," Lady Blodgett said. "Your uncle Charles held him in the utmost regard."

"From what I recall of my great-uncle, Professor, that is indeed the highest of compliments. And no doubt well deserved."

"I was a great admirer of his, as well," the professor said gruffly. "Always wanted to join one of his expeditions, but the time was never quite right."

"But now you are accompanying me, and I am most grateful to have a man of your expertise and obvious wisdom."

"You just met the man," India said without thinking. "How can you possibly say that?"

"Uncle Charles was an excellent judge of character," Mr. Saunders said smoothly. "Any man who had his respect has mine, as well. I must say, Miss Prendergast, I am somewhat shocked that you would not understand that." A chastising note sounded in his voice.

Four pairs of accusatory eyes turned toward India. Not the least bit fair. She was not the practiced charlatan here. Obviously why he had won them over and she had not. Still, this was not a good way to begin a journey of indeterminate length. For someone who preferred to act with reason rather than succumbing to emotion, she was apparently letting her feelings about Mr. Saunders color her judgment. And if one wished to best an op-

ponent, one might wish to employ his tactics. She was
not used to chicanery, but two could play at his game.
How difficult could it be?

"Please forgive me, all of you. I spoke without thinking." She heaved an overly dramatic sigh. "I am trying very hard to keep my emotions in check but not
knowing where Cousin Heloise is…" She sniffed back
a nonexistent tear, surprised to note it was not quite as
feigned as she had expected.

"You poor dear." Mrs. Greer cast her a sympathetic
glance.

"Apology accepted, Miss Prendergast." Mr. Saunders
nodded and turned to the others. "We leave for Paris
tomorrow. If we take the morning train to Dover, we
can be in Paris by nightfall."

"Paris?" India stared.

"Paris." Mrs. Greer fairly sighed the word. "Did you
hear that, Frederick? We're going to Paris." She leaned
toward Lady Blodgett in a confidential manner. "I have
always dreamed of going to Paris."

"As have I," Lady Blodgett said with a weak smile.
"Charles always intended to take me, but somehow,
the opportune time never arose. My friend Persephone
speaks quite fondly of it. Of course, it's been years since
she's been there."

"I spent some time there as a student," the professor
added. "I doubt it's changed much. Paris never does."

"Paris?" India glared at Mr. Saunders. This was not
what they had discussed.

"We, too, have some final arrangements to make."
Professor Greer stood and offered his hand to his wife.
"Come along, Estelle."

"Oh my, yes." Mrs. Greer took his hand and rose to
her feet. Mr. Saunders stood at once. The man was at

least cognizant of polite behavior. "This has all happened so quickly. There is a great deal to do before we can leave. Why, we have to pack our bags and confer with the servants and arrange for—"

"Then we won't keep you a moment longer." Lady Blodgett stood, as well. "Allow me to see you out." She glanced at her nephew. "I suspect you and Miss Prendergast have much to discuss before your departure."

Mr. Saunders glanced at India. "I would think so."

The older lady's gaze shifted from her nephew to India and back. "I will leave you to it then." She took Mrs. Greer's arm and herded the couple toward the hall. "I can't tell you how envious I am. Perhaps, one day, I, too…"

Mr. Saunders closed the doors behind them.

India stood and crossed her arms over her chest. "Paris?"

"I believe that's the third time you've said that."

"It bears repeating. If I recall correctly, you originally suggested following in Heloise's footsteps. And I agreed." She drew her brows together. "Her footsteps did not begin in Paris."

"No, they did not," he said mildly, crossing the room to a cabinet and opening the doors. "Would you care for a brandy or whisky? Or perhaps sherry would be more to your liking."

"I have tea." She waved impatiently at her cup.

"Ah yes, well, so you do."

"I have never been one for overindulgence in spirits."

"Imagine my surprise."

"Besides, it's entirely too early in the day for spirits."

"How did I know you were going to say that?" He poured himself a glass of something amber and probably horribly inebriating.

She ignored the question. "I do hope indulging in alcohol at all hours is not something you plan to make a habit of during our travels."

"As long as my *habits* do not interfere in our purposes, I would say they are none of your concern."

She paused to summon a measure of calm. She couldn't find Heloise without this beastly creature, and, as much as she disapproved of nearly everything about him, it made no sense not to attempt to get along with him. *Still...*

"Mr. Saunders." She drew a calming breath. "I do not appreciate you changing our plans without informing me."

He glanced at her, took a deep swallow of his drink, then refilled his glass. As if dealing with her required strong spirits.

"First of all, Miss Prendergast, they are not *our* plans." He returned to his chair, gestured for her to sit, then resumed his seat. "They are *my* plans. You insisted upon coming. It's only because my aunt agreed that you should that I am allowing you to do so."

She gasped. "Allowing me?"

"Yes," he said in a hard tone. "Allowing you."

"Whether you *allow* me to accompany you or not, I was not about to *allow* you to look for my cousin without supervision."

"Supervision?" His brow rose as if she had just made the most amusing comment.

"I daresay someone needs to keep an eye on you."

"You don't trust me, do you, Miss Prendergast?"

"Absolutely not."

"Why not?" He leaned forward in what appeared to be genuine curiosity. "You don't even know me."

"Your reputation does not foster trust, Mr. Saunders."

"I see." He studied her curiously. "I would have

thought you were the type of woman who judged people on their own merits rather than what gossips have had to say about them."

Heat washed up her face. "I am indeed, but I am not a fool. When one person says a piece of fruit is a plum, there's a possibility it may not be a plum. However, when dozens of people identify it as a plum, the chances are very good that it is indeed a plum."

"I see." He continued his perusal of her as if she were an insect in a glass case. "You're very sure of yourself, aren't you?"

"I've never had any reason to doubt myself or my judgment."

"Oh, this will be an enjoyable trip," he said under his breath.

"I am not here to enjoy myself," she said staunchly.

"Understandable, of course."

"I am very concerned about my cousin." The oddest lump formed in her throat, and she cleared it. "Indeed, she is my only concern."

"Do not mistake my words, Miss Prendergast," he said in a serious manner. "I, too, am concerned that we find Lady Heloise safe and well. However, it has been my observation that even the most serious of ventures progresses more easily when one attempts to appreciate new experiences."

"I have no intention of appreciating anything."

"No, I didn't think you would."

She ignored him. "I do wish you would answer my question. Why are we starting in Paris?"

"Because the last letter you received from her came from Paris."

"How did you know that?"

"Good God, Miss Prendergast, you needn't look at

me as if I were some sort of nefarious villain intent on doing you and your cousin harm."

Admittedly, she had little more than gossip and her suspicions as to his character. Not that he probably didn't deserve it.

"Until you prove otherwise, Mr. Saunders…" She shrugged.

He stared at her for a moment, then laughed.

"This is not amusing."

"On the contrary, it—you—" he raised his glass to her "—are most amusing."

"Imagine my delight in your assessment of me," she snapped. "Now, once again—how did you know her last letter was from Paris?"

"When we first met, you said her last letter was from France and you specifically said it was from Paris in each and every letter you sent to the Travelers Society."

She stared at him. "You actually read them?"

"Of course I did." He sipped his drink. "If you recall, I had already begun an effort to locate her before you so politely introduced yourself."

"I will grant you that," she said reluctantly. Perhaps on this one point she was not being fair.

"Thank you." He thought for a moment. "It simply seemed to me it was logical to begin our search in the last place we know Lady Heloise to have visited, rather than going back to where she was previously. Don't you agree?"

"That does make sense." She nodded slowly.

"Then I'm right?"

She clenched her teeth. "Yes, I suppose you are."

"Excellent." He grinned.

"Don't be smug, Mr. Saunders. It's most unbecoming."

"Nonetheless, I find it hard to resist. I can't imagine you admitting that I may be right about something to be more than an infrequent occurrence. I intend to savor it when it happens."

"As well you should, as I, too, am fairly certain it will be extremely rare."

He grinned another most disarming grin. It was all she could do to ignore it.

"Did you bring your cousin's letters?" he said, abruptly changing the subject.

She nodded.

"May I read them?"

She started to refuse, then realized it was not an unreasonable request. And while he might not have her trust, a little cooperation between them might be beneficial. "May I ask why?"

"There may be something in them that could prove of value. Something you might have overlooked."

"That's possible I suppose." She grabbed her bag and rummaged through it.

"And I am right once again," he murmured. She pretended not to hear him. "If these are of a personal nature—"

"No, not at all." She pulled out a packet of letters and handed it to him. "Heloise wrote of the sights, where she was staying and assorted travel details. Nothing especially personal at all."

He shuffled through the letters. "Is that unusual? For them to be so impersonal, that is?"

"I didn't say they were impersonal, although I suppose they might be construed as such. As for whether or not that's unusual, I can't really say." She thought for a moment. "Heloise and I haven't corresponded since my school years. If I recall correctly, those letters were about the details of her day-to-day life. Her letters now

are about travel and the sights she's seeing. This is very
new to her, and she was extremely excited about her
travels. It simply stands to reason that detailing what
she sees would be what she'd write about."

"Of course." He nodded. "May I return these to you
in the morning?"

"Certainly, and I should take my leave, as well." She
rose to her feet, Mr. Saunders standing at once. She
could not fault the man's grasp of manners. "I, too, have
a great many details to attend to before our departure."
She nodded and started toward the door.

India was the first to admit her greatest flaw was
impatience. Now that arrangements were made, she
was almost as eager as the Greers to begin their travels. Eager and possibly even a bit excited. The thought
pulled her up short. There was nothing to be excited
about. This was Heloise's adventure, not hers.

"One more thing, Miss Prendergast, before you go."

She turned back to him. "Yes?"

"As we are to be traveling companions, and will be
spending a considerable amount of time in each other's
company, I would appreciate it if you would give the
slightest bit of consideration to the possibility that I am
not as wicked as you apparently think." He smiled in a
most engaging way. She ignored it.

"That remains to be seen, Mr. Saunders. Although I
should warn you—" she flicked her gaze over him in a
dismissive manner "—I have never been fond of plums."

CHAPTER SIX

"AND HOW LONG do you expect this endeavor to take?" Uncle Edward studied Derek from behind the massive desk in the library in his London house. Now in his sixty-first year, the Earl of Danby was still a fine figure of a man with graying hair and piercing blue eyes that seemed to notice all sorts of things one wished they wouldn't. Derek had been the recipient of that look before. He resisted the urge to squirm in his chair like a guilty schoolboy.

"Quite honestly, sir—" Derek braced himself " I have no idea."

Derek would have liked nothing better than to have avoided this conversation altogether, but in the months since Uncle Edward's mandate that he reform his care-free ways, he'd been working with the earl's estate, property and business managers. No one had been more surprised than Derek to discover he not only had a knack for numbers and business; he enjoyed it. Abandoning his new duties for as long as it took to find Lady Heloise would not sit well with his uncle. At least not without an explanation.

"I see." Uncle Edward considered him in a non-committal manner.

"Frankly, sir —" Derek leaned forward and met his uncle's gaze firmly "—I don't see that I have a choice. While I did look into hiring private investigators to locate Lady Heloise, such efforts will take funding beyond my resources and a great deal of time."

"You could have asked me for the money," Uncle Edward said, his tone deceptively mild.

"I could have, and I did consider it." Derek chose his words with care. The earl was a clever man, and now was not the time for anything other than complete honesty. "But Lady Blodgett is my mother's aunt and not a relation of yours."

"As much as I haven't seen her in years, I have always been fond of Guinevere. She helped me with an awkward situation once. I wish she had come to me with her financial problems."

"She would never do that, sir. Indeed, as far as I am aware, she never mentioned any difficulties to my mother." Without question, Mother would have insisted Aunt Guinevere accept her help. "But as a member of my family she is my responsibility."

"One does take responsibility for family."

Derek started to say that was something he'd learned from his uncle but thought better of it. Uncle Edward took a dim view of those who curried favor too overtly, even with the truth. Instead he nodded. "Which is why I did not think it was appropriate to ask for your help in this."

"So you intend to use your own resources?" The earl's brow twitched.

"Such as they are." Derek couldn't resist a grin. "It seems in recent months, I haven't been squandering my allowance in the manner I once did."

Uncle Edward stared at him for an intense moment. "I am aware of that."

Family money supported Derek, as it had his father before his death and his mother between her first and second husbands. Derek barely remembered his father, but Uncle Edward had said on more than one occasion how reliable and responsible Henry Saunders had been. How his twin brother had taken a significant role in the management of family affairs. As Uncle Edward always made such comments in an especially meaningful manner, the point was not lost on Derek.

"I would have preferred not to have told you about any of this at all."

The earl nodded. "Understandable."

Still, Derek hadn't told his uncle everything. While he had admitted that Aunt Guinevere and her friends had started the Lady Travelers Society and had subsequently misplaced a member, he'd thought it best not to reveal his conviction that the elderly ladies were engaged in fraudulent activities. That would not sit well with the Earl of Danby. Nor would the scandal that would surely erupt if Lady Heloise was not located. He had no doubt Miss Prendergast would make the whole mess horribly public. And there was no reason why she shouldn't.

"But I did not feel I could shirk the duties you have entrusted to me without telling you why I chose to do so."

"Prudent of you." Uncle Edward tapped his pen thoughtfully on his desk. "And you feel the need to take this upon yourself?"

"I'm afraid so. I don't see any other option. I'm not sure I trust anyone else to do this with the expedience I think it warrants. And I do think time is of the essence."

"Nor will anyone put the effort into it that you will, am I correct?"

"I believe so, sir."

"Then you have considered the possibility that something dire might have happened to Lady Heloise."

"Frankly, that is my greatest fear." Derek shook his head. "The responsibility would then fall fully on Aunt Guinevere and her friends. It would devastate them, sir, and destroy their organization's reputation as well as their good names."

"Without question." Uncle Edward paused. "Do you think it's wise to bring Lady Heloise's niece along with you?"

"I think it's a disaster in the making." Derek shuddered. "But I have no choice in the matter. She threatened to follow if I did not permit her to accompany me, and Aunt Guinevere pointed out the blame would then be laid at my feet if anything happened to her."

"She's right there."

"Oh, and it's not Lady Heloise's niece but her cousin. Second cousin actually. She is Lady Heloise's ward." Derek had thought it wise to check into Miss Prendergast's background and had called on the services of an old friend, Phineas Chapman, who had turned a brilliant mind to the art of investigation. It seemed there wasn't much to uncover.

India Prendergast had been orphaned as a young girl when her missionary parents had died of some unknown tropical illness in the South Seas. She'd then made her home with Lady Heloise, apparently her only relative. She had graduated with honors from the prestigious Miss Bicklesham's Academy for Accomplished Young Ladies. Derek knew quite a few women whose formative years had been spent at Miss Bicklesham's. Fortunately, the lessons of propriety and decorum taught at the academy did not impress themselves upon those ladies in the way they obviously did Miss Prendergast.

She'd been briefly employed as a governess and had an even shorter tenure as a teacher at Miss Bicklesham's before becoming the secretarial assistant to Sir Martin Luckthorne. Derek had never heard of the man, but apparently he was well regarded in assorted intellectual, scientific and antiquarian circles. While only in his early forties, he was considered somewhat reclusive and a bit eccentric. There was no Lady Luckthorne, which one might think would cast a pall of impropriety over Miss Prendergast's employment if, of course, one had not made Miss Prendergast's acquaintance.

According to Chapman, Miss Prendergast had never been engaged, her name had never been linked to any man's and, at the age of twenty-nine, she was considered a true spinster. Apparently there had been no effort to see her wed, either. Odd, as Chapman said—although Lady Heloise lived frugally—she did seem to have a surprisingly significant fortune. But Miss Prendergast had had no coming-out season, no introduction to society; indeed, society seemed to have no idea of her existence. Odder still, given Lady Heloise's resources, that Miss Prendergast chose to be employed rather than work at charitable causes or those things with which most ladies occupied their time. Aside from her life with Lady Heloise and her work with Sir Martin, there was little to say about Miss India Prendergast.

"So you intend to wander aimlessly around Paris looking for this woman?"

"Not aimlessly," Derek said. "I do have something of a plan. I intend to check with hotels and the embassy, make inquiries at the train station and wherever else she might have been and that sort of thing. If necessary, we will progress on to the next point in her itinerary." It seemed quite clever when he'd first thought

of it but, saying it aloud to his uncle, it did seem rather
aimless at that.

"I am inclined to offer you my assistance, Derek,"
the earl said.

"I didn't ask—"

His uncle held up a hand to stop him. "Precisely why
I intend to give it." He leaned forward over his desk
and met Derek's gaze firmly. "If something has happened to Lady Heloise, the situation will only be worse
if Miss Prendergast is present when such information
is discovered."

"I don't even want to consider that possibility, sir."

"Nor do I, but it is a possibility. Admittedly a dismal one, but a possibility nonetheless. Here's what I'm
going to suggest." He paused thoughtfully. "First, I am
pleased that you have taken on the task of protecting
your great-aunt and her cohorts. There is nothing in
this world more important than family and a family's
good name."

Derek nodded.

"Secondly, I have a fair number of influential connections as well as more money than even you can
spend in a lifetime. I can afford to send out a small
army of investigators to track down a missing traveler in a swift and efficient manner. Men who are well
trained and know what they're doing."

It was indeed a generous offer. "Still, sir, it is my
problem."

"Correct me if I'm wrong, but isn't your objective
to find Lady Heloise as quickly as possible so as to ap-
pease Miss Prendergast, thereby avoiding destroying
an old lady's good name?"

As well as keep her out of prison. "Yes, sir."

"And shouldn't you employ every means at your disposal to do so?"

"Yes, of course, but—"

"And am I not offering assistance that might help you do just that?"

"Nonetheless, sir, this is my responsibility."

"Good God, you're stubborn." Uncle Edward grinned. "But then, so am I. Here's my proposal. Travel as planned with Miss Prendergast to Paris and keep her there. The longer she's out of London, the less likely she is to cause problems for Lady Blodgett. You did say she had contacted the police?"

Derek nodded.

"You will restrict your search to the confines of Paris. I will hire trained investigators to proceed with the utmost haste in searching elsewhere."

Derek drew his brows together. "Regardless of my lack of training, you do realize there is every possibility that I will find Lady Heloise."

"If she is alive and well, there is indeed. And we will hope for that. Do not mistake my words, Derek. You are an intelligent man, and my offer is not due to any lack of confidence in you. Rather, I want to help. Besides, I have always been fond of a good mystery." The older man's eyes twinkled in a way Derek could not recall having seen in a long time. In recent years, whenever they talked, the look in his uncle's eyes tended toward irritation. "I don't know if you're aware of it, but I am quite fond of detective novels and stories of mystery. And, as much as I hate to admit it, all these responsibilities I am currently training you for tend not to be terribly exciting. After a while, one does long for a taste of adventure."

"Determining the whereabouts of an elderly lady does not strike me as a significant adventure, sir."

"One takes what one can get, my boy. I'd accompany you if I could but that's impossible at the moment. Still, the idea of managing a search like this, being the mastermind behind it, if you will, sounds rather like an adventure."

"Mastermind?" Derek's brow rose.

"Excellent word. It denotes power, perception, a fine intellect and perhaps a touch of wickedness." His uncle grinned. "Give me a week. Better yet—a fortnight."

His uncle was right. If his purpose was to find Lady Heloise as quickly as possible, he would be an idiot to turn down help.

"Why not a month?" he said blithely.

"Excellent." Uncle Edward beamed.

"I wasn't serious." Derek glared. "How am I to keep Miss Prendergast in Paris for a month?"

"Come now, Derek—it's Paris." Uncle Edward settled back in his chair and considered him thoughtfully. "You can't have forgotten the charms of Paris. You've been there in recent years. I know. I paid for it."

"Well, yes, but—"

"Aside from the fact that the entire world is flocking to the Paris Exposition, Paris itself has always had a certain charm—part utter elegance, part ancient history and part Bohemian decadence."

"Decadence will not appeal to Miss Prendergast."

"She's a woman, isn't she?"

"One would think." Nonetheless it was hard to picture the very disapproving India Prendergast in Paris.

"And you are a man with a rather significant reputation when it comes to women."

Derek started to deny it, but what was the point?

"Between your charms and those of the City of Light, I can't imagine you can't come up with dozens of ways to delay Miss Prendergast."

"But an entire month in Paris…" Derek shook his head. "I'm not sure that's possible."

"It may not take a month for either of us to find Lady Heloise. I shall telegraph you to keep you apprised of my progress." The earl chuckled. "I think it sounds like fun."

"Fun?" Derek snorted. "You haven't met Miss Prendergast."

His uncle waved off the comment. "She's simply an obstacle tossed in your way to make things more interesting."

"Good God, Uncle Edward, this is not a game."

"You're right, of course." Uncle Edward had the grace to look chagrined. "Why don't we just call it a test?"

"A test?" Derek stared.

"Or would you rather make it a wager?" A wicked gleam shone in Uncle Edward's eyes.

"A wager," Derek said slowly. He'd always loved a good wager. Still, his uncle wanted him to mend his wild ways. As much as he wanted to agree, the thought occurred to him that perhaps this was the test. "I'm not sure that's wise, Uncle."

The earl snorted back a laugh. "Bloody hell, man, I never intended to break your spirit. An interesting wager between two honorable men is not objectionable."

"Given what's at stake, I'm not sure a wager is appropriate."

"Perhaps." His uncle shrugged. "Then we are back to a test. Succeed in keeping Miss Prendergast occupied while I use my resources to learn what happened to her cousin. And then avoid dragging your great-aunt's name through the mud, as well as evade any legal problems that might arise from all this—" Uncle Edward was apparently even more perceptive than Derek realized "—and it will prove to me that you do indeed have what it takes to handle my affairs after I'm gone. Any idiot can inherit a title and a fortune, Derek, but managing property, finances and, more important, people takes experience, skill and instinct."

"And if I pass this test of yours?"

"Then I shall withdraw the threat of leaving you penniless." Uncle Edward grinned.

Derek stared at the older man. "I'm not quite sure I believe you."

"Wise of you." His uncle chuckled. "Show me that you can manage a situation as fraught with disaster as this one and you have my word. You will inherit everything you deserve."

"Everything I deserve?" Derek was fairly certain his uncle's phrasing left something to be desired. "Who decides what I deserve?"

Uncle Edward laughed. "Excellent catch, my boy." He sobered. "But I am serious about this. If you pull this off, then you will have earned your inheritance as well as my respect. There's nothing I can do about who inherits my title, but I'll be damned if I'll leave my money and property to a man I don't respect. Prove to me you can be that man."

"I shall try, sir."

"Then I can ask nothing more. But regardless of how this turns out, I will still expect you to continue to tread the straight and narrower path you have been walking of late." His grin widened if possible. "I just won't be such an ass about it."

"Oh well, that makes it all worthwhile then," Derek said without thinking, then winced. He hadn't meant to be quite so glib. Uncle Edward had never taken Derek's quips particularly well, especially when they were aimed at him.

But Uncle Edward laughed, and Derek had the distinct impression they had just crossed some sort of threshold in their relationship. Helped, no doubt, by Derek's embrace of his uncle's edict about reforming his questionable behavior. For the first time, Derek felt like an adult in his uncle's presence. A feeling strengthened by the look of respect in the older man's eyes. As well as the laughter.

"You're enjoying this, aren't you, sir?"

"Why wouldn't I enjoy seeing my heir live up to expectations?"

Derek blew a long breath. "I hope I can."

"As do I. Indeed, you may well be on the way to becoming the man I always thought you could be. A man your father would be proud of." The earl pinned him with a hard look. "Don't muck it up."

CHAPTER SEVEN

There are moments of tedium in the course of travel when one is confined to a train carriage or ship's cabin that provide the perfect opportunity to study the places one is headed. The clever lady traveler will be prepared with books not only on the current state of one's destination but on its history, as well. However, fictional tales of misadventure or mayhem are best avoided as they will serve only to make even the most stalwart lady traveler uneasy.

—The Lady Travelers Society Guide

INDIA STARED AT the ornate white ceiling embellished with entwined plaster swags and flowers and, for a moment, couldn't determine exactly where she was. *Of course.* She was in Paris, where even the beds were decadent. Although apparently, when it came to blissful slumber, there was something to be said for a certain amount of decadence. She struggled to sit upright in spite of the soft, cushiony mattress that seemed determined to seduce her back to sleep under downy covers and the scent of fresh-washed linen. Pity she was made of sterner stuff.

She couldn't remember ever having slept so soundly. Perhaps, when she returned to London, she'd look into replacing her firm, sensible mattress with something a bit more self-indulgent. Although her excellent night's sleep probably had less to do with the bed and everything to do with her overwhelming fatigue. Who would have thought doing nothing more than sitting on trains and steamboats would be quite so exhausting? She'd done nothing of any merit all day yesterday save to change from train to boat and back to another train. Although travel was not without its perils. She had quickly learned Mrs. Greer had an unending reserve of completely inconsequential topics she delighted in expounding upon given the slightest opportunity. In that, she and her husband were well matched, although his chosen topics were of a more intellectual nature— the influence of classical thought on the architecture of the last century as opposed to his wife's ponderings on whether the French would be relying more on feathers or silk flowers for the decoration of hats this year. India's hats were sensible, practical creations and in no need of such frippery.

Never in her entire life had India imagined she would be going to Paris—that bastion of sin and debauchery. Whereas Heloise had gone on and on about the delights of Paris—the innovation, art, history and food— and couldn't wait to sample it all for herself, India was perfectly happy with the impressive history, practical innovation, notable art and solid food of her native England. France held no particular lure for India, nor did the French. She'd never met a Frenchman but had heard they were uniformly rude and condescending. She was not fond of being condescended to by anyone.

While India preferred not to be bothered by idle chatter, she'd had no choice but to engage in conversation during meals with the Greers and Mr. Saunders— Derek, he'd insisted she call him as they were to be traveling companions for the foreseeable future. As Mrs. Greer—Estelle—was already doing so, it seemed rude of India not to. But the rest of the day she avoided unnecessary discussion by claiming to be engrossed in one of the books she had brought with her—although admittedly reading *Dyke Darrel, The Railroad Detective*, a story of murder, theft and all manner of mayhem may not have been wise when one was actually traveling by rail. Why, such a story might put a less rational person than herself in the position of looking with distrust at every suspicious person on the train. Although there did seem to be a significant number of questionable travelers—especially once they were in France. India would have been much better off rereading her copy of *Mr. Bazalgette's Agent* about the indomitable Miss Miriam Lea, although the very idea of a female detective was totally absurd, if oddly compelling.

India drew her knees up to her chest, wrapped her arms around them and studied the room. She'd barely paid any attention to her surroundings upon their arrival last night. Far larger than her bedchamber at home, the room allotted her was colored in muted shades of lilac and blue. It was at once serene and calming and distinctly welcoming. Lace curtains fluttered slightly at the long windows at the end of the room. The furniture was delicate in appearance, colored in aging shades of white, accented with burnished gold. From the pastel Aubusson rug on the floor to small, crystal sconces on the wall, the room spoke of wealth and heritage and feminine grace. It was as far from her own taste as if some obstinate, contrary creature had designed it with annoying her in mind, and yet she rather liked it.

By the time they'd actually set foot on Parisian soil, it had been quite late. The professor had arranged for their baggage to be collected from the *Salle des Bagages*, and insisted upon waiting to accompany the luggage while Derek had found transportation and escorted the two ladies to their lodgings. India had assumed they would be staying at a hotel, but Derek explained, given the Paris Exposition opened its doors last month—as did its remarkably ugly iron tower centerpiece—hotel rooms had been booked for months. He said it was fortunate that he had a relative with a large house in the center of the city. India was far too tired to care at that point, although now she wondered at the wisdom of staying in the private home of a relation of his, even if he was right and they had little choice. They were no doubt lucky to have a roof over their heads at all, let alone one quite as opulent as this.

Professor Greer was probably no more than a few minutes behind them, but neither India nor Estelle could keep their eyes open. They were both whisked off immediately to their respective rooms by friendly, smiling maids who chattered the entire time in a manner reminiscent of finches. Poor Estelle's French was minimal, but India was quite adept at languages and had studied French, Italian and German. Admittedly, she had never spoken anything but English outside of a classroom.

A knock sounded at her door, and before she could respond, it flew open.

"Good morning, mademoiselle." A pretty dark-haired girl, one of the maids from last night—Suzette, if India recalled correctly—breezed into the room carrying a tray bearing a plate of pastries, a pot and a cup. "I hope you slept well."

"Quite well, thank you." And apparently she was starving. The food they'd purchased from vendors yesterday was no more than adequate, and they had all eaten sparingly. "You speak English?"

"I have been studying the English for some time, mademoiselle." Suzette set the pot on a side table, then deftly unfolded short legs under the tray and set it in front of India on the bed. India stared at the golden pastries accompanied by a dish of raspberries. It was not at all her usual kind of breakfast—lightly buttered toast, coddled eggs and a small slice of ham. No, this was…*French.* "My fiancé, Jerome, and I will settle in America after we marry. One of us should know the language. Jerome is a carver of stone. His cousin is in America and writes that there is very much work for a man with Jerome's skills."

She filled the cup with a rich, dark chocolate. Good Lord, India hadn't had chocolate in longer than she could remember. Leave it to the immoral, irresponsible French to have chocolate on an ordinary day. The aroma drifted past India's nose, and her stomach growled. She picked up the cup and took a sip, resisting the urge to sigh with delight. It tasted every bit as wonderful as it smelled. Perhaps in this, and this alone, the French were on to something.

"He is a true artist, mademoiselle. What the man can do with his hands…" Suzette heaved a heartfelt sigh, and India wasn't entirely sure if she was still talking about stone. "But he is not, oh…*adept* at words. So I will translate American for him, and he will earn our fortune." She beamed at India.

"That sounds like an excellent plan." India broke off a piece of a croissant and popped it in her mouth. It fairly melted on her tongue. There may well be something to be said for decadence—at least at breakfast. "Tell me, Suzette, where exactly am I?"

"Why, you are in Paris, mademoiselle," she said cautiously and inched toward the door. "You did not know that?"

"Yes, of course." She gestured with the pastry in her hand. "But whose house is this? I was so tired when we arrived, I'm afraid that has slipped my mind."

"Ah." Suzette's expression cleared. "I see. This is the home of the Marquess of Brookings," she announced with a flourish.

"Brookings?" India swallowed the bite of croissant in her mouth. "He's English then?"

"Indeed he is, but his mother was Parisian." Suzette smirked with satisfaction. "This was his mother's family's house."

"And he lives here?"

"As well as in England, but he is here as often as possible."

"But why?"

Suzette stared as if the very question was mad. "Because it is Paris."

"Even so, he is English," India persisted. After all, why would a subject of Her Majesty's choose to live anywhere but England? "It makes no sense to me."

"And it makes no sense to a Parisian to live anywhere but Paris."

"But he's English."

"I would suggest you ask his lordship why he chooses to live where he does," Suzette said firmly. "I do not gossip about my employer."

"Of course not. I never thought— I am sorry."

Suzette waved off the apology as if India's comments were already forgotten. "I am to assist you during your stay. Please call for me at any time. Is there anything else you need at the moment?"

"Yes, actually, I was wondering…" India held her arms out. Her sleeves dripped with delicate lace, an extravagant lace-trimmed ruffle plunged down the center of her chest, far lower than any nightgown she'd ever even imagined wearing. "Whose gown is this?"

As their luggage had not arrived with them last night, she had been provided with borrowed nightclothes. She'd paid no attention; she'd practically fallen into bed and was asleep in minutes. The gown was as decadent as the bed. Pale peach in color—to complement the room no doubt—silky against her skin, with no weight to the fabric at all, and far sheerer than anything any respectable woman would ever wear, even in the privacy of the bedroom. She could see more than the mere shadow of her arm in the sleeve and was afraid to get out from under the protection of the covers for fear of what she might reveal. "The marquess's wife perhaps?"

Suzette scoffed as if India had just said something absurd. "The marquess is not married."

"Then whose gown is this?"

"I am not entirely certain, mademoiselle." Suzette frowned thoughtfully. "Probably a mistress but I do not know which one."

India stared in shock. "He has more than one?"

"Oh no, not at the same time," Suzette said matter-of-factly. "That would be…difficult."

India snorted. "One would think." She did need to get out of bed. "Has my luggage arrived?"

Suzette shrugged. "I have not seen it, mademoiselle."

"I'm sure it's here somewhere." India sighed. "Very well then, until it's located, I shall have to make do with what I was wearing yesterday."

"Yes, of course, mademoiselle." Suzette nodded.

"Your clothes are being brushed and pressed. I shall bring them as soon as they are ready."

"I do appreciate that, but what am I to wear until then?" India certainly couldn't leave her room dressed like a tart.

"Ah!" Suzette brightened and stepped to the chaise near the foot of the bed. She picked up a garment matching the gown India wore and displayed it with pride. "There is as well a dressing gown to match the negligee."

It was no more substantial than what she had on, but hopefully adding another layer would help. Regardless, she had no intention of leaving her room until she was properly attired.

"I see you're awake," a male voice sounded from the hall. "You slept much later than I expected. I rather thought you'd be an early riser." A tall, dashing gentleman with hair colored a rich walnut and an infectious grin strode into the room. He looked to be about the same age as Derek and had the same lighthearted nature. "Forgive my impatience, but I've been looking forward to meeting you."

India yanked the covers up to her chin. "Have you?"

He chuckled. "Derek has told me a great deal about you."

"Has he?" Shock at this intrusion was apparently robbing her of all ability to speak in words more than one syllable long. But then she'd never had a handsome devil invade her bedroom before. A certain amount of stunned paralysis was probably to be expected.

"Oh my, yes." His gaze raked over her in an admiring manner. "But apparently he left out some important facts."

Heat washed up her face. Why, the man was flirting with her! How terribly forward. She clutched the covers tighter. "I beg your pardon, but I can't imagine, even in Paris, one invades a lady's bedchamber without so much as a by-your-leave."

"The door was open." He shook his head in a chastising manner. "I don't think you can really call it an invasion if the door is open. An open door is more like, oh, an invitation."

"I did not invite you!"

"And yet." He grinned in a manner that was at once boyishly endearing and completely wicked. "Here I am. Allow me to introduce myself. I am your host, Percival St. James, Marquess of Brookings." He swept an exaggerated bow. "And I am at your service."

"Very nice to meet you, my lord," she said without thinking, then tightened her grip on the covers with one hand and waved her free hand at the door. "And if you are truly at my service, you will take your leave at once."

"I am truly at your service," he said staunchly, although she suspected her definition of "at your service" and his were decidedly different. "And my friends call me Percy or Val, one of which I prefer to the other, but it makes no difference as anything is better than Percival. Don't you agree?"

She stared, not entirely sure what to say. "I suppose."

"As I am certain we are going to be friends, which would you prefer to call me, Miss Prendergast?"

"I do not share your certainty, and I will call you Lord Brookings," she said firmly. "Anything else would be most inappropriate."

"Precisely the point." He grinned and glanced at the maid. "Suzette, if you would be so good as to see if Miss Prendergast's clothes are ready."

"Yes, my lord." She bobbed a curtsy, aimed India a quick glance of encouragement and took her leave.

"And leave the door open if you will," India called after her.

"Come now, India—"

"Miss Prendergast."

"You are perfectly safe in my presence. In spite of what you may have heard, I have never ravaged a woman who did not wish to be ravaged. And with great enthusiasm I might add."

"Given that I am in bed wearing the clothes of one of your mistresses, that is good to know." India paused. "And I haven't heard anything."

He stared at her. "Really?"

"Really."

"Nothing at all?" He frowned. "My reputation has not preceded me?"

"I'd never so much as heard your name until a few minutes ago."

"That's rather distressing."

She stared in disbelief. "Why?"

"It does one no good to have a certain reputation if no one knows about it. Are you sure you've never heard of me?" he added hopefully.

Good Lord, the silly man was actually bothered that she'd never heard of his no doubt sordid reputation. She felt the tiniest bit sorry for him and dismissed the feeling at once. What on earth was she thinking? "Perhaps I have never heard of you because I am not active in society."

"Oh, well then." His expression brightened. "That makes perfect sense." He stepped closer and perched on the side of the bed.

She slid to the center of the mattress, nearly upending the tray in the process. "You're sitting on my bed!"

"Indeed I am." He glanced around and patted the bed beside him. "I hope you found it to your liking."

"Yes, yes, it was quite comfortable. Now if you would be so good as to remove yourself from my bed, I would be most appreciative."

"But this is convenient as well as comfortable." He pinned her with a firm look. "You didn't expect me to keep talking to you from the other side of the room."

"You were closer to the foot of the bed than the other side of the room."

"And now I am closer still." He grinned. Again. This was completely absurd. There was a man—a stranger—sitting on her bed! And as much as she tried to maintain her indignation, he was rather disarming. Which was every bit as annoying as the man himself. "I can tell you all sorts of stories."

"I don't care!"

He ignored her. "Some of them are even true, but most are simply the stuff of gossip. As you haven't heard any of the stories about me it compels me, as your host and a man with an unsavory reputation—"

"Well earned I suspect." She glared at him.

"I would say the tales of my misadventures are somewhere between well earned and a complete exaggeration." He paused. "Perhaps not a complete exaggeration."

She raised a brow.

"Possibly embellished more than exaggerated, although one or two might be fairly accurate." He waggled his brows at her in a most disconcerting way. If she wasn't so irritated, she might have laughed. "I would imagine it all depends on who is telling the story. You know how these things are."

"I don't know how these things are nor do I wish to. Now." She aimed a pointed finger at the door. "If you would be so good as to get out of my room, my lord, I—"

"Percy. Or Val. Your choice." He reached over and selected a piece of her pastry.

"Lord Brookings," she forced a hard note to her voice, "if you don't leave at once, I shall…I shall scream. That's what I'll do, I'll scream. And quite loudly."

"Because you fear for your virtue?" He considered her curiously and took a bite of the pastry.

"Not as much as I fear for my croissants!"

"I doubt that you have ever in your entire life screamed, quite loudly or otherwise," he said mildly. "Unless of course it was at the unexpected appearance of a rat, but certainly not out of fear or rage or frustration. You don't strike me as that type of woman."

For a moment she considered lying, but what was the point? "I have never felt the need before as I usually have my emotions well in hand."

"But not today." He smirked, and she had the immediate impulse to smack his face.

"On the contrary, my lord, I am in complete control of my emotions as well as being both rational and logical." She summoned a measure of calm. "As you will not depart willingly, it seems to me, if I were to scream as loudly as possible, you would then do exactly as I ask and leave my room."

"You expect me to scamper away like a frightened bunny?" He tossed the rest of the croissant in his mouth.

"I'm not sure I would have used the term *frightened bunny* but…" She met his gaze firmly. "Yes, I do. Regardless of whatever reputation you claim to have, no man in his right mind wishes to have a woman's scream echoing through his home. It tends to frighten servants, who will then seek other positions. And I imagine finding good servants in Paris is every bit as difficult as it is in London."

"You have no idea," he murmured and reached for another pastry.

"I would further suspect, even in Paris, neighbors who hear a woman's scream—" she nodded at the open window "—might well be inclined to summon the police. Particularly if they lived next door to a foreign scoundrel with a scandalous reputation."

He stared at her for a moment, then laughed. "Touché, India—"

"Miss Prendergast."

"Derek calls you India."

She rolled her gaze toward the ceiling. "Mr. Saunders and I will be spending a great deal of time together, accompanied by Professor and Mrs. Greer. In the interest of expediency, it was decided we would call one another by our given names. There is absolutely no reason why you and I should be so personal."

"Except that I am your gracious host."

"And while you do have my gratitude, I am still not inclined to call you Percival, Percy, Val or anything other than Lord Brookings."

"I see." He took a bite of her croissant and chewed thoughtfully, studying her the entire time.

She picked up a raspberry and tossed it in her mouth. If the man was trying to make her uncomfortable, he was failing. Admittedly, she might have been a bit nonplussed when he had first appeared in her room. Who wouldn't be given she was in a strange bed dressed like a harlot? Perhaps their absurd sparring was to blame, or possibly the chocolate, but she had regained her normal disposition. She had no intention of letting this arrogant, presumptuous relation of Derek's get the better of her. Why, it would be almost as bad as if Derek was doing it himself.

"I shall make a bargain with you, India," he said at last.

"Miss Prendergast." She smiled pleasantly.

"Believe it or not, it is remarkably difficult to scream."

"I can't imagine that."

"But you have never before screamed. One must let go of all one's reservations. Put one's heart and soul into it, if you will. I doubt that a woman like you can do it."

"What exactly do you mean?" She drew her brows together. "A woman like me?"

"Derek says you're cool and collected. Not the least bit emotional." He lowered his voice in a confidential manner. "Even somewhat cold."

"Does he?" India wasn't sure why something she'd always prided herself on now bothered her just the tiniest bit.

"He does." Lord Brookings nodded, a challenge in his eye.

She met his gaze directly. "Good."

He laughed. "I shall make you a wager, India."

"Miss Prendergast. And I never wager."

"You see, I don't believe you can overcome your reserve, your unyielding conviction as to what is proper and what is not. Therefore, if you can toss your inhibitions aside and truly release a bloodcurdling yell, I shall, from then on, quite properly call you Miss Prendergast."

"Good Lord." For a moment, she could have sworn she was governess again. "How old are you?"

He grinned.

"And are you really a marquess?"

"I am."

"And that is an English title? Not some frivolous foreign designation?"

"I am the eighth Marquess of Brookings. My father was the seventh, my grandfather the sixth and so on. I have the papers to prove it if you wish to see them."

"That's not necessary."

"So what's it to be, India? Although I must say I like the sound of India and Percy. It fairly reeks of England, and yet I think it has a certain flair to it." He reached for her last croissant. "Although, perhaps India and Val are even more—"

Before she could think better of it, India opened her mouth and screamed.

CHAPTER EIGHT

A WOMAN'S SCREAM ripped through the house, reverberating off lofty ceilings and echoing off marbled floors. Derek started, frozen in midstep on the stairs, and knew with unerring certainty whose scream it was. *Bloody hell.*

He sprinted toward India's room, just down the hall from his, taking the steps of the broad, curving stairway two at a time. He and Val had talked for long hours after their arrival last night, and Derek knew there were no other guests staying at the grand house. He had left the professor and his wife downstairs in the breakfast room, probably too far away to hear, although he wouldn't be at all surprised to find them right behind him. No one could miss that scream.

What was wrong now? India had made a noticeable attempt yesterday not to be overly critical of very nearly everything but she did not take well to the inconveniences of travel. It was obvious she'd had little travel experience except perhaps for the occasional trip from London to the country.

He reached the second floor and headed toward her room. India was in no real danger. He was confident of that. Although one never knew what—or who—one might run into in the halls of Val's Parisian domicile. The last time Derek was here, there had been a precocious monkey—the adored pet of Val's paramour at the time—that had been clever enough to escape his leash

and evade capture for nearly a month, living off scraps
in the kitchen and terrifying both servants and guests
alike. For a small creature, he had been extremely unpleasant and rather threatening. Val broke it off with
his owner the moment the beast was captured. Derek
suspected the animal was no more than a convenient
excuse.

Derek reached India's room and pulled up short.
Even a monkey wouldn't have been a greater shock
than the sight that greeted him.

The indomitable, unyielding, eminently proper Miss
India Prendergast was sitting upright in her bed—still
in her nightclothes—covers clutched nearly to her chin
in one hand, a tray balanced on her lap, glaring at Val,
who sat on the edge of her bed. More shocking still
was India herself.

Her hair was loose and hung around her shoulders
in clouds of unsuspected curls that caught the light and
shimmered with gold highlights. Curls that were usually
ruthlessly imprisoned in a knot on the top of her head,
so tight it made his scalp ache to look at it. Her skin was
flushed, no doubt with annoyance, and her green eyes
sparkled—again, probably with annoyance. But it was
most becoming. He could see little of her nightwear—
a peachy shade and most flattering to her coloring—
except for her arms. The almost transparent fabric was
enhanced by creamy lace that caressed her wrists and
whispered against the bedclothes. She was the picture
of charming dishabille, an illusion at once angelic and
seductive. A vision that fairly begged to be kissed. It
was the oddest thought—kissing India Prendergast—
but Derek couldn't quite dismiss it. He would wager
Val had thought the same thing.

Val reached a hand toward her tray. She smacked it away, and the illusion shattered.

"Good God, Miss Prendergast." Derek stepped into the room. "Are you all right? What on earth is going on here?"

She gave Val a scathing look, then turned her attention to Derek. "This man is trying to steal my croissants, Mr. Saunders. As he has already taken two of them, and there is only one left—" her narrowed gaze shifted back to Val "—I could not allow that."

"They're excellent croissants, Derek." Val looked mournfully at the remaining croissant. "You should try one."

"I did," Derek said slowly. "At breakfast." This was about pastry? He stared at India. "You screamed because he took your croissant?"

For the first time since he'd met her, she looked distinctly uncomfortable. "Not exactly."

"Not at all," Val said. "She screamed because I challenged her to do so. Or perhaps *dared* is a better word." He grinned at India. "What do you think, Miss Prendergast? Was it a challenge or a dare? Or..." He paused in a meaningful manner. "Was it a wager?"

"I told you—I do not wager," she said in a manner entirely too lofty for a woman who had screamed not to defend her honor but to protect her pastry. "And you know perfectly well why I screamed."

"Val." Derek summoned a hard tone. "Why did she scream?"

Val shrugged. "I have no idea."

"Utter nonsense. You know exactly why." India huffed. "I asked him to leave as his presence is unwanted as well as being highly inappropriate."

Val slanted him an unrepentant grin.

"I threatened to scream if he did not take his leave. He didn't, so I did."

"And an impressive scream it was, too." Admiration curved Val's lips. "I didn't think she had it in her."

"And yet it didn't seem to work," she said coolly.

For a moment, Derek thought there was a glint of amusement in her eyes, but then Val had always been skilled at amusing women. Still, for whatever reason, the thought that Val could make her smile was irritating.

"I'd wager you could hear it all over the house," Val said smugly.

"I'd wager you could hear it all over the city." Derek nodded at India. "Well done, Miss Prendergast."

"Thank you, Mr. Saunders." A satisfied note sounded in her voice, and this time there was no mistake. India was definitely trying not to smile. Perhaps there was hope for her, after all.

"You said you call him Derek." Val's eyes narrowed.

"Apparently, when I am entertaining incorrigible gentlemen in my bedchamber, I prefer more formal, proper terms of address."

Val laughed, and Derek couldn't resist a grin. This was going to be an interesting stay. He moved farther into the room, grabbed a chair and positioned it on the opposite side of the bed from Val.

She raised a brow. "Oh, do join us, Mr. Saunders."

"I would be delighted." He ignored the sarcasm in her voice and sat down. "While you have obviously already met, allow me to properly, formally introduce the Marquess of Brookings, my stepbrother."

"Your what?" India stared in disbelief.

"Derek's mother was my stepmother."

"Val's father was my mother's second husband."

"That explains so much," she said under her breath.

"You were right, Derek," Val said with a regretful shake of his head. "She is stuffy."

"You said I was stuffy as well as calm, unemotional and cold?" She turned to Derek. "Dare I ask what else you said about me?"

Derek threw his stepbrother an annoyed look. Did the man ever know when to hold his tongue? "I'm afraid Lord Brookings has taken my comments out of context."

"Oh, I don't think I did," Val said. "I distinctly remember you saying all of that as well as calling her stubborn, suspicious, overly proper and something of a pain—"

"It scarcely matters what Mr. Saunders thinks of me." India waved off the comments. "Nor does it matter what I think of Mr. Saunders."

A wicked glint sparkled in Val's eyes. "What do you think of Mr. Saunders?"

"What do I think?" Her green eyes met Derek's. "Oh, I have no doubt Mr. Saunders knows exactly what I think of him."

Her gaze stayed locked with his, and for a moment the oddest sense of regret washed through him.

"But I don't know what you think of him, and I would pay a great deal to know." Val grinned. "I daresay it might well be one of the most amusing things I've heard in a long time." A maid appeared in the doorway and caught his attention. "If you will pardon me for a moment." He stood, moved to the maid and they exchanged a few quiet words.

Val grimaced. "It appears the gendarmes are here, and I need to speak with them. This is a most respectable neighborhood, and it seems someone in the vicinity reported a woman's screams."

"Not the first time I imagine," India said wryly.

Val tossed them an unrepentant smirk and took his leave.

"India," Derek began, bracing himself. "Please accept my apology for my comments. I am sorry if they offended you in any way."

"Goodness, I can't imagine why they would. They certainly come as no surprise." She shrugged. "I am never offended by the truth."

"Still, it was rude of me and I never intended—"

"For me to learn of them?"

"Well, yes." He still couldn't believe Val had betrayed his confidence. "I shall have a few well-chosen words to say to my stepbrother about this."

"You needn't bother." She paused. "I suppose no one especially wants to hear themselves described as stuffy, unfeeling and cold—"

He winced.

"And while the words themselves do seem rather harsh, they are not inaccurate. I am…" She thought for a moment. "Reserved, if you will. I don't believe in displaying my emotions, nor do I allow them to dictate my behavior. And I do believe that the rules of proper behavior should be adhered to. I am well aware of my own nature and how I appear to others. Especially those who do not know me."

"I suspect your friends probably know better."

"My friends…" She hesitated, then raised her chin in a resolute manner. "Yes, I would imagine they do."

"If you are amenable to the idea…" He chose his words with care. "I would like to offer the hand of friendship."

"Good Lord, Derek." She stared in obvious disbelief. "You don't like me, and I certainly don't like you. Why on earth would I want to be friends?"

"I don't dislike you," he said quickly, but she was right. The woman was perhaps the most stodgy, opinionated creature he'd ever met. Still, they were stuck with each other. He drew a deep breath. "For one thing—we share a common purpose. We both want to locate Lady Heloise and make certain of her safety. It's going to be much less difficult if we aren't at each other's throats."

"You may have a point there."

"In addition, we are to be together for the foreseeable future. I would prefer to spend my time with a friend rather than a foe."

"But I don't trust you."

"I am more than willing not to trust you, either, which gives us something in common on which to base a friendship."

"I don't think friendships are built on mutual distrust."

"Then we shall be the first." He flashed her a grin.

"That's absurd." She frowned. "Why, friendships are based on shared admiration and respect. I have no respect for you at all."

"Then I shall simply have to earn your respect." He was fairly certain it would not be easy, but then, thus far, nothing about India Prendergast was. "Although we do already have one thing between us on which to base a friendship."

"I can't imagine what that is."

"Honesty."

She raised a brow. "And yet we distrust each other."

"But we are honest about it."

She studied him closely. "It would be entirely dishonest of me to say I am willing to accept your offer of friendship. But, in the spirit of cooperation, I am willing to attempt a certain level of cordiality between us."

"I can ask for nothing more."

"I do have a condition."

"Anything."

"As I have been entertaining gentlemen in my room, while I am still in my bed, dressed in my nightclothes—which even you would agree is the height of impropriety—"

He nodded.

"I believe you should rescind your description of me as stuffy."

"Well." He grimaced. "You did scream."

"My scream was directed more at encouraging his lordship to leave than any concern about proper behavior on my part."

"I'll give you that. Very well then." This was actually going far better than he'd expected. "You are not nearly as stuffy as one would have thought."

"Thank you. Now, perhaps you would consider—"

"I should leave you to dress." He rose to his feet. "I think we should start our efforts today at the hotel Lady Heloise mentioned in her letters. I suggest we depart as soon as you are ready."

"My thoughts exactly."

"One more thing we have in common."

"Unfortunately…"

"Unless you have another idea?"

"It's not that. But my maid—Suzette—says she has not seen my luggage. I was forced to borrow this—" she glanced down and winced "—*garment* to sleep in last night."

"I see. Then the nightclothes are not yours?"

"Dear Lord, no." Indignation rang in her voice. "I would never wear something this…this flimsy. And suggestive. And indecent."

"No, of course not." It was a pity really. He suspected what he could not see of her in the nightgown was even more delicious than what he could. "I would imagine your nightclothes to be of good solid linen, unencumbered by silliness like lace or ruffles."

"Simply because one is abed doesn't mean one should abandon good judgment and proper attire," she said primly. "But that is beside the point. As I was saying, Suzette has not seen my luggage."

"She hasn't?" He knew this was coming. It might have been wiser for him to have said something right away, but while Derek considered himself fairly courageous under most circumstances, this was not one of them.

"No, which means I am forced to wear the same clothes I wore yesterday, and they are being freshened. I'm afraid we will have to delay our start until Suzette returns with my clothing."

"Oh well." He sighed. "It can't be helped I suppose. We can't have you running about the streets naked. Even in Paris, that would be frowned upon." He started toward the door.

"Derek."

He paused. "Yes?"

"I can't help but notice you are not wearing what you wore yesterday." Her brow furrowed. "Am I to assume you have your luggage?"

He winced and turned back toward her. "I do."

"And have Professor and Mrs. Greer their luggage?"

"As far as I know."

"Then, as our luggage traveled together, mine should be somewhere in the house. Delivered to the wrong room perhaps. Don't you think?"

"One would think that. I know," he said brightly. "Why don't I check for you?"

She breathed a sigh of relief. "I would be most grateful."

"I am happy to do it, as any responsible friend would."

"In the meantime, I will wait for Suzette to return."

"And I will see you downstairs whenever you are ready." He smiled and took his leave, closing her door behind him.

It did indeed stand to reason that her trunk would be somewhere in the house. If, of course, it had arrived at the house in the first place. Which was contingent upon whether or not—when it was checked at the beginning of their journey—it was appropriately labeled for Paris and not, oh, say, Prague. An understandable mistake really. There was nothing more annoying than to have to delay one's travel plans and be compelled to stay longer in a city than intended in hopes of recovering one's luggage. But if one wished to ever see one's belongings again, there was little choice. And who knew how long it might take?

Derek ignored a tiny twinge of guilt. When all this was over, he would replace India's wardrobe and anything else she might have brought along with her. And there was always the possibility that her errant trunk would make its way back to England. Eventually.

Uncle Edward would argue that, ultimately, this was in India's and her cousin's best interests as well as Aunt Guinevere's. His resources were far more likely to track down Lady Heloise than Derek and India were. Still, she would never see it that way.

Even so, diverting her luggage off to the ends of the earth was not the best way to start a friendship.

CHAPTER NINE

*As much as it may be an affront to the sensibilities
of a proper Englishwoman, one must understand
the customs of a foreign land are often far different from what one is used to. Embracing local
customs will endear one to the native population
as well as provide an amusing story to relate upon
one's return home.*

—The Lady Travelers Society Guide

WHERE WAS THE blasted man?

India waited in the foyer and resisted the urge to
tap her foot with impatience. She'd sent word to Derek
through Suzette that she was ready to leave and now
wished to do so without further delay. Admittedly, their
late start could partially be laid to rest at her feet, given
she had not risen as early as was her custom. Even so,
it did seem that it took an eternity to get her clothes returned. She felt much more her usual self in her own
clothing with her hair in its usual coiffure. Ready to
face the world and get on with the search for Heloise.
And more than ready to put this morning behind her.

She wasn't at all sure what had come over her. In
hindsight, she had indeed done all she could to get Lord
Brookings to leave her room. Short of leaping out of bed
and escorting him bodily to the door, she didn't know
what else she could have tried. It was most annoying.

But oddly enough, she'd found the man—as well as his stepbrother—rather amusing. And she shouldn't have. There was nothing amusing about impropriety.

Even though there was no blood between them, she was not at all surprised to learn of Derek and Lord Brookings familial connection. Both men shared a certain air of confidence, both obviously relied on their dashing looks and charming natures, and both were entirely too flirtatious for their own good, or the good of any woman who unwittingly crossed their paths. Derek was a bit less obvious about it than his lordship, although she never would have imagined any man could be surer of himself than Derek. But she had noted the oddest look in Derek's eyes when he had first entered her room that didn't speak at all of confidence. It was rather something akin to revelation.

It wasn't until he'd left and she'd assessed her appearance in the antiquated pier mirror by the window that she suspected what that look might have meant. It was absurd, but, for a moment, India wasn't entirely sure the image reflected was her. She didn't look at all like her usual self. Her hair had reverted to its natural state and was a riot of annoying curls, the bane of her existence. Her face was decidedly flushed, no doubt with frustration over her attempts to rid the room of Lord Brookings, which made her eyes look somewhat greener than they were. And thank God neither man had seen more of her in the negligee than her arms. The disgraceful garment clung to her in all sorts of ways it shouldn't, defining and revealing curves she didn't realize could look quite so fetching. In a terribly immoral way, of course. All in all, she had no idea who the tousled creature staring back from the mirror was. The image was both shocking and, perhaps, a bit intriguing, but it certainly wasn't India Prendergast. Or at least not the India Prendergast she'd always seen in the mirror before. Regardless, it was a momentary aberration and nothing more significant than that. The blame could be placed squarely on the negligee, the circumstances, the decadent boudoir and even Paris itself.

And despite how amusing she might on occasion find Derek, she could not let that deter her from the reasons she was with him in the first place. One—and the most important—was to locate Heloise and make certain she was safe. And two—find some way to prove Derek was indeed the mastermind behind the fraudulent Lady Travelers Society—an immoral, illegal enterprise created for the sole purpose of separating women, particularly older women, from their savings. India hadn't been able to save Heloise from his plot, but she would prevent him from fleecing anyone else. It was the responsible—the *right* thing to do. And India prided herself on always being right, morally as well as every other way.

"I see you're ready to go." Derek descended the stairway, a spring in his step, to join her in the foyer.

"I am." She nodded. "Have you managed to find my trunk?"

"Not yet, but I have the entire staff looking for it." He smiled in an encouraging manner. "This is an extremely large house, and your trunk could have been put anywhere. However, I am certain that your luggage will be recovered by the time we return."

"I do hope so," she said, the confident note in her voice belying the niggling fear that she might never see her things again. In terms of possessions, she didn't have a great deal to lose. The trunk itself was somewhat battered—it had once served to transport her things to and from Miss Bicklesham's—but losing it would be devastating.

She had packed sparsely with an eye toward economy. A few dresses suitable for traveling, a couple of additional blouses, an extra skirt, undergarments of course, nightclothes, a pair of boots and a second pair of sturdy walking shoes. She'd also brought a simple gown appropriate for evening and slippers to match, should that become necessary—which she assumed it wouldn't. This was not a pleasure trip. Still, one should be properly prepared. According to Heloise, being properly prepared for any eventuality was practically the motto of the Lady Travelers Society. In that piece of advice alone the society was competent. India did wonder if any of the pamphlets Heloise had brought home from the society dealt with the loss of one's luggage.

"Unless you have some objection, Professor Greer and his wife would like to see some of the city, and I didn't think it was necessary for them to accompany us. Don't you agree?"

"Absolutely," India said with relief. "I suspect they would only hinder our progress."

"My thoughts exactly. Besides, Mrs. Greer has always wanted to see Paris, and who knows how long we'll stay? This might be her only chance."

"Then she should certainly take it."

"Excellent." Derek nodded. "Now then, I have reread Lady Heloise's letters and perused her itinerary. You have her photograph with you, I assume."

"I do."

"Very good." Derek pulled a small notebook and a Baedeker guide from his coat pocket. "I have made a number of notes as to how to proceed."

"You made notes?"

"I wished to organize my thoughts and our efforts."

She studied him closely. "You do not strike me as the sort of man who takes well to organization."

"Then I am delighted that I have surprised you," he said in a pleasant manner. "In recent months I have seen the benefit of organization when one has something one wishes to accomplish quickly and efficiently."

"It's most…admirable." *And shocking.* Of all the things she expected from him, organization and efficiency were not among them.

"Furthermore, we need a definite plan of action, unless you intend to simply wander the streets of Paris calling Lady Heloise's name?"

"No, of course not." Although she really hadn't given any consideration as to how to actually find her cousin.

"I didn't think so. Therefore, I have taken the liberty of devising a plan of sorts." He glanced at her. "Do you have an idea?"

"No." She had no more than a vague thought in the back of her mind about making inquiries at places Heloise had mentioned in her letters. "Not yet."

"Should we wait until you do?"

She did not for a moment believe the innocent note in his voice. "I suggest we follow your plan until such time as it needs revision."

"Very well then." He flipped open his notebook. "Unfortunately, her itinerary strikes me as rather vague and a bit haphazard as to arrival dates and departures. Nor does it indicate which hotel she intended to stay in—"

"Rather a serious omission—don't you think?" she asked pointedly. "One would imagine such pertinent information would be included on an itinerary created by a travelers society and assistance agency."

"Itineraries change, India, as plans for travel progress," he said, his attention never leaving his notebook. "In addition, people don't always go where they're expected to go. It's part of the adventure, to head toward an unforeseen destination because it strikes you as interesting. Is the schedule your cousin left with you her final itinerary?"

"I'm not sure." Blast it all. India had scarcely given Heloise's itinerary more than a second glance when her cousin had given it to her. Admittedly, that had been when Heloise had first announced her intention to travel. A scant two weeks later the older woman was off, and, while India had glanced at the places Heloise had intended to visit, she'd paid no notice whatsoever to the details of her lodging. "She did mention she would stay in Paris as long as it took to see everything she wished to see."

"That would have been good to know," he said under his breath. "In her first letter from Paris, she says her room in 'this grand hotel' is more than adequate."

"Then obviously she was staying at the Grand Hotel. I suggest we make our way there and inquire after her." India couldn't quite keep the note of triumph out of her voice. While it was the logical place to start, it was also her suggestion.

"I agree." He smiled pleasantly. "Which Grand Hotel?"

"What do you mean which Grand Hotel? *The* Grand Hotel."

"And herein lies our first problem."

She narrowed her eyes. "I don't see a problem. It seems very straightforward and sensible to me."

"Perhaps it would if you were more prepared."

She stared. "I beg your pardon?"

"Did you bring a guidebook to Paris with you? Do you have a listing of hotels? Did you think to ask your cousin exactly where she planned to stay in Paris or anywhere else?"

"No, but—"

"I suggest you take a look at this." He handed her the Baedeker.

She took the book and opened it. "And what, pray tell, am I looking for?"

"You're looking for the Grand Hotel of course." He paused. "You will also find the Grand Hotel du Louvre, the Grand Hotel de Port Mahon, the Grand Hotel Normandy, the Grand Hotel de Chateaudun, the Grand Hotel—"

"How many Grand Hotels are there?"

"I counted twenty-seven in the guidebook. I have made a list of each and every one." He paused. "But I might have missed some."

"Good Lord." She paged through the guide. "What utter insanity. How very…*French*!"

"I daresay there are a few Grand Hotels in London, as well," he observed mildly. It was most annoying.

"A few is a far different matter than dozens! How can such a thing be permitted?"

"I doubt it can be prevented."

"Even so—"

"You must admit—it's an excellent name for a hotel. It conjures up an impressive image of hospitality and service."

"They can't all be grand," she muttered, skimming the small, tight print.

"Probably not, but I can't imagine a hotel attracting much business by calling itself the *Almost Grand Hotel* or the *Less Than Grand Hotel*. And would you really wish to stay at lodgings called the *Tiny, Trivial and Insignificant Hotel*?"

She closed the book and glared at him. "Now you're being silly. And this is not the time."

"Indeed I am, and it's the perfect time." He put his notebook back in his pocket. "I am trying to impart a certain lightheartedness to what is surely going to be a very long afternoon. And more than likely, just the first."

"Well, I have no intention of being lighthearted." She handed him the guide.

"No." He accepted the book and opened it. "I didn't think you did." He found the page he wanted, studied it for a moment, then shut the book smartly and replaced it in his pocket. "I suggest we start at the first Grand Hotel listed, the one that is simply the Grand Hotel, as it is one of the largest hotels in Paris." He accepted his hat from the butler and stepped toward the door. "There is every possibility we will be lucky and find your cousin firmly established there with not a care in the world, having completely forgotten about details like correspondence."

"Do you really think so?" The sooner they found Heloise, the sooner India could return to her well-ordered existence.

"I don't know her as you do, but I do think it's possible." A footman opened the door, and Derek waved India through ahead of him. "Not a very likely possibility, but stranger things have happened."

"Yes, I suppose." Stranger things certainly had. For one—India had never imagined she'd leave England at all, let alone travel to Paris to stay in a grand manor in the heart of the city with a dashing scoundrel for a host and an even bigger scoundrel by her side.

"Cheer up, India," Derek said. "Very nearly all the grand hotels are on the Right Bank."

"Are they near one another then?"

"Not really." He chuckled. "But at least the haystack hiding our needle is reduced a bit in size."

Derek hailed a cab and directed the driver to their first stop. Derek's French was not as precise as hers but was less academic, friendlier perhaps. While she had no problem following the conversation, she decided to allow him to do most of the talking. After all, he had experience visiting other countries whereas she had never stepped foot outside of England.

Perhaps it was some misguided impulse on his part to share those days of his past travel or perhaps he was simply trying to be informative, but he spent the duration of their ride pointing out sights of questionable interest and expounding on the redesigning of the French capital that had begun some twenty or so years ago. From his tone, it was impossible to determine whether he approved of the changes in the city or not. But—in spite of her lack of interest in all things French—India rather liked the newly broadened boulevards and the impressive buildings that blended one into the next, their pale stone facades, matching ironwork and mansard roofs giving the impression of continuation, as if each side of the street was one endless structure. There was a sense of order here that she found both comforting and refreshing.

The first Grand Hotel—*the* Grand Hotel—was as imposing as its name. It was the same architectural style as the other buildings she'd admired and took up an entire city block. The hotel was highly recommended by Baedeker, the guidebook listing it as one of the most impressive in the city with somewhere between six hundred and seven hundred rooms.

They stepped into the lobby, and it struck India as more a palace than a hotel—not that she'd ever been in either—with a dazzling display of marble and crystal, painted decoration and gilt embellishment. Opulence and grandeur shimmered in the very air around them. This was a setting more befitting a dream than reality. It might well have taken one's breath away if one was impressed by such an overt exhibit of extravagance and excess. India certainly wasn't.

"Extraordinary place, isn't it?" Derek glanced around with a smile. "I read once that it was the largest hotel in the world when it first opened. It might still be."

"It certainly is *grand*," she murmured.

As was the clientele. Judging by the universal air of wealth and importance of the well-dressed guests, they obviously took these ostentatious surroundings as their due. India had never been concerned about fashion. Her serviceable gray wool dress was more than acceptable for her needs. That it was not the latest style had never bothered her. But for the first time in her life—amid the grandeur of the hotel lobby—India felt out of place and more than a little dowdy. As if she should have come in through a servants' entrance and not the front doors. As much as she tried to dismiss the feeling she couldn't quite manage. Derek, however, fit right in.

She caught his arm. "I don't think this is right," she said in a low voice. "This type of hotel would never suit Heloise."

"Why not?" He glanced around the lobby. "I think it's quite impressive."

"As well as quite expensive." She shook her head.

"The cost of a hotel like this would be well above my cousin's resources."

Derek cast her a puzzled look. "Are you sure?"

"Without question," she said firmly. "This can't possibly be the right Grand Hotel."

"Well, we are here now." Derek nodded toward the registration counter. "The clerk on the end appears to have a good command of English. Why don't you wait here and I'll talk to him?"

"Very well." As there were no other women standing at the counter, it seemed a good idea. Besides, a well-dressed man like Derek would surely get more respect, and therefore more information, than an ordinary woman in serviceable gray wool. "Don't forget the photograph." She pulled it out of her bag and handed it to him.

Derek took it, strode off and India tried not to feel like she was somewhere she shouldn't be, an imposter who didn't belong. It was nonsense, of course. She raised her chin and adopted an air of mild disdain. As if she was neither aware of how out of place she appeared nor did she care. Although for some unknown reason, she did.

Derek returned quickly. "He didn't recognize her. Apparently all older Englishwomen look alike." He handed her the photograph. "And she's not registered."

"Well, was she registered six weeks ago?" Goodness, did the man not even know what he should and shouldn't ask?

He paused. "The clerk said the hotel prides itself on preserving the privacy of its guests, so he couldn't say."

"He couldn't say or wouldn't say?"

He grimaced. "He said hotel policy forbids it."

"Did you tell him a woman is missing? Did you tell

him her last known location was his hotel? That if she was not found, his hotel might well be held to blame? Or, at the very least, subject to gossip and public scrutiny? I can't imagine any hotel would wish to be known as the last place a missing Englishwoman was seen."

Derek's brow furrowed. "That's not entirely accurate, India. We don't know which grand hotel your cousin's letter referred to."

"He doesn't know that."

"India Prendergast!" He gasped in mock horror. "I never expected you of all people to advocate deception."

"Oh, come now, Derek." She stared in disbelief. Certainly Derek had admitted right from the start that he had no particular investigative skills, but surely this was little more than common sense. "Have you never read a novel of detection? Of mystery?"

It was his turn to stare. "Have you ever dealt with a French hotel clerk?"

"Did he frighten you?"

"No, he did not frighten me." The muscles of Derek's jaw twitched.

"Then go right back there and demand to see the register. Or insist he look at the register." She thought for a moment. "And give him money."

"Money?"

"Money." She nodded. "Money often changes hands when one is seeking information."

"I had no idea," he said wryly. "Do you have an amount in mind?"

"No, but surely you've done this sort of thing before."

"Bribed someone to get information he's not at liberty to disclose? Surprisingly enough, I've never needed to."

"That is surprising, and I wouldn't call it a bribe. More of a…oh, a gratuity."

"How much of a *gratuity* would you recommend?"

"I don't know." She shrugged. "Ten francs."

"Ten francs? That's rather exorbitant, don't you think? My pockets are not endless."

"Haven't you collected dues this month?" she said under her breath."

His brows drew together in confusion. "What?"

"Nothing." She waved away his question. She had already decided it was best not to let him know of her suspicions.

"I could get a room here for ten francs." He paused. "Well, half a room."

"Then it should do the trick." She waved him off. "Go on."

He heaved a resigned sigh.

"And don't forget to mention Heloise was last seen here. That's very important in terms of encouraging his cooperation."

"I shall keep that in mind," he muttered and returned to the desk clerk. India didn't actually see money change hands, but the desk clerk left for what was probably only a few minutes but seemed much longer. At last he returned and spoke briefly with Derek. Derek nodded and started toward her, the expression on his face annoyingly noncommittal.

"Did you learn anything?"

"Yes." He took her elbow and steered her toward the door.

India's heart jumped. "Tell me."

"In the last six weeks, this hotel—as well as every other hotel in Paris—has been full to bursting with guests." He hailed a cab. "A shockingly large percentage of which have been English or American. Our friend at

the front desk apparently can't tell the difference. There
is a world exposition here, you know."

"I don't care."

He leveled her a disparaging look and handed her
into the cab. "A great many other people do, including,
I believe, your cousin."

India nodded. "That is one of the reasons she planned
on staying for a time in Paris."

"She and everyone else. Although the desk clerk says
he did not see her name in the register, it is entirely
possible he is mistaken. And just as possible he's not."

India's heart sank. The news was not unexpected.
She didn't think they would be so lucky as to find Heloise the first place they looked. She forced an uncon-
cerned note to her voice. "Then it's on to the next Grand
Hotel."

"I've already given directions to the driver." He
paused. "How long did your cousin plan to stay in
Paris?"

"She wasn't entirely sure. Her plans were—"

"Vague? Indecisive? Undetermined?"

"No," she said sharply. "Flexible."

"Flexible?" Skepticism rang in his voice.

"Yes. She had never been to a world exposition before, and she fully intended to see everything there was
to see. As well as everything there is to see in Paris.
She has always dreamed of traveling, and Paris is one
of the places she most wanted to see. She is quite fond
of art as well and planned to spend a great deal of time
at the Louvre. She also wanted to climb that iron monstrosity that is now towering over the city."

"Monsieur Eiffel's tower? You don't like it?"

"I think it's hideous." She shuddered.

He chuckled. "In that you're not alone. There's a great deal of debate about the tower. I, for one, like it."

"Why?"

"First of all, it's an impressive feat of engineering, a symbol of progress—of how far man has come in the world if you will. Secondly—it's the tallest structure on earth, also most impressive. And third—I like how something made of iron can look so light and delicate."

She stared at him. "That's rather fanciful of you."

"I can be fanciful on occasion."

"No doubt." She sniffed.

"Besides, it looks like climbing it will be a great deal of fun."

"We're not here to have fun, Derek."

"Nor shall we," he said firmly, but his eyes twinkled. "Don't you have any desire to see this fascinating city laid out before you? As if you were a bird in flight?"

"Not especially."

"But you've never been to Paris, have you?"

"No." She shrugged. "I've never traveled outside England."

"Why not?"

Obviously, the man was not going to let this go. "I've never had the opportunity, nor have I had the desire. I'm perfectly happy in my own country, and I see no need to trudge about the world in search of adventure. Or for whatever other reasons people abandon hearth and home for. England has everything I want or need."

"Which explains why you chose not to accompany Lady Heloise," he said slowly.

"A fact I now regret. If I had, perhaps she would not be…misplaced." Or at least, India would know where she was.

"Given the flexibility of her schedule combined with

her desire to fully explore the exposition and Paris it-self... I'd say it's entirely possible she may yet be in Paris."

"It's equally possible Paris was not as intriguing as she'd hoped, and she's gone on to Italy or Switzerland or parts as yet unknown," she said with far more irritation than his comment warranted. At least, this comment.

No, it was what he'd said about India choosing not to accompany Heloise. She really hadn't made a choice. She'd thought nothing of it at the time, but when Helo-ise had announced she was going to spend upward of half a year traveling Europe, she had not included her younger cousin in her plans. Certainly, such a trip was not something India would have joined in anyway, but Derek was wrong. India had not chosen not to travel with Heloise.

Cousin Heloise, who'd never done anything even re-motely daring or adventurous in her entire life, had never asked her.

CHAPTER TEN

DEREK SLANTED A quick glance at India beside him in the cab. They'd managed three hotels yesterday before he'd insisted they return to change for dinner. Not that India had anything to wear other than her staid gray traveling dress. He did feel rather bad about that, but it couldn't be helped. Anything he could do to keep them in Paris he would indeed do. The number of Grand Hotels in the city was a help he hadn't expected.

Thus far today they had checked two more Grand Hotels off the list in his notebook—a rather brilliant idea on his part. He had never in his life thought to impress a woman with efficiency, organization and—God help him—a list, but it did indeed seem to warm India's frosty heart.

It probably wasn't at all fair of him to think of her heart as frosty. As much as she tried to hide it, it was obvious to him that she was worried about her cousin. And he had once or twice seen what might possibly be the hint of a genuine smile. India was the only woman he'd ever met with such an unrelenting grip on her emotions. It was at once admirable and terrifying. On occasion, he had noticed a look in her eye that indicated the control she so tightly held might be on the verge of slipping away. But that was rare, and who knew what might happen if someone wound as tight as India were to let go? On one hand, he would pay to see that happen.

On the other, it might be best to be as far away from her as possible when she was at last pushed over the edge.

Even so, there had been something about her yesterday morning in her room when she was very nearly relaxed. Something far more appealing than he had suspected. He was fairly certain Val had noticed. Derek's past sins and indiscretions paled in comparison to his stepbrother's, not that there had ever been any sort of competition between the two. India was just the kind of challenge Val would enjoy. The fact that she'd looked unexpectedly delicious would only make that challenge more enticing. Derek was not about to let the man seduce India. For good or ill, she was under his protection and he would not see her hurt. It was not far-fetched to assume she had little experience with men. Especially men of Val's ilk.

"I need to send a telegram," she said abruptly.

"A postcard would be less costly," he pointed out.

"And it takes a great deal longer to reach its destination."

"Of course, but—"

"Derek." She pinned him with a hard look. "If you are making assumptions about my finances, I can assure you I have funds sufficient to pay my expenses for at least the next six weeks. I am hopeful we will not be gone that long."

"As am I." He thought for a moment. He didn't wish to insult her, but only a fool would fail to note the offhand comments she'd made or how her dress—while not quite shabby—was well worn. "Should you find your expenses exceeding your budget, I do hope you will allow me to assist you."

She raised a brow. "Financially?"

"Well, yes."

"Correct me if I'm wrong, but aren't you here in the first place because you couldn't afford the cost of a detective agency to track down my cousin?"

"True enough." He nodded and wondered how much his uncle was paying.

"A hundred or so pounds a month doesn't seem to go very far, does it?" she said quietly.

What on earth was she talking about? "What?"

"Nothing important. It simply seems to me that your funds, too, are limited."

"Nonetheless—"

"And I have no intention of discussing the matter further. No, Derek." She shook her head. "It must be a telegram, and it must be sent today. And I should like to send it as soon as possible."

"I thought we'd stop for a bite to eat first." He paused. "And perhaps a glass of wine."

"Wine?" The disapproval in her voice matched the look in her eyes. "In the middle of the day?"

"Shocking, I know, but we are in Paris." He gestured at the passing scene. "Paris is known for its sidewalk cafés, and we do have to eat."

"I'm not particularly hungry."

"And yet I am famished," he said firmly. "I would very much like to savor a good *poulet* or *poisson*."

"As much as a nicely broiled chicken or a well-poached piece of salmon does sound tempting, I would prefer to send my telegram first." She set her jaw in the stubborn manner he was already beginning to recognize.

"And then we can eat?"

She heaved a long-suffering sigh. "Yes."

"Excellent." He pulled out his guidebook, flipped to a listing of telegraph offices, then directed the driver to the one closest. A few minutes later, he helped India out of the cab. "Should I go in with you?"

"I don't think that's necessary." She considered the door to the telegraph office with the same look a general might have when preparing for battle. "My French is excellent, and I shouldn't have any problems."

"Very well then." The cafés and restaurants on either side of the street appeared acceptable. The neighborhood was more than respectable and seemed to be frequented as much by tourists and foreigners as Parisians. He gestured at the restaurant to the right of the office. "I shall obtain a table and wait for you there."

She nodded, squared her shoulders slightly—not really necessary as her posture was never less than perfect—and strode into the office. Derek rather pitied the poor clerk inside.

He procured an outdoor table—not too close to the street and the gutter—ordered a carafe of the house wine and two glasses. It had been a good five years or so since he had last been in Paris but, aside from the construction that had been ongoing in the city for decades, very little had changed. Cafés had always been an excellent way to observe the inhabitants of the French capital. It was easy to differentiate between native Parisians passing by, their manner unhurried and relaxed as if they relished in the savoring of life itself, and the tourists that flocked here to see the sights—their expressions intent and determined. As if they hadn't a moment to waste in their quest to visit the Louvre and the Cathedral of Notre Dame and all else Paris offered, and no doubt they probably hadn't. Lady Heloise was wise to plan an extended stay here, although it would certainly help if she had determined in advance just how long she intended that stay to be. In spite of the lax nature of the travel plans prepared for Lady Heloise by the Lady Travelers Society, there was something here that made no sense. He couldn't quite put his finger on it. But then, in his experience, women rarely made a great deal of sense. An annoying trait that tended to increase with age. His mother and Aunt Guinevere were sterling examples of that.

"Is that for me?"

Derek jumped to his feet. He hadn't seen India coming, an error on his part. It didn't seem wise to allow this woman to catch him unawares. He pulled out her chair and she sat down. "You mean the wine?"

"Yes." She eyed the still-empty glass.

"Indeed it is." He took his seat and filled her glass. "I would have ordered for you, but I didn't know if you really did prefer fish to chicken."

"In this particular case, I should probably allow you to select for me as you are familiar with the food in this country and I am not." She slid the glass away. "And I told you, I do not drink wine in the middle of the day."

"Actually, you said nothing of the sort." He pushed the glass back toward her. "You did, however, imply there was something improper about a glass of wine in the middle of the day."

"And indeed—" she slid the glass toward him again "—there is."

"Not in Paris." He moved the glass back. "Do you ever loosen your corset, India? Ever?"

Her eyes widened. "My corset is none of your concern! I daresay, even in Paris, one does not discuss one's corset with a gentleman. Of course a gentleman would never bring up such a subject in the first place."

"Certainly not with you."

"I shall take that as a compliment," she said in a lofty manner, picked up the glass and took a healthy sip.

He resisted the urge to grin with triumph. There was something about annoying India Prendergast that was very nearly irresistible.

"If you are hoping to see me intoxicated, I assure you your efforts are in vain." She smirked. "I frequently have wine with dinner."

He laughed. "And I assure you, that is the farthest thing from my mind. I was hoping for no more than an enjoyable meal and equally enjoyable company."

"I doubt that you have found my company enjoyable thus far."

"You have a great deal on your mind." He signaled to a waiter and ordered them both a delicious-looking chicken stew he'd spotted at another table. "It's to be expected really that you would be preoccupied. You're worried about your cousin."

"Thank you," she said when the waiter left. "I am concerned. Heloise has never traveled anywhere, and she has a tendency to be a bit flighty and impractical. She's always been something of a dreamer."

"I imagine you are practical enough for the two of you."

"There is nothing wrong with being practical. Or sensible. I see the world as it is, Derek. Not as I wish it would be."

"How do you wish it would be?"

She stared at him. "I am perfectly happy with the world as it is."

"Your cousin wished to travel. Surely you have dreams, as well?"

"Not really." She thought for a moment, then shrugged. "Nothing comes to mind."

"I find that hard to believe. Even the most content among us has something they would wish for."

"I might ask you the same thing. What do you dream of? What do you want?"

"I want not to disappoint," he said without thinking, but the moment the words left his lips he wished he could take them back.

"Not to disappoint who?"

"Anyone, everyone." He resisted the urge to squirm in his seat. This was entirely too…revealing. He wasn't sure why he'd admitted this in the first place, and to her of all people. Of course, he hadn't known what he'd wanted at all until the words had come out, an unanticipated revelation that bore further scrutiny but not at the moment. And not with India.

"Come now, Derek," she said mildly. "I daresay not being a disappointment is what everyone wants. It's like wanting to be good instead of bad."

"I shall make you a bargain, India." He leaned forward slightly and stared into her eyes. "If you will not belittle my wishes, then I will not disparage the fact that you have none."

Her cheeks colored. Guilt stabbed him. He ignored it and changed the subject. "Tell me more about your cousin."

"Why?" she said with as much relief as distrust. She was obviously as uncomfortable with the turn their conversation had taken as he.

"You needn't be so suspicious, I simply think knowing as much as I can about her might be helpful."

"I can't imagine it would hurt."

"Then I am right." He grinned. "Again."

"Savor it, Derek, as it is so rare."

He laughed. "I take it your cousin is somewhat frugal."

"Why would you say that?"

"Do you intend to be wary of every question I ask?"

"Probably," she said coolly and lifted her glass to her lips. He would have wagered she did so to hide a smile.

"You were surprised at the first Grand Hotel we visited."

She nodded. "Heloise does not squander her money. She has a very limited income—only a trust left to her by her father. He was the Earl of Crenfield, a title that went to a distant relative along with most of the family's wealth and property. Heloise was left a house in London and a trust that provides a modest annual income."

"Oh?" *Modest* was not the word he would use.

"She became my guardian when my parents died. I was eleven at the time. My parents left a small sum in savings, which went toward my education. Heloise provided the rest. She is most generous, but her income is minimal." She paused. "I would hate to be a burden on her."

"Which explains why you chose to seek employment."

"I suppose it does." She took another sip of her wine. "But I enjoy my financial independence. I daresay, even if Heloise had a huge fortune, I suspect I would want to do something other than sit around and embroider or watercolor."

"You could wed," he said in an offhand manner.

"I've never met a man I could imagine shackling myself to for the rest of my days." She shuddered. "I can't think of a worse fate."

"Have you no desire for love?"

"Love, Derek, at least the romantic kind, is the height of irrational, illogical, foolish absurdity. And romance is nothing more than a silly lure for love. People live for love or die for love, or the lack of it. They write bad poetry over it and make worse decisions. Love makes people forget their responsibilities and do imbecilic things. No indeed." She shook her head with a bit more vehemence than was necessary, but that might have been the wine. "I have never been the least bit enamored of love nor do I intend to be. And I realized years ago that some of us are simply not suited for marriage."

"Oh?"

"I would think a successful marriage—at least the only kind I would consider—would require a certain amount of compromise. I have never even heard of a man who is willing to compromise, especially not when it comes to marriage." She wrinkled her nose in a delightfully unguarded manner. "And I have never been good at compromise."

He sucked in a sharp breath. "No!"

She ignored him. "I simply see no reason to compromise when I am right. And I am always right."

He laughed. Before he could debate her statement, their food arrived. The chicken and vegetable dish cooked in a rich wine sauce was as good as it had looked, and they were both too busy enjoying the tasty cuisine to say much of anything beyond murmurs of appreciation and satisfaction.

"Might I ask who you were so adamant about telegraphing?" he said when they were nearly finished.

"It's none of your concern." Her glass was empty, and he refilled it, surprised that she did not protest. "But it's not a secret. My employer asked me to telegraph him regularly and inform him of our progress." She raised her glass to him. "He doesn't trust you, either."

He gasped in feigned dismay. "And what, pray tell, have I done to earn his distrust?"

"Good Lord, Derek, you have quite a reputation."

"Yes, you mentioned that in London."

"It bears repeating. You can't be so dim as to not be aware of your tarnished image."

"I am well aware of it. However, I am in the process of reform."

She stared at him for a long moment, then snorted in disbelief. "Come now. Men like you do not reform."

"Men like me?"

"Your misdeeds are public knowledge. Your name can scarcely come up in conversation without someone relating one unfortunate incident or another." She set down her glass and ticked the points off on her fingers. "One of your best known indiscretions involved Lady Philbury—"

"Who was estranged from her husband," he said casually.

"But married nonetheless. There was an incident centered on an indecent painting—"

"A youthful error in judgment on my part." He waved off her comment. "Surely such transgressions can be forgiven?"

"But never forgotten. There was a questionable sporting event in Hyde Park. A race I believe."

"Scarcely worth mentioning." He snorted in dismissal. "And might I point out neither animal nor human suffered the tiniest injury. Other than perhaps to their dignity."

"There was a wager involving the auction of undergarments of a royal personage."

He winced. "Yes, well, that was perhaps not one of my finer moments. Although it really wasn't my idea."

"Giving credit to someone else does not absolve you of responsibility," she said primly. "There was a masked ball where the ladies in question—"

"That's quite enough, but thank you for allowing me to relive my wicked ways." He grinned. In hindsight, there were a great many things he'd done, and nearly as many that he'd failed to do, that now struck him as foolish and asinine. But nearly all of them had been fun at the time.

"Ways you say are in the past."

"The very definition of *reform*."

"That remains to be seen."

"One does have to grow up at some point, you know." He smiled wryly. "Whether one wants to or not."

"One can only hope. But you can see why your past behavior does not engender complete trust in someone like Sir Martin."

"I gather he is most trustworthy."

"Well, he's not prone to silly pranks and disgraceful behavior, so in that respect, yes. He is also honorable, respectable and quite brilliant."

"He sounds perfect."

"Good Lord, no." She scoffed. "He is disorganized, prone to distraction and rarely sees anything through to completion."

"I see. Quite a handful then for Lady Luckthorne," he said even though he already knew there was no Lady Luckthorne.

"Oh, there is no Lady Luckthorne."

"Then who manages his household, his staff, his social engagements? That sort of thing."

"I do, of course."

"I thought you were a secretarial assistant?"

"I fear the term is rather broad when it comes to Sir Martin." She sipped her wine. "I do very nearly everything he needs so that he needn't waste his valuable time and can spend it in more beneficial pursuits. Mostly of an intellectual or academic or scientific nature. Experiments and inventions and the like. As well as research, writing, collecting—that sort of thing."

"And this honorable, respectable, brilliant gentleman sees nothing the least bit improper about an unmarried man working in close proximity with an unmarried woman in his own home."

"Not at all." She waved off the charge. "As there is nothing nor has there ever been anything untoward between us. Not that I would permit such a thing."

"No doubt," he said under his breath.

Her eyes narrowed. "What do you mean by that?"

"Scandal, my dear India, is as often as not in the eyes of the beholder. As aboveboard and innocent as it might be, some people might view your employment with Sir Martin to be more of an *arrangement* than a legitimate position." He braced himself.

She stared at him for a long moment, then snorted back what might have been a laugh. "Then *some people* have never met either Sir Martin or myself."

"Yes, well, trust me when I say it's not necessary to know someone personally to spread tales about their misdeeds. I am a prime example of that."

"In your case, there are witnesses to your misadventures." She smiled in a smug manner. "Dozens I would say, perhaps hundreds."

"And there are no witnesses as to what transpires between an odd sort of chap and his lovely assistant behind closed doors."

"Do not attempt to charm me, Derek, with words like *lovely*. It will not work. And furthermore nothing goes on behind closed doors with Sir Martin. I do feel a certain…sisterly affection for him. In the manner I imagine I would an older brother. And I'm certain any feelings that he might have for me are very much the same." She paused to finish her wine. "Goodness, I've worked for the man for eight years. I would think he would have said something by now if he felt otherwise."

"And if he did?"

"I would leave his employment at once." She held out her glass to be refilled yet again. "I will not allow myself to be put in an awkward position."

"And yet you insisted on traveling with me."

"That's entirely different. *We*—" she aimed a pointed finger at him "—are traveling in pursuit of a higher purpose. A noble calling, if you will. We are off to rescue Heloise."

"Whether she wants rescuing or not."

"And we have chaperones," she added. "Nothing here for witnesses to spread gossip about."

"Come now, India, I would have thought you far smarter than that." He met her gaze directly. "Surely you realize, whether it's true or not, the most interesting, most tantalizing, juiciest gossip is about that behavior that has no witnesses at all."

"Regardless, that doesn't mean one can do whatever one wants. There are rules, Derek. And rules are meant to be followed."

"Always?"

"Yes," she said firmly, then paused. "Although I suppose there might be extreme circumstances under which it might be acceptable to bend or even break a rule. I can't think of an example offhand, but I am willing to acknowledge the possibility."

"How very broad-minded of you," he said with a grin and raised his glass to her. "Here's to finding an example."

CHAPTER ELEVEN

*One should keep in mind where one is bound
when selecting attire for a journey. A wardrobe
for the Egyptian desert would not be appropriate in the Bavarian Alps. However, one can never
go far afield with a good-quality skirt and sturdy
walking boots. The knowledgeable lady traveler
always checks her luggage more than once to
make certain it is properly labeled. Lost luggage
will disrupt the trip of even the most steadfast
among us.*

—The Lady Travelers Society Guide

EVEN AT THE house she shared with Heloise in London,
India dressed for dinner. It was proper and expected.
But her gray suit was simply not up to the task of dining yet again in Lord Brookings's ornate Parisian dining
room with its mural-painted walls and sparkling gold-
and-crystal chandelier. Still, she made do—she had no
choice. It would have been rude to have stayed in her
room. Nonetheless, being impolite might well have been
better than being present at dinner. She wouldn't have
believed it possible but she felt even more out of place
at the table with his lordship, Derek and the Greers than
she had in the lobby of the first Grand Hotel although
the second, third and all the way through today's seventh, while not quite as grand, were still impressive.

It was early evening when Derek decreed they were finished for the day and insisted they return to his step-brother's house. Her trunk had still not been located, but Suzette assured her it had probably simply been placed in the wrong room, more than likely in the wrong wing, and every effort was being made to find it. India wasn't sure she completely believed the woman. What she'd seen of the household staff did not inspire confidence in their efficiency. It was not the least bit surprising that they had misplaced her trunk. However, she had to admit, the food here was excellent, if a bit rich. Still, there was too much on her mind to enjoy the meal or partake in the lively conversation. No one seemed to notice.

It was obvious that Estelle had fallen under the spell of both Derek and Lord Brookings, given the way the older lady fluttered her lashes and emitted the occasional giggle, not to mention the look of adoration in her eyes. As if she were a schoolgirl and not a woman in her late fifties.

Professor Greer seemed to have succumbed to their charms, as well, and much of the conversation consisted of reminiscences of his student days in Paris thirty-some years ago. The three men dedicated a considerable amount of time to comparing and contrasting the Paris of today—with its newly widened boulevards and recently constructed edifices—with the Paris of the professor's youth. And as much as he appreciated the modern look of the city, he did speak longingly of twisted medieval streets, narrow passageways and ancient buildings. There was a touch of longing, as well, in his memories of some of the more unsavory entertainments Paris had offered, and Lord Brookings as-

sured him some things never change. Thankfully, Derek
quickly directed the conversation toward other topics.

No, India would have preferred to avoid dinner altogether and wouldn't have minded avoiding Derek, as
well. She had not been inebriated at the café, but the
wine had served to loosen her tongue. But when she reflected upon their conversation, there was little she said
that she would not have said without the wine. Although
she probably owed him an apology. Her dismissal of his
desire not to disappoint was beyond rude; it was petty
of her and unkind. A distinct sense of shame washed
through her at the thought. He'd been nothing but nice
to her, and she'd returned his kindness with sarcasm
and disdain. Indeed, she couldn't help but wonder if
he wasn't quite the scoundrel she'd thought he was but
rather misguided in his attempt to prove his worth. It
was a thought worth further consideration.

She excused herself after dinner, pleading weari-
ness, which was not entirely untrue. Once more, she was
forced to sleep in the same frilly nightwear she'd worn
since her arrival while Suzette again took her clothes to
be cleaned. While she wasn't used to such luxury, the
silken feel of the garment against her skin was delightful. The thought crossed her mind that she might wish to
pamper herself and indulge in something similar when
she returned home. And indulge in a mattress that was
as welcoming as this one. Silly musings of course, no
doubt attributable to this city and this house.

India had awoken this morning with renewed determination. She had again slept later than usual but
woke earlier than the past two mornings, intending to
join the rest of the household downstairs for breakfast.
She'd surrendered to Suzette's insistence on helping her
dress and arranging her hair—even if the end result was

decidedly more French than she would have preferred with her usual knot higher on her head and annoying tendrils of curls fringing her face. Suzette had declared it quite fetching, and India had wished to escape more than she'd wished to argue.

"Good morning," she said brightly, entering the dining room. His lordship wasn't present, no doubt this was entirely too early for him, but Derek and the Greers were engaged in animated conversation. Derek and the professor both stood at her arrival.

"Good morning, my dear." Professor Greer smiled. "You look lovely today."

"You do indeed, India." Estelle nodded with enthusiasm. "Paris obviously agrees with you."

"I wouldn't wager on that." Derek studied her curiously. "Is there something different about you today?"

"Nothing I can think of." India resisted the urge to pat her hair back into its usual place. Her glance strayed to the sideboard. "Is that an English breakfast?"

"With a few French pastries thrown in for good measure." Delight sounded in Estelle's voice. "His lordship apparently appreciates the benefit of both French and English offerings at breakfast. Frederick and I think it's a custom we might well adopt ourselves when we return home."

"Lord Brookings has always believed in taking the best of both cultures," Derek added. "There's a specially blended coffee, as well."

"How very…worldly of him." India gestured to the others to take their seats, then hurried to the sideboard. It was a breakfast to rival even the heartiest offering to be found in England: eggs cooked three different ways, sausages, an assortment of cheeses, fish and fruit, as well as croissants and several other types of pastries.

For a fleeting moment, she envied those whose wealth allowed them to indulge this way every morning. She filled her plate and took a seat at the table.

"Derek," she began, "as much as I am eager to return to our search today, I'm afraid there will be an unavoidable delay."

His brow rose. "A delay?"

She nodded. "I cannot continue to wear the same clothes day after day. As everyone has assured me my trunk must be here somewhere, I intend to take my maid and go through every room in this house until I find it." India pulled apart a croissant and popped a bite in her mouth.

Derek and the professor traded glances.

"I do hope you intend to ask Lord Brookings before you go barging about his house, India," Estelle said.

"I have every intention of doing so, but thank you for pointing that out to me." India stabbed a piece of sausage. The sausages were particularly good.

"I hate to be the bearer of bad tidings, my dear," the professor began, then glanced at Derek, who nodded in an encouraging manner. "But I was unaware your trunk was missing until this morning."

Perhaps Heloise's cook could learn to make French pastries.

"Frederick and Estelle had already left for the day when you awoke yesterday," Derek said.

"Thank you for your concern, Professor," India said and took a bite of eggs cooked with mushrooms and herbs. It was all she could do not to moan with delight.

"It's more than concern really." The professor cleared his throat. "I very much fear I am responsible."

India froze, her fork halfway to her mouth. "Oh?"

"If I recall correctly, when I claimed our luggage the

other night," Professor Greer began, "it seemed more than sufficient for four people. There were a number of valises—I'm not sure exactly how many—and three trunks."

"One of which was mine," Derek said.

Estelle winced. "The others were ours."

"I do apologize, but I had no idea we were missing your baggage." Professor Greer shook his head. "I certainly would have said something at the time if I had realized we were one trunk short."

"So my trunk is not in the house," India said slowly.

"Apparently not." Derek considered her with the same look one might give an unexploded bomb that could detonate at any moment. "However, the instant the professor informed me this morning, I personally returned to the station to see if your trunk was there with other lost bags."

"And?" She held her breath.

"And…it wasn't," Derek said reluctantly. "It's entirely possible it was somehow misdirected, and instead of coming to Paris it went off on its own travels."

She set the fork down. "Where?"

Derek hesitated. "That does seem to be the question."

She drew a deep breath and struggled to stay calm. "And do you have an answer?"

"Not yet." Derek grimaced. "But I assure you, I am doing everything possible to recover your trunk. Val is lending his assistance, as well. I have no doubt it will turn up." He paused. "Eventually."

"Eventually?" She could barely choke out the word. *"Eventually?"*

"Sooner or later," he said weakly.

"Yes, I know what *eventually* means," she said sharply, her voice rising in spite of her best efforts.

"These things happen when one travels, my dear."
Estelle reached over and patted her hand. "I have never
traveled myself, of course, but I understand this does
happen on occasion. Why, one of the brochures from the
Lady Travelers Society deals with this very subject and
offers excellent advice on how to manage without one's
own things until one's luggage is recovered."

India had never experienced panic before, but what
was surely panic rose within her now. "You belong to
the Lady Travelers Society?"

"Oh my, yes." Estelle dimpled. "I have from very
nearly the beginning."

And wasn't that a revelation? Still, it scarcely mattered at the moment. Not when her stomach was twisting, and she could barely drag air into her lungs. Her
vision narrowed, and the oddest black dots clouded the
edge of her sight.

"If you will excuse me." India got to her feet and
braced her hands on the table, her knees unsteady as if
they might fail her at any moment. Dear Lord, was this
what it felt like to faint? She was not the type of woman
who fainted. Indeed, she'd always had a certain con-
tempt for women who fainted to avoid a pressing problem. In that, she might have been too harsh.

"Are you all right?" Derek jumped to his feet and
circled the table toward her.

The professor frowned with alarm as he, too, stood.
"You look extraordinarily pale."

"No, I'm fine." She pulled in a deep breath, then
another.

"Are you sure?" Derek was beside her now, concern
in his voice and his eyes. As well as a touch of what
might well be guilt. "You don't look well."

Indeed, he should feel guilty. He was the one who had seen to the luggage at the beginning of their journey.

"No, really, I'm quite all right." She straightened, her momentary distress swept aside by anger. Which would serve no one well. She needed to take her leave, at once, before she said something that would only make matters worse. "I think I shall retire to my room and consider all this." She mustered a weak smile. "Thank you for your concern." She quickly took her leave.

With every step, her ire eased. If one looked at this in a rational, sensible way, it probably wasn't Derek's fault, not completely. Oh certainly, he was responsible for the luggage, but as for the rest of it... It was simply easier to direct her fury at him than to place the blame where it belonged—squarely at her feet. But it had seemed such a clever idea at the time.

Martin had gone on and on about the dangers of travel. About thieves and pickpockets in cities like Paris. About the threats to women traveling even with companions. About how one could be knocked over the head and lose everything. It therefore didn't seem at all wise to carry her funds in her traveling valise or on her person. Why, in her books of detection and mystery, where valuables were secreted in hidden places, no one ever found them until the final chapter. What could be safer than putting the bulk of her traveling funds in a hidden compartment in her trunk?

It had never been mentioned that the trunk itself could be lost!

She reached her room, closed the door behind her and collapsed against it. Good Lord, what was she going to do? She and Derek had agreed from the beginning that they would each pay their own expenses. The only money she had at the moment was what Martin had

given her for telegraphs, and that would not last. At least
as long as they remained in Paris, she did not have to
pay for a hotel room. But when they left...she shuddered
at the thought. She could not under any circumstances
take money from Derek. That would be the same as
taking it from ladies like Heloise herself.

She pushed away from the door and paced the room.
There were few options. She could use what little money
she had to return to England and abandon her search for
Heloise—praying her cousin would at some point realize she had failed in her correspondence and write to
her. Of course, that was assuming Heloise was indeed
fine. It was also dependent upon prayer, and India was
not confident in divine intervention. Surely God had
other things to concern himself with than lost cousins
and lost luggage. Besides, he'd never seemed to listen
to her before.

No, the only real choice was to stretch what little
she had and—should it be absolutely necessary—wire
Martin for funds. He wouldn't be at all averse to assisting her, but she hated the very thought of admitting her
stupidity and asking for rescue. She was not a helpless
female and did not want to be seen as one. Nor did she
wish to be further indebted to Martin. She was already
in his debt for her employment. She would send a final
telegram, make up some sort of excuse as to why she
wouldn't be telegraphing him further and then make
that money last as long as possible. And she would repay
him every bit of it when she returned home.

A knock sounded at her door.

"Yes?"

The door opened, and Estelle poked her head in.
"My dear girl, are you all right? Everyone is worried
about you."

"That's very kind of you." India forced a smile. "But you needn't worry, I'm fine."

"Oh, well, then, I'll leave you be." Disappointment flickered through the older woman's eyes, and she turned to go. It really was quite nice of her—of all of them really—to worry about her. Especially given that she might not be the most congenial traveling companion.

"Don't go," India said without thinking. "That wasn't entirely true."

"Oh?"

"I'm not the least bit fine, I'm afraid." India brushed an annoying tendril of hair away from her face. "Please, come in."

"Of course." Estelle's face brightened, and she fairly bounced into the room. "You poor child. What can I do to help?"

"I don't know." India indicated an upholstered chair. "Do sit down." Estelle settled in the chair and waited expectantly. India resumed pacing. "I've never not known what to do, at least not as far as I can remember. My life is usually well ordered and controlled. Things are not generally out of my hands."

"This is an awkward situation." Sympathy sounded in Estelle's voice. "Although we are in Paris, so it's not as bad as it could be."

India paused in midstep. "I don't see how it could be worse."

"Nonsense. This is the fashion capital of the world, you know. I can't imagine anything more fun than replenishing one's wardrobe in Paris, even if one has limited means. It's an opportunity that does not often come along, at least for most of us. And you have the perfect excuse."

India stared. "I hadn't even thought about clothes."

"Well, you simply can't continue to wear the same thing day after day." Estelle's gaze traveled over the gray dress from bodice to hem and back. "It's beginning to look a bit—" she winced "—sad."

"It is being cleaned every night."

"Clean is one thing, dear. Worn is something else altogether."

India glanced down at the dependable garment. "I think it's holding up well."

"Come now, India." Estelle's tone was gentle, as if she were trying to make a small child see reason. "Do you really?"

"Yes," she said staunchly. "I do."

Estelle's brow arched upward.

"I've never been particularly concerned with fashion."

"I've noticed, dear."

"I prefer to choose my clothes for practical reasons— appropriateness and reliability, that sort of thing."

"Not for appearance then?"

"No." India shrugged.

"Never?"

"I've never seen the need."

"I see." Estelle considered her thoughtfully. "Have you never put on a new gown or a dress and enjoyed how it not only made you look but how it made you feel?"

"No." India had never even considered such a thing.

"Goodness, even I have that experience very nearly every time I don a new frock. Admittedly, it's been some time since the view in the mirror was as fetching as it once was…" A wistful smile curved Estelle's lips. "But enough of that. It's past time you had that same experience, too. Come along, India." She rose to her feet. "We have shopping to do."

"I can't."

"Of course you can." Estelle waved off India's objection. "As we shall certainly be here for some time, we shall order you some new clothes at once. Until then, there are a few shops here where clothes are sold ready-to-wear. I have already, out of mild curiosity, stopped at a few, and their charges are quite reasonable. Purchasing ready-made clothing is not something I would normally endorse, you understand, but necessity dictates a modicum of sacrifice. Although the purchase of Paris fashions, even those not made to order, is scarcely—"

"I can't purchase any clothes." India's voice rose.

"Not only can you but you must," Estelle said firmly.

"No, you don't understand—I can't." India drew a deep breath. "Most of my money is hidden in my trunk."

Estelle's mouth dropped open, and her eyes widened.

"Is there a Lady Travelers Society pamphlet for that?" The panic India had thought laid to rest threatened to return in full force.

"I don't know." Estelle stared. "But there certainly should be a pamphlet. 'What to Do When One Is in a Foreign Country with No Money.' I shall suggest it when we return." She hesitated. "But I suspect the first thing it might say is don't put your money in luggage that could go astray."

"Yes, well, that would be good advice." India continued to pace. "I realize it sounds, oh, unwise—"

Estelle snorted, then coughed.

"But it did seem like such a clever idea at the time." Still, what had she been thinking? Why, she'd been so caught up in worry about Heloise and preparing for a trip she'd never previously considered, with a man she didn't trust, and Martin was going on and on about rogues and gypsies, and obviously she wasn't thinking at all. India prided herself on her intelligence but, apparently, when one's intellect failed, it did so in a spectacular manner. "I see now it was a stupid mistake. Why, if anyone else had done something this absurd—"

"You'd call them an idiot." Estelle nodded. "And in no uncertain terms, I'd wager."

India stared at the older woman. She'd never worried about what other people thought of her; it simply wasn't important. She lived her life as she pleased. Of course, she'd never had a season, never been officially out in society, never even been to a ball. And never particularly cared about what she considered foolish nonsense. Was it even remotely possible that all those things she'd never done—never wanted to do—had made her into the kind of shrew who was so unyielding she couldn't forgive fault in other people? Who saw nothing wrong in pointing out the flaws of others? Who spoke her mind regardless of what insult she might cause? Who belittled a man's sincere desire not to disappoint?

Estelle was right. India would be the first to call someone who had made as ridiculous a mistake as she had an idiot. That was exactly what she would do. And she'd do so with a great deal of disdain and superiority.

"You're right." India sank down on the bed. "I probably would. How terribly…awful of me."

"I'm not sure *awful* is the right word," Estelle said. India shot her a skeptical look.

"Although I suspect it's fairly close. However…" Estelle adopted a no-nonsense attitude. "One cannot change if one doesn't recognize there's a problem, dear. You are an intelligent, outspoken, independent woman, and I see nothing wrong with that." She smiled. "But you might consider accepting that the rest of us are flawed, mortal creatures who might not live up to your standards of perfection."

India nodded slowly. "I could consider that."

"And that's all we can hope for. Now then, there's little I can do about your finances, although I'm sure I can scrape together a bit of a loan. For now…" Estelle studied her closely. "Stand up for a moment so that I may get a good look at you."

"Why?" India asked but stood nonetheless.

"Turn around please." Estelle twirled her finger. "Slowly."

"All right but why am I doing this?"

"So I can best determine which of the articles of clothing I brought with me would be suitable for you."

"Oh, I couldn't—"

"But you will. I insist, and I will not take no for an answer." Estelle stood and circled India. "My things will need a few alterations here and there but nothing significant I wouldn't think. We are of a similar height and while our bosoms are comparable, I'm afraid the rest of me is a bit more curved than you are."

Stout was a more appropriate word. India cringed to herself. If she was to be less judgmental and, well, nicer, she needed to start now. If Estelle wanted to call herself curved, then curved she should be.

"I'm not unskilled with a needle and thread myself, but I would imagine one of the maids here is probably more adept than I am." Estelle's brow furrowed with thought. "I brought far more than I can possibly ever wear, but one never knows what one might encounter when traveling."

"Is that advice from a Lady Travelers Society pamphlet?"

"Yes, I believe it is," Estelle said absently, gathering some of the gray wool between her fingers and pulling it tighter. "You're not quite as plump as I thought you were. It's simply that your clothes are a bit ill fitting."

"They are quite comfortable."

"I imagine they are," the older woman murmured. "I have several things that will do for you. At least one will take no more than a stitch here and there. I'll fetch it at once and find a maid, as well."

"Thank you, Estelle." Wearing Estelle's clothes would not have been her choice, but the offer was very kind. And the older woman was right—the gray wool was looking tired. While India was only of moderate means and had never given a second thought to fashion, she did prefer to look neat and precise.

Estelle turned to go.

"One more thing." India hesitated. "I would appreciate it if you would not mention my financial difficulty to Mr. Saunders."

"I think he will notice eventually."

"Not if I'm careful. And not if we do indeed find my cousin soon, which we will surely do as we have only twenty or so more Grand Hotels at which to inquire." Although it did seem rather a lot. She refused to consider their next step if Heloise was not at a Grand Hotel. If the word *grand* in her letter was nothing more than a description. Would they then have to inquire at every hotel with a grand appearance? And what if they didn't find her in Paris at all? "And I did carry a little money with me." India wasn't used to asking anyone for anything, but pride did need to be set aside on occasion. "I would hate for him to know how foolish

I was." Strange, how important it seemed. Whatever else Derek might think of her, she would hate for him to think she was stupid.

"I can certainly understand that." Estelle nodded. "Very well then, this shall be our secret."

"Once again, you have my gratitude." India released a relieved breath. "You're being very kind, and I've done nothing to merit it."

"Nonsense. I have no doubt you'd do the very same thing for me if our positions were reversed."

India wasn't entirely sure of that, but it was rather nice that Estelle thought so.

"I am also hoping that you and I can be friends."

Friends? It had occurred to India the other day when Derek had mentioned something about her friends that, aside from Heloise and Martin, she had none. She'd never given it a second thought, and it had certainly never bothered her before. Odd that it did so now.

She smiled. "I would like that."

"Good. Then as your friend, I must be honest and admit that providing you with a few garments is a benefit to me, as well. It gives me the opportunity to buy a few things here for myself." Estelle grinned in what could only be called a wicked manner. "And I have always wanted a gown made in Paris."

CHAPTER TWELVE

"I HAVE GIVEN this situation a great deal of thought," Professor Greer said in a ponderous tone, as if he was about to make an announcement of importance or impart some gem of academic wisdom. For a moment, it was as though Derek had returned to the classroom.

"Which situation would that be, Professor?" Derek checked his pocket watch, then glanced once again at the parlor door. India had sent one of the maids to tell him she would meet him at this hour to continue their Grand Hotel search. She was late, which didn't bother him at all really. Anything that extended their stay in Paris—even by as little as half an hour—was a benefit.

"Miss Prendergast's lost luggage for one thing."

"Nothing can be done about that, I'm afraid." Derek shrugged in a helpless manner. "The best we can do is hope it makes its way to Paris. I gave the clerk at the station our address here and Miss Prendergast's name, as well as pointed out she is the guest of the Marquess of Brookings. I further stated his lordship would be most grateful if Miss Prendergast's trunk was recovered."

"I daresay there isn't more you can do than that." The professor nodded thoughtfully. "Until then, however, Estelle and I would like to offer our services in the Paris search for Lady Heloise. Miss Prendergast was obviously quite distressed at learning her trunk had gone astray, so it occurred to me the sooner we find her cousin, the sooner we can leave Paris."

"That occurred to you, did it?"

"It did." He nodded. "There is nothing that upsets a lady more than knowing she has nothing to wear."

Derek chuckled. "Miss Prendergast is not your usual female."

"Yes, I have noticed that, as well. Still you cannot deny her dismay about the loss of her things."

"She did seem quite distraught." Indeed, she was far more upset than Derek would have expected. Although perhaps she was simply tired of her gray dress. Derek certainly was.

"I realize we are here only in the capacity of chaperone, but we would like to help." The professor paused. "Do you and Miss Prendergast still suspect Lady Heloise may be staying in one of the numerous Grand Hotels in the city?"

"We do."

"It will take a great deal of time to inquire at all of them, won't it?"

"Well, we do want to be thorough and ask all the appropriate questions."

The professor nodded.

"We've already visited the first seven on the list. There are only twenty or so left."

"It will proceed much more quickly if my wife and I assist you. We can make inquires at half of those remaining. Divide and conquer, you know."

"That's most generous of you." The last thing Derek wanted was to shorten their stay in Paris by speeding up the search. "But we couldn't possibly accept your help."

The professor frowned. "Why on earth not? The very

reason you're in Paris in the first place is to search for
Lady Heloise."

"Of course, but…" Why on earth indeed? Derek
struggled for a plausible reason. "Miss Prendergast and
I have it well in hand."

"It seems to be going rather slowly to me."

"On the contrary, we are progressing steadily, leaving no stone unturned and all." And yet no plausible
reason came to mind.

"I daresay—"

"However, while I am confident we can make inquiries at the Grand Hotels without assistance," Derek said
slowly, "there is something you can do."

The professor smiled knowingly. "I thought there
might be."

"Lady Heloise had long wanted to visit Paris, and
she intended to see everything there was to see here."

"Quite right," the professor said. "My wife expresses
the same sentiment. I, of course, have seen it all before, but I, too, would like to reacquaint myself with
the sights of the city."

"Then we shall kill two birds with one stone, as they
say." Derek nodded. "You and Mrs. Greer can continue
your own tour of Paris, and, in the process, inquire at
the various monuments and museums if anyone has
seen a woman matching Lady Heloise's description.
You have seen her photograph, haven't you?"

"Miss Prendergast showed it to us on the train."

"Excellent." Derek beamed. "That will be a great
help."

"It seems rather inefficient to me," the professor said.

"It is. But then we are looking for an older lady
whose plans were not the least bit efficient or organized."

"You do have a point."

"I can think of no other way to go about this. She only sent two letters from Paris. In one, she wrote about a driving tour she took of the city, and in the other, she wrote in great detail about a daylong visit to the Louvre."

"We can certainly query the attendants in the various galleries," Professor Greer said, "as well as talk to those purveyors of driving tours around the city."

"And, as you do, you will be able to see all the sights of Paris for yourselves." Derek leaned toward him and lowered his voice in a confidential manner. "I would imagine Mrs. Greer would be most displeased if you didn't. Unlike you, she has never been to Paris, and unless you plan on returning—"

"Probably not." A regretful note sounded in the professor's voice.

"Then this is her only opportunity." Derek shook his head mournfully. "I would not want to be the one to deprive her of that."

"Neither would I." The older gentleman shuddered.

"In which case, this shall work brilliantly," Derek said with an encouraging smile.

"It still strikes me as a haphazard way to search for Lady Heloise."

"Professor," Derek said sincerely, "if you have a better idea, I am certainly willing to consider it."

"I wish I did." He shook his head. "I'm afraid finding lost items has never been my forte. It's an enormous city, and given the influx of more travelers than usual for the exposition and the opening of Monsieur Eiffel's tower, it seems rather futile, doesn't it?"

"Yes, I'm afraid it does." Derek considered the other man for a moment. The professor was a good sort and could no doubt be trusted. And Derek could certainly use an ally. "Might I confide something to you? In the strictest of confidence?"

"Certainly."

"My uncle offered to assist in our quest by hiring detectives. He suggested I keep Miss Prendergast searching for Lady Heloise in Paris while his investigators retrace her path and try to locate her. It will keep Miss Prendergast's mind off the possibility that something terrible has happened to her cousin. And if something has, well, it might be best if she and I are not the ones to discover that."

Professor Greer nodded.

"The longer we keep her here, the better the chances that my uncle's endeavors will bear fruit."

"I see."

"There is one other thing." Derek chose his words with care. "Miss Prendergast does not trust me. I have not lived a spotless life, but I assure you, while my misdeeds might have walked the edge of scandal, they did not include violations of the law." At least not any serious, important laws.

"That is good to know." The professor chuckled wryly, then sobered. "I know better than most the kinds of ill-conceived behavior young men are prone to. However, even in the most reckless youth, I have usually been able to ascertain his true nature. See what kind of a man he will eventually become, that sort of thing. I have long prided myself on my judgment of a man's character." He met Derek's gaze directly. "I am confident you are a good man."

The oddest flush of pride washed through Derek. "Thank you, sir." He paused. "There is one other matter."

"Go on."

"While I wish to find Lady Heloise, I also wish to

protect my great-aunt. Miss Prendergast is convinced the Lady Travelers Society is to blame for her cousin's disappearance through ineptitude or incompetence or misrepresentation. I have discovered that before we left England, she spoke to police about the society."

Professor Greer's eyes widened in indignation. "I cannot believe anyone would think such a thing about any endeavor involving Lady Blodgett."

"Fortunately, neither did the authorities. As long as Miss Prendergast is in Paris, she is not trying to convince police to badger my great-aunt." He heaved an overly dramatic sigh. "Poor old thing."

"Why, I can't imagine such an indignity!" The professor practically sputtered with outrage. "I have known Lady Blodgett for longer than I care to admit, and I considered Sir Charles not only a fellow enthusiast in the pursuit of knowledge but a true friend. We cannot allow so much as a hint of illegality to fall on dear Lady Blodgett's head."

"My thoughts exactly," Derek said with relief. "I should tell you, as well, I received a telegram from my uncle this morning. He thinks there might be good news soon."

"I do hope so. For now, though." He squared his shoulders. "We shall carry on."

"I would appreciate if you not mention the telegram to Miss Prendergast. I would hate to get her hopes up."

"I won't say anything to Estelle, either. I've never known the woman to keep her mouth shut about anything. But you may rest assured Derek, unlike my wife, I am the very soul of discretion. I will not breathe a word of this."

"A word of what?" India appeared in the doorway. *Bloody hell.* How much had she heard?

"Nothing of significance." Derek adopted a casual tone.

"No, indeed, my dear. Nothing of significance, nothing at all," the professor said in an overly jovial manner. "Just the sort of thing one man says to another when waiting for ladies to make an appearance. Eh, Derek." He nudged Derek with his elbow in a show of masculine solidarity. "You know how gentlemen are."

"I'm afraid I don't." Her eyes narrowed with suspicion. "Do explain it to me."

Derek forced a chuckle. "I'm afraid explaining the complexity of the male mind would take entirely more time than we wish to spend today."

"Oh, I find that hard to believe," she said, pulling on a glove. "Furthermore, I would debate your use of the word *complexity*."

"And I must find my wife." Professor Greer started for the door. "We are off to the Louvre today, and there is much to see." He glanced at India long enough to see she was not looking at him, then winked broadly at Derek, one conspirator to another. *Good Lord.* Derek bit back a groan. Still, at least the professor would now be on his side.

"Well?" India demanded. "Are you going to tell me what the professor was not going to say a word about?"

"Absolutely not. I would never betray his confidence. Why, you would probably go running right to Estelle and the next thing you know…"

"What?"

He had been too busy evading her suspicions to pay any attention but now he couldn't help but notice how… how *frilly* she looked.

"It's impolite to stare, you know."

"I am aware of that." Still, he couldn't help himself. She was distinctly frilly and ruffled and beribboned.

Her dress was a deep shade of vivid purple, the bodice festooned with ruffled lace, the skirt split to reveal a black-and-white-striped underskirt. He struggled to restrain a laugh. "My apologies, India, but I can't help myself. My gaze is as drawn to you as a moth to a flame."

"Understandable but bad mannered nonetheless." She paused, then grimaced. "It's dreadful, isn't it?"

"I don't know that *dreadful* is the right word." He swept his gaze over the purple concoction with its ruffles and stripes and tried not to cringe. "Frankly, I thought your stern gray dress was rather awful."

She shot him a menacing look.

"Although the gray does suit you," he murmured. "And it might well be fashionable somewhere."

She ignored him. "Estelle was kind enough to offer me some of her things and had a maid do a few quick alterations. By the time I realized how truly terrible the dresses were, it was too late to refuse the offer. And I did not want to offend her."

"I find that hard to believe."

She glared at him.

He shrugged. "My apologies, but thus far, I have not noticed any overt concern on your part for the feelings of others. In the beginning, I attributed that to worry about your cousin, but the longer we are together—"

"Yes, yes, I've been made aware of that." She heaved a resigned sigh. "And I am trying to cultivate a more pleasant disposition." She held her arms out and glanced down at her dress. "This is apparently the price one pays for being nice."

"I'm sure you'll get your reward in heaven."

"I would have to."

"It fits well though." He studied her with a critical eye. He had seen more than his share of well-dressed ladies in the latest styles. "Better than your gray I would say."

She frowned. "Estelle said the same thing."

"Perhaps that should give you a hint."

"A hint?"

"All right, a smack across the face then." He grinned. "Even if you are not pursuing marriage, I don't know why anyone in their right mind—male or female— would not want to look their best."

"I do look my best." A defensive note sounded in her voice. "I am unfailingly neat and most presentable in my appearance."

"Your appearance—" he knew this was a mistake and yet he couldn't seem to stop himself "—fairly screams your sensible, rational, efficient nature."

"I see nothing wrong with that," she said in a lofty manner.

"It also says you are unyielding, unwilling to even consider compromise, always right, unfailingly stubborn—"

"You needn't continue, Derek. You have made your point," she said sharply and shook her head. "Women who fuss about their appearance tend to be silly, useless creatures, and I have no desire to be one of them. I do not wish to be measured by how I look, but rather for my abilities."

"Surely you realize one does not necessarily preclude the other? It has been my observation that when people look their best they generally do their best. It's a matter of confidence."

"I have never lacked for confidence."

"Disdaining what everyone else cares about is not confidence. I would say it's more concealment. Or protection."

"Nonsense." A blush colored her face.

"So, just out of idle curiosity mind you..." He studied the ensemble. "Are the other things Estelle loaned you—"

"Equally distressing?" She nodded. "This was the best of the lot." She sighed. "She is a very nice woman."

"Paris is known for its fashion. You could certainly buy something here—"

"No, I think not," she said quickly. "I would hate to offend Estelle by the implication that her taste is questionable."

"My, you are making an effort."

"I am trying." Resolve rang in her voice.

He had to give her credit. For any woman—even one who claimed not to place much store in appearance— to dress in such an ill-suited ensemble simply to avoid offending someone else, did indeed point to a certain decency of character.

"Are we ready?"

His brow shot upward. "To appear in public?"

"I'm afraid so."

"What will people say?" He grinned.

"I've never cared what people say." She paused. "But I suspect they will wonder at your intelligence for escorting a woman who dresses in such a manner."

"I shall try to endure it bravely." He offered her his arm.

"Oh, I wouldn't be that confident if I were you." This time he was sure her smile was genuine, as was the teasing look in her eye. There was no doubt that this India Prendergast was not the same woman who had left England. Whether that was for good or ill remained to be seen. She took his arm, and they started toward the hall. "There's a hat that matches the dress."

INDIA WAS RIGHT. The hat was absurd. But it did go well with the dress. And as the day went on, India's ensemble looked less and less ridiculous. Derek realized it was only in contrast to her usual severe style of dress that made it seem so frivolous. In truth, it softened her entire appearance. And possibly her demeanor, as well.

It could have been her determination to be more pleasant in nature or it might have been the magic of Paris at last spinning its spell, but there was a marked difference in the woman by his side today. As if—with the wearing of well-fitting, utterly feminine attire—a burden of responsibility and sensibility had eased from her shoulders. Certainly she was still concerned about her cousin and her missing trunk—as evidenced by the worry that creased her brow whenever the topics arose—but even that did not appear to distress her the way it had this morning.

She scarcely protested at all when he ordered wine with their midday meal, and her objection struck him as more cursory than legitimate. And she'd given in fairly easily to his suggestion that they take a respite from their tour of Grand Hotels to stroll through the Jardin des Tuileries. With the Arc de Triomphe visible at the far end and the garden's water basins, riotous blooms and classical statues, there was no better place on a fine June day to truly feel the spirit of Paris.

Indeed, while their late start meant they only managed to check three more Grand Hotels off his list, it was obvious India had enjoyed their day, in spite of her clear determination not to. Her green eyes sparkled with interest, and there was color in her cheeks. Although he had seen a hint that first morning they'd talked in her room, this new India was unexpected. He would never have described her as beautiful, but today she was surprisingly appealing. The kind of woman one wanted to know better. Shocking what a change of heart and clothing could do for a woman.

Beyond that, she was interesting. She had firm views on literature, an excellent knowledge of antiquities—as he discovered when they'd passed by a store window with a display of ancient coins—and was better versed than he on the issues of the day. Unlike most women he knew, she did not hesitate to express her opinion when it might conflict with his own. India Prendergast was not the type of woman to hide her intelligence, and he found that both intriguing and delightful.

But the more he enjoyed her company, the more he wanted to be with her, the more his conscience nagged at him. He hadn't been honest with her, and he couldn't ignore a growing sense of unease. Guilt probably. Certainly all he was really hiding was his uncle's involvement in searching for Lady Heloise. Of course, Derek had sent her luggage astray in an effort to lengthen their stay in Paris, which probably was unforgivable. As much as his conscience might bother him, he vowed never to let her know about that. As for the rest, Aunt Guinevere was family and as such was his responsibility. Until India's cousin was found safely, his greataunt's future was at stake. Keeping India in Paris—and away from the authorities—was still an excellent idea. Besides, when one really considered everything, he was doing nothing more than extending a lady's stay in one of the most exciting cities in the world. Pity the one woman in the world who wouldn't appreciate that was the one he needed to keep here.

Even as he dressed for dinner, he couldn't get his mind off this new India. Would she be wearing the purple dress again or did Estelle have something else in mind for her? He rather hoped so. He did like surprises. Good ones anyway.

Bloody hell. He paused in his efforts to knot his necktie and stared in the mirror. He was beginning to like her. Perhaps more than like her. This was certainly a surprise and he wasn't sure if it was good or very, very bad.

India Prendergast was the exact opposite of everything he'd ever wanted in a woman. She was soundly practical, terribly sensible and horribly annoying. She knew everything, or at least she thought she did. She was stubborn and determined and overly concerned with propriety. And he had serious concerns over whether she ever indulged in anything he would consider fun. In very nearly every way he could think of, she wasn't at all his type of female, not the type he was usually attracted to. The type he dreamed about. The type he fell in love with.

This was not, by any means, love. The very idea was ridiculous. He'd been in love several times, and whatever he was feeling now was nothing like that. No, love in his experience was swift and all-consuming and, for good or ill, brief.

One did not fall in love with the indomitable India Prendergast. Even if she was clever and independent and self-assured. Even if her smile seemed a reward for good behavior. Even if the best moments of the day were those spent with her, especially those when he was driving her mad. And hadn't the thought of kissing her lingered in his mind? He grinned at his image. It made no sense, but there it was. In a few short days, she had become a part of his life. Filled a hole he hadn't known was empty.

Had he already lost his heart to India Prendergast?

It was an interesting question. A question fraught with both excitement and terror. A question that, at the moment, he couldn't answer. Not really. Even more interesting was whether it was even remotely possible that he could win her heart. Finding her cousin and keeping Aunt Guinevere and her friends out of prison paled in comparison to that.

But there was no question about one thing.

In more ways than he had imagined, India Prendergast was the biggest challenge of his life.

CHAPTER THIRTEEN

One should prepare oneself for travel by investigating in advance the places one intends to visit through lectures and books and the experiences of friends. It is always wise to know which places in a foreign locale are welcoming to visitors and which are hostile. Which are suitable and respectable for lady travelers, and which to avoid at all costs. Not availing oneself of such information in advance can be at best awkward, at worst scandalous, even dangerous.

—The Lady Travelers Society Guide

A SHARP RAPPING like the sound of a small, determined bird sounded at her door.

"Come—"

"India, I need your assistance." Estelle burst into the room. "Or possibly your advice. Although I'm not certain I will listen to it. I wouldn't have bothered you, but this is most concerning. There are consequences and repercussions, and, well, you understand."

"Not in the least, but please, come in." India waved her into the room. She'd been reading *Mr. Bazalgette's Agent* and was nearly ready to put the book down and prepare for bed. It had been an exceptionally trying day.

Still, there was nothing better than lending assistance and giving advice. Why, those were two of the things she did best and among the reasons Martin valued her so highly. Resolving Estelle's difficulty—whatever it might be—was just the sort of thing India needed to feel more like herself. Besides, Estelle had helped India when she needed it. India could do no less for her. "How may I help?"

"I'm not sure, but you are so terribly competent and rational and sensible." Estelle pressed her lips together in a determined manner. "Competent, rational and sensible are exactly what is needed at the moment."

"You have always struck me as extremely rational and sensible," India said although Estelle seemed neither rational nor sensible at the moment.

"That seems to be eluding me tonight." The older woman blew an annoyed breath. "It's about Frederick."

"Has something happened to him?" Concern squeezed India's heart. "He seemed fine at dinner. Is he ill?"

"No, no, it's nothing like that. I almost wish it were."

"Then what on earth is the matter?"

"Frederick and Lord Brookings have gone to…well, I don't know how to put this delicately."

"Nor is it necessary," India said firmly. "When one is as distraught as you are, the time for delicacy has passed."

"You're right of course." Estelle adopted a resolute expression. "They've gone to an…establishment. In Montmartre."

India stared. "I have no idea what that means."

"You really need to do at least a modicum of inquiry before you travel again, dear," Estelle said in a chastising manner. "Montmartre is a district of Paris known for its less-than-respectable entertainment. Cabarets and dance halls and the like. Some of which feature women clad in most suggestive costumes or even none at all. The area is frequented by artists and writers and students and is considered quite Bohemian."

"I see."

"Frederick is unfailingly cognizant of proper behavior, but we are in Paris, after all." Estelle turned on her heel and paced the room. "I assure you this is not at all like him. He does not usually frequent that sort of place."

"What sort of place?" India asked, although she was beginning to have her suspicions.

"I suppose it's to be expected. What man wouldn't seize the opportunity to relive a few moments of his lost youth? I certainly wouldn't mind reliving a few moments of my younger days. That's how it all began, you know. All that talk at dinner with Frederick going on and on about his time here when he was a student."

"Yes, of course." In truth, India had paid no attention whatsoever.

"It's not as if I don't trust him," Estelle continued. "I do. Implicitly. After all, if we don't have trust between us after all these years, what do we have? Trust between a man and woman is everything, and we have trusted one another from the beginning. I'm not sure love is possible without trust."

"Probably not." India had no idea what to say. "I'm afraid I'm not sure what the problem is. If you are not concerned about this outing with Lord Brookings—"

"I'm concerned about who might see him and his lordship." She paused. "Although I daresay, Lord Brookings won't be. He does seem to be that sort of man, doesn't he?"

"If you mean the sort of man who doesn't care about appearances, who is self-centered, irresponsible and entirely too arrogant? Then yes, that is an accurate description of his lordship."

"You don't like him, do you?"

"Oddly enough, I think I do like him." India shook her head. "It's hard not to like him."

"As do I—where was I?"

"Your concern about someone seeing the professor at this establishment."

"Yes, well, it seems every time we turn around here, we are running into someone we know. Frederick has quite a respected reputation in certain circles, academic for the most part, and of course he's a member of the Explorers Club and various other organizations." She shook her head. "I had no idea Paris would be so crowded with subjects of Her Majesty although I suppose it is a *world* exhibition, isn't it?"

"Go on."

"Just this morning, we crossed paths at the Louvre with several ladies I know from London, and I joined them for refreshments while Frederick examined a display of medieval manuscripts. The ladies were bemoaning the fact that their husbands were determined to visit Montmartre. The group included Mrs. Marlow, the wife of George Marlow." Her eyes narrowed. "If Frederick has any sort of rival, George Marlow would be it. He's always been envious of Frederick's accomplishments."

"I still don't understand."

"If Marlow—if *anyone* from London—sees Frederick there…" She shuddered. "They will deny it, but men gossip far more than they would have us believe. Mark my words, in less than a day after they return home, everyone will know Frederick was spotted at highly unsuitable places. That beastly Marlow will make certain of it. You know how these things are—the gossip will grow out of all proportions. It will ruin him."

"But won't these gentlemen be tarnished with the same brush?"

"Frederick is held to a higher standard. This is a very delicate time. I'm not supposed to say anything—" she glanced from side to side as if to make sure they were alone and lowered her voice "—but there is talk that the queen is considering a knighthood for him. And you know how Her Majesty is about things like this."

"So I have heard." India could well imagine the queen would not be at all inclined to knight a man who was seen in questionable surroundings, even far from home. Her Majesty was known to be intolerant of the merest hint of impropriety.

"I had no idea he was going tonight. Why, he and Lord Brookings and Derek retired to the billiards room after dinner. I went to our rooms to read and dozed off. When I woke, Frederick had still not returned. That's when I discovered he and his lordship had decided on a foray to Montmartre."

"It seems to me," India said, "you are anticipating a problem that does not yet exist. It's rather far-fetched to think that in a city the size of Paris two acquaintances from London will encounter one another."

"Men, my dear India, are men." Estelle cast her a condescending look. "They are all prone to adventures of a disconcerting nature. I would not be the least bit surprised if Marlow wasn't in Montmartre at this very moment."

"Still—"

"I will not allow Frederick's chances at a knighthood to be shattered because of one ill-advised venture." Estelle folded her arms over her chest. "Therefore, I intend to fetch him myself and bring him back."

India stared. "Surely you're not serious."

"I have never been more serious." A determined look shone in Estelle's eyes. "I have supported that man through nearly forty years of marriage, and I will not fail him now. A knighthood would be his crowning achievement, and he deserves it. And I deserve to be Lady Greer."

India shook her head. "This does not strike me as a good idea."

"I didn't say it was a good idea, but it is the only one I have." She squared her shoulders. "And I would very much appreciate it if you would accompany me."

"Because two Englishwomen on such an excursion would be less improper than just one?"

"Because your French is much better than mine." Estelle grimaced. "And I prefer not to go by myself. If you have a better idea…"

"I wish I did." India thought for a moment. Estelle's plan was unwise and ill conceived. Her reasoning was based on nothing more than emotion and distress. India had not known the older woman long but she had no doubt she would indeed try to find her wandering husband alone if India refused to accompany her. "Although I believe I know who might." She started toward the hall. "Come along."

"Where?" Estelle hurried behind her.

"If there's anyone among us who would know best how to evade scandal, it would be he who has experienced it firsthand." She glanced over her shoulder. "Unless Derek accompanied your husband and his lordship—"

"He didn't. At least according to the butler, but I believe Derek has already retired for the night."

"Well then, we shall have to beard the lion in his den." India headed toward Derek's rooms.

"Are you sure?" Doubt sounded in Estelle's voice. "I've never visited a man in his bedroom before. I'm not sure that's appropriate."

India glanced at her. "*Now* you are considering what is and is not appropriate?"

Estelle shrugged.

"Regardless…" India stopped before Derek's door. Estelle had come to India for help, and help she would have. India gathered her courage and knocked sharply on his door. "A knighthood is at stake."

A moment later the door opened. Derek, clad in a deep red dressing gown, stared at her. "What?" His gaze skipped to Estelle, then back to India. "Ladies," he said cautiously. "To what do I owe this unexpected pleasure?"

"We have need of your assistance," India said firmly, ignoring how rakishly charming he looked.

"Do you?" He stepped back and waved them into his room. "Come in then, by all means."

India stepped into his room, Estelle right on her heels. India had never been in a gentleman's bedroom before and never imagined she would be. Especially not with said gentleman dressed in attire unsuitable to receive female callers.

"Oh, this is nice." Estelle glanced around the room approvingly.

It was indeed nice. Twice as big as India's, it was a suite of rooms really. A sitting area complete with a sofa and desk adjoined a bedchamber via an open archway. Whereas the furniture in her room was in shades of pastels and white and decidedly feminine in nature, his had a distinctly masculine flair with carved, dark woods. Her gaze was irresistibly drawn to the adjoining room, where an enormous armoire and an equally enormous mahogany bed dominated the space. Heat washed up her face, and she jerked her gaze back to Derek. Which was no better at all.

His dressing gown was the color of a rich claret, deep and decidedly sinful and worn over trousers. A fringed sash cinched his waist and a white shirt was open at his throat. The man was the epitome of, well, seduction. Only the fact that his hair was slightly ruffled, as if he'd run his hands through it, giving him an appealing boyish quality, saved him from looking positively dangerous. She glanced at Estelle, who stared at Derek in open admiration.

His gaze shifted between the women. "I assume you're here for a reason."

"Yes, of course." India cleared her throat. "The professor needs your help."

"Oh?"

"His lordship has taken the professor to a questionable establishment in Montmartre."

Estelle continued to stare. India groaned to herself. You would think the woman had never seen a dashing scoundrel in a dressing gown before. She probably hadn't, but she was married, after all. Admittedly, while the professor and Derek were both men, that's where the similarity ended. India nudged the other woman.

"Oh." Estelle started. "Yes, of course." She drew a deep breath. "I believe they intended to make an evening of it."

"I know," Derek said. "They discussed stopping in

at the Folies Bergère when we were having port and cigars in the billiards room."

"I'm rather impressed that you thought better than to accompany them to such a place," India said.

"I didn't think better of it." He shrugged. "I simply had no desire to go."

"Regardless, that's to our benefit." She nodded at Estelle.

Again, he looked from one woman to the other. "I'm not sure what you want from me."

"We want you to find the professor before acquaintances of his from London spot him in surroundings that can only be described as immoral, which would surely lead to his disgrace and ultimate ruin," India said.

"Disgrace and ultimate ruin?" He chuckled. "Aren't you being a bit dramatic? It's not uncommon for tourists to visit the sights of Montmartre."

India traded glances with Estelle.

"It really is a matter of disgrace and ultimate ruin." Estelle chewed on her lower lip. "I'm not at liberty to tell you why, but please believe me this is crucial for Frederick's future."

He studied her for a long moment. "Very well," he said at last. "It will take me a few minutes to change. Then I will be on my way."

"Excellent." Estelle nodded. "I shall meet you in the foyer."

India braced herself. "*We* shall meet you in the foyer."

Estelle smiled at her gratefully.

"I have no intention of bringing the two of you along with me." Derek stared in disbelief. "This is not the sort of area for well-bred English ladies. It's frequented by men and…working women for the most part."

"The fate of my husband is at stake." Estelle raised

her chin in a determined manner. "I will not be left behind."

"And Estelle is my...my friend." India doubted she'd ever said that before about anyone other than Heloise or Martin. "She came to me for help, and I will not abandon her now." India crossed her arms over her chest. "Are we going or not?"

"Very well." His jaw tightened. "But you'll limit your observations to what you can see on the street. And you will both stay in the carriage."

"We can agree to that," India glanced at Estelle, who nodded. "Five minutes then," India said and ushered Estelle out the door.

Before she could follow, Derek stepped close and lowered his voice. "I can do this myself, you know."

"No doubt." India shrugged. "But Estelle is determined, and I cannot allow her to go without me."

"Because you don't trust me." His eyes narrowed. "I assure you I am more than capable of finding the professor and returning him safely to his wife."

"I am well aware of that, and in this particular case, I do trust you." Even as she said the words, she knew they were true. "But Estelle asked for my help. Therefore, I consider this *quest* my responsibility, and I intend to see it through to the end."

"That's the most absurd thing I've ever heard but I know better than to try to argue with you." He heaved a frustrated sigh and stepped back. "Now, unless you intend to assist me in changing my clothing—"

"*That* I'm certain you can manage without me." She nodded and took her leave.

A quarter of an hour later they were in one of his lordship's closed carriages headed for Montmartre. It did seem to take forever or perhaps it was simply that the silence in the carriage was deafening. Derek was not at all happy with them and apparently thought it better not to say anything at all than to continue to express his annoyance. *Fine.* India would rather listen to her own thoughts than listen to him. Especially as he was probably right.

She should have convinced Estelle to let Derek come alone. This was not the sort of thing India did. Ever. She was at all times cognizant of the need for propriety. She was not prone to, nor had she ever had, any secret desire for adventure. Nonetheless, she had the oddest sense of anticipation. It was ridiculous and yet there it was.

At last they pulled up on the opposite side of the street from a large, decorative building plastered with playbills on the ground floor. On the upper story, multiple window panes were divided by ornate columns. The edifice was topped by wrought stonework running the width of the building, with a curved and graceful design and a sort of crown in the center. Immediately beneath the crown were the words *Folies Bergère.* The place fairly reeked of immorality and indiscretion and decadence. Although immorality, indiscretion and decadence apparently had a great deal of appeal. Even at this late hour, the streets were crowded with vehicles and pedestrians.

"This is where they said they were going." Derek nodded at the building. "It's a sort of cabaret or music hall."

"It's very busy, isn't it?" Estelle murmured.

"It's extremely popular." He glanced at India. "What do you think?"

"Sin is usually popular," she said with a casual shrug. "We will indeed remain in the carriage. I believe you were right."

He raised a brow. "Again?"

"Again. And you needn't be smug about it."

He chuckled. "Oh, but I enjoy being smug." He grabbed the door handle. "I would wager the doorman knows Val by sight. It won't take me long to see if he's here or not." He opened the door and smiled wickedly at India. "You should probably give me a token for luck."

Estelle nodded. "Like a knight of old going off to do battle."

"Don't be absurd. He's venturing into a veritable den of iniquity not a duel to the death. And I daresay it's not the first time."

"Still, a token for luck. A glove perhaps or—" his smile widened "—a kiss."

India arched a brow in disdain, but the oddest thing happened to the pit of her stomach.

Estelle clucked her tongue. "Goodness, Derek, you are naughty."

He grinned in an unrepentant manner. "I know." He nodded at India. "She likes it."

India gasped. "I most certainly do not!"

He laughed, stepped out of the carriage and turned back to India. "Are you certain about that kiss?"

"Quite certain," she said firmly, ignoring a vague sense of regret. Still, a kiss? She would never so much as consider such a thing. "Besides, a kiss here in this part of Paris, at this time of night, well, I can only imagine what an observer might think. People would jump to all sorts of conclusions, and Estelle and I wouldn't be the least bit safe. Even in the carriage."

"Now *you're* probably right."

"I know." It was her turn to sound smug.

"I shouldn't be long." He nodded and headed toward the music hall.

Estelle switched to the opposite side of the carriage, and both women tried not to stare at the passing scene. They couldn't help themselves. It was impossible to ignore. Here were the pleasure seekers of Paris. Well-dressed gentlemen reeking of wealth and elegance mingled with working men, rougher in appearance in clothes that had seen better days. The women, too, were mostly of a working class although, judging from the appearance of a great many, not all their work was respectable.

Estelle nodded toward a particularly garish-looking woman. "Do you think that she is, well—"

"Yes, I think she probably is," India said uneasily. She was not so sheltered as to be unaware of women who sold their bodies, and probably their souls, to survive. God knows there were plenty in London. Nor was she so narrow-minded as to believe these women had a choice. More than likely circumstances of birth and poverty had left them few options in life. Legitimate work for women, especially those of the lowest classes, was scarce. Why even someone such as herself—of good family and modest means—had little opportunity for honest employment. She was well aware that a dire fate was never far from any woman who had no husband or family to depend upon.

"India!" Estelle grabbed her arm. "Look, across the street—isn't that Frederick?"

"I can't tell. He's too far away." India peered at the top-hatted figure headed away from them.

"I can't make him out. My eyes aren't as good as they used to be." Estelle reached for the door.

"You'll never catch him. I'll go." Even as India opened the door, she knew this was not her brightest idea. "Stay here."

She jumped out of the carriage, dodged the oncoming traffic and fairly sprinted to the other side of the street. She hurried after the man, striding ahead of her at a leisurely speed. Somewhere in the back of her mind, she noted he was unaccompanied and wondered where Lord Brookings was.

"Professor," she called. He was still a few strides away. She picked up her pace. "Professor." She reached out and grabbed his arm.

He turned, and she realized her mistake.

"I beg your pardon." He directed a disgusted look at her hand on his arm.

She released him at once. "My apologies. I thought you were someone else."

"No doubt." He was the right height and build as the professor and even sported the same style of beard, and he was certainly English, but there the resemblance ended.

"I am sorry." She took a step back.

"As well you should be." His bushy brows drew together. "An Englishwoman like yourself. I assure you, I am not in the market for what you are selling."

"Not in the—oh!" She gasped, indignation washed though her. "I'll have you know I am not selling anything. This was an honest mistake."

"A mistake perhaps but allow me to question the honesty of it." He huffed, turned and strode away.

For a moment, India could only stare. How dare he! Why, she'd never been so insulted in her life! Just because a respectable woman wore a purple dress in a questionable area of a city did not mean she was an... *unfortunate*! That *gentleman*—although one did have to question that—deserved a stern dressing-down on the insulting consequences of jumping to conclusions.

And she was just the woman to do it! She took a step after him and caught sight of Estelle gesturing from the window of the carriage. India pulled up short.

What on earth was she thinking? Certainly his insult had earned him an impassioned rebuke, but nothing, save perhaps a measure of self-satisfaction, could be gained by going after the man. And what would Derek say if he knew she'd left the carriage after she'd said she wouldn't? She turned toward the carriage.

"What a shame, mademoiselle." A large, dark-eyed brute with an unrestrained mustache and stubble on his chin stepped in her path. His French was not as refined as hers, but she had no trouble understanding his words. Or the look in his eye. "To be tossed aside that way. Stupid English." He turned his head and spit in a most revolting manner.

"I beg your pardon." She drew herself up to her full if inadequate height. "*I* am English."

"My apologies, mademoiselle. But you are the English rose, and he is a fool." He leaned close, the garlic on his breath nearly overwhelming. "And I am a lover of flowers." He grabbed her arm.

"Unhand me at once." She tried to shake off his hand, but his grip tightened. She couldn't recall ever having been afraid before, but what was surely fear rose in her throat.

"I would do as she asks if I were you," a familiar voice said casually.

Relief washed through her. "Derek, I—"

"Shut up, India," he said in English, then returned his attention to her admirer. "It would be in your best interest to release her."

"Why? She is available, is she not?" A predatory gleam showed in the brute's eyes. The man was a good

half a foot taller than Derek, broader and harder looking. Derek was obviously no match for this man. "And
I like them small and spirited."

Derek stepped closer to the man and spoke low into
his ear. The brute's eyes widened; he let her go at once
and leaped back. He crossed himself, staring at her as
if she were the devil incarnate. *"Mon Dieu."* He turned
and sprinted away.

"Come along, India." Derek grabbed her elbow and
hurried her toward the carriage. "Now."

"What did you say to him?" She looked over her
shoulder. Her assailant hadn't so much as slowed his
step.

"I told him I was a doctor, you were my patient who
had escaped from my care and you were highly con-
tagious."

India could barely keep up with him. "What did you
say I had?"

"You don't want to know," he said in hard, clipped
tones. They reached the carriage, he yanked open the
door and practically tossed her inside. She plopped
down beside Estelle, who patted her hand in encouragement. Derek gave directions to the driver, then took his
seat. She couldn't see his face in the dark interior, but
it wasn't necessary to know he was annoyed with her.

"Are you all right?" Estelle asked, concern in her
voice.

"Quite." India summoned a measure of calm. "Obviously that was not the professor."

"But it was very brave of you to go after him."

"Brave?" Derek fairly sputtered with outrage. More
than merely annoyed then. "*Stupid* is a more accurate
term."

"I have always heard there was a fine line between

bravery and stupidity," Estelle said, obviously trying
to be helpful.

"Derek, I—"

"That was the most irresponsible, foolish thing I have
ever seen." Anger underlay his words. "You promised
to stay in the carriage."

"We thought we saw the professor, and we didn't
want him to get away."

"It didn't seem stupid at the time," Estelle added.

"I expected better. From both of you," he snapped.
"Do you know what might have happened to you?"

"I believe I have some idea." India folded her hands
together in her lap to still their shaking. She pulled in a
deep, calming breath. "And I am never irresponsible."

"Ha!"

"So, am I to assume you did not find my husband?"
Estelle ventured.

"I did not," he said sharply. "The doorman told me
he and my brother were there briefly and then left. Apparently to return home."

"Oh, that is good to hear." Estelle breathed a sigh
of relief.

"Derek." India braced herself. "In hindsight, as much
as it pains me to say this…" She was not used to admitting her mistakes. She was not used to making mistakes.
This was far more difficult than she had imagined.
"While it did seem necessary at the time, I did not give
my actions due consideration. I acted upon impulse—
which I might point out I am not prone to do—as well
as in a most, well, less than responsible manner. I have
no excuse. I don't understand it myself—"

"It was an adventure, dear," Estelle said under her
breath. "One can never underestimate the lure of adventure. I suspect it causes even the most rational among

us to do foolish things they would never think of doing otherwise."

"Thank you, Estelle. Nonetheless, it was…" India blew a long breath. "Stupid. You were right, Derek."

Silence hung heavy in the carriage for an endless moment.

"Well." A desperate note sounded in Estelle's voice. "That's that then. I'm sure we can put this behind us now and, well…"

India nodded. "Excellent idea. I know I intend to never mention it again."

A disgruntled snort sounded from Derek's side of the carriage.

The moment they arrived at Lord Brookings's, Estelle bolted from the carriage, muttering her thanks in her wake. His lordship's expertly trained footman opened the door, and she shot into the house as if the hounds of hell were at her heels. India didn't blame her. She would have dashed toward the house herself, but she suspected escaping Derek's ire was not going to be that easy. Not that she didn't deserve it. He helped her out of the carriage, and they started for the door.

"India." He stopped.

She turned toward him, his face illuminated by the flickering gaslight. "Yes?"

"I owe you an apology."

"Don't be absurd," she said in a gracious and relieved manner. "You were upset, understandably so. It was a, well, awkward—"

"Awkward?" he said slowly.

"I suppose *perilous* might be a better word."

"Do you think so?"

"Oh my, yes." She nodded. "He was much bigger

than you. I don't know what might have happened had
you needed to resort to fisticuffs."

"I assure you I would have held my own." He paused.
"For the first minute or two."

"Fortunately, you were cleverer than that, and physical means were not necessary."

"India—"

"But as I was saying," she said quickly. It did seem
better not to allow him to get a word in. "You had every
right to be angry, and no apology is necessary."

He stared in disbelief. "You think my apology is because I was angry? Justifiably angry? You understand
the danger of the situation was not just for myself?"

She shifted from foot to foot uneasily. "Yes, I suppose."

"I'm apologizing for suggesting I kiss you." He
clasped his hands behind his back. "I know how you
are about impropriety. Therefore, you have my apology."

"Then you didn't want to kiss me?" she said without thinking. Not that she wanted him to kiss her, of
course. That would indeed be improper. And she wasn't
sure one's first kiss should be in a notorious district in
a decadent city.

"Oh, make no mistake, India, I would like nothing
better than to kiss you. This was not the first time it has
occurred to me." He paused as if debating his words.
"However, it seemed an apology was called for on my
part as you were willing to apologize to me."

It was her turn to stare. "I didn't apologize."

"You said I was right. You admitted you should have
stayed in the carriage."

"It was an admission, an acknowledgment if you
will, of my mistake." She shrugged. "I didn't actually
apologize for it."

"Don't you think you should?" He stepped closer and glared down at her. "If not for ignoring your promise to stay in the carriage, then for, at the very least, scaring the hell out of me?" His voice rose, and there was genuine concern in his tone. "Do you have any idea how I felt when I saw you in the hands of that animal? I have never been so terrified in my life!"

She stared up at him. "Oh."

"Oh?" He stepped closer, so close she could see the rise and fall of his chest with every breath. *"Oh?"*

"Oh…" Close enough to pull her into his arms and kiss her, if he was so inclined. Her heart thudded in her chest. "Oh, I…I apologize? I obviously wasn't thinking, and I am truly sorry."

"Apology accepted." Was he so inclined? He stared down at her. "You are not infallible, India Prendergast."

She nodded. "I am aware of that."

"Good." His gaze shifted to her lips, then back to her eyes. "Please try to keep it in mind in the future."

"Yes, of course." She leaned closer.

A footman peered out the open door.

Derek took a step back. "I shall see you in the morning, then, to resume our Grand Hotel search."

She nodded. "In the morning."

He accompanied her into the house and bid her goodnight. She started up the stairs. She knew without looking his gaze followed her. What was he thinking? Did he regret not kissing her? And did he still wish to kiss her? India had never been kissed before and had never paid any attention to that omission in her life. Now…

She reached her room, closed the door behind her and sank onto the bed. Odd, the fact that he had wanted to kiss her, had confessed that tonight was not the first time the thought had occurred to him, eclipsed the other events of the night.

She had nearly been kissed. By a rogue, a scoundrel, a man who had no doubt kissed dozens—even hundreds—of women. He was probably quite skilled at it. Still, he hadn't kissed her and by now had probably changed his mind about kissing her altogether. Which was for the best really.

Why, she had no desire to kiss Derek Saunders. None whatsoever. So it made absolutely no sense that she had the awful, sinking feeling that she had just taken the wrong turn at a crossroads.

And her life would never be the same.

CHAPTER FOURTEEN

IF DEREK COULD act as if nothing whatsoever had happened between them, then so could India. While she was grateful he had not mentioned the events of last night, it was annoying that he had as well ignored the whole matter of his desire to kiss her. If indeed he still had that desire. Not that she cared. No, it was best to put the entire night behind them and continue on with their quest.

Today they'd made progress, but they were barely halfway through Derek's list of Grand Hotels. India vowed to herself never to stay in a hotel with the word *grand* in its name. She'd had quite enough of them already, thank you. Even so, she was not about to give up.

Where was Heloise? Admittedly, she'd been showing the strangest tendencies toward independence in the weeks before she'd joined the Lady Travelers Society. But independence did not preclude common sense and courtesy. Surely, she would have known that India would worry if she allowed her correspondence to lapse. Although, now that she thought about it, India realized, while her cousin had said she would write, she'd made no promises as to frequency. And Heloise did have a tendency to pay little attention to the details of life she deemed unimportant. The chances were very good that nothing distressing had happened to her at all. India did hope so. She loved the older woman, and would not rest until she was assured of her safety.

And then what? an annoying voice whispered in the back of her head. *Will you drag her home? Insist she abandon this adventure of hers and return to the rather ordinary life she lives? The life you both live?*

India ignored it. She would cross that road when she came to it. First, she had to find Heloise. And hopefully trap a scoundrel in the process. Even if Derek wasn't quite the devil she had originally thought. In fact, she was reluctantly beginning to like him, which had nothing to do with his alleged desire to kiss her. Regardless, as any good detective would tell you, the first step in an investigation is to know your subject.

India dressed for dinner early and slipped down to his lordship's library, where Suzette said he was often found before dinner. She knocked on the half-open door, then pushed it wider and stepped into the room. "Good evening, your lordship."

"You do realize people who don't wait for an invitation often find themselves in awkward situations," Lord Brookings said, his gaze firmly on papers spread on the desk in front of him.

"And who would know that better than you?" she said lightly.

"Indeed, I have been caught unawares any number of times." He stood and circled the desk toward her. "It has proven most awkward."

She arched a brow. "For you?"

"For everyone else." He grinned in an entirely too knowing manner.

"The door was open. I believe an open door is an invitation."

"There is nothing I like better than having my words

thrown back at me by a lovely woman. Well then, welcome." He took her hand and raised it to his lips. "And to what do I owe the honor of this visit, India? I've not seen you alone since I visited you in your bed and you insisted I call you Miss Prendergast."

"You remember that, do you?"

"It was one of the most memorable moments of my life." He brushed his lips across her hand, his gaze never wavering from hers.

"I doubt that, but surely then you recall I won our little wager." She pulled her hand from his.

"Ah yes." He heaved an overly heartfelt sigh. "Miss Prendergast it is to be then."

She couldn't help but grin. The man was incorrigible and annoyingly amusing.

"I see Mrs. Greer's taste in fashion continues to astound."

She glanced down at the evening ensemble. Estelle really did bring more clothes than she could possibly ever wear but she was so gracious about loaning them, India was hard-pressed to object to the style. "I understood plaid was quite the current rage."

"In Scotland perhaps." He propped a hip on the corner of his desk. "Now then, as you have dared to brave the inner sanctum of the scandalous Lord Brookings, I assume you are not here simply to pass the time until dinner."

"No." She wasn't entirely sure how to phrase this. "I was hoping you would answer a few questions for me."

"Anything."

"About Mr. Saunders."

"Oh." His brows drew together. "It's like that, is it?"

"It's like what?"

"Usually, when a woman wants to talk about another man it's because she harbors some feelings for him."

"I can assure you I harbor no feelings for Mr. Saunders other than perhaps friendship," she said quickly, ignoring the heat that washed up her face. Why his lordship's charge would make her blush was beyond her. It probably had to do with that kiss nonsense. Still, Derek had indeed offered friendship even if she hadn't accepted.

"No." He studied her curiously. "Of course not."

"It is for no other reason than the pursuit of that friendship that I thought it would be beneficial if I knew more about him."

"I daresay everything there is to know about my brother is public knowledge." He chuckled. "Derek has no real secrets, at least not as far as I am aware."

"Then you will be revealing no confidences." She perched on a nearby chair and smiled pleasantly. "Is he a good man?" It wasn't the question she had intended to ask, but it did seem important.

"Yes," Lord Brookings said without hesitation. "I have known Derek for most of his life. His mother—and the only mother I have ever known—married my father when I was nine and Derek was eight. We grew up together. I consider him my brother in everything but blood. Admittedly, he has engaged in any number of activities that one might consider reckless and even outrageous, but then so have I." He flashed her an unapologetic grin. "However, I have never seen him hurt anyone nor have I ever seen him be deliberately unkind."

She nodded. "That's very…interesting."

"I should add, last night, when he set forth to rescue Professor Greer, he did so at his own peril."

"Did he?" She forced a light tone, but unease settled in her stomach.

"Derek's uncle has told him in no uncertain terms that he will not tolerate any further hint of scandal. So, if the professor's reputation was at risk, so, too, was my brother's."

"I see." That certainly put a different light on the evening and perhaps explained why Derek hadn't accompanied his lordship and the professor in the first place.

"I would put my life in his hands without a second thought. Does that answer your question?"

"Yes, I suppose it does."

If his lordship was lying he was quite good at it. No, there wasn't a doubt in her mind that he believed what he'd said. The oddest sense of relief washed through her. The more time she spent with Derek, the more he wasn't at all as she had expected.

Why, the man had actually eased her discomfort about her appearance in Estelle's borrowed clothing, pointing out that, while this was not how she usually dressed, she did not look as absurd as she had first feared. Indeed, he claimed she looked rather fetching. She wasn't sure she believed him, but no one stopped and stared in horror at her. He had also drawn her attention several times to other ladies garbed in apparel even more fussy than hers. It was quite kind of him really, and she wondered if he might not be a rather nice sort beneath his dashing good looks and wicked smiles. He had made a list, after all. One had to give him credit for that. He'd also insisted on showing her some of the sights of Paris between Grand Hotel stops. That, too, was surprisingly thoughtful in spite of her lack of interest. Now, knowing the risk he'd taken for the professor, her opinion of him notched upward.

Which made it all the more unpleasant to search for proof as to his wrongdoing.

"I was curious, there are any number of rumors about his financial circumstances, but I distrust gossip. What are the state of Mr. Saunders finances?"

"Now that is the question of a woman who is looking for a husband and wants assurances about the gentleman she has set her cap for."

"I assure you," she said firmly, "I am not looking for a husband—"

"Not in that dress."

"And even if I was, Mr. Saunders would not be of interest to me." It did seem important to let his stepbrother know she had no intentions toward Derek. Set her cap indeed.

"I must say I find that difficult to believe. Most women think Derek irresistible."

"I imagine there have been a great number of women," she said in an offhand manner.

"A great number?" He chuckled. "I'm not sure what a great number is. Dozens? Hundreds?"

"Many," she said sharply.

"My, my, Miss Prendergast." His brow rose. "That sounds a bit like jealousy."

"Don't be absurd." She rolled her gaze toward the ceiling. "I just told you I have no intentions toward Derek other than friendship."

"Of course not. But other women consider Derek a brilliant catch. His prospects are excellent, he is the heir to an impressive title and even I can admit he is not unattractive. Not quite as handsome and dashing as his brother—"

She snorted.

"But acceptable." He considered her thoughtfully. "Why aren't you looking for a husband?"

"Oh for goodness' sake." Why was everyone so disturbed by her lack of interest in marriage? It was right on the tip of her tongue to tell him it was none of his concern, but why not answer the man? She had nothing to hide, and she did want answers from him, after all. "For one thing, my lord—"

"Val. Or Percy." He shrugged. "It doesn't matter. And, yes, I know I agreed to call you Miss Prendergast, but it makes me feel like an antiquity to have someone no more than a few years younger than I refer to me by my title. Especially when discussing matters as personal as my stepbrother's life and your opposition to marriage."

"I never said I was opposed to marriage, *Percy*."

"Val would have been better," he said under his breath.

"I simply came to the realization years ago that some of us are not intended for marriage."

"I've heard that from a man but never from a woman."

"Well, now you have."

He stared at her as if she had suddenly grown two heads. "Why?"

"I was starting to explain but you interrupted me, *Percy*."

He winced.

"I shall be thirty on my next birthday, a confirmed spinster by anyone's definition. I have neither the wealth nor the heritage nor the appearance that most men look for in a wife. Those looking to improve their position in life will not achieve that by marriage with me. Is that satisfactory?"

"No." He shook his head. "Not in the least. For one

thing, any man who marries a woman for those attributes only deserves what he gets."

"Forgive me for pointing this out, but that's rather easy for you to say. You don't need to marry for money or position. Most people are not that fortunate."

"You're absolutely right. I firmly intend to marry for nothing less than undying love."

"Good God, you're a romantic!" And far less jaded than she had assumed.

"Shocking, isn't it?"

"I scarcely know what to say."

"My brother considers himself a romantic, as well." He nodded. "You should know that, India."

"Miss Prendergast, and it makes no difference to me as I am not interested in him as anything other than a friend. A good friend, perhaps, but a friend nonetheless. And if I were—" She knew she should hold her tongue but couldn't seem to help herself. It had occurred to her late in the night, no doubt brought about by the kissing, or lack of kissing, incident, and she couldn't get the thought out of her head. "Derek and I are from entirely different worlds and would never suit. He is to be an earl, and I work for my living. Only in silly stories would such a match be possible."

"I like silly stories. I always have."

"How wonderful for you, but this is not a story." This was becoming more and more annoying. She was not here to talk about her life nor did she wish to discuss why a match with Derek was impossible. Even if she was interested in such a thing which she certainly wasn't. "Furthermore, my dowry is respectable but not what someone like Derek would expect."

"Derek is in no need of a generous dowry. He'll inherit a substantial fortune along with his title."

"His wife will be a countess. A countess needs to at least be the daughter of someone titled."

"What a snob you are, India."

"*Miss Prendergast*, and I am most certainly not a snob. I simply know how the world works in matters like this."

"A snob." He shook his head in a mournful manner. "A dreadful, nose-in-the-air snob."

"This entire conversation is absurd," she snapped. "I have no desire to marry Derek, and he has no particular interest in me."

His lordship cast her a skeptical look. "Are you sure?"

"Of course I'm sure." She waved off the ridiculous question. He hadn't kissed her, after all, and he'd had every opportunity to do so. A man who said he wanted to kiss you and then made no effort to do so had obviously changed his mind. Or had come to his senses. "For one thing, as I said, we are not suited for each other, and if you were to ask him, I'm certain he would agree. For another, men like him—and you for that matter—"

"Men like me?" He grinned. "Do go on, India."

"Miss Prendergast!" This was perhaps the silliest conversation she'd ever been engaged in, but that was no reason to lose her temper. Again. The control of her emotions she'd always prided herself on had eroded since the moment she'd left London. Or perhaps the moment she'd met Derek. She drew a calming breath. "As I was saying, men like you and Mr. Saunders—men of prominence because of wealth or family or expectations—usually give some sort of indication as to their interest. Mr. Saunders has done absolutely nothing to so much as imply he has any regard for me that goes beyond the bounds of friendship."

"And you've had a great deal of experience with men like him?" he asked in a mild manner.

"Not a great deal, no." And by great deal she meant none. But everyone knew men like Derek did not marry women like her. No matter how much of a romantic they considered themselves. "This is ridiculous."

"You're right, and I do apologize." Although he didn't sound the least bit remorseful. "It was nothing more than an exercise in possibilities. And whether you wish to believe it or not, there are few things I like better than a rousing debate with a lovely, intelligent woman. I know I enjoyed it."

"Well, I did not," she said sharply. "And I do wish you would stop trying to charm your way past my—"

"Reluctance to so much as hint that you might find life even a tiny bit amusing?"

"That's not what I was going to say." She paused. "But perhaps. And you needn't keep calling me lovely. I am well aware of how very ordinary I am."

"My dear Miss Prendergast." Genuine surprise shone in his eyes. "The first time I met you, you were sitting upright in a bed, your face flushed, your hair tousled. Those captivating green eyes sparkled with indignation. You were wearing something delightfully naughty— and vaguely familiar—with the covers clutched up to your neck and a plate of croissants in your lap. You were very nearly irresistible."

She stared at him for a long moment. "Are you mad?"

"I daresay, I have rarely been more sane."

"Well…" She had no idea how to respond. She'd never thought of herself as anything other than distinctly average. "Thank you?"

"Of course, after that morning you insisted on wearing that dreadful gray thing day after day." He shivered.

"You may not realize it, but while Mrs. Greer's clothes tend to be a bit brighter and somewhat fussier than is my personal preference in lady's garments, they do show off your estimable assets."

She stared. "I have assets?"

He frowned in disbelief. "Has no one ever said this to you before?"

"Not that I recall."

"Perhaps when one is appreciated for her efficiency and intelligence, no one is concerned about the rest of her." He shrugged. "Pity."

"Assets," she murmured. She rather liked that.

"And you're doing something—" he gestured at her head "—different with your hair. It's not as...clenched."

She patted her hair and resisted the urge to tuck away the tendrils of curls now drifting around her face. "Suzette has been doing my hair."

"I should have known." He studied her with a critical eye. "It's quite flattering. You should continue to wear it that way."

"Perhaps," she said weakly. Lord Brookings was an outrageous flirt, but he did seem sincere. She'd stopped being concerned about her appearance years ago. In hindsight, perhaps that was a mistake.

The bong of the dinner bell reverberated through the house. "And there's the call for dinner." He offered his arm.

She hadn't realized it was so late. She sighed and took his arm. "You haven't fully answered my questions."

"I know. Wicked of me, wasn't it?"

"Yes, it was. My only concern is to lend Mr. Saunders my assistance." Derek Saunders might well be a scoundrel, but he might be worth redeeming.

"In what?"

"In becoming the man I believe he wants to be." And hadn't Derek said so himself? Hadn't he said his desire in life was not to disappoint?

"In becoming his father."

"His father?" India released his arm and took a step back. "I'm not sure I understand."

"I never met the man, of course, but from what I've heard, Derek's father was one of those people who was respected by everyone."

"I can't imagine anyone not liking Derek," she said firmly. "He's quite charming and…personable."

"Henry, Derek's father, was brilliant and competent and responsible. He and his brother, the earl, were twins, although not identical, and apparently quite fond of each other. Not always the case between the heir and the spare, you know. It's my understanding Henry worked closely with his brother in all matters pertaining to the family's interests. Furthermore, there was never a hint of anything disreputable associated with Henry Saunders. Unless, of course—and this is hearsay mind you—one considers the uproar over his marriage to Mother."

"His family didn't approve?"

"As I said, this is just something I've picked up through the years. Nothing more than gossip really."

"Go on."

"Why, Miss Prendergast," he chastised. "I had no idea you were so fond of gossip."

"Something that happened thirty some years ago is no longer gossip but more in the realm of history," she said in a lofty manner.

"Interesting way you have of bending the rules." He chuckled. "I shall have to remember that."

"Now, if you would be so kind as to finish the story."

"Apparently, Mother's family was not as prosperous as it had once been. Her father was a viscount who'd had some disastrous setbacks due to—oh, let's call it bad investments, shall we?"

"Investments?"

"Of a speculative nature. Gambling, Miss Prendergast."

"Oh." She stared. "I see."

"Still, the family name was respectable enough." He paused. "Until of course, Henry and Mother ran off together."

Surprise widened her eyes. "Oh?"

"Which certainly wouldn't have caused the kind of gossip that lingers through the years except, of course, for the tiny problem that Henry was supposed to marry her older sister." He lowered his voice in a confidential manner. "The way I heard the story, someone left someone at the altar."

"Who?" She knew she shouldn't be quite this eager to hear the sordid details, but it was a very long time ago. Which did indeed make it less like gossip and more like history.

"I have no idea." He shrugged. "Unfortunately, the details are murky at that point."

"That is unfortunate," she murmured.

"Miss Prendergast! You astound me. I never imagined you to be interested in such rubbish." Laughter sparked in his eyes. "Tsk, tsk."

"I'm not interested in gossip," she said. "I am simply interested in helping Mr. Saunders."

"Of course you are."

"As his friend."

"Perhaps you are, at that." His lordship studied her for a long moment. "You asked about his finances." He offered his arm again, and she placed her hand on the inside of his elbow. "Derek has always received a substantial allowance from his uncle. And has always gone through it with rapt abandon so he is continually on the verge of having nothing at all." Once again they started toward the door. "In recent months, however, he's seemed quite solvent. Frugal living, no doubt."

"No doubt." Her heart sank. Derek's solvency coincided with the success of the Lady Travelers Society. Which did seem proof of his misdeeds. Still, even a good man could be led astray. The strangest idea was nibbling at the back of her mind.

"I hold Derek in great affection, Miss Prendergast. You should know that." There was the vaguest hint of a threat in his words.

"That is good to know."

"You should also know—" he grinned "—I am far wiser than I would appear."

"One can only hope, Percy, one can only hope."

CHAPTER FIFTEEN

It is not uncommon for a lady traveler, especially one who is inexperienced, to find herself feeling like a different person altogether when in completely new surroundings. One must decide for oneself whether to embrace that or disregard it.
—The Lady Travelers Society Guide

INDIA WASN'T FEELING at all her usual self but lighter somehow, not quite as somber. As if a weight had lifted. Ridiculous notion, of course. She hadn't changed, not in any significant way. Nonetheless, two days ago she'd borrowed another woman's overly fussy clothing and resolved to be a better person. On the very same day she'd ignored caution to accost a stranger in the streets with the best of intentions and had been told by a dashing scoundrel that he'd had thoughts of kissing her. Yesterday, a handsome rogue had claimed she had *assets*. And today, while the reflection looking back from her mirror did not seem especially changed, she was decidedly different. Oddly enough, she didn't seem to mind.

The blame could be placed on Paris itself. The city's legendary charms might well be too much even for a sensible woman like India to resist. Or perhaps Derek was to blame, although she couldn't imagine ever fully trusting the man. Still, like the city, his charm was difficult to ignore completely. Nor could she fault his deportment. He was at all times a gentleman aside from a momentary lapse when he had asked for a kiss. She had nearly put that nonsense out of her head altogether. Furthermore, he had not brought up their misadventure in Montmartre, and she was eternally grateful.

It was also hard to ignore how unfailingly pleasant the man was to very nearly everyone. He gave Professor Greer the deference due his position, and it was obvious the professor held him in great affection in return. He flirted outrageously—but not at all seriously—with Estelle, who obviously adored his attentions. And he treated the servants politely and respectfully, as if they were social equals. The ways in which Derek's character was admirable were adding up.

Even so, the man was not to be trusted. There was the matter of his improved finances, after all. And he was definitely hiding something. There was a telegram he'd received that he'd failed to mention. Logically, she realized it might have nothing to do with Heloise, but it was the same day she'd overheard Derek and the professor agree to keep some sort of secret. One would have to be blind not to put two and two together. Still, it was becoming more and more difficult to keep in mind that Derek was the mastermind behind the Lady Travelers Society and, as such, was taking advantage of the desires of older women for the adventure to be found in travel. But God help her, she liked him. And liking him was accompanied by a few startling revelations.

She'd never in her life been so *aware* of anyone before. It was as if she sensed his presence in a room before she turned around. Felt his gaze on her before her eyes met his. Noted his scent—there was a faint hint of spice about him—the timbre of his laugh, the tiny mannerisms that were his alone. It was unnerving and annoying and extremely confusing. Try as she might, she couldn't seem to get the realization that the man had become important to her out of her head. Absurd of course, and best to ignore the very idea altogether. Besides, there were far greater issues to concern herself with. First and foremost was finding Heloise.

Today she intended to send her last telegram to Martin. Telegrams were charged by the word—although why it cost more to send a telegram from Paris to England than to Italy made no sense to her—and there was a ten-word minimum. If ten words was the cheapest she could send, ten words it would be.

"You've seemed unusually preoccupied all morning," Derek said beside her in the cab. They were headed toward the nearest telegraph office and had just left the Grand Hotel Louvois—although it scarcely mattered which Grand Hotel they had come from or which was next on Derek's list. They were all starting to swim together in her head in one enormous tableaux of marble and gilt and crystal. The French did seem to have a penchant for extravagant decor, even if not every Grand Hotel was as grand as its name.

"I am trying to compose my telegram."

He chuckled. "I wouldn't think it would be that difficult. 'Haven't found Lady Heloise. Still looking. Sincerely, Miss Prendergast.'"

"Thank you," she said coolly, trying not to give him the satisfaction of a smile. "It is more complicated than that."

"I might be of help if you tell me what you wish to say."

She was not about to admit she was trying to think of some plausible reason why she would not be sending further telegrams so that she might save the money for other expenses. "It's a most gracious offer, but I think I can come up with an appropriate message."

The cab pulled to a stop. Derek exited, then extended a hand to help her out.

"I still think 'Haven't found Lady Heloise. Still looking. Sincerely, Miss Prendergast' is appropriate."

"I shall consider it then," she said primly.

He grinned. "You're just saying that to make me feel appreciated."

"Of course I am." She adjusted her parasol over her shoulder and gazed up into his blue eyes. "And how very perceptive of you to notice that."

"I can be very perceptive and it is good to know." His gaze shifted from her eyes to her lips and back. "That I am appreciated, that is."

"I daresay any number of women appreciate you," she said in as flippant as manner as she could manage given he was still holding her hand.

"Any number of women are not you."

"I would think that would work in your favor."

"I would have thought so, as well." The oddest look flashed through his eyes, as though he was trying to find the answer to a question but wasn't entirely certain of the question itself. "Now I'm not quite as sure."

For a moment, neither of them could do more than stare. As if something inexplicable had trapped them in an embrace of awareness. Surely, he didn't intend to kiss her now? Here? Without warning, she recalled her words to Lord Brookings. Regardless of any unexpected feelings she might have for Derek, there could never be anything between them. He was a man of the world, destined to be an earl. She was a practical woman who worked for her living.

India pulled her hand away just as he released it. The

moment of intensity between them shifted, abruptly awkward and uncomfortable.

"Well, I should…" She gestured toward the telegraph office.

"Yes, I suppose, you should." A frown creased his forehead. "Would you like me to accompany you, or shall I wait for you here?"

"I will only be a moment." She nodded and hurried into the building.

What on earth was wrong with her? She had abandoned the idea of romance years ago, foolish concept that it was. In spite of his admission that he wished to kiss her, romance had never even crossed her mind until this very minute. Until Derek's gaze had locked with hers and what was surely no more than an instant had seemed forever. She'd long ago given up any desire or belief in romance—in true love and that sort of nonsense. But had she done so because it struck her as irrational and absurd, or because it was something she would never know? Odd how the experiences of one's youth could affect the rest of one's life. It made no sense whatsoever but there it was.

No, it was fortunate he hadn't kissed her as there could never be anything of a romantic nature between them. And a kiss would surely lead to something more. That was the nature of things. His was a world of wealth and society and power. And hers was one of organization and precision in the assistance of a man dedicated to intellectual pursuits. The differences between their worlds were insurmountable despite what romantic novels or fairy tales might claim. Besides, she had a fairly clear idea of the type of woman that would suit Derek. Someone accomplished and sophisticated, of impec-

cable heritage and, of course, beautiful. The next Earl
of Danby would settle for no less.

Romance was out of the question, but she could indeed be his friend. And that would have to suffice. With
every passing day, she was more and more convinced
that he was a decent man at heart. One couldn't spend
nearly all one's time in the company of a man without
discerning his true character. He had simply been led
astray, out of desperation no doubt. A man destined to
be an earl had a great deal of expectations placed on
him. It was entirely possible that all Derek needed to
mend his larcenous ways was the influence of a good
woman. A good woman who was also a good friend.
And hadn't he already offered the hand of friendship?
Time to accept that offer—if only for his own benefit.

The idea that had simmered in the back of her
thoughts now blossomed into resolve. Determination
washed through her and with it a sort of missionary
zeal. This might have been the kind of thing her parents felt although she'd been fairly certain, even as a
girl, they were much more interested in the adventure of
exotic places and the excitement of foreign shores than
the saving of souls. Regardless, for the first time since
India's arrival in Paris, at least one matter was firmly in
her hands. She was not used to feeling as if events were
swirling out of her control, as if she were adrift and at
the mercy of others. It was most disquieting.

She was accustomed to managing very nearly everything. Hadn't she run Heloise's household ever since
she'd finished at Miss Bicklesham's? And didn't she
supervise Martin's household as well as everything else
he needed? Really, when one looked at it, she managed
more than their households, she managed their lives

and did so with efficiency and economy. Both would be lost without her.

And there was no time like the present to begin Derek's true reformation. But first she had to send her telegram to assure Martin of her well-being. It was simple enough:

Search progressing. All is well. No further telegrams necessary. Prendergast.

India was nothing if not efficient. And the most efficient way to help a friend chart a new, legitimate course for his life was with honesty. Poor man was probably not entirely used to honesty. Charm and honesty rarely went hand in hand.

India dispatched the telegram, then joined Derek outside. "Did you dismiss the cab? I thought you wished to find a café."

"I do, but as it is such a lovely day, I thought we could walk rather than ride." He inhaled and released an exaggerated breath. "Stimulate the appetite, invigorate the mind, that sort of thing."

"I have yet to notice your appetite needing any stimulation whatsoever. Indeed, if you did not demand a daily break for sustenance, we could visit at least one more Grand Hotel every day. One would think you'd never had a decent meal the way you insist on interrupting our efforts for food."

He laughed. "Even you must admit you haven't eaten a meal yet that wasn't extremely tasty."

"I'll grant you that." She narrowed her eyes. "Is this another one of your attempts to show me Paris?"

"You are the most suspicious woman I have ever met." He shook his head in a mournful manner. "You've made it quite clear that you have no desire to see what

Paris has to offer which I consider a very great pity. I am simply suggesting a bit of exercise and there's no better place for that than right here."

She arched a brow. "Oh?"

"Good Lord, India." He waved at the street in a grand gesture. "We are on the Avenue des Champs-Élysées, one of the most fashionable promenades in Paris. It is not nearly as busy at this hour as it will be later in the day, so it's perfect for a leisurely stroll. We can walk toward the magnificent Arc de Triomphe—"

"Which you have insisted on expounding upon every time we've driven by," she pointed out.

"Then we shall head toward the Place de la Concorde instead, which many people feel is the true center of Paris. If I recall correctly, there are any number of charming cafés in the vicinity." He offered his arm.

"Very well then." She sighed and took his arm. "I see nothing wrong with a nice, *brisk* walk."

"You do enjoy having things your own way."

"Doesn't everyone?"

He chuckled, and they started off. A row of perfectly spaced trees and a strip of lawn separated the sidewalk from the street. Whatever else one might think about Paris, it was nicely laid out.

"Did you manage the appropriate wording for your telegram?" Derek asked offhandedly. "Something to keep the inestimable Sir Martin informed?"

"I don't believe I've ever called him inestimable."

"I stand corrected. I was extrapolating. As you have called him brilliant, respectable and honorable." He shrugged. "Inestimable seemed appropriate."

"You might as well call him Sir Martin the Great." It was really quite pleasant strolling beneath the shade of the trees. No wonder those they passed by—fashionably dressed elegant ladies, nannies with charges by the hand or in prams, well-appointed gentlemen—seemed in no particular hurry.

"Don't you?"

"Of course not." She scoffed. "He's simply my employer and, to a certain extent, my friend."

"He's more than your friend." He glanced at her. "Any man who wants a woman to telegraph him every few days thinks of her as far more than a friend."

She started and nearly tripped.

"You can't deny it, can you?" he said in an annoyingly smug manner.

"I have no need to deny it." She sniffed in disdain. "It simply isn't true and therefore doesn't warrant a denial."

"Methinks thou dost protest too much."

"You needn't quote Shakespeare—and inaccurately I might add—to make your point. And I am scarcely protesting at all, simply pointing out the facts." And Martin was the last thing she wished to discuss. "The building we're passing." She nodded at the huge, glass and iron structure. "It strongly resembles the Chrystal Palace in London."

"It's the Palais de l'Industrie and was indeed constructed to rival the Chrystal Palace. And you have changed the subject."

"Very well then. I understand you had a telegram the other day."

A decidedly satisfied smile lifted the corners of his lips. "And changing it yet again."

"In point of fact, I am returning to the original subject of my telegram to Sir Martin. Which reminded me that you had recently received a telegram, at least according to my maid." She adopted a casual tone. "Was it important?"

"Not really," Derek said. "It was from my uncle."

"I thought perhaps it was from Lady Blodgett. I hoped she might have had some news about my cousin."

"I'm afraid not."

"Or perhaps she wished to keep you informed about the activities of the Lady Travelers Society." She kept her voice light and her gaze on the tall Egyptian obelisk at the end of the avenue. "It does seem to be quite a profitable enterprise."

"I'm not sure *profitable* is the right word."

"Miss Honeywell told me the membership continues to grow."

"Membership is closed at the moment," he said firmly.

"Still, in dues alone I would suspect it brings in a significant amount of money."

"There does seem to be a lot of interest." He paused. "I wouldn't have imagined quite so many women would wish to join an organization dedicated to travel. As there are, it turned out to be a rather brilliant idea."

She nodded. "And a lucrative one."

He stopped in midstep. "Why do you keep saying that?"

"If one gives any credence to rumor, your finances are not particularly sound. In addition, you have made a few comments about the state of your pockets."

"My pockets are just fine, thank you." His jaw tensed, and they resumed walking.

"It just seems to me if you are unable to afford this search for my cousin, someone must be paying the bills. I simply assumed that was the Lady Travelers Society."

"I wouldn't assume anything, India. I assure you I am indeed paying my own way."

"Thanks to the dues from unsuspecting females," she murmured.

Again he stopped to stare at her. "What are you—"

"What did you and the professor wish to keep from me yesterday?" she said abruptly.

"Nothing of any interest." His brows drew together in annoyance. "You still don't trust me, do you?"

"No, I don't." She sighed. "Which makes this all the more difficult. I very much fear I am beginning to like you. I think, underneath it all, you might well be a good man."

"Underneath what?"

She waved off his question. "In spite of the fact that I do indeed distrust you, I find I am starting to enjoy your company."

He snorted in disbelief.

"Come now, Derek—you can't be all that surprised. Why, men like you depend on their charm. And even someone as sensible and rational as myself is bound to succumb to it at some point. You are like an endless stream of water, and I am a rock starting to wear away." They paused at an intersection to wait for a break in the relentless stream of traffic. If this is what the Champs-élysées was like when it wasn't busy, she couldn't imagine the scene when it was. "Furthermore, I am now willing to accept the hand of friendship you offered at the beginning of our travels."

"You just said you still don't trust me."

"I daresay, any number of people have friends they don't entirely trust.

"True enough but—"

"Who other people choose as friends is not my concern. As your friend, my only concern is you. And I'm certain, with a little effort—" she favored him with a brilliant smile "—you can earn my trust."

"I'm so glad one of us is confident," he said and steered her quickly across the street.

"Which is of little importance really." She shrugged. "The only truly important matter is finding my cousin. As for everything else…" She heaved a heartfelt sigh. "If you would just be honest with me about your involvement with the Lady Travelers Society."

He pulled up short. "My what?"

The street ended in a huge, open rectangular plaza. The obelisk was centered between two enormous iron fountains colored black and green. Water droplets sparkled in the sunlight and danced over gilded accents. Precisely aligned lampposts outlined the border between the pavement and the street and statues marked the corners. The park Derek had insisted they walk through a few days ago lay beyond the square. "Is this it then? The Place de la Concorde? The true center of Paris?"

"Yes, yes." Impatience rang in his voice. "What—"

"Isn't this where the guillotine—"

"Yes," he snapped. "And as gratified as I am to know that you've listened to something I've said, this is not the time. What involvement? I have no idea what you're talking about."

"Don't be absurd—of course you do." She glanced from side to side. "You can certainly see everything from here, can't you? A bridge over the Seine on the right and the arch behind us. Why you can even see that dreadful tower."

"India." A warning sounded in his voice.

"My, my Derek, which of us doesn't wish to see Paris now?" she said pleasantly. It was rather nice annoying him for a change. Still, perhaps it was time. "I'm talking about the fact that the Lady Travelers Society is a fraud. You're taking funds for the arrangement of travel without the slightest ability to do so. It's a sham designed to do nothing more than put money in the pockets of the man behind it." She met his gaze directly. "The man hiding behind three sweet elderly ladies."

"The man…" His eyes widened with realization. His voice rose. "You mean me?"

"Yes, I mean you. Who else could I possibly mean? I assume you are in this scheme alone." She frowned. "Unless there is someone else involved?"

"No." He shook his head, a stunned look on his face. She'd seen the very same expression on the face of one of her young charges during her brief, ill-fated period as a governess when the devil child had been caught adding pepper to his sister's porridge. "There's no one else."

"Excellent." She nodded. "Otherwise this would be most awkward."

"Awkward?"

"In detective novels I have read when one miscreant decides to mend his wicked ways, a partner is not always willing to do so. It can then be quite unpleasant."

"In detective novels." He paused. "Which are works of fiction."

"True, but they claim to be based on realistic events. I see no reason not to believe that."

"No reason whatsoever except they are fiction," he said. "What makes you think I am willing to mend my wicked ways?"

She wasn't sure what to say now that he'd admitted his fraudulent activities. How did one convince a man to abandon a moneymaking scheme? None of the detective novels she had read dealt with that particular question. Scoundrels rarely repented unless they were caught and even then were never truly sincere. "Aren't you?"

He took her elbow and steered her to a nearby bench. "Now then, why do you think I am willing to change? You noted that the Lady Travelers Society is extremely profitable."

She settled on the bench and positioned her parasol to block the sun. "And you said you were reforming."

"I was not referring to this."

"Goodness, Derek, one can't reform partially. One can't pick and choose which part of one's life in which to do better."

"On the contrary, India." He smiled. "One can do exactly that."

She widened her eyes. "This is not some foolish lark you're engaged in. This is wrong, morally, *legally* wrong. And think of the scandal, Derek. For the future Earl of Danby to be arrested for fraudulent activities, why, that's a far cry from a silly, drunken prank." She leaned forward and met his gaze firmly. "As your friend, it's my duty to point that out as well as assist you in mending your wicked ways."

"And if I wish to continue my wicked ways? At least the profitable ones?"

"Then I shall employ every resource possible to see you receive what you deserve."

"So much for friendship."

"Sarcasm, Derek, is ill advised at the moment." She glared at him. "I don't think you're treating this with the gravity it merits. I would hate to see you end up in prison or...or worse."

He raised a brow. "Worse than prison?"

"Infinitely worse." As the daughter of missionaries, India considered herself a good Christian. Admittedly, she had never been concerned with the trappings of religion, firmly believing Sunday services should be reserved for those whose souls were in need of redemption. Hers was not, although Derek's obviously was. "Eternal damnation." She raised her chin. "Hell if you will."

He chuckled. "I suspect I will know a great many people there."

"No doubt," she said sharply. "But hell is surely where you are headed."

"You would hate to see that, would you?"

She heaved a resigned sigh. "Apparently."

"As would I." He stared at her for a long moment. "I shall make you a deal, India. I have already put a stop to additional memberships, but there's nothing more I can do until we return to London. Until then, I will give you every opportunity to convince me to abandon the immoral, illegal and yet highly profitable path you believe I am on that will surely lead to incarceration and the fires of hell. Reform me, India—save me." He crossed his arms over his chest and trapped her gaze with his. "If you can."

CHAPTER SIXTEEN

"Oh, I HAVE no doubt of it." India nodded and idly twirled her parasol. "And I am certain you will come to believe, eventually, that this is the best course."

"We shall see," Derek said with a confident smile.

He'd been accused of many things before but never of fleecing women out of their savings. Still, as long as India thought he was behind the Lady Travelers Society she would not turn her attention toward his great-aunt and the other ladies. This was nothing more than a guess on her part. She had no real proof of his guilt, and no real proof of the fraudulent nature of the Lady Travelers Society. Even the misplacing of Lady Heloise could be attributed to incompetence rather than outright fraud. He stifled a grin at the thought of how indignant Aunt Guinevere and her cohorts would be if they knew India thought they were nothing more than innocent pawns in his game of deceit.

"Dare I ask what happens if you fail?" he asked.

"I have no intention of failing. Your freedom and your immortal soul are at stake."

"Still, if you do…" He sat on the bench beside her and heaved a dramatic sigh. "I'm the one to suffer the consequences. You face no penalty at all but are free to go on your merry way."

"But I shall feel badly about it." She thought for a moment. "Quite badly. I imagine seeing you go to prison or knowing you will burn forever in the fires of hell—" he winced "—will also provoke a great deal of guilt." She grimaced. "As I have taken the responsibility for your salvation upon myself."

"Scant comfort, knowing you feel badly or guilty." He shook his head in a mournful manner. "It doesn't seem fair, does it?"

"It seems perfectly fair to me as I am not the one whose wicked ways need mending. The world is not fair, Derek. Surely you know that."

"Even so, it does seem to me that you should face some sort of penalty for failure."

"I have already said I will feel quite badly should I fail." She pressed her lips together. "I am not fond of failure nor do I intend to experience it in this particular instance."

"My immortal soul thanks you."

"Derek, I don't think—"

"I think it is past time to find a café." He stood and offered his hand to help her up. "If we are to discuss my dire fate should your efforts at reformation fail—"

"Which they won't," she said firmly, rising to her feet.

"Then I would prefer to do so with a plate of excellent food before me and a glass of wine in my hand." He escorted her to the street.

"Very well." She paused. "I am possibly a bit hungry myself."

"Obviously the price one pays for taking on a project of this magnitude." He hailed a cab, assisted her up and directed the driver to a café Val had recommended.

"I'm not sure it's quite that bad…"

By the time they reached their destination on the other side of the Pont Neuf bridge over the barge-laden

Seine, ordered their meal and had glasses of wine in front of them, Derek had—if not an actual plan—then certainly an excellent idea.

"I have been giving your resolve to reform me a fair amount of consideration."

"I assumed as much as you have been extraordinarily quiet."

"There is a great deal to consider." He searched for the right words. "As we are agreed that, should you fail, the only one who truly suffers is me."

She opened her mouth to protest, and he held out his hand to stop her.

"Yes, yes, I know you will feel badly—"

"Very badly."

"Very badly then, which will be of no comfort to me if I am in prison or broiling in eternal flames."

She shrugged. "I'm not sure that can be helped."

"Therefore, while I have already agreed to allow you to try to convince me of the need to change my path to incarceration or damnation—in this life or the next—I should have some say in how you intend to proceed."

Her brows drew together. "What do you mean?"

"Well, do you have a plan in mind as to how to rescue me?"

"Not a plan exactly—it has only just today occurred to me that you can be saved." She thought for a moment. "However, for one thing, merely being in the company of a woman who is not the type of woman you are usually with should have something of an influence on you."

"You intend to be a good influence?"

"I already am a good influence."

"You were very nearly the cause of my being beaten senseless in the streets of Montmartre."

"Yes, but that was in pursuit of a good deed," she said in a lofty manner. Apparently, the more dangerous aspects of that evening had faded in favor of the ultimate goal.

"I see. And please, do tell me what kind of woman I am usually with."

"You know full well what kind of woman." She sniffed.

"No, I'm afraid I don't." He smiled pleasantly and sipped his wine. "Enlighten me, if you will."

"Very well." She paused. "A man of your position is expected to find a wife of a similar level of society. The female equivalent of yourself, if you will."

"Good Lord, I hope not," he said mildly.

She ignored him. "These are the types of women I went to school with. They are concerned only with the social season, their next gown and the next ball. They delight in gossip, regardless of whether it's true or not—and have no concern for anyone they do not consider worthy, up to their social standards, if you will. They are not stupid by any means but do not engage in pursuits of an intellectual nature for fear allowing anyone to know they are intelligent will somehow detract from their worth. They occupy their time with frivolous activities, change their ensembles numerous times a day, treat servants as if they were less than human and—should they engage in charitable activities—do so only for the sake of appearance." She took a sip of wine. "Appearance, you know, is everything."

He stared. "And this is the kind of woman you think I should marry?"

"I didn't say that, Derek. I said this is the kind of woman you are expected to marry."

"Perhaps before you save my soul you should save

me from that." It did sound like a fate worse than eternal damnation.

"I'm afraid your destiny is sealed. You are to be an earl, and that is the kind of woman suitable to be a countess."

"Shallow, insipid, self-centered, devious and cruel?"

"Take heart, Derek." Her eyes twinkled in a way that could only be called wicked. "They spend a great deal of time and money on their appearance, and they are hardly ever truly ugly."

"Yes, that is something to cling to," he muttered. India must have hated her years at Miss Bicklesham's if this was the kind of girl she'd met there. Although, while overly harsh, her assessment was not entirely inaccurate. "However, that particular aspect of my future is not the current point of discussion. We were talking about what you stand to lose if you fail."

"I won't."

He ignored her. "By the time we conclude our efforts today, we will only have seven Grand Hotels remaining. I anticipate another day and a half or so to visit the rest unless, of course, we find Lady Heloise. Barring that, we shall then have to consider our next step."

She nodded.

"However, while I have agreed to allow you to convince me to abandon a, as you continue to point out, very profitable enterprise—"

"A swindle."

"And we have both acknowledged my penalty should you fail will be much greater than your own—"

"I expect the guilt to be substantial."

"Then I have a few conditions, terms, if you will."

Suspicion flashed in her eyes. "What kind of conditions?"

"I think, at the very least, you should allow me to show you the sights of Paris."

"I believe you have been showing me the sights of Paris."

"Pointing out places of interest from a cab, a few minutes in a park and a stroll down an avenue is scarcely showing you the sights."

"But we are here to search for Heloise, nothing more. When we finish with the hotels—"

"There are other places we should inquire at. Places Lady Heloise would have visited."

"I was given to understand the professor and his wife had taken that upon themselves."

"They have but there are a great many places to see in Paris. Why, the Louvre alone will take days. While I have every confidence in Frederick and Estelle, it does seem to me she is far more interested in seeing Paris and shopping than finding Lady Heloise and he is attempting to rediscover the Paris of his youth."

She sighed. "You do have a point I suppose—"

"Allowing me to show you Paris will give us the opportunity to add our inquiries to the Greers, lessening the chances that they missed something important and increasing the possibilities of finding Lady Heloise."

"Perhaps."

"In no more than two days, we will have completed querying the twenty-seven Grand Hotels listed in the guidebook."

"Then what? Should we leave Paris for the next city on Heloise's itinerary? I believe that's Lyon."

"Oh, I think leaving Paris is ill advised."

He might have been mistaken, but he could have sworn a look of relief passed over her face. It vanished as quickly as it appeared. "Do you?"

"I do." He nodded. "First of all, Lady Heloise's last letters were from Paris."

"Yes, but—"

"Secondly, your best chance of recovering your lost trunk is to stay in Paris. When it's found, this is where it will be brought."

"I hadn't thought of that," she murmured. "Still, if we have exhausted our efforts here—"

"Oh, but we haven't." He pulled out his notebook. "It struck me that your cousin's use of the word *grand* might have nothing to do with the name of the hotel. Therefore, it seemed expedient to compile a list of the hotels in Paris that cater primarily to English visitors."

She stared at him. "Why didn't you think of that sooner?"

"The point is that I have thought of it now." He passed the notebook to her.

She scanned the list. "Perhaps it would be wise to abandon the Grand Hotels altogether in favor of these."

"I don't think that's a good idea," he said quickly although she couldn't possibly be as weary of the endless list of Grand Hotels as he was. "We need to stay the course we've begun. It would be inefficient to do otherwise." He shook his head. "She could very well be at the next hotel we call on. Or there could be some record of her. Haphazard is not the way to conduct a search, India."

"I wasn't suggesting—"

"However, when we have at last made our way through the Grand Hotels, I wish to take a respite from our search. I have no intention of leaving Paris without seeing the exposition." He took a sip of wine. "It's my understanding that it is a spectacle of progress and mankind's accomplishments as well as a taste of cultures far different from our own. We can visit the markets of Cairo and a Japanese village. And the entire city is talking about the American Wild West show. I would hate to miss that. The world has come to Paris and—through no fault of our own—so have we. I like to think of it as fate."

"I sincerely doubt—"

"This is the sort of thing that only comes along once in a lifetime."

"And this is a sight of Paris you wish to show me?"

"It's the newest sight of Paris and where I wish to begin. Besides, I would be derelict in my duties as your friend if I allowed you to miss it." He studied her for a moment. She didn't look especially interested, but she wasn't protesting, either. At least not yet. "I first visited Paris as a boy, and I've been here a number of other times. And while I do want to reacquaint myself with those places in the city that have attracted visitors for centuries, I don't want to fail to see what—according to the papers—thousands of foreign visitors are flocking to. Why, the Gallery of Machines alone is worth the effort."

"Is it?"

"And think, India, of the opportunities that a day spent seeing the marvels of invention and curiosities from around the world will give your campaign to reform me. I shall be so busy soaking up the wonders of progress that your incessant tirade about the Lady Travelers Society will sink into my conscience without so much as a protest."

"I don't believe I mentioned an incessant tirade." It was all the woman could do to keep a smile from her lips although—to give her credit—she gave it a sterling effort. But there was nothing that could hide the sparkle of amusement in her eyes. "Although, now that you have mentioned it, an incessant tirade seems a rather brilliant suggestion."

"Thank you."

She laughed, a light, musical sort of sound almost tentative in nature as if it wasn't used to being displayed. It certainly hadn't been around him. Indeed, this was the first time he'd heard her laugh, and it did the oddest things to the pit of his stomach and possibly his heart. It struck him that if her smile was a reward, her laughter was a gift.

"Then you agree to my terms? You will share Paris with me?"

She hesitated.

"I have always considered Paris a special place. And I have never shown it to a lady before." His gaze met hers. "I would consider it a great honor if you would allow me to show you those sights that make this city remarkable."

"I've never especially wanted to see Paris." Her gaze remained meshed with his.

"India, I believe when an unexpected opportunity comes along, especially one that is not likely to come along again, one should throw caution aside and seize it. Carpe diem, as it were."

"The thought of seizing the day has never occurred to me. Nor has tossing caution aside for any reason." She paused. "But then I'm not sure I've ever been confronted with an unexpected opportunity before."

"And now you have." He resisted the urge to reach for her hand. "What do you say, India?"

"Well…yes, I suppose. But only as part of my efforts to save your eternal soul," she added quickly.

"I can't imagine you doing it for any other reason." He grinned. Even the guidebooks agreed there was enough of worth in Paris to keep a visitor busy for months. And surely they wouldn't need that long.

His uncle's resources would no doubt find Lady Heloise soon, hopefully safe and in one piece. Derek would allow India to save him and make the grand gesture of giving up the Lady Travelers Society or, at the very least, transform it into something entirely legitimate. By then, Derek would know how he truly felt about Miss India Prendergast, beyond a simple wish to kiss her. And furthermore, what he needed to do about it.

Still, he couldn't ignore the nagging thought in the back of his mind that there was nothing simple about this at all.

CHAPTER SEVENTEEN

Guidebooks are indispensable and should be carried at all times. But do not rely on them to the exclusion of unforeseen possibilities. Some of the best travel adventures are those that are not planned.

—The Lady Travelers Society Guide

"WHEN YOU SAID you wished to show me the sights, I had no idea you wanted to show me everything at once." India gazed out over the city of Paris at her feet and tried not to think about just how high up this highest platform of the Eiffel Tower really was. Or rather tried not to think how far it was to the ground. And tried very hard to ignore words like *plummet* or *tumble* or *thud*, which kept popping into her head.

Derek rested his forearms on the railing and leaned forward, which did not strike her as wise. "I thought this would be a unique opportunity to see the city as few have seen it before."

"Aside from birds?"

He chuckled, his gaze firmly fixed on the vista spread before him.

"Well, you did say opportunities should be seized," she murmured and returned to her perusal of the City of Light—which Derek had explained had more to do with the city's position in the last century as a place of enlightenment and education than being the first city in Europe to illuminate its streets with gas lighting. He did seem to relish sharing such insights.

She hadn't expected—or particularly wanted—to go up in the architectural monstrosity that could be seen from everywhere in the city. In that, she was apparently alone. If she'd thought the boulevards and streets of Paris were crowded, they paled in comparison to the hordes of Parisians and visitors that swarmed into the exposition. They waited in long queues for lemonade and souvenirs and especially their turn to begin the terrifying series of elevators that would take them to this highest public platform of the Eiffel Tower. She was fairly certain she'd never heard so many different languages in one place before. She and Derek had avoided waiting too long in the warm afternoon sun thanks to Lord Brookings, who supplied two special tickets that allowed them to move to the front of the queue.

India had never thought she was afraid of heights but then—until today—she'd never been tested. The elevators provided a relatively smooth ride but had an appalling tendency to jerk now and then on the way to the summit. While there were gasps of alarm from several of those in the elevator car with them, India was pleased that she had not so much as uttered a word. It was not easy.

"I can't tell you how delighted I am that you chose to accept my advice," Derek said with a satisfied grin, his attention still directed toward the view.

"I wouldn't become accustomed to it if I were you."

"I wouldn't dream of such a thing."

The platform seemed steady enough although there was a bit of a breeze, and India was certain the entire structure swayed with the light wind. In that, she might have been mistaken as no one else seemed to notice. There were far more people up here than she would have considered safe, but Derek had assured her this level was constructed to hold as many as nine hundred visitors. Even so, it was not overly reassuring. Derek was a fount of knowledge about the Eiffel Tower, the exposition and Paris itself. It was as if she had a personal guide, which was really rather nice and far more interesting than she would have expected. And she was willing to admit—however reluctantly—that the view was indeed magnificent.

"Did you know, on a clear day you can see as far as fifty miles?"

"Why, I had no idea," she said drily.

"You can deny it all you want, but I am well aware you are enjoying this."

"Am I?"

"You are. I can see it in your face and even you have to admit seeing Paris spread out before us is remarkable."

She started to deny it, but it was absurd. He was right. "I believe I am enjoying this at that."

"Why do you do that?"

"Do what?"

"Refuse to admit that you might well be enjoying something you did not expect to enjoy."

"Nonsense. I just said I was enjoying this."

"Reluctantly."

"I do apologize if I did not muster up the proper level of enthusiasm," she said lightly.

"I think you even enjoyed Montmartre."

"Everything looks better in hindsight, Derek." She bit back a smile. The further away they moved from that night, the more, well, adventurous it became. Certainly, she had never sought adventure, but it did seem when adventure presented itself, it was irrational to waste the experience. Only as a lesson learned, of course.

"I suppose if you admit you're enjoying something then you would have to admit that you might, just might, have been wrong," he said thoughtfully.

"I don't refuse to admit when I'm wrong." She sniffed. "It's simply that I am never wrong."

His brow rose.

"If one is right, there is no need to doubt one's actions. Especially if one has responsibilities for the well-being of others." Although she was beginning to lose track of how many times she'd been wrong since she'd met Derek.

"You were wrong about coming up here."

"On the contrary, I never said a word in protest."

He snorted. "You didn't have to. It was apparent."

She was about to deny it when it struck her that, once again, he was right. Whether it was habit or inclination she did exactly what he was charging. Without warning, she saw herself as an old woman, complaining about everything that wasn't done precisely to her liking and refusing to acknowledge when something was better than she expected. When she was wrong. As that would surely be a sign of...what? Weakness? Dependence? Not accepting one's duty? She had no idea, but it was a horrible image and certainly the end of the path she was on. Worse, it did seem that woman was not merely old but alone. As a glimpse of the future it was terrifying. But was it unavoidable, as well?

"India?" he said cautiously. "You look distraught. I am sorry if I—"

"Well, you did," she said sharply. "Even if you've said nothing that probably isn't true." She drew a deep breath. "Ever since I arrived in Paris, ever since I met you, it seems everyone I meet is determined to point out my...my flaws to me. Flaws I was quite frankly unaware of. No one has ever seen fit to mention them before."

"Perhaps you didn't give them a chance."

"Perhaps it was better that way!"

"Perhaps," he said mildly and wisely changed the subject. "If we follow the railing to the left, we should be able to see the Cathedral of Notre Dame."

"I believe I will enjoy that." She glared and moved in the direction he indicated. "I can hardly wait to see what flaws God might see fit to point out to me."

He choked back a laugh behind her. She ignored him. She was not the least bit amused.

From this distance, the cathedral looked like little more than a child's toy but then everything below them did. Carriages, omnibuses, tramway cars were nothing more than moving shapes. People were no bigger than minuscule insects. It was an interesting perspective on the world, and her irritation faded.

She braced her hands on the railing and stared out at the cathedral and beyond. She had heard that travel broadened one's mind. She wasn't sure if her mind had been broadened at all, but her eyes had certainly been opened. She had already realized she had a propensity for intolerance and a greater tendency toward impatience than she had thought, especially with the flaws of others. Now she was discovering she had a great many unsuspected flaws herself. Flaws she should probably correct. But not today. Determination squared her chin. Today, she had a scoundrel to redeem.

"Derek." She glanced at him beside her. "I've been thinking."

"Oh good, I was afraid you hadn't," he said in a resigned manner.

She frowned. "What do you mean by that?"

"In the two days since I agreed to let you try to convince me to reform, for lack of a better word, you have begun every conversation on the subject with 'I've been thinking.'"

"And you have cut off every conversation."

"Because I had no intention of listening to you until you began fulfilling your end of the bargain."

"I'm here now, aren't I?" She waved at the panorama around them. "On top of the highest structure man has ever built."

"But you're not very gracious about it."

"I am bloody delighted!"

He lowered his voice. "We are beginning to attract attention. It scarcely matters to me but—"

"Once more you're right." She forced a smile. "Is that better?"

"If you mean the alleged smile—it's somewhat frightening." He returned his gaze to the panoramic view. "However, I am made of sterner stuff than to let an insincere smile dissuade me."

"That is good to know." She widened her smile although she suspected it did look more like her stomach hurt than anything remotely pleasant. Regardless, it was the best she could manage at the moment. "I was only going to say that I was wondering if my cousin had made it up here. Going to the top of the Eiffel Tower was one of the things she hoped to do in Paris."

"Then I can't imagine she would have missed it." He paused. "Which could indicate we might be close to finding her."

"Are we?"

"The elevators only began operating last week. I can't imagine even the intrepid Lady Heloise would wish to climb the steps."

"No, she's not overly fond of steps."

"If she was here as recently as last week, she might still be here."

India nodded. "The exposition and the tower were two of the reasons she intended to linger for a while in Paris. That and the art."

"I think you mentioned her interest in art before."

"Heloise adores art and has studied it for most of her life. She also fancies herself an artist. She has a studio of sorts on the top floor of the house and spends a great deal of time with her paints and brushes and canvases."

"Rather frivolous, don't you think?" he teased.

"Not at all," she said staunchly, then sighed. "Yes, I'm afraid I do. Especially as, well, she's not very good at it. The walls of the house are covered with her efforts. She's quite proud of them."

"And you have never told her the truth?"

"Goodness, Derek, I would never tell her that."

"That's very kind of you."

She glanced at him but his attention was still on the scenic view. "You're surprised."

He chuckled.

"I deserve that I suppose. But Heloise has been very kind to me. She is my family." She hesitated then plunged ahead. "Heloise was my mother's cousin. My parents were engaged in missionary work when they died. I had just started at Miss Bicklesham's—I was always boarding at some school or another as my parents were rarely in England. Heloise was named my guardian and my home has been with her ever since.

She managed to continue to fund my education even though her income is limited."

"Is it?"

She nodded. "I owe her a great deal. She's been both mother and dearest friend to me." Her throat tightened. "I don't know what I would do without her."

"Or what she would do without you?"

"Perhaps." She pushed aside the disconcerting thought of never seeing Heloise again. "I took over management of her household and very nearly everything else when I finished school. She has only the vaguest idea how to run a house. She never concerns herself with what she deems unimportant details. She does see to the household accounts but only because I stand over her and force her to do so although she has always been concerned about money." She smiled. "But Heloise is not what one would call organized."

"Imagine my surprise."

"This excursion of hers is a perfect example. Right from the beginning, she was not definitive in her travel plans. She said she might be gone anywhere from six months to a year and fully intended to stay as long as she wished anywhere that caught her fancy." She thought for a moment. "I did not pay as much attention to the details as I should have. I'm not sure I thought she would really leave."

He nodded.

"You've mentioned the lax nature of her itinerary—" she glanced at him "—for which I blame the Lady Travelers Society as much as I blame Heloise."

"As well you should."

She turned toward him. "The other day you derided me because I have no desires, nothing I particularly want. I admit I don't understand it, but Heloise wanted to see for herself things she had only seen in paintings or photographs. It was her dream. I had no idea she was doing it, but it seems she set aside money for years—small bits and pieces she could ill afford really, so that she might one day see the world beyond England's shores. I suspect she gave up a fresh canvas here or a new tube of paint there to save funds for this trip of hers. I imagine in that respect, she was not unlike most of the members of the Lady Travelers Society."

He studied her thoughtfully. "In that they wish to see the world?"

"And they are willing to sacrifice to do so." Determination strengthened her voice. "I saw the ladies at the meeting, Derek. They were not wealthy. Women with money do not attend lectures and meetings about travel. They travel. They do not have to save their pennies to finance their dreams. The women you are taking money from do."

An undefined emotion washed across his face. Guilt perhaps? Or regret?

"One could say you are stealing their dreams."

He winced. "It sounds awful when you put it like that."

"It is awful."

"I had not looked at it in quite that way." He shook his head. "It certainly deserves further consideration."

"Good." At the moment, that was all she could ask for. But the very fact that he would consider what she had said was gratifying. As was the expression on his face. She was right—underneath it all, Derek was a good man.

"For someone who admits she has no dreams…" He studied her closely. "You seem to understand quite a lot about them."

"Do I?" She smiled. "I assure you no one is more surprised at that than I."

His gaze searched hers. "There is so much more to you than you would have people see."

"I imagine that could be said about any of us."

"I very much want to kiss you, India Prendergast."

"Still?" She stared up at him.

He chuckled. "Apparently."

"Why?" It was the first thing that came to mind.

"Any number of reasons, I suspect." Bewilderment shone in his blue eyes, then resolve. "None of which I wish to detail at the moment."

"But—" She glanced around. No one seemed to be paying the least bit of attention to them. "Here? Now?" Her pulse sped up.

"We are on the top of the world." His gaze slipped to her lips and back. "I can't think of a better place or time."

She swallowed hard. "But there are a great many people here,"

"And yet." He stepped closer. "I see only you."

Her heart thudded in her chest. "Everyone will stare."

"Let them."

Butterflies fluttered in her stomach. "Kissing in public, Derek, that's highly improper and, well, scandalous."

He shrugged. "I don't care."

"Of course not, you've done worse." She shook her head. "But I care."

"You said you didn't care about what other people think."

"I lied." She sighed. "Besides, it's pointless."

"Pointless?" He narrowed his gaze in confusion.

"There can never be anything between us." This was

much harder to say than she'd imagined. "I believe we agreed on that."

"I don't recall agreeing to anything quite that absurd."

"It was implied." She turned back toward the view. "When we discussed the type of woman you are expected to marry. I am not that woman."

"Nor do I believe I said anything about marriage." Amusement sounded in his voice.

"I am well aware of that. I am not so stuffy as to believe a kiss is a commitment to eternity."

"God forbid."

She ignored him. "But a kiss is more than just a frivolous moment. At least it should be. And it is for most of us. Perhaps not for you."

"I have always liked frivolous moments."

"And I am not the least bit frivolous. I have always thought a kiss to be something of a…a promise."

"A beginning then?" he said cautiously.

"Well, yes. But as anything between us other than friendship is impossible, it seems foolish to begin something that cannot end well."

"I don't understand this at all." He paused. "Have you never been kissed, India?"

"I am not in the habit of randomly kissing gentlemen." *Or kissing anyone at all.*

"There is nothing random about this. As I have already confessed, I have given the idea of kissing you a great deal of thought. And more so in recent days."

"Well then perhaps *spontaneous* is a better word." She shrugged. "As I assume you did not plan for this particular moment."

"No." Frustration sounded in his voice. "And while

it might have been spontaneous a moment ago, I assure you the spontaneity of it has passed."

"Then you no longer wish to kiss me?" She held her breath.

"Oh, I still wish to kiss you." He heaved a resigned sigh. "But this is obviously not the right moment."

"Obviously." She ignored the unexpected disappointment that washed through her. "If that's settled then…" She had the most absurd desire to flee. "If you will pardon me for a moment, I wish to…um…see the view elsewhere…" She turned and stepped away, circling around the tourists in her path.

Good Lord! She stopped short. What on earth was she running from? She was nearly thirty years old and had never been kissed! She'd never so much as given it a second thought before, but now it struck her as truly awful. And somewhat pathetic. And shouldn't she do something about it? Carpe diem, after all.

Before she could think better of it, she swiveled on her heel and marched back to Derek.

"Yes?" His brow rose.

She grabbed the lapels of his coat, rose on her tiptoes and pressed her lips to his. The most remarkable spark of something electric and quite wonderful shot through her at the feel of his warm lips against hers. He smelled vaguely of warm spice and tasted faintly of lemonade and summer.

She released him, stepped back and caught her breath. "There."

"There?" He looked as taken aback as she felt.

"Now I have been kissed on the Eiffel Tower," she said with a surprisingly firm nod given something had replaced her stomach with a quivering mass of aspic.

"On the contrary, my dear Miss Prendergast. *I* have been kissed on the Eiffel Tower. You have not."

"You did kiss me back."

"A natural response to being kissed, but you caught me by surprise." He shook his head in a mournful manner. "It was not my best effort."

She frowned. "The, well, *quality* of the kiss cannot be blamed on me. Indeed, I thought it was…"

"Adequate, no more than adequate. And you're absolutely right—it cannot be blamed on you." He pulled her into his arms and stared intently down at her. "But my dear Miss Prendergast, this can." He pressed his lips to hers.

For a moment, she froze. Then unexpected heat swept through her, and she thought she would surely melt into a small puddle of heretofore unsuspected sensation and something…more. He angled his mouth harder over hers. Her lips opened slightly, and her breath mingled with his and…and *adequate* was the farthest thing from her mind. And she knew without question or doubt, this kiss, this moment, this man would linger in her thoughts, in her heart for the rest of her days. Still, it wasn't a promise or a beginning, it was no more than a foolish error in judgment.

She pulled back and struggled to catch her breath. "People are staring, Mr. Saunders." She stared up at him. "You should, well, release me, I think."

"I thought you didn't care what people say?" He stared down at her.

"I don't care what they say. I care what they see." She drew a deep breath and pushed out of his arms. "This was…" She shook her head. "A dreadful mistake."

"What?" His brows drew together. "Why?"

"Because I am…" She impatiently brushed a strand

of hair away from her face. "*Eroding* as it were. With every minute, you are wearing me away. What I think. How I feel. The rules I have always lived my life by." She shook her head. "And this cannot end well."

"Why?"

"You know why!"

"No, I don't." He glared at her. "And that nonsense you keep bringing up about the type of woman I am supposed to be with is nothing but...*nonsense*. Complete and utter foolishness. And you are far too intelligent to believe that."

"It's simply the way things are." Her voice rose. "You can protest it all you want, but you cannot deny the facts of it."

"No." He shook his head. "That's not what this is about at all." He studied her intently. Realization dawned on his face. "You really don't trust me, do you?"

As much as she had decided he was, somewhere deep inside, a decent man, he was also right. "I've made no effort to conceal that."

"I understand your reticence to trust me when we first met. Now, however, I thought I had proved myself to be most trustworthy."

"Somewhat, I suppose, perhaps, but—"

"But it doesn't matter, does it?" He glared at her with equal parts anger and disbelief. "You haven't trusted me from the beginning, and you are unwilling to bend so much as the tiniest bit to admit that just possibly, once again, you were wrong."

"That's not entirely fair." She raised her chin.

"The world is not fair, India—remember?"

"I..." She stared at him for a long moment. This was neither the time nor the place to discuss whatever feelings she—or he—might have. Nor did she have any idea what to say. This was not the kind of problem she knew how to solve. She straightened her shoulders. "I have no desire to discuss this further. Any of it."

Someone behind them cleared his throat, and Derek stepped back. The most awful sense of mortification swept over her, and she did so wish she was the type of woman who fainted.

"I should like to leave now," she said coolly.

"And I should like to take another turn around the platform." He leaned toward her, lowering his voice. "And the discussion is far from over." He nodded and strode off.

She turned back to the endless view of Paris and stared unseeing into the distance. Somewhere, in a part of her mind not oddly still and numb, she noted people continuing to move past her. She heard excited comments about the view and the remarkable nature of the tower. The world, even here at the tallest manmade pinnacle, continued as it always had, as it always would.

But India would never be the same. Something inside her had changed. Twisted. Shattered. The question was why, and she had no answer. Regardless, it seemed to hold a great deal of pain.

Derek returned a few minutes later. "If you're ready…"

"More than ready," she murmured and accompanied him toward the elevators. They joined the crowd waiting for the next ride down.

The ride to the ground, including the changing of elevators, was fraught with tension. As if they were each tied to the end of a taut rope that neither could break or ease. The silence between them on the return to the house was broken only by an occasional terse question on his part or hers. They'd originally planned to explore some of the exposition but neither now seemed inclined to do anything other than retreat to Lord Brookings's house.

For the first time in her life, India didn't know what to say and thought it best to say nothing. She was by turns angry, regretful and astonished. None of this would have happened if he had not announced he wished to kiss her. Why on earth did he have to do that? What was he thinking? And if he really wanted to kiss her, why? Did he harbor feelings of affection for her? Perhaps he should have mentioned that. And why couldn't she stop thinking about it? About him?

Much of the blame really should be put on her. Whatever possessed her to make such a spectacle of herself? She'd kissed him! She'd never kissed a man before. Had never wanted to. And who would have imagined how... *moving* that kiss would be? Although it did pale in comparison to the kiss he gave her.

After what seemed like forever, they arrived at the house. He escorted her inside, then turned to her in the foyer.

"Once again, I owe you an apology, India," he said coolly. "I put you in an awkward position in public, and for that I am truly sorry. Apparently, whenever I wish to kiss you, it does not end well. However, it was a kiss. Nothing more than that. And you're right. It was a mistake. Good day." He started toward the parlor, then paused and returned. "I nearly forgot." He pulled a large coin from his waistcoat pocket and handed it to her. "Something to remind you of the day." He nodded and took his leave.

She stared after him for a long moment.

She'd been kissed for the first time. In a public place. By a man who was as much scoundrel as gentleman. A man with whom there could be no future. A man who now was obviously furious with her.

She looked down at the object in her hand. It wasn't a coin but a medal. On the side facing her was a depiction of the Eiffel Tower dwarfing world monuments including Saint Paul's Cathedral and the pyramids, together with the dates of the tower's construction and opening. She turned it over. On the other side, in French, was written that this was a souvenir of ascending to the summit of the Eiffel Tower. She'd never had a souvenir before.

How terribly ironic that now she had a souvenir of a day she couldn't possibly ever forget.

CHAPTER EIGHTEEN

"SHE'S INSANE, I tell you." Derek strode into the parlor. "The woman is mad, utterly completely mad."

Val leaned against the mantel. His eyes widened at the appearance of his brother.

"I can't believe that I thought, perhaps, for no more than a moment really, it just popped into my head and—"

"Someone you met on the street no doubt," Val said in a manner that struck Derek as anxious, and nodded toward a high-backed chair.

"Don't be absurd." Derek stalked to the cabinet where Val kept good Scottish whisky and fine Spanish sherry for whatever lady might be with him at the moment. "Admittedly, the thought had crossed my mind, only when we had discussed why she didn't want to be married. Have you ever heard such words from a female? I've never met a woman like her. She's an enigma. The most confusing creature on earth." He yanked the cabinet doors open. "We seem to have discussed marriage quite a bit in a theoretical, philosophical sort of way but not as it pertained to the two of us. At least not the two of us together. I never mentioned anything remotely like spending the rest of our days together." He grabbed the decanter of whisky. "All I wanted was to kiss her. One, simple kiss—not a lifelong commitment!"

Val winced. "I really don't think—"

"Worse—she rejected me!" He sloshed a healthy portion into a glass. "Not that there was anything to reject. But it's insulting nonetheless. And offensive. And unpleasant." He tossed back a fast swallow. "*Most* unpleasant. Rather like being stabbed. In…in the heart! Yes, that's it exactly. Even if one isn't certain one's heart is engaged, she stabbed me in the heart nonetheless. The woman made assumptions based on nothing more than a request for a kiss. She simply skipped over any number of—I don't know—steps I suppose, that this sort of thing requires." He downed the rest of the whisky.

"Steps?" Val stared with a look that might have been horror on his face and jerked his head sharply toward the chair. What on earth was the matter with him?

"Yes—steps! In this day and age, one kiss does not mean 'marry me.' One does not plunge into marriage." Derek refilled the glass "Particularly not with a woman who drives you stark, raving mad! What kind of woman refuses to marry you when you haven't asked? When you haven't even thought about it?"

"I have no idea," Val said cautiously.

"I'll tell you what kind of woman!" He took a large swallow. "The kind who—"

"No!" Desperation sounded in Val's voice.

"Well, I for one would like to hear that." A familiar voice rang from the back of the room.

Val cringed.

"Mother?" Derek turned and stared.

The Marchioness of Westvale rose in the graceful manner she had long ago perfected from a chair in the shadows of the room. "Good day, Derek. You're looking well."

Val groaned.

FREE Merchandise is 'in the Cards' for you!

Dear Reader,

We're giving away FREE MERCHANDISE!

Seriously, we'd like to reward you for reading this novel by giving you **FREE MERCHANDISE** worth over $20 retail. And no purchase is necessary!

You see the Jack of Hearts sticker above? Paste that sticker in the box on the Free Merchandise Voucher inside. Return the Voucher today... and we'll send you Free Merchandise!

Thanks again for reading one of our novels—and enjoy your Free Merchandise with our compliments!

Pam Powers

Pam Powers

P.S. Look inside to see what Free Merchandise is **"in the cards"** for you!

We'd like to send you two free books, similar to the one you are enjoying now, from the Harlequin® Historical series. Your two books have a combined cover price of over $10 retail, but they are yours to keep absolutely FREE! We'll even send you 2 wonderful surprise gifts. You can't lose!

LAURA MARTIN

Heiress on the Run

LOUISE ALLEN

Surrender to the Marquess

His defiant lady

REMEMBER: Your Free Merchandise, consisting of **2 Free Books** and **2 Free Gifts**, is worth over $20 retail! No purchase is necessary, so please send for your Free Merchandise today.

Get TWO FREE GIFTS!

We'll also send you 2 wonderful FREE GIFTS (worth about $10 retail), in addition to your 2 Free books!

Visit us at:
www.ReaderService.com

YOUR FREE MERCHANDISE INCLUDES...

2 FREE Books **AND** 2 FREE Mystery Gifts

FREE MERCHANDISE VOUCHER

2 FREE BOOKS and **2 FREE GIFTS**

Please send my Free Merchandise, consisting of
2 Free Books and **2 Free Mystery Gifts**.
I understand that I am under no obligation to buy
anything, as explained on the back of this card.

246/349 HDL GLUP

Please Print

FIRST NAME

LAST NAME

ADDRESS

APT.#   CITY

STATE/PROV.   ZIP/POSTAL CODE

NO PURCHASE NECESSARY!

FP-517-FM17

Derek threw his brother an annoyed look. "Why didn't you tell me she was here?"

Val snorted. "I tried."

"Your poor dear brother practically snapped his neck off trying to indicate there was someone else in the room. You were simply too agitated to notice. Although I must say I'm delighted he didn't succeed. Your tirade was entirely too interesting to miss." Mother smiled pleasantly.

"I'm glad you enjoyed it." He moved to her and kissed her cheek.

"I must say, your presence in Paris is an unexpected surprise."

"As is yours." His mind raced back over everything he had said since he'd stepped into the room. *Bloody hell.*

Celia Newell, the Marchioness of Westvale—formerly Mrs. Saunders and then the Marchioness of Brookings—was, to most of the world, a charming, attractive woman who did not look at all her true age, not that even her sons knew exactly what that age was. She was a perfect hostess and a delightful conversationalist. She was a sought-after guest at dinner parties or country house sojourns or any kind of social event. But when something caught her interest she was, as well, very much like a dog with a bone. Derek braced himself. Unless Stephen, Lord Westvale, had managed to curb her innate tendencies toward meddling in the five years of their marriage, she would never let Derek's display of ire pass unmentioned. Especially as it concerned a woman.

"Is it really?" She cast Val a chastising glance. "You didn't tell him we were coming?"

Val shrugged uneasily. "It slipped my mind?"

"Percival." Mother's brow furrowed delicately. "You

are hosting a ball in this very house not more than five days from now. I do hope that didn't slip your mind, as well."

"You're having a ball?" Derek stared. "Here?"

Val ignored him. "Of course not, Mother," Val said smoothly. "You simply had the arrangements well in hand when you were last here, so I wasn't the least bit worried about it."

She studied him suspiciously for a moment, then nodded. "Aside from final details, I suppose there's little left to do." She turned her attention back to Derek. "Stephen and I were here last month for the opening of the exposition. I must say I was surprised by how many people I know are here. Why, London society must be totally bereft of anyone of interest at all. Although the season is winding down, I suppose." She sank back into her chair. "There hasn't been a grand ball in this house for years." She aimed a hard look at her stepson. "Of course, if Percival had a wife, I'm certain that social oversight would be corrected."

"Keep in mind, I spend only a few months here every year. Paris is not my primary residence," Val pointed out, wisely avoiding any reference to his unmarried state. He had come very close once, a few years ago, and had yet to again find whatever it was he was looking for in a wife. But there was no question he quite enjoyed his unencumbered status.

Mother, however, took Val's—and Derek's, too, for that matter—failure to wed as a personal affront. Fortunately, Lord Westvale proved a continuing distraction from her crusade to see her sons married. Derek rued the inevitable day when the couple became too comfortable with each other and Mother could fully turn her attentions back to her unmarried sons.

"Nonetheless, there are social obligations that do need to be fulfilled on occasion," she said firmly.

"Yes, Mother." Val nodded, playing dutiful son to the hilt.

And leaving Mother free to give Derek her full attention. "When I last saw you in London, you made no mention of coming to Paris."

"When we last spoke, I didn't know I would be." Exactly how much should he tell her?

Her brow arched upward. "So this was unanticipated on your part? A spur of the moment sort of thing?"

On one hand, the more she knew, the more she might be able to help. "One could say that."

"And Edward did not protest?"

On the other, the more she knew, the more dangerous she might be. "Not at all."

She studied him closely. He resisted the urge to shift from foot to foot like a guilty schoolboy. "That doesn't sound like Edward. He was quite serious about you— how did he put it?"

"Accepting your responsibilities, giving up a pointless life of excess, debauchery and misdeeds? Becoming a man?" Val offered.

"Thank you." Derek clenched his teeth. "I had forgotten the exact wording."

"Anything I can do to help." Val's expression was solemn, but amusement shone in his eyes. "I think you need to tell her everything."

"Again, you have my thanks," Derek snapped, but Val was probably right. Besides, one way or another, Mother would surely find out everything anyway. She always did. "Very well." He added another splash of whisky to his glass, then drew a deep breath. "When you and Lord Westvale left London, you charged me with looking after Aunt Guinevere. A duty, I might add, that you have not shouldered particularly well."

"Nonsense." She sniffed. "I call on Aunt Guinevere frequently. Dear, sweet, fragile lady that she is."

Val snorted back a laugh and headed toward the whisky decanter.

"Then you are aware that she and two of her dearest friends have started an organization ostensibly to assist women with information and travel arrangements but that in truth does little more than provide her and the other ladies a steady income?"

"Why, how very clever of Aunt Guinevere." Mother beamed, deftly managing to avoid answering the question.

Derek gritted his teeth. "And did you know they are offering services they are not competent to provide nor do they feel compelled to provide? Which might well be seen as, oh I don't know—fraud?"

"I'm certain that's nothing more than a misunderstanding." Mother waved off the charge. "No doubt one that can be rectified."

"Well, it would have been easier to *rectify* had they not lost one of their members!"

"Surely they can't be blamed for that," Mother said slowly.

"Surely they can!" Derek glared at his mother. It was past time she accepted some of the responsibility for this mess. God knew he had.

"Percival?" She craned her neck and peered around Derek. "Some sherry, if you please."

"Already poured, Mother." Val stepped around his brother and handed her a glass. "I suspected you might need this." He took a position slightly behind her chair and shot his brother a knowing smirk.

"You are a thoughtful son. Thank you, dear." Mother took a sip, no doubt as much for a moment to consider Derek's words as for the bracing effects of the wine. "None of which explains why you are in Paris."

Val leaned over the back of the chair and addressed his mother. "This is where it gets really good."

She glanced at Val. "I thought the really good part had to do with the woman who won't marry him."

"Stop talking as if I'm not here." Derek blew a frustrated breath. "And there are no good parts. This is not some sort of French farce."

"And yet we are in France," Mother murmured.

"I'm here because this is the last place we know that Lady Heloise Snuggs visited."

Mother's eyes narrowed. "And who is that?"

Derek heaved a long-suffering sigh. "She is the Lady Travelers Society member who seems to have disappeared."

"Lady Heloise Snuggs?" Mother shook her head. "I don't know her. Although I believe I might have known a Snuggs once. Charming fellow if I'm thinking of the right person." She glanced at Val. "One meets so many people."

Val raised his glass to her. "And more than a few Snuggs."

"And you're trying to find her?" Mother asked.

"Exactly." Derek nodded.

"Which does explain why you are here. Now then…" Mother sipped her sherry. "You said this is the last place *we* knew, I should like to know who *we* is, as I'm assuming it's not Percival."

"I have nothing to do with this," Val said quickly.

"I didn't think so, dear. And, more important, who is the woman you haven't asked to marry you but wouldn't do so anyway?" Mother's tone was pleasant but there was a familiar look in her eye. Derek had always thought it similar to that of a predator right before pouncing on its prey.

"*We* would be myself and Miss India Prendergast. Lady Heloise's cousin."

"Her much younger cousin." Val leaned forward. "A rather interesting woman, Mother. Quite efficient and intelligent, obviously as she has refused to marry Derek—"

"I didn't ask her!"

"Too proper for my taste, wound too tight if you will," Val continued, "but surprisingly attractive in spite of her dreadful clothes." He shuddered. "Excellent lungs on her, too."

"I see," Mother murmured, a speculative look in her eye. "So you are traveling with an unmarried woman, Derek?"

"I assure you we are appropriately chaperoned." Derek threw a silent prayer of thanks in the direction of England and Aunt Guinevere. "Professor and Mrs. Greer are accompanying us. He was a colleague of Uncle Charles."

"I have never heard of him." Mother shrugged, then shot a quelling glance at Val. "Don't say it, dear."

Val gasped in feigned indignation. "I wasn't going to say a word about your lack of acquaintances—or interest—in all things academic."

Mother gave him the kind of look both he and Val had lived in fear of as boys. From the time Mother had married Val's father she had treated him exactly as she treated Derek. And he adored her for it.

"I have interests in any number of diverse subjects, several academic in nature. Admittedly, I find some more worthy of note than others." She pinned Val with a firm look. "You would do well to remember that."

"Yes, Mother," he said solemnly but his eyes gleamed with laughter.

As did hers. Until she returned her attention to her younger son. "When would you suggest I meet Miss Prendergast?"

"Why do you want to meet her?" Derek said without thinking.

Val winced.

"Why wouldn't I want to meet her?"

"I don't know," he said slowly. "It just doesn't strike me as a wise idea."

"Nonsense. For one thing we are all houseguests together." She glanced at Val. "I would like to meet the professor and his wife, as well."

"Dinner tonight, I would think," Val said.

"I don't know that I wish to wait that long to meet the woman who refuses to marry my son." She smiled. "Tell me about her."

"I'm not sure there is much more to tell," Derek said cautiously.

"Really?" Mother raised a brow. "Nothing more than she is a cousin of a Snuggs, intelligent, proper and has poor taste in clothing?"

"I think she's rather intriguing," Val said.

"I can tell her that." Derek huffed. "After all, she is my—"

"Your what?" A wicked light shone in his brother's eyes.

"Your what, dear?" Mother asked, a similar light in her eyes.

"My responsibility," he said firmly.

"Is she indeed?" Mother studied him.

"Speaking of responsibilities, a telegram came for you earlier." Val pulled a paper out of his waistcoat pocket and handed it to his brother, knowing full well he had just changed the subject. Derek shot him a grateful look.

Derek scanned the message. It was from Uncle Edward, who was notoriously tight with his wording in such things, as if a few pennies here or there made a great deal of difference to his net worth. Apparently one of the detectives he had hired was now in Paris with information about Lady Heloise. Derek was to meet with him tomorrow at his hotel. Thankfully not a Grand Hotel.

"Good news?" Mother asked hopefully.

"With any luck." As much as Derek had been unexpectedly enjoying India's company, as much as he was perplexed by this inescapable attraction to her, as much as he couldn't quite determine exactly what he was feeling at the moment, finding Lady Heloise and getting on with his life had a great deal of appeal. Still, as annoyed as he was with the woman, not seeing India every day was not something he wished to consider. Nor did he need to. Yet. "Uncle Edward has hired investigators to help locate Lady Heloise while Miss Prendergast and I search for her here. I am to meet with one of his detectives tomorrow morning."

"A detective?" Mother's eyes widened. "How very exciting."

"It's not exciting. It's a necessity." Something that might well have been guilt sharpened his tone. Aside from all else that had happened today, he couldn't get the idea that the Lady Travelers Society had been stealing women's dreams out of his head. "One that would not be needed at all if Aunt Guinevere had not been forced to find some way of improving her finances. If you had paid more attention to her perhaps you would have noticed she was very nearly at poverty's doorstep."

Val cringed.

Mother stared at him for a long moment. "My mother, God rest her soul, used to say there was no one in the world more independent than her sister. When your uncle Charles was away on one of his expeditions, my mother would invite Guinevere to stay with us. She never once accepted, saying she was able to take care of herself and she preferred to do so."

"That might well be, but now she is getting on in years, and she needs assistance and attention," Derek said sharply. Admittedly, he had shirked his familial responsibilities up to this point, but now that he had been made aware of Aunt Guinevere's plight, he was willing to do whatever was needed to make certain the elderly lady—and her friends—were taken care of. Mother needed to acknowledge her failure in this, as well. "She deserves better than to be abandoned by her family."

"Abandoned?" Mother's eyes narrowed. "I'll have you know, I call on Guinevere at least once and usually twice a month when I am in town. In addition, every month, I send a carriage for her so that she might join me for tea or join us for dinner. Fully half the time, she begs off—claiming a previous commitment. When she does come, she often brings her two old friends with her and they are most welcome." Mother met Derek's gaze directly. "At no time has Guinevere ever given me so much as a hint that she had financial problems of any kind. Indeed, she has always led me to believe Uncle Charles left her quite well off."

"Even so—"

"Furthermore, Derek, I am not so scatterbrained, nor am I so absorbed in my own life, as to ignore a family member in need, particularly not Aunt Guinevere. I love the dear woman. But she has never said a word about financial difficulties nor has she ever implied that all was not well."

"I can't imagine it's easy for a woman who has lived her entire life depending mostly on herself to admit that she can no longer do so," Val said. "Pride and all that."

"No doubt," Mother said coolly. "Guinevere has not been abandoned by me, Derek. And I quite resent that you think so."

He winced. "My apologies, Mother. That might have been unfair of me."

"It was more than unfair. It was offensive, unkind and undeserved."

She was right. Was there so much as a single woman alive he would not do battle with today? "I am truly sorry."

"However, given the way you burst into the room, you have obviously already had a difficult day so I suppose your thoughtless comments can be attributed to your foul mood. And therefore overlooked."

Val snorted.

"I appreciate that, Mother," Derek said under his breath.

"And I assure you, my aunt and I will have a long chat about this very thing the moment I return to London. If I have been lax in my obligations toward her, have no doubt, I will rectify that." Mother's tone hardened. "I'm certain we can devise a plan to provide her—"

"They," Derek said.

Mother frowned. "They?"

"They—Aunt Guinevere, Mrs. Higginbotham and

Mrs. Fitzhew-Wellmore." Derek shrugged in a helpless manner. "They are like sisters."

"Like the Three Musketeers." Val nodded. "One for all and all for one, that sort of thing."

"I suspect, whatever financial support we are able to provide, Aunt Guinevere will share it with the others."

"Of course, I should have realized that. The three of them are indeed bound together by affection and history. They have been close for as long as I can remember. Quite a daunting and yet amusing trio. Ophelia and Persephone are every bit as unique in character as Guinevere. I find them all quite enjoyable." She paused. "Perhaps something can be done with this Lady Travelers Society of theirs."

"Something legitimate," Derek said quickly.

"Without question." Mother frowned. "And I don't know why you think it was necessary to point that out. I should hate for dear Aunt Guinevere or her friends to be incarcerated." She considered the matter for a moment. "I shall have to talk to Stephen about this. I daresay he'll come up with some sort of clever idea. He's quite brilliant, you know."

Derek and Val traded long-suffering glances.

"Where is Lord Westvale?" Derek asked.

"He had business to attend to. Stephen has some sort of business very nearly everywhere we go." Mother rolled her gaze toward the ceiling. She had never been tolerant of *business*. "He should return shortly. You'll see him at dinner." She finished her sherry and held her now-empty glass out to Val. He dutifully took it and crossed the room to refill the glass. "Now, what are you doing to find your Lady Heloise? I assume you're not simply waiting for your uncle's efforts to bear fruit."

"No, we most certainly are not." Derek swirled the

whisky in his glass. "We are continuing to canvass those places Lady Heloise intended to visit. And, as one of her letters referred to the Grand Hotel she was staying in, Miss Prendergast and I have been checking all the hotels in Paris with the word *grand* in the name—"

Mother stared. "All of them? That must have taken forever."

"Very nearly." Val returned and handed Mother her glass.

"Indeed it has, but Uncle Edward thought it best to keep Miss Prendergast in Paris as long as possible while his investigators try to find her cousin. We've not had any luck yet." He took a thoughtful sip. "But I have noticed the oddest thing."

"Apart from the sheer number of Grand Hotels?" Val grinned.

Derek ignored him. "I have reread all of Lady Heloise's letters to her cousin. They are quite interesting and full of the details of travel but…" He wasn't sure how significant it was but it was certainly of interest. "Everything she writes, every description, every detail is taken practically word for word from one of the Baedeker guidebooks."

"So, one could have stayed in the comfort of one's own home and written the letters?" Mother asked. "What an intriguing idea."

"Except for the postmarks, of course. And the fact that Lady Heloise has long wanted to travel and was extremely excited about finally doing so. But one would think she would have used her own words, her own way of relating what she was seeing. As she is something of an artist, I would think her observations would be a bit more descriptive, more colorful, if you will, than what I've read in her notes. Still…"

"Still, one does have to wonder if she was ever in Paris at all. Or France, either, for that matter." Val raised his glass. "The plot thickens, as they say."

"Indeed, it does," Mother murmured. "Have you checked Galignani's?"

"Galignani's?" Derek shot his brother a questioning look.

Val shrugged. "It's a bookshop."

"Goodness, Percival," Mother chastised. "It's much more than that. Galignani's publishes a paper—*Galignani's Messenger*—that has daily lists of all the English and American visitors to Paris. It also publishes a weekly list of all English and American visitors to the other major cities of the continent."

Derek stared. "So this paper would tell me when Lady Heloise arrived and—by extrapolation—when or if she left?"

Mother nodded. "Without question."

Derek gritted his teeth and glared at his brother. "Why didn't you tell me about this?"

"I didn't think of it. Sorry."

"I'll stop at Galignani's after I'm done with the detective tomorrow." Derek nodded. "It would have been beneficial to have known this sooner."

Val shrugged.

"And how do you plan to explain your absence to the always suspicious Miss Prendergast?" Val smiled in a smug manner. "It's obvious she doesn't trust you." He paused. "But I think she likes you."

"Not that I've noticed." Derek heaved a frustrated sigh. Although she did say she was beginning to like him. Not enough to marry him of course—not that he had asked. "I daresay she'll be grateful for a morning apart. Our day together did not go well."

"Because she won't marry you." Sympathy sounded in Mother's voice.

"I never asked!"

"Well, now you know the answer should you ever decide to ask." Val sipped his whisky. "I'd say that's most convenient. Saves you a great deal of trouble."

"I have no intention of asking India Prendergast to marry me," he said in a hard tone, wondering why his words didn't ring entirely true.

"Regardless, I wish to meet her." Mother studied her younger son thoughtfully. "I don't believe I have ever heard you proclaim with such vehemence that a woman was driving you mad before."

"I daresay, I've said that about any number of women."

Mother smiled in an altogether too-knowing manner.

Derek groaned to himself. The last thing he wanted—the last thing he needed—was his mother's interference. Whatever he felt about India, whatever this was between them, his mother had no place in it. Not that a simple fact like that would stop her.

"Percival." Mother directed her attention to Val, and Derek breathed a sigh of relief. "We do need to discuss the arrangements for the ball. I shall confer with the cook and the rest of the staff tomorrow, although I am certain all is in order."

Val shrugged. "One can only hope."

"One can do more than merely hope," she said in a no-nonsense manner and rose to her feet. "Travel is always so tiring. I believe I shall retire to my rooms before tea. Percival, please tell the butler I expect tea to be served promptly at half-past four, here in the parlor." She paused. "No, I'd rather have tea in my rooms, I think. I believe I would prefer privacy. And would you please inform Miss Prendergast I would be honored if she would join me."

"Why?" Derek said without thinking. Any brief sense of relief was dashed aside and replaced by a large, heavy weight in his stomach.

"Why? Come now, dear. Why wouldn't I want to meet the woman who does not wish to marry my son?"

"Why indeed," Val added. Derek considered the possibility of thrashing him when the opportunity arose.

He forced a weak smile. "Of course."

"I am quite looking forward to it." That predatory light was back in her eyes. "I suspect we have a great deal to talk about."

Precisely what Derek feared.

CHAPTER NINETEEN

Regardless of where wanderlust leads a lady trav-
eler one should not discount the pleasure to be
found in acquiring native goods as souvenirs of
travel as well as gifts for those left behind. They
are usually quite reasonably priced.
                              —The Lady Travelers Society Guide

"So, Miss Prendergast." Lady Westvale set down her
cup, folded her hands in her lap and smiled pleasantly.
"Do tell me why you won't marry my son."

India choked on the bite of biscuit in her mouth, a
bite that had been quite tasty a moment ago and now
was reminiscent of sawdust. She covered her mouth
with her hand. "I beg your pardon?"

"Oh dear." Her ladyship refilled India's cup. "I've
startled you, haven't I? A bit more tea perhaps?"

"Thank you," India gasped out the words and accepted the cup.

"Tea is often helpful when one has choked on something, oh, unexpected."

India sipped the tea and struggled to regain her composure.

It wasn't easy. She'd been more than a little apprehensive ever since she'd received the invitation—
although summons was more accurate—to join Derek's
mother, the Marchioness of Westvale, in her rooms for

tea. The suite of rooms Lord and Lady Westvale occupied was even larger than Derek's and decorated in a
manner less feminine than India's but quite lovely, with
darker carved wood furnishings and light, pastel fab-
rics. If one had to imagine the sort of rooms suitable for
a marquess and his wife, this suite would not be far off.

No one had mentioned the marquess and marchioness were expected, and India suspected his mother's
appearance was a surprise to Derek, as well. Surely he
would have said something otherwise. Prepared India
in some manner. Not that her preparation was necessary. In spite of everything that had passed between
them, she was nothing more than his friend. Nor would
she ever be.

Within minutes the marchioness had alleviated India's misgivings. She was surprisingly friendly, engaging and quite lovely. Somewhere past her fiftieth year
India surmised—a guess based more on Derek's age
than his mother's appearance—she was no taller than
India, with pale blond hair and eyes the same shape and
color as her son's. India found herself enjoying their
light conversation about Paris and the challenges of
travel.

Most of the comments had come from Derek's
mother, who appeared to be doing her best to put India
at ease. And indeed, her efforts had worked. Until now.
India hadn't expected to have to explain her reasoning
again today and definitely not to Derek's mother.

"Is that better?" Lady Westvale asked.

India nodded. "Much."

"Good, then we can continue." Lady Westvale stud-
ied her curiously. "Now then, Miss Prendergast." Lady
Westvale paused. "May I call you India? Lovely name.
So wonderfully exotic."

"Thank you." India smiled weakly. "Yes, of course."

"Excellent. As I was saying, most women fall all over themselves at the prospect of marriage to Derek. I am curious as to why you do not."

"Well…" India chose her words with care. "It seems to me, as Derek has not asked me to marry him, my reasons for believing such a match is impossible are irrelevant."

"But interesting nonetheless."

"I doubt that."

"Come now, India, let's not be sly with one another." The marchioness's blue eyes—her *son's* eyes—narrowed slightly. "You would not be the first woman to realize men usually want exactly what they can't have. If this is how you intend to entrap my son into marriage, I assure you, he is not as gullible as he appears."

India sucked in a short breath. "And I assure you, I am doing no such thing! I consider Derek nothing more than a friend. And, as his friend, I am trying to help him in his efforts of reformation."

"Reformation?"

India said the first thing that popped into her head. "Live up to his father's memory, that sort of thing."

"His father's memory?" the marchioness said slowly.

"Well, yes." It wasn't entirely true but it wasn't exactly a lie, either. But India was not about to tell a marchioness her son had been engaged in duping unsuspecting women out of their money. Nor was she going to allow the woman to think she had designs on her son. She stiffened her spine. "Your suspicions as to my true intent could not be more inaccurate."

"Are they?"

"They are indeed. I am well aware that I am not the type of woman Derek is expected to marry."

"How very interesting," Lady Westvale murmured. "Why not?"

"Why not?" India stared at the other woman, but she seemed genuinely interested in the answer. "My family, while respectable, is not noteworthy in society or otherwise. I have no fortune to speak of. I am of ordinary appearance. Furthermore, I am gainfully employed in a position other than that of a governess or teacher or companion. Even you must admit that alone is unusual enough to throw doubt upon my suitability as a potential match for Derek." She huffed. "Why am I the only one who seems to understand this?"

"I found it most understandable." The marchioness paused. "Who doesn't?"

"Your sons don't. Neither Derek nor Lord Brookings."

"They are good boys." Lady Westvale beamed with pride.

"Good boys?" India stared. She knew she should hold her tongue, but that was one of the most ludicrous statements she'd ever heard. "Forgive me for saying it, Lady Westvale, but Derek has a notorious reputation—"

His mother scoffed. "Foolish nonsense for the most part."

"And his lordship apparently has a reputation every bit as disgraceful. One that he is so pleased with, he is actually indignant when no one knows of it."

"I find that charming, don't you?"

"I do not."

Her ladyship frowned. "That's rather stuffy of you."

"I daresay—"

"Might I point out to you—"

"Lady Westvale—"

"You had your turn, dear, now it's mine," the older

woman said firmly. "I am well aware of the reputations of both my sons. However, to the best of my knowledge, neither Derek nor Percival has ever knowingly hurt anyone. I daresay there are any number of so-called respectable people in the world who cannot say the same." She pinned India with a hard look. "Don't you agree?"

"Yes, I suppose."

The marchioness nodded. "Nor has either of them ever involved an, oh, *innocent* in any sort of misadventure. They have never ruined a young woman's reputation. The incidents they are credited with—"

"*Charged* with."

"Interpretation, India. Eye of the beholder and all that." Lady Westvale waved off the comment. "Regardless, the mistakes they have made have never been truly wicked but rather…naughty. Do you understand what I'm saying?"

"I understand that you're their mother," India said slowly. "And, as such, I would expect you to defend them."

"You're right, of course. I will always defend my sons. And while they may well have done any number of things that society looks askance at, they are good men with good hearts." She pressed her lips together in a hard smile. "And I am proud of them."

Would she be proud of Derek if she knew about his connection to the Lady Travelers Society? It scarcely mattered; that would soon be at an end. In spite of their altercation, she was confident he would indeed do what was right.

"Now then, I understand your luggage went astray."

"Unfortunately." India nodded, relieved at the abrupt change of subject. "It's one of the reasons why we are forced to linger in Paris. Although admittedly, we still have not made inquiries at any number of places my cousin might have been."

"There are few better cities in the world to linger in than Paris." The marchioness selected one of the almond biscuits India had become quite fond of, took a bite, then considered India thoughtfully. "Are you aware that we are hosting a ball here in a few days?"

A ball? India's mouth was abruptly dry, and she shook her head. "No one has said anything to me." But then why would they? She was a guest in the house but not the type one would invite to a ball. "I can arrange to remain in my room while it's under way."

Lady Westvale stared. "Why?" Realization dawned on her face. "Oh, I see." She nodded in sympathy. "We shall have to do something about that."

"About what?"

"Your clothes, of course." She considered the pale blue India had chosen for tea and winced. "I understand your chaperone loaned you some attire."

Of the two day dresses, one dinner ensemble and a gown for evening wear Estelle had loaned her, this one had seemed the least objectionable of the lot. Apparently, not in the countess's eyes. "Mrs. Greer has been quite kind."

"Yes, well kindness is one thing—taste is something else again. I dare not ask what kind of evening gown she might have provided."

"It's…sufficient." India wrinkled her nose. It was the worst sort of betrayal of Estelle's kindness but the gown—somewhere between a brilliant pink and pale scarlet in color—with flounces and ruffles and flowers fashioned from silk, was perhaps the fussiest thing India had ever encountered. Worse, even with Suzette's expert alterations, it made her look like a stuffed sausage. "I really didn't anticipate having to wear it."

"Nor should you." The marchioness nodded firmly. "This is Paris, home to the finest dressmakers in the world and it would be wrong not to avail ourselves of their services. You and I shall make a day of it tomorrow. We will go to some of my favorite places and have you suitably attired in no time."

"I do appreciate the offer, Lady Westvale, but I'm afraid that's not possible." She drew a deep breath. "I don't have any money. I've lost it."

"Lost it?" The marchioness cast her a sympathetic look. "Gambling?"

"No."

She winced. "Blackmail then?"

India bit back a gasp. "Most certainly not."

"Dear Lord." Lady Westvale stared. "You haven't given it to a dashing scoundrel who promises to pay it back when he inherits but then vanishes never to be seen again?"

India's eyes widened. "I have managed to avoid that."

"Good. There are few things more foolish than that." Lady Westvale breathed a sigh of relief. "But I can't think of any other way you might have lost your money."

"You don't understand. I actually *lost* it. Misplaced it, if you will. I don't know where it is." Regardless of how many times India admitted her error in judgment, it continued to sound stupid. "I hid it in my trunk."

"The missing trunk?"

India nodded.

"Apparently there is something more foolish than being taken in by a handsome stranger."

"Yes, well so it seems," India admitted.

"Percival said you were efficient." The marchioness

considered her. "This does not sound the least bit efficient to me."

"It seemed a good idea at the time," India said weakly.

"Goodness, my dear." Lady Westvale shook her head. "When traveling, you should always hide your funds in your boot. Or in a special pocket affixed to your underpinnings. Or, better yet, travel with a gentleman whose job it is to keep track of necessities like money."

"I shall remember that."

"See that you do." She nodded firmly. "Put it in your trunk, indeed."

India winced.

"However, you misunderstood. I was not suggesting you purchase a new wardrobe." The marchioness favored her with a brilliant smile. "I intend to purchase one for you."

India choked again. "But why?"

"You do need to stop doing that, dear. It's unbecoming and possibly hazardous." She lowered her voice in a confidential manner. "I was once at a dinner party when a somewhat portly gentleman choked on a bit of roasted quail. Why, he turned all sorts of dreadful colors before the stout woman seated next to him thumped him quite vigorously on the back. Which sent the quail flying across the table, much to the dismay of the person sitting opposite him." She paused. "Although, if I recall correctly, the gentleman became quite enamored of the lady who had so thoughtfully struck him. One thing led to another, and they were quite happily wed shortly thereafter. Indeed, they delight in telling the story of how they became acquainted when she saved him from imminent death."

"How...fortuitous?"

"It was that. However—" she gestured in an absent

manner "—I have strayed from the matter at hand, which is your need for suitable clothing and my determination to purchase it for you."

"And I don't understand why you wish to do so." India couldn't quite hide the stubborn note in her voice.

"Any number of reasons. First of all—" she ticked the points off on her fingers "—you don't wish to marry my son. Regardless of the questionable soundness of your reasoning, you do impress me as being honest. And I am an excellent judge of character. That wasn't always true but one of the few benefits of growing older is that you do learn a few things along the way. And honesty, my dear, should always be rewarded."

"Thank you," India murmured.

"Secondly, one could say that my dear Aunt Guinevere is responsible for your search for the missing Lady Heloise in the first place. Which means it's her fault your clothes—and your money—are missing. You deserve compensation for that."

"Still—"

"Furthermore, my husband has a substantial fortune. Even more than I can ever possibly spend, although I do consider it my purpose in life to do my best." She flashed India a satisfied grin. "Providing you with a new wardrobe is barely worth noting."

"And it is most generous of you but—"

"And—" she pinned India with a no-nonsense look "—we are having a ball here in five days. As a guest in this house, your appearance will reflect on your hosts. Make no mistake, India, you are expected to attend. Percival and I would be deeply offended and highly insulted if you do not. We would consider it extremely rude. And you do strike me as the type of woman who would not wish to be impolite."

"No of course not. But…I've never been to a ball," India blurted.

Lady Westvale's eyes widened. "Never?"

India shook her head. "I'm afraid not."

"But you do know how to dance?" the marchioness asked cautiously, as if she was afraid of the answer.

"They did teach us at Miss Bicklesham's."

"Miss Bicklesham's Academy for Accomplished Young Ladies?"

India nodded.

"Excellent institution." She frowned. "But you do not strike me as a typical Miss Bicklesham's graduate."

India raised her chin. "Thank you."

Lady Westvale laughed. "That's one less thing to worry about. Now then, as for your new clothes, we should make a list of what is absolutely necessary, what would be wise to acquire and what is simply for fun."

"Lady Westvale." India drew a deep breath. "I do appreciate your kind offer but I cannot allow you to purchase clothing for me. I would feel obligated to reimburse you, and I'm afraid I will never be able to do so."

"My dear young woman, I'm afraid you don't understand. Allow me to explain." Lady Westvale thought for a moment. "My mother died when I was quite young, my stepsisters were never especially fond of me, and, as my father was always notoriously short on funds, I did not have a season. It was not until I married that I had the financial resources to indulge in things like fine dresses and exquisite shoes and elaborate hats. I quite enjoy shopping now that I have the means to do so. It is a great deal of fun. Indeed, I consider it something of an art, and I am very good at it.

"However, I have two sons and, as much as I love them dearly, I have long regretted not having had a daughter. There is nothing to be done about it now, of course, but there you have it." She smiled wistfully. "I have always been most envious of those friends of mine who have had the pleasure of shopping for or with a daughter. I would consider it a very great favor if you would allow me to do so with you. And I do promise not to be too extravagant."

"I see." India didn't know what to say. On one hand, clothes had never been important to her before. On the other, Paris—or something—had changed her. She'd begun to wonder if perhaps being sensible and practical and efficient didn't have to mean she always needed to look sensible and practical and efficient.

"You may give my proposal due consideration of course but I will warn you, I will not accept any answer other than yes." Her eyes gleamed with excitement. "We shall start visiting my favorite dressmakers first thing in the morning."

"I'm afraid that's not possible," India said, ignoring an unexpected stab of regret. "Derek and I need to continue to look for my cousin."

"Derek is well capable of continuing the search on his own for a day or two," Lady Westvale said firmly, then sipped her tea. "And it will do you good, as well, to think about something other than the missing Lady Heloise. I can't imagine this has been easy for you."

"I am worried. She is my only family, and I do miss her but…" India wasn't sure why she was saying this, but Lady Westvale wasn't nearly as intimidating as India had initially feared. She was really rather nice. "It has come to my attention that there may well be things about Heloise I didn't know. Things I paid no attention to or things she didn't wish me to know. It's been something of a revelation, and I'm not sure how I feel about it all."

"I understand completely." The marchioness nodded in sympathy. "I doubt that anyone truly knows another person as well as we might think we do."

"Probably not."

"Furthermore, things don't always turn out as we expect them to."

"I never expected to be in Paris."

"I would imagine you never expected to be friends with my son, either. You did say you consider yourself his friend?"

India nodded. "I do."

"How very interesting," she said thoughtfully. "That you are willing to be his friend, that is. When you're not willing to consider marriage to him."

"I thought you understood." Why would no one leave this alone? India braced herself. "I'm not suitable for marriage to him, and under no stretch of the imagination would I be considered appropriate to be a countess."

"I do apologize." Lady Westvale shook her head in a mournful manner. "I had no idea you had, well, a criminal propensity."

India could barely get out the words. "I most certainly do not! I have never broken any sort of law."

"Your family then." Lady Westvale broke off a piece of biscuit and popped it in her mouth.

"My family is most respectable." Indignation raised India's voice. "My parents were missionaries, and my cousin is the daughter of the previous Earl of Crenfield."

"Good, decent people?"

"Without question!"

"Respectable, law-abiding and good is all anyone can ever ask, dear." She paused. "Then, correct me if

I'm wrong, but your only real objection to a match between you and my son is that such a match would not
be correct as society sees such things?"

"Yes." India nodded. "I am not a silly, foolish creature—" in spite of the evidence of her missing funds
"—who believes in romantic nonsense. I understand
the manner in which the world works."

"I've never been overly fond of the way the world
works. I think it's frequently cruel and often absurd.
Tell me, India, do you like Derek?"

"Yes, of course."

"Why?"

"I don't know. He's quite nice." She considered the
question. "I didn't think so at first, or perhaps I simply
didn't expect it, but I think so now. He's very thoughtful of others and treats people with kindness. He helped
the professor when he was under no obligation to do
so. He's quite clever. That, too, I did not expect, and
saved me from an awkward situation." At the risk of his
own safety. "He has insisted on showing me the sights
of Paris in spite of my reluctance. And I must admit, I
am enjoying it." And enjoying as well being with him.
"He seems to make people feel, I don't know, special
perhaps. He is respectful toward the professor, engaging him in all sorts of academic discussions. Why, you
can see the man practically preen under Derek's attention. And he flirts outrageously with Mrs. Greer, which
I found quite distasteful in the beginning, but she adores
it. I'm not sure why, but it's obvious that she does.

"He's more, I don't know, observant I think is the
right word, than I anticipated. He sees things about me,
notices things, that no one has ever seen or noticed before." It was really rather remarkable now that she put
it into words. "Not all of them nice, mind you, but all

of them startlingly perceptive. Aside from a few instances, he's quite candid. I'm not certain that I trust him, at least I didn't in the beginning, but now…" she said more to herself than to the marchioness.

Now what?

Did she indeed at last trust him? She did have faith in him, confident that he would do what was right. Didn't faith and trust go hand in hand?

Her breath caught at the revelation. Hadn't she told him just this afternoon that she still didn't trust him? Was that something she'd said because she was supposed to say it? Because she never expected to feel differently? But, if he was indeed a good man, a decent man, a man willing to reform, a man who was everything she'd just told his mother he was, why wouldn't she trust him?

"Now?" Lady Westvale prompted.

"Now I…I like him." Perhaps she more than liked him.

"I see."

India shrugged helplessly.

"My, this is interesting," the marchioness murmured, then drew a deep breath. "You should know something about my son, India. Derek has been in love any number of times that I know of and I suspect several more that I don't. In each and every instance, the lady was eminently suitable to be the next Countess of Danby. They were all exactly the type of woman you say he is expected to marry. And yet, not one of those instances led to marriage or even an engagement."

India couldn't help herself. "Why not?"

"Because, even though they were right in terms of money and position and everything else you—and society for that matter—seem to think is appropriate, they were not right for him."

"That is…interesting."

"My dear India. One of the nicest things about having a title and money—especially money—is that you can do very much as you wish and people forgive you for it. I never once married for position or financial considerations. Derek's father was a second son with no prospects whatsoever. My second husband, Percival's father, was a marquess with a sizable fortune but not when I married him. He was not poor, of course—I long ago realized true poverty would not suit me, but I had no idea he was heir to a cousin's title and wealth. And my husband now, my dearest Stephen, has both money and title—another marquess, which was ever so convenient—and did so when I married him, but I would have married him if he'd had nothing at all." She smiled in a knowing manner. "Money and position, my dear, are not as difficult to find as a good man. Particularly one who claims your heart. I have been extraordinarily lucky. Love, in this world, is remarkably hard to find. I have been well loved by three wonderful men and I have loved them in return."

She paused thoughtfully. "If I had known I would lose Henry, Derek's father, as soon as I did, I would have cherished every moment. I feel the same about Percival's father, Arthur. But one never knows what one has until it's gone." Resolve sounded in her voice. "I will not make the same mistake with Stephen. I make certain he knows, every single day, in words and deed, how much I care for him."

India smiled. "That's quite lovely."

"Yes, well, as I said one hopefully learns something as one travels the path of life," she said in a brusque manner as if she had said more than she had intended. "I'm not sure why I have told you all this except that I suppose I wanted you to know that the example I set for my sons is not one of concern for the matters that society deems important. Both Derek and Percival intend to marry for love, which is probably why they have not wed." She sighed. "That's a problem I have yet to solve. I simply want them to be happy, and the right woman will do that for them. I know the right man did that for me. All three of them."

CHAPTER TWENTY

"I THINK YOU should tell her everything."

Derek stopped in midpace and stared at his brother. "Do you really?"

"Well, your other alternative is to tell her absolutely nothing. I'm not sure one option is particularly better than the other." Val shrugged. "But apparently your Miss Prendergast is especially fond of novels of detection. She might well appreciate the twists and turns the search for her cousin has taken."

"Do you realize when you sit behind your grandfather's desk in this imposing library, you look like you actually know what you're saying."

"I do know that." Val planted his palms flat on the desk in an all-encompassing gesture, looking not unlike a king surveying his domain. "It's why I sit here. I am wise beyond my years, brother."

"In your eyes only."

"Come now, I have just given you excellent advice. It's not my fault that you refuse to take it."

"You've just explained my choices. Choices I am already well aware of. You've given me no advice whatsoever."

"Again." Val smirked. "Beyond my years."

"Good Lord," Derek muttered and resumed pacing.

At least he didn't need to make a decision at the moment. India and his mother were now in their third day of laying siege to the dress shops of Paris. He'd barely seen her at all, except in passing, since their kiss and subsequent argument. But then he'd been avoiding dinner, and, according to Estelle, so had India. Which was probably for the best.

"As much as I love Mother, as much as I am grateful she is keeping India occupied, the idea of the two of them spending so much time together strikes fear into my heart. They've forged some sort of unholy alliance. That union cannot possibly bode well." He paused and looked at his brother. "What do you think they talk about?"

"Oh, Mother probably goes on about the newest fashions and latest style and what color is de rigueur this season. And your Miss Prendergast undoubtedly loses no opportunity to point out what miscreants Mother's sons are."

"That sounds right." Derek sighed and continued to pace.

He shouldn't have kissed her. It was a mistake. Oh, not kissing her exactly but kissing her then and there, although he had apologized even if she did kiss him first. And while not his finest moment, there had been the loveliest sense of promise in her kiss.

She'd been so delightfully tempting with those green eyes and perfect posture and ever-so-earnest manner. He wasn't sure when she'd stopped being annoying and had become irresistible. Although she did continue to be fairly annoying, which oddly enough simply added to her appeal. Nor was he sure which one of them was responsible for that debacle on top of the world—probably both. But he had been truly wounded that even now, after spending so much time together, after he had told her things he'd never told anyone, she still did not trust him. Bloody hell, he was putting up with her campaign to convince him to give up his wicked ways! What more could a man do for a woman?

"I think what you need is practice."

"Practice?" Derek rolled his gaze at the ceiling. "And what, pray tell, do you think I need to practice?"

"Perhaps *practice* is not as good a word as, oh, *rehearsal*."

"Rehearsal?" Derek raised a brow. "Like a stage play?"

"Exactly." Val leaned back in his chair. "I shall play the role of Miss Prendergast and you shall be you."

"This is absurd," Derek said and plopped into a chair.

"I prefer to think of it as brilliant."

Derek snorted.

"Now then, Mr. Saunders," Val adopted an overly high falsetto and sat up rigidly straight in his chair. "You scandalous beast of a scoundrel you, tell me what you learned from the detective."

"She doesn't sound like that." Derek bit back a grin.

"Oh come now, you naughty, naughty boy, I sound exactly like this." Val wagged his finger. "Now, you wicked man, answer my question."

"Very well." He thought for a moment. "The detective—"

"What detective?"

"The one hired by my uncle." Derek had met with him two days ago, seen him yesterday and then again today.

Val gasped in an exaggerated manner. "Your uncle hired detectives?"

Derek nodded. "He wished to help."

"What a brilliant idea." Val narrowed his eyes and pursed his lips. "Why didn't you tell me, you rogue, you?"

"I…" Why didn't he tell her? Because even at the beginning he'd wanted to prove something to her? Or to himself? "I don't know," he said sharply. "Go on."

"You haven't answered my question, you wayward reprobate." Val heaved an overly dramatic sigh. "What did the detective tell you?"

"His investigation showed Lady Heloise never arrived in Paris." A fact Derek had confirmed for himself by checking the lists of visitors kept at Galignani's. "Nor was she apparently ever in France at all."

"Not in France!" Val clapped his hands to his cheeks. "Goodness, how can you say such a thing, you vile creature! I received letters from her from Le Havre and Rouen and Trouville as well as Paris."

"Letters that were all taken word for word from guidebooks."

"Poor, dear Heloise has never been very original." Val heaved another heartfelt sigh.

"You do realize you sound ridiculous."

"No more ridiculous than I feel." Val fluttered his lashes. "Do go on, you villainous cad."

"The letters were indeed written by your cousin but…" This was where the whole thing became rather messy.

"Yes?" Val's falsetto was even higher if possible.

"But she did not mail them." Derek paused. "Mademoiselle Marquette, her maid, mailed them for her."

Derek had spent much of the day accompanying Uncle Edward's detective to and from the picturesque village of Chantilly, northeast of Paris, an hour or so away by train. According to the investigator, this was the home of Mademoiselle Marquette's family. It wasn't at all hard to find the woman, but it took much prodding, appeals to her better nature and threatening to involve the authorities to get the truth from her.

She admitted Lady Heloise had entrusted her to post letters destined for India from various locations in France, including Paris. Mademoiselle Marquette was further expected to continue on to travel throughout Switzerland, Italy, Greece and a number of other places for a full six months, funding for said travel provided by Lady Heloise. The woman was charged with sending the letters Lady Heloise had written back to India from the places she visited. It was an interesting scheme and would have progressed exactly as planned had not Mademoiselle Marquette decided to pay a visit to her home. She was then so overcome with missing her family, she decided it would do no harm to stay for a while. Apparently, it had taken her several weeks to come to the realization that now that she had returned to the bosom of her family she did not wish to leave, and her obligation to mail Lady Heloise's letters paled in comparison to her own desires.

Mademoiselle Marquette declared she had sent all the remaining letters back to Lady Heloise in recent days as well as arranged to return the funds she'd been given for travel, minus a bit for her troubles, which she insisted she deserved. While her loyalty to her employer did not extend to continuing her ruse, it apparently did apply to revealing why Lady Heloise had initiated this scheme in the first place and where she was currently. The maid assured Derek Lady Heloise was safe and well but adamantly refused to reveal the lady's present location. She did, however, imply Lady Heloise had never left England. Uncle Edward's detective was confident, with this information, she would soon be found.

Upon their return to Paris, Derek sent a telegram to

his uncle, asking to be informed the moment the older lady was located.

"Oh, my goodness." Val rested a limp wrist against his forehead. "Why would she do such a thing? And where is she now?"

"I don't know." Derek blew a frustrated breath. "I don't have the answer to any of that."

"And that may well be your biggest quandary at the moment," Val said, resuming his usual voice.

"I have already realized that, but thank you for pointing it out."

"I believe my initial advice is still the best course. Tell her everything. At the very least it will prove to her this is not the fault of the Lady Travelers Society, and by association, Lady Blodgett's or yours. As much as it will disappoint her to know she was wrong about you—that you have not been defrauding helpless women out of their savings."

"I'm not sure it's worth it." Derek had been wrestling with this ever since he'd learned the truth.

"Why? Because then she will no longer need to reform you?" Val's eyes narrowed in a speculative manner. "Or because then she can return to England, and your continuing association will be at an end?"

"Actually," Derek said slowly, "I hadn't considered any of that, but I suppose it is worth noting."

"As you've become quite fond of her." Val paused. "No, that's not entirely accurate. I've become quite fond of her, oddly enough. You like her."

"She's easy to like."

"No, she's not." Val snorted. "Although I will say she seems to have loosened, if you will, during her stay here. She is not stretched as taut as she first was."

"I believe her stay in Paris has been something of a revelation for her."

"Paris will do that." He shrugged. "Or perhaps it's your influence."

"Possible, I suppose. We are entirely different creatures." And yet he was hard-pressed to imagine his life continuing without her.

"You're afraid you'll lose her if you tell her about her cousin, aren't you?"

"That's shockingly perceptive of you."

"It's the desk." Val grinned, then sobered. "I've never known you to be a coward."

"I've never had so much at stake before."

Val stared. "I'm right then. You do have feelings for her."

"So it would appear." He shrugged in a helpless manner. "I want to protect her, Val, and I'm not sure I can. Not from this."

"Regardless, if you care for her, it's even more important that you tell her what you've discovered. If you don't, it will be that much worse when she finds out."

"Worse?" Derek said sharply. "How could it possibly be worse than discovering her only family, the woman who has been as much a mother to her as a cousin, the woman who gave her a home when she needed one, has concocted an elaborate scheme to deceive her?"

"Because as hard as that will be for her to learn—" Val met his brother's gaze "—she will never forgive you for knowing and not telling her."

For a long moment the brothers stared in silence.

"You're right. I hate to say it, but you're right. However…" Derek thought for a moment. "I believe it's best not to tell her any of this until I know where Lady Heloise is. Right now, regardless of how much we've learned, there are still more questions than answers. For her to know Lady Heloise concocted all this but not to know where she is will only increase India's concern. She's likely to think all sorts of dire things."

"Admittedly, it might be wiser to wait." Val grimaced. "Or it could be an unforgivable mistake. I still think you need to tell her everything you've found thus far."

"If you were in my shoes, would you?"

"It's the wisest course but…" Val shook his head. "I don't know. I am eternally grateful I am not in your shoes."

"The ball is the day after tomorrow," Derek said. "Mother says India has never been to a ball."

Val's brow rose. "What, never?"

"Apparently not. I would hate to ruin it for her. And by then we might have Lady Heloise's location, as well." He drew a deep breath. "But regardless, I'll tell her after the ball."

Val drummed his fingers thoughtfully on the desk. "What kind of woman has never been to a ball?"

"The kind who never had a season, who never came out in society. The kind who feels it's her responsibility to earn her own way, who believes things like balls and social events to be frivolous and silly." Derek's jaw tightened. "The kind who believes the woman who raised her has a limited income."

"Lady Heloise?"

Derek nodded. "According to my information, she has a substantial fortune that India is unaware of."

Val stared at his brother. "Lady Heloise appears to have a lot of secrets."

"And I am not going to be the one to reveal those secrets." Learning Lady Heloise not only deceived her

about her alleged travels but that she had lied to India
her entire life might well devastate her. India did not
trust easily, and Derek did not want to be the one to
shatter the trust she had in her guardian. "But I'm afraid
you're right. If she learns any of this and then finds out
I knew and didn't tell her…"

"Nasty bit of business, Derek." Sympathy shone in
Val's eyes. "She may never forgive you if you tell her—
blame the messenger and all. And she may never forgive you if you don't."

ENOUGH WAS ENOUGH. In spite of the sense of looming
disaster, Derek joined the rest of the house for dinner.
India made an appearance, as well, and he could not
help but wonder—or perhaps hope—that she missed
him as much as he missed her. Still, she made no effort
to speak with him privately nor did he. Apparently he
truly was a coward when it came to her.

Dinner had the feel of a party to it. Mother played
her accustomed role of perfect hostess to the hilt, encouraging and directing conversation around the table.
Much of the talk had to do with preparations for the
upcoming ball, and Mother made certain the Greers
and India understood how delighted she was that they
would be in attendance. Derek wasn't sure if that was
as much for the older couple's benefit as for India's.
And when his mother wasn't steering the discussion,
his stepfather was. Westvale had a heretofore unknown
interest in medieval architecture and had apparently
read one of the professor's books. His stepfather also
had the unexpected ability to make such an obscure
topic interesting for those who were not as well versed
in it as Professor Greer. Val took it upon himself to
flirt enthusiastically with Estelle and attempted to do

so with India, as well. Estelle delighted in his attention, and even India seemed amused. In spite of his best intentions, Derek spent most of the meal studying her.

India was still wearing one of the dresses Estelle had loaned her—Mother had mentioned India's new clothes were to be delivered in the next few days, thanks to her influence and the added incentive of his stepfather's fortune. Derek realized his brother was right about India. She was more at ease than she had been when they'd first started out on the quest to find Lady Heloise. Would that vanish when she knew the truth? He still had two more days until he would be forced to find out.

Through the course of the meal, every now and then when Derek's gaze returned to India, she would be watching him. Her expression gave no indication of what she was thinking but her gaze would meet his with a sort of bemused acknowledgment. And what was surely a promise, although admittedly that might have only been in his head.

If this was the woman he wanted, and with every passing day, any doubt about that faded, then he needed to do something. Something romantic and irresistible. And he needed to do it before he told her about her cousin. If he didn't want to lose her, in the next two days, he would have to win her heart. And offer her his. A grand romantic gesture was obviously called for.

By the time dinner had ended Derek had acknowledged what he had already suspected. For good or ill, he had fallen in love with the indomitable Miss India Prendergast.

And he had the power to ruin her life.

CHAPTER TWENTY-ONE

This guide would be remiss if it failed to mention the necessary yet distasteful topic of money. As there is no certain method to safeguard one's traveling funds against thieves, highwaymen, gypsies, scoundrels and one's own incompetence, we shall not attempt to provide one. Our apologies.
—The Lady Travelers Society Guide

"GOOD DAY, INDIA," Derek said, stepping out from behind the grouping of potted palms that flanked each side of the closed ballroom doors.

"Derek!" India pulled up short, her breath caught in her throat. "I didn't see you."

"I was trying to find a button that popped off my coat and rolled away under the foliage." He chuckled. "Although I suppose I could have been hiding."

She raised a brow. "From me?"

"I would hate to scare you away."

"Nonsense. I see nothing to be scared about. Not really." Although she had been something of a coward. She needed to apologize and perhaps confess or whatever else might be necessary to set things right with Derek. Last night was the first time she'd seen him for more than a moment since their altercation at the Eiffel Tower. Thanks to Lady Westvale, India had had barely any time in the last few days to dwell on what had passed between them. Still, their quarrel, as well as the kisses they'd shared, refused to be banished from her mind, especially late at night when sleep eluded her. And when she did sleep, her slumber was filled with dreams of flying like a bird over the city of Paris, or the feel of his lips pressing against hers and the distinct longing for more, or the hurt in his blue eyes.

She never should have told him she didn't trust him. Her heart twisted every time she remembered the look on his face. If she believed in him—and she did—surely she trusted him, as well. Pity, she hadn't realized that sooner. At least she now knew she was wrong. Now she wondered what else she was wrong about. "Although I suspect matters like this are always difficult."

"Matters like this?"

"I have been the worst sort of coward, Derek." She straightened her shoulders and met his gaze firmly, ignoring the way her heart beat faster in her chest. "It has always been difficult for me to admit when I'm wrong—"

"As you are never wrong."

"Apparently, in that, too, I'm wrong. It is something of a revelation." She wasn't exactly sure what to say next even though she'd rehearsed this over and over. "Paris seems to be fraught with all sorts of revelations for me."

"Being in unfamiliar surroundings can have that effect on people."

"Quite possible I suppose."

"I must say you look lovely today." His gaze skimmed over her in an approving manner. "This new way of wearing your hair is most becoming."

"How kind of you to say." Suzette continued to do her hair in a softer style that framed her face. India had to admit she rather liked it.

"Is that one of the new dresses?"

"It is."

He grinned. "My mother has excellent taste."

"And I am delighted to be the beneficiary of it." India glanced down at the new dress and smiled with satisfaction. "It arrived this morning."

She couldn't remember ever having a dress that was as lovely as it was practical. The new day dress was a fetching salmon color, with a draped overskirt and a touch of lace at the neck, wrists and waist. It was far and away the frilliest thing she'd ever owned but not nearly as fussy as Estelle's gowns. India still found it hard to believe, but Estelle was right. There was nothing like a new dress to make you feel, well, new. And not the least bit ordinary.

India had been assisting Lady Westvale with preparations for the ball all morning. Preparations that had come to an abrupt halt the moment several of India's new dresses were delivered. Derek's mother had insisted India try each one on before they did anything else. The older woman had been very much like a child with a new toy at Christmas. India wasn't at all sure how she felt about being a new toy, but she'd been nearly as excited as her ladyship.

As much as she had tried to rein in Lady Westvale's enthusiastic assault on the dressmakers of Paris, even India was no match for the older lady's resolve. The more India had protested, the more determined Lady Westvale became until India finally realized the only way to curb the lady's excesses was to capitulate. Still, the end result was four day dresses, three dresses suitable for evening, two dresses for traveling and a ball gown. None of which, her ladyship had insisted, would do by themselves, and the appropriate shoes, hats, gloves and everything else Lady Westvale deemed necessary was ordered or purchased. And all, India suspected, at exorbitant prices as Lady Westvale wanted everything as quickly as possible. India could never repay her, not merely for her expenditures but for her kindness.

"But I'm afraid your mother was entirely too generous. I can't even imagine the total expenditure." India shook her head. "I can never repay her."

"Nor does she wish to be repaid," Derek said firmly. "She has had a great deal of fun, and I am grateful to you for giving that to her. And grateful as well that you have kept her occupied." He lowered his voice in a confidential manner. "There is nothing more dangerous than my mother with time on her hands."

"I can imagine," India murmured.

The past three days with his mother had confirmed that India was right about the kind of man Derek truly was. Certainly one should take what a man's mother said about him with a grain of salt, but Lady Westvale was far too clever to simply detail Derek's good points. Instead she regaled India with stories about Derek and Lord Brookings's boyhood. Stories about the time Derek had talked his brother into giving him his collection of foreign coins to add to his own savings so the boys could purchase a horse that was being mistreated. The horse had been old and had died some months later, but both boys learned that the reward of helping those who cannot help themselves was as much for those who give as those who receive. Or the time he had been forced against his will to ask a less-than-pretty wallflower to dance, only to discover she was quite nice and very sweet when one looked past her plain appearance. That, too, was a lesson that things aren't always as they appear that Lady Westvale said her sons had never forgotten.

India wasn't sure how it happened, but she found herself telling Derek's mother things she had never told anyone. During one of her dress fittings, Lady Westvale was curious as to why India thought herself ordinary in appearance. Without thinking, India told her that during her school years, there was a young man who would come to escort his sister home for holidays. While India had thought it her secret, apparently some of the other girls noticed that India had a crush on the young gentleman, and she overheard them say the youthful Lord So-and-So would never give someone as ordinary as India Prendergast so much as a second look. Why, she'd be lucky ever to find a husband. Odd, that until Lady Westvale had asked, India would have said she didn't remember the incident at all. The older lady had pointed out, whether India recognized it or not, she was no longer ordinary but rather striking in appearance with her green eyes and ripe figure and, of course, well-fitting, stylish clothing. Lady Westvale had also noted that, while she herself had been considered a beauty in her youth, when she was a young girl, she was more than a little plump. Some of us, she'd said to India, blossom at our own pace.

When they had stopped at a charming café—but then Lady Westvale had declared nearly all the cafés in Paris to be charming—for tea and she had again brought up her desire for her sons to find love, India had mentioned in an offhand manner that she was not especially enamored of love and considered romance a silly notion. She'd also confessed that her parents' union had been considered a love match, a great romance that had ultimately led them to abandon home and family to wander the world together in search of adventure, in the guise of spreading the word of God. The older woman agreed that abandoning one's responsibilities to a child was selfish and unforgivable but that could not be blamed on love. The fault she'd said, quoting Shakespeare—apparently it ran in the family—is not in our stars but in ourselves, and added that the very best thing about love was that it knows no bounds but is open and endless. Indeed, when one has opened one's heart to one person it's easy to love others, as well. Before India could respond, Lady Westvale had gone on to another topic, but her words lingered in India's head.

"What were you wrong about this time, India?" Derek asked abruptly.

"You," she said without thinking, then plunged ahead. "Or rather me. When I said I didn't trust you—" she shook her head "—I shouldn't have said it as it isn't true."

"It isn't?" Caution sounded in his voice.

"I didn't realize it at the time but..." She met his gaze directly. "If I believe that you, at heart, are a good, decent man, if I have faith that you can indeed reform, and be a better man, the man I think you want to be, then, whether I wish to acknowledge it or not, I do trust you." She drew a steadying breath. "I am truly sorry that I did not say so when I should have."

He stared at her. "I see."

"And I am indeed a coward, not only because I refuse to face that I am—or have been of late—frequently wrong..." *In for a penny*, she supposed. She braced herself. "But because I like you, Derek Saunders. I like you a great deal, and I find it somewhat terrifying."

"I—"

She held out her hand to stop him. "I didn't expect to

like you at all. Nor did I ever expect to trust you even the tiniest bit." The words seemed to come of their own accord. "And I liked kissing you. But as much as I liked kissing you, I liked you kissing me more. While I would prefer to think that the enjoyment of it had more to do with who you were kissing than the fact that you no doubt have had a great deal of practice—"

"I can assure you—"

"I would not be averse to you kissing me again." She raised her chin. "Frequently and with a great deal of enthusiasm." She ignored the heat washing up her face. How could she have said that? What was she thinking?

"I see," he said thoughtfully.

"Goodness, Derek." She huffed. "You cannot continue to respond with 'I see.' That's a most unsatisfactory answer. It says nothing at all. What exactly do you see?"

"I see that what you are trying to say is more or less in the way of an apology."

"It is an apology, I thought that was apparent. And quite sincere, too, I might add."

"As well as a confession."

"Yes, well, perhaps," she said weakly.

"There is no perhaps about it." He stepped closer and stared down at her. "You said you liked kissing me, you liked my kissing you and you would not be disinclined to do so again. I'm fairly certain that's a confession."

"Very well then." She raised a shoulder in a casual shrug. "It's a confession."

"I see." He grinned. He was close enough to kiss her again if he was so inclined.

"And what do you see this time?" Her pulse pounded in her ears.

"I see a lovely woman who is clever and stubborn and perhaps the most annoying creature I have ever met."

"Oh?"

"I have a confession to make, as well. I said kissing you was a mistake. The mistake was in the time and place." He lowered his head, his lips close to hers. "Not in the kiss itself."

"Then do you intend to kiss me again?" She held her breath.

"I do."

"Now?" The word was little more than an odd sort of squeak.

"No." He straightened.

Her heart plummeted. "I see."

He laughed. "You're right. 'I see' is not a good response."

"Well, I don't know how else to respond," she said sharply, ignoring the overwhelming sense of disappointment and dismay that rushed through her. "I was quite clear about my feelings regarding our previous kissing and my willingness to do so again and you said—"

"Good God, India, shut up." He pulled her into his arms and pressed his lips to hers in a kiss hard and fast and utterly intoxicating. Far too quickly he released her and shook his head. "You drive me stark, raving mad."

"Do I?" She struggled to catch her breath. "Good."

"Furthermore, the next time I kiss you—" his eyes narrowed "—and make no mistake, I fully intend to kiss you again, it will be at a place and time of my choosing. It will not be in a public place, it will not be for luck and it will not be simply to stop your incessant arguing!"

"Excellent." She glared at him, but it was extraordinarily difficult to maintain her indignation when all she wanted to do was throw herself back into his arms. "I shall expect nothing less."

"Then we are agreed!" He blew a long breath. "You

are unlike any woman I have ever met, India Prendergast. You are the most confusing, annoying—"

"You've already mentioned annoying."

"It bears repeating." He shook his head. "Nonetheless, I can think of nothing but you."

She stared at him for a long moment, then cast him a brilliant smile. "How truly delightful."

"I'm glad you think so."

"You should know I find you extremely annoying, as well."

"Then we are well suited." A slow smile spread across his face. "Now, I believe you were to meet my mother in the ballroom."

"She wanted to arrange the urns I think."

"Very well then." He opened the ballroom doors and ushered her inside.

The doors were at the top of a short flight of eight or so steps allowing one to see the entire ballroom at a glance upon entering. Huge vases and urns were clustered around the perimeter awaiting the flowers that were to be delivered later today. The room itself was paneled in shades of white adorned with plaster swags and intricate molding. Crystal sconces matched a huge chandelier hanging from a ceiling painted with scenes of the heavens. White marble columns defined galleries along two walls. A balcony hung over the far end, above a series of glass-paned doors leading into the gardens. Every architectural detail was accented and highlighted with gilt. It was so decidedly *French* and every bit as grand as the very nicest Grand Hotels they'd seen.

"Ahem."

India's attention jerked toward the sound of a throat being cleared. Lord Westvale, Lord Brookings and Professor Greer stood at the bottom of the steps, off to one side. Derek's mother was nowhere in sight.

India's gaze shifted from the three gentlemen to Derek, who grinned in a satisfied manner.

"Dare I ask what this is about?" she said cautiously.

"My mother told me you had never been to a ball."

"The opportunity has never presented itself." Nor had she ever particularly wished to attend a ball.

"But you do know how to dance?"

"Of course. Miss Bicklesham's has excellent instructors." If she recalled correctly, she had excelled at dancing. Although, admittedly, she'd never danced with a male partner before.

"No doubt. However, as it has been some time, I thought you might wish for a bit of practice before tomorrow night," he said in an offhand manner as if this was of no importance at all. But it was. "My stepfather, my brother and the professor have offered to provide you with partners."

Lord Westvale stepped forward. "I believe the first dance is mine, Miss Prendergast."

"Well?" An uncertain smile played on Derek's lips.

"You arranged this," she said slowly.

He nodded. "I did."

Somehow the man knew she would be apprehensive about attending a ball, about being in a situation she'd never been in before. She would be ill at ease and out of place. And he did what he could to make it easier for her. It was the nicest thing anyone had ever done for her.

She leaned close to him and spoke softly into his ear. "You can be shockingly thoughtful, Mr. Saunders."

"Do try to keep that in mind, Miss Prendergast," he said quietly. She could hear the smile in his voice.

She straightened, then moved down the steps to greet Lord Westvale.

He offered his arm and escorted her toward the center of the floor. Derek waved in the direction of the balcony, and a moment later, the strains of a sedate waltz played on a violin drifted over the room.

Surprise caught her breath. "Derek arranged for music?"

"Derek arranged for everything, my dear." The marquess took her right hand in his left and placed his other hand lightly on the small of her back. She rested her free hand on his arm below his shoulder. "Ready?"

"I am." She forced a light laugh. "I do so love to waltz," she lied.

God bless him, his lordship was as thoughtful as his stepson. He steered her around the floor with a gentle hand, guiding and directing her steps. He didn't so much as wince when she stepped on his toes, and he smoothly saved her from falling when she stumbled over her own.

"Did you enjoy your shopping excursion with my wife?" his lordship asked pleasantly after she had begun to feel at ease enough to move with the music rather than against it.

"I've never experienced anything quite like it, my lord."

He chuckled. "Celia considers shopping something of a cross between art and sport."

"She may well be the nicest woman I have ever met."

"She speaks highly of you, as well." He steered her through a simple turn, and she followed with scarcely any effort at all. "She also said you are concerned about her expenditures. You needn't be. My wife knows the value of the patronage of the Marchioness of Westvale to the merchants she deals with as do they. I am always rather astonished when her bills come in to find they are far less than I would have expected."

"That is something of a relief."

"It scarcely matters really. My fortune is more than sufficient. I inherited great wealth, and assorted business enterprises have enabled me to increase it. My father would be shocked, of course, to know that I have dabbled in business, but the world has changed since his day." He paused. "Derek has been assisting his uncle in recent months with the earl's business pursuits, management of his properties and that sort of thing. I hear he's doing more than satisfactory. Derek's inheritance will be quite significant."

"So I have heard."

"I understand from my wife that Derek's financial future is of no particular concern to you."

"Her ladyship is wrong, my lord." Fortune aside, she was not right for Derek, and she did not wish to explain that yet again. Although perhaps in that, too, she was wrong. "I want nothing more than for Derek to receive exactly what he deserves."

He studied her. "Are we still speaking of his inheritance?"

"I can't imagine what else we would be talking about." She shrugged and promptly tripped.

His lordship managed to keep her upright with barely noticeable effort. "I have always thought it beneficial to be able to talk while I dance but perhaps until you are more…"

"Accomplished?"

He smiled. "I was going to say confident. At any rate, perhaps we should forgo conversation and concentrate on the steps for now."

"I think that is indeed a good idea." She smiled up at him and tried to concentrate on her feet and the music even though the more she danced, the less she had to think about it.

Every now and then she would catch sight of Derek with the other men, and her heart would do the oddest things. The effort he'd gone to was most impressive and rather touching. There was far more to the man than she had ever imagined.

What did Derek deserve? The more she'd grown to know him, the more her opinions had changed. She no longer wanted to see him thrown in prison. And, as he would make right the fraudulent nature of the Lady Travelers Society, that was no longer necessary.

The music drew to a close. Lord Westvale released her and stepped back. "Excellent effort, Miss Prendergast. Why, a few more turns around the floor and no one will ever suspect you don't dance every night."

"Thank you, my lord," she said with a grateful smile.

"If I might give you one piece of advice." He leaned close and lowered his voice. "You have a rather strong tendency to try to lead. Most partners are not fond of having to battle for control at every step."

She winced. "I shall keep that in mind."

He flashed her an encouraging smile, then nodded at the professor waiting to take his place.

"I quite enjoy dancing, India, but I fear I am not as fine a dancer as his lordship," the professor said, assuming the correct position.

"I can't imagine such a thing."

The music began, another waltz, this one a bit more sprightly, and they started off. With every note, more and more of what she'd been taught came back to her. Why, this was actually enjoyable. A realization helped by the fact that Professor Greer's skill on the dance floor was more comparable to India's than to Derek's stepfather. But what he lacked in proficiency, he made up for in enthusiasm.

The professor cleared his throat. "I am most impressed by the effort Derek went to on your behalf today."

"As am I." India shook her head. "It was very kind of him."

"I am well aware that you are not overly fond of him."

"On the contrary, Professor. We have forged a firm friendship."

"I see." The professor paused to lead her through a turn. "I have grown quite fond of Derek, as has Estelle. He flirts outrageously with her, you know."

"Yes, sir, I have noticed that."

"She quite enjoys it."

"I have noticed that, as well." She drew her brows together. "You don't find it bothersome?"

"Why should I?"

"You just said it was outrageous."

"Precisely why she adores it." He chuckled. "I have no concerns as to my wife's fealty or affections, India. As you are still young, I doubt you will be able to understand this, but when Derek flirts with Estelle, she feels her youth again. There is nothing like the attentions of a dashing, handsome young man to make a woman remember when that was a common occurrence. He understands that, as well. And I am the, oh, how to phrase this delicately, beneficiary, if you will, of her remembrances."

India summoned an awkward smile.

"I do hope I haven't shocked you."

"No, of course not." She swallowed hard. "Not at all."

"One doesn't spend a lifetime molding the minds of young men without learning a thing or two about them in the process. I consider myself an excellent judge of character. Derek is a good man, India."

"You're certain of that, are you?" She adopted a teasing tone.

"As certain as experience allows. But I assure you, I cannot recall being in error in my assessment of a man's nature." The music faded, and the professor guided her to a halt with a bit of an unexpected flourish. "Even the finest among us makes mistakes, India. Through errors in judgment or even good intentions. You would be wise to remember that."

"Thank you, Professor, I shall."

"I believe it is my turn." Lord Brookings's voice sounded behind her.

"India." The professor took her hand and raised it to his lips. "This has been my pleasure. And I fully intend to claim at least one dance tomorrow night." He placed her hand in Lord Brookings's, nodded a bow and walked away.

"I should warn you, Miss Prendergast." A wicked twinkle shone in Lord Brookings's eyes. He placed his free hand firmly on her back, glanced in Derek's direction and the music began. "You have saved the best for last."

"Have I, my lord?"

"Apparently, I shall have to prove it to you. Although, I must say, for a woman who has never been to a ball, you are doing far better than I expected."

"I was well taught," she said in a prim manner, then smiled. "But I will admit, I have had little opportunity to dance since I learned at Miss Bicklesham's. I thought I'd forgotten everything. I find it reassuring how quickly it has all come back to me."

"You may be one of those people to whom it comes easily."

"Then I am grateful for that. I would hate to be an embarrassment." She paused. "I must say, I'd forgotten as well how much I liked dancing."

"Then you should do it more often," he said firmly. "Life is entirely too short not to indulge in those things that bring pleasure. And dancing is perhaps the most innocent among those."

"I would never be so bold or so foolish as to ask what else brings you pleasure, my lord."

"Why, Miss Prendergast." He stared down at her. "I do believe you are flirting with me."

"On the contrary, Lord Brookings—"

His brow shot upward.

"Percy." She laughed. "I have never flirted in my entire life."

"It appears, under the appropriate circumstances, that comes easily to you, as well." He led her through a quick turn and she followed him with relative ease. "Excellent, Miss Prendergast. You are doing extremely well."

"I am quite enjoying it."

"Derek thought you might." His tone was matter-of-fact. "My brother went to a great deal of trouble to arrange this for you."

"It was extremely thoughtful of him."

"He can be quite thoughtful, even when one least expects it. He always has been," he added in an offhand manner. "Although I can't imagine he would have done all this for anyone else."

"Only me?" she said lightly.

"Only you." His gaze met hers, and she nearly stumbled at the honesty in his eyes.

At once the truth hit her. These men weren't merely helping her dance; they were laying out a case in Derek's favor. Regaling her with his good points. It was a concerted effort to—what? Win her over? The idea that Derek had asked these men to not only dance with her but make mention of his virtues was an outrage, and she should be furious. But the fact that he had gone to all this trouble so that she might see him in a better light was most endearing. How could she possibly be annoyed with him for that?

"The lady who captures his heart will be a lucky creature indeed." Sincerity colored his words. "No woman could ever do better. He will spend the rest of his life making her happy.

She stared up at him. "I have no idea what to say to that."

"Say nothing, Miss Prendergast." He smiled and executed a quick spin. "Simply remember it."

The tempo of the music increased and the rest of the dance was spent in a thoughtful silence. At least on India's part. His lordship was no doubt letting her dwell on his comment, beast of a man that he was.

"Miss Prendergast, I look forward to our next dance," he said when the music had ended. "Now, unfortunately, I must relinquish you to my brother." Derek stepped up beside him. Lord Brookings cast him a pitying look. "Not as accomplished a dancer, not as handsome or as clever but not totally objectionable."

"Ah, brother." Derek shook his head in a mournful manner. "The fictional world you live in must be a strange and lonely place."

"Strange perhaps." A knowing grin curved his lips.

"But never lonely." He nodded, turned and strode across the floor.

"Miss Prendergast," Derek began, "may I have the honor of this dance?"

"I'm not sure another dance is necessary, Mr. Saunders." She furrowed her brow thoughtfully. "I feel quite confident now, and your mother will be wondering where I have disappeared to."

"My mother will be wondering no such thing, and another dance is always necessary." He signaled to the violinist, and the music started once again.

"Still…" She shook her head even as she moved into his arms. "I don't know…"

"Trust me, Miss Prendergast." He gazed down at her, held her a bit more tightly than was proper and moved to the music.

"I do, Mr. Saunders." Her throat tightened. "I do."

He smiled, his eyes shining with something unknown, something extraordinary. Shivers raced up her spine. "Then you feel more comfortable, about the ball, that is?"

"Yes, I believe I do. Thank you."

"It was my pleasure."

They moved together effortlessly, and she suspected he was making accommodations for her because they couldn't possibly dance this well together. As if their feet were barely touching the floor.

"It was most kind of their lordships and the professor to take the time to assist me." She studied him curiously. "Are you aware that each and every one also took the opportunity to extol your virtues?"

"No!" He gasped. "Did they?"

"Unceasingly."

He grinned.

"Your stepfather spoke of your expectations and your interest in business, your brother pointed out the thoughtfulness of your nature and the professor commented on your flirtation with his wife."

"Oh?" Caution sounded in Derek's voice.

"He's quite appreciative of it."

"Excellent," he said with relief. "I should mention, in the spirit of honesty, I did suggest that if they wished to mention a few of my more noble qualities to you, I would not object."

"They served you well."

"Friends and family do that for you."

The oddest pang shot through her. She glanced at the room flashing by and noticed they were now alone. "They seem to have taken their leave. Part of your plan?"

"It's a very good plan," he said firmly. "Although I do find it interesting that what I consider my best qualities were not the ones they chose."

"I suppose we rarely see ourselves as others do." Still, hadn't she been seeing herself through the eyes of others since this all began? "It can be quite startling."

"Particularly if one thinks one is always right."

"Yes, well, that does make it more difficult." She smiled wryly. "Aside from extolling your virtues and the practicality of refreshing my dance skills, this is all part and parcel of a romantic endeavor on your part, isn't it?"

He glanced around in surprise. "By God, it is!" He shook his head. "I had no idea."

She laughed.

He stared at her, a bemused smile on his lips. "When we first met you never smiled at me at all. Let alone laughed."

She stared in surprise. "What utter nonsense, of course I smiled."

"You did not. Or at least, not a genuine smile. I wasn't sure you knew how." He led her through a more complicated set of steps than she had attempted thus far, and she scarcely noticed.

"How dreadful of me."

"Not really. We did not get off on the best foot, if you recall. Eventually I realized I would have to earn your smile."

"And I believe you have," she said lightly.

"Have I really?" His gaze searched hers. "Because when you smile at me it feels as if I've been given a gift." His arms tightened around her. "A gift I am hard-pressed to live without."

"Then I shall have to give it to you more often." The music drew to a close, and they came to a halt. But his arms stayed around her, and she made no effort to move.

"I should warn you. I am claiming the first dance tomorrow and the last."

"How very forward of you," she teased.

"I know." He grinned. "You like it."

"Perhaps. Derek." She summoned her courage. "I was wrong about something else."

Once again he gasped in an exaggerated fashion. "Not you!"

"About the type of woman you are supposed to marry. I see now I might possibly…" She hesitated. There would be no going back.

"Yes?"

"I might have been mistaken." She smiled up at him.

"Might have been?" He grinned and pulled her closer. "Say it, India."

"Very well." She couldn't help but laugh. What

Derek had done for her, all this was just so wonderfully…perfect. "I may have been, possibly—"

His brow arched.

"Probably…" She sighed. "I was wrong. Without question, undoubtedly, undeniably wrong."

"Why, Miss Prendergast." He lowered his head down, and she raised her lips to meet his. "You say the most alluring things."

"Miss Prendergast!" An outraged voice sounded from across the room. "What is the meaning of this?"

CHAPTER TWENTY-TWO

"I BEG YOUR PARDON." Derek stepped forward. Who in the hell was this? "I don't know who you are but—"

"Derek." India placed her hand on his arm to stop him, her gaze locked on the newcomer. Shock shone on her face. "Allow me to introduce Sir Martin Luckthorne." She drew a deep breath. "My employer."

"And friend." Luckthorne stepped closer. "Your very close friend."

This is Sir Martin? Surely not. According to Derek's information Sir Martin was in his forties, scholarly and considered somewhat eccentric. This man looked far younger than his years, appeared to be in excellent condition judging by the breadth of his shoulders, had an air of solid determination about him and was not what one would call unattractive. This was India's employer for the past eight years without so much as a hint of impropriety? What was wrong with the man?

"I must say, India." Luckthorne frowned. "I did not expect this."

"And I did not expect you." India shook her head, still obviously stunned by the new arrival. "What are you doing here?" She narrowed her eyes. "And what did you not expect?"

"I did not expect to see you standing in some man's arms—"

"Or Derek Saunders, if you will, rather than *some*

man," Derek said. "Although I suppose I might have been called *some man* on occasion."

"*The* Derek Saunders?" Luckthorne stared.

She stepped toward him. "Martin—"

"The rogue? The scoundrel? The mastermind behind the plot to defraud hapless women out of their savings?" Luckthorne's indignation rang in the ballroom.

A bit overdone really.

"Did you call me a mastermind?" Derek said in an aside to India.

"Yes." She grimaced. "But that scarcely matters at the moment."

"And yet I am rather flattered." He chuckled.

"Flattered?" Luckthorne sputtered.

"Come now, Sir Martin," Derek said coolly. "The word *mastermind* denotes both power and intelligence. Why would I not be flattered?"

"You forget scoundrel, as well!"

"I chose to ignore it. And rogue." He shrugged. "Not the least bit complimentary. I much prefer mastermind. What say you, India? Is it scoundrel or mastermind?"

"Regardless, it—*you*—are most annoying, and this is beside the point," she said sharply and directed her attention back to her employer. "Once again, what are you doing here?"

"I assumed, as you did not telegraph as per our agreement, that something had gone horribly wrong and you needed my help." He squared his shoulders. "You needed rescue."

India stared. "From what?"

"A mastermind perhaps?" Derek said in an overly innocent manner.

"I can now see I may have been mistaken." Luckthorne shot Derek a scathing glare.

"In my last telegram I distinctly told you I would not send additional telegrams."

"You said—" He pulled a telegram from his waistcoat pocket. "'Search progressing. All is well. No further telegrams necessary. Prendergast.' What was I supposed to think?"

"You were supposed to think the search was progressing, everything was fine and there was no need for continued telegrams!" She glared. "I really don't understand why you didn't."

"Perhaps because this—" he waved the telegram at her "—was vague and ambiguous and—"

"I only had ten words! I believe I did quite well under the circumstances."

"It sounded rather clear to me," Derek said under his breath.

"It sounded like someone who was being held against her will!"

"Against my will?" She scoffed. "That's the most absurd thing I have ever heard. You of all people should know I would never allow anyone to hold me against my will."

"She has you there," Derek murmured.

"You gave me your word that you would send a telegram every three days—"

Derek snorted in derision.

"And I have never known you to go back on your word." Luckthorne shook his head. "So naturally, I assumed the worst. You are the most responsible person I know."

"The tide has apparently turned there." Even so... Derek frowned. "Why didn't you continue to telegraph him?"

She hesitated. "I needed the money he gave me for the telegrams."

"Why?" Luckthorne's brows drew together. "You assured me before you left that you had more than enough to see you through for several months."

"Yes, indeed, India." Derek narrowed his gaze. "I, too, thought you had suitable funding."

"I did." Her gaze shifted between Derek and her employer; then she rolled her eyes toward the ceiling and heaved a resigned sigh. "But I lost it."

"Lost it? You?" Luckthorne stared in confusion. "I find that hard to believe." He slanted a suspicious look at Derek. "Are you certain it wasn't stolen?"

Bloody hell. Was Luckthorne charging him with stealing India's money? *Good.* No one could possibly blame him now for taking the man outside and thrashing him thoroughly. He adopted a cold smile. He intended to enjoy this. "Are you implying that I stole Miss Prendergast's money?"

"Don't be absurd," India said quickly. "You're not. Are you, Martin?"

Luckthorne hesitated, studying Derek warily. No doubt considering whether he stood a chance in a physical confrontation. "No, of course not," the coward said at last. "But you should have telegraphed me, India. I would have sent you whatever you needed."

"Why didn't you tell *me*?" Derek stared at her. She was obviously loath to continue. He'd never seen her so hesitant before. "How did you lose your money?"

"I didn't want to telegraph you," she said to Luckthorne, "because I was embarrassed, and I didn't want to ask for your help. It might have been foolish, but there it is." She turned to Derek. "I didn't want to tell you because I didn't want you to think I was an idiot."

"You are perhaps the most intelligent woman I have ever met," Derek said.

"As much as I hate to shatter that illusion…" She met his gaze and cringed. "I hid most of my money in my trunk."

Good God. Luckthorne's suspicions weren't entirely wrong. "The trunk that went astray?"

She nodded.

"Oh, well…" Any vague thought he might have had about confessing his role in her missing trunk at some point in the far distant future vanished. "That is awkward."

"At the very least." She shook her head. "I thought it would be safer than carrying it all with me."

"Oh, I'm sure it's safe." Derek tried and failed to adopt a confident tone. No, this was a secret he would have to take to his grave. "Wherever it is."

"You do understand how humiliating I find this."

Genuine guilt ripped through him.

"In hindsight it seems so stupid."

"Mistakes like this are bound to happen when one is not an experienced traveler," Derek said in as supportive a tone as he could manage. "Your trunk could have easily arrived exactly where it was supposed to be. It was a stroke of bad luck that it didn't."

"Regardless, this is no longer of any consequence," Luckthorne said firmly. "I am here now, and I intend to return with you immediately to London."

"You what?" India's voice rose and her eyes widened.

"It's obviously past time. Why, I scarcely recognized you." He glared at her. "What have you done to yourself?"

Her hand flew to her hair. "I am doing my hair a bit differently."

"And your dress!"

"I quite like it, Martin." A hard tone colored her words.

It was difficult not to wince. Derek almost pitied the man as he was clearly not as intelligent as Derek had heard. Only a fool would fail to recognize that note in India's voice.

"It's not at all like you. Why…" Luckthorne waved at her dress as if to brush it away. "It isn't even gray!"

"She looks lovely," Derek said mildly.

"I am well aware of that," Luckthorne snapped.

"And are you also aware that you are my employer?" India said sharply. "*Only* my employer."

"I am indeed! Which is precisely why—"

"Sir Martin!" Mother's voice rang out over the ballroom. She swept down the stairs and headed toward them. "How delightful to see you again."

"Do you know her?" India said in a low voice to Luckthorne.

"No." He stared at the oncoming marchioness as if he were a reclusive feline and she a very exuberant lapdog. Derek had never seen anyone look quite so apprehensive at his mother's approach, well, not when she was being this charming. "At least I don't think I do. Who is she?"

"Lady Westvale," India said under her breath. "And for God's sakes, Martin, don't let on that you don't remember her as she obviously has met you."

"My dear man, I must apologize for not greeting you when you arrived." Mother beamed and sailed toward them, extending her hand. "You will be staying here with us I hope? For the ball?"

"The ball?" He took her hand and bowed awkwardly over it.

"Lord and Lady Westvale and her son Lord Brookings are hosting a ball here tomorrow night," India said.

"I had planned to stay at a hotel." Luckthorne released Mother's hand and straightened. "And return to London tomorrow."

"Oh, my dear man, that will never do." Mother shook her head. "There is a world exposition here, you know. There is not a room to be had anywhere in Paris." She cast him a triumphant smile. "You will absolutely have to stay here."

"Nonetheless, I really don't think—"

"Furthermore, I would be most distraught if you did not remain for the ball." Mother sighed in an overly dramatic manner. "There hasn't been a ball in this house for years and I would hate for dear India's friend—"

"Employer," Derek said.

"—to miss what will surely be a festive and most enjoyable evening."

"I have not been to a ball in some time," Luckthorne said uneasily.

"Then this is the perfect opportunity for you." Mother glanced at India. "Don't you agree?"

"I know I have no intention of missing it." A stubborn note sounded in India's voice. Derek had heard that tone before. Surely Luckthorne had, too.

"I am here only to offer my assistance to Miss Prendergast. And I would prefer to waste no time in returning to London."

"Goodness, Sir Martin." Mother smiled engagingly. "Stealing the time for a bit of frivolity now and again makes life much more enjoyable."

"I assure you—"

"Besides," she continued in a casual manner. "If you stay for the ball, you will have the rest of today and all day tomorrow to attend the exposition. Why, the exhibits of the latest inventions and scientific advancements alone would be well worth your time."

Derek might have known Mother would find a man's Achilles' heel and use it to her advantage. While he would have preferred she get rid of Luckthorne altogether, he wasn't entirely sure the man wouldn't manage to convince India to return with him.

"I hadn't considered that," Luckthorne said thoughtfully. "I had no intention of attending the exposition but I suppose, as I am in Paris…"

"It would be a dreadful shame if a man of your accomplishments missed this spectacle of man's progress and achievements," Mother pointed out.

"Perhaps you're right." Luckthorne nodded. "Very well then, I shall stay through tomorrow, and we shall return to London on the day after."

"Wonderful." Mother beamed and turned toward her son, a satisfied gleam in her eyes. "I suspect India would like to have a word with Sir Martin as he has come such a long way to offer his assistance."

"Thank you, Lady Westvale. Indeed, I have a great deal to say to Sir Martin." India's words were measured and controlled, but it was clear to Derek she was not the least bit happy with her employer. He resisted the urge to grin with delight.

"Derek, if you would join me?" Mother took his arm. "I need your opinion on a matter of some importance."

He glanced at India. She gave the slightest nod of her head. "Of course." He nodded at Luckthorne. "Sir Martin."

"Saunders," the man replied curtly.

Derek steered his mother toward the stairs. "What is this matter of some importance you wish my opinion on?"

"I believe the weather is quite lovely for June. What do you think?"

He stared down at her. "You wanted my opinion on the weather?"

"Goodness, Derek. I thought you were intelligent enough to understand I simply wished to give India a moment alone with Sir Martin without being overly obvious."

"Why?"

"Because she needs to straighten a few things out with him."

They started up the stairs. "You noticed that, did you?"

"Didn't you?"

"Apparently not." He was too busy noticing Luckthorne's overly possessive attitude. He should have thrashed the man when he had the chance. "You've never met him before, have you?"

"Of course not."

"Then how did you know—"

"My dear boy." She shook her head. "Do you really think I would allow you to be smitten with a woman I know nothing about?"

"Smitten?"

"You needn't deny it. I am your mother, I know these things. While India and I were refurbishing her wardrobe, Stephen made a few inquiries into her background. Naturally, Sir Martin, as her employer, was also of interest."

"Naturally."

She slanted him a sharp look. "Sometimes, I cannot tell if you're annoyed or amused."

"I'm not annoyed, Mother. I'm most appreciative." He smiled. "Although it was not necessary. I did the same thing before we left London. And I suspect India made inquiries about me, as well."

"How very clever of her." She smiled in a too-smug manner. "I have always wanted an intelligent woman for you. And for your brother, as well. Beauty is fleeting, but a clever woman will keep you on your toes for the rest of your days."

He chuckled. "You want that for me, do you?"

"Good Lord, Derek." She cast him a wry look. "You would be quite unbearable otherwise."

"WELL?" MARTIN CROSSED his arms over his chest in the manner of a parent reprimanding a child. He could not have picked a worse stance. "What do you have to say for yourself?"

"What do *I* have to say for myself?" India could scarcely get out the words. Aside from any number of times since she'd met Derek, she didn't think she'd ever been quite so furious with a man in her life.

"You are supposed to be searching for poor Lady Heloise and instead I find you in a grand mansion in the heart of Paris in the arms of a scoundrel you wished to see thrown in prison!"

"Yes, well, I might have been wrong about that," she snapped.

"*You* are never wrong! And why are you still in Paris? Shouldn't you be traveling the continent by now?"

"We have not yet exhausted our search here."

"You've been here nearly a fortnight. How difficult can it be to find one mere woman? I found you easily enough."

"Then I suggest you attempt it, Martin!" India clenched her teeth and prayed for calm. "According to the papers, approximately one hundred thousand people attend the exposition every day, a fair percentage of them English speaking. They are at every other attraction in Paris, as well, and they have filled the hotels. It is far more difficult to find a *mere* woman in a crowd of her own countrymen than it is if she appeared out of place. Do you understand?"

"I understand completely. Neither you nor that cad are the least bit equipped to find a woman lost in the streets of Paris or anywhere else." He set his jaw in a determined manner she'd never seen before. "The moment we return to London, I shall do what I should have done in the first place. I will hire someone to find Lady Heloise, and there's to be no more discussion about it!"

She stared at him. This was not the Martin she knew. Not the man she'd worked for, and with, for eight years. This was some overbearing, pompous, arrogant tyrant of a beast who thought simply because he paid her a salary he could control her entire life.

"In which case..." She squared her shoulders. "I shall be obliged to submit my letter of resignation."

For a long moment he stared in disbelief. Then he sighed in surrender. "Very well then, I won't."

"You never argue with me," she said slowly. "You chastise, you parry—on occasion you tease. We are never at odds. You never disagree with me. Indeed, you act as if you don't have a care in the world." Realization widened her eyes. "Because you haven't! Not when I'm there."

He toyed with his collar as if it were entirely too tight and refused to meet her gaze.

"That's it, isn't it? You're not as concerned about my safety or locating Heloise as you are that I'm gone and you have to fend for yourself."

"Now see here, India." An injured note sounded in

his voice. "I was worried about you. Admittedly, it has been difficult for me without you. This is the first time you've been gone for more than a day or two in eight years and I didn't like it." He sighed. "I didn't like it one bit."

"Yet another surprise."

"I was alone, left to my own devices. I couldn't think—not about anything of significance. My mind kept drifting to mundane matters, like what I should tell the cook to prepare for dinner or perhaps I should look at the morning post or what I should wear to Wednesday's lecture." He paused and pinned her with a helpless look. "I had no idea there were so many minuscule details to attend to in a day. It's exhausting, India."

"Is it?" She crossed her arms over her chest.

"Good God, yes. Worse, I was lonely. I am accustomed to having you to discuss with what I wish to discuss. You are an enormous part of my work and my life. I didn't realize how important until you were gone. And I admit, I don't like having to take care of everything, but more I don't like you not being there." He waved at her in a petulant gesture, like a small child. "And I don't like *that*!"

"What?" She frowned. "Are you referring to my appearance?"

"Yes," he said in a lofty manner. "I don't like it."

"Everyone else does. But more important—" she wasn't sure she'd actually admitted this to herself "—I like it."

"Well, I won't have it. It makes you look entirely too...too attractive."

"Is that a compliment?"

"It's an admission. I have always thought you most

attractive, quite lovely really, but you never did anything to, well, display your charms."

She choked.

"And therefore no other man seemed to see what I was well aware of. Which was most convenient." He met her gaze directly. "I did not want to lose you."

"Oh." Surprise widened her eyes. She had no idea how to respond to this admission. "Even so, Martin." She drew a steadying breath. "There was no need to follow me to another country."

"There was every need." He huffed. "These weeks without you have brought me to my senses." He clasped his hands behind his back as he often did when making some sort of pronouncement. "I believe I'm in love with you, India."

"Of course you are."

His eyes widened. "You're not surprised?"

"Why should I be? I take care of nearly everything in your life. Why wouldn't you think yourself in love with me? At least at the moment."

"Forever," he said staunchly.

"Goodness, Martin, the timing alone is questionable. If you were in love with me, I suspect you would have had some inkling before now."

"Oh, but I have." He stepped toward her eagerly. "I have had far more than an inkling."

"And yet you've said nothing."

"There was no need to say anything. Life was well organized and efficient and pleasant. I didn't have a care in the world. It wasn't until you left that I realized how much I needed you. And loved you," he added quickly.

"What you need—" she chose her words with care "—is someone to take care of you."

"Part and parcel, I believe." He studied her closely.

"You cannot tell me you do not harbor some affection for me, as well."

"I do indeed, Martin. You are my dear, dear friend. I feel for you as I imagine one might feel for a brother."

"A brother?" He frowned.

"A *cherished* brother."

"That's not what I thought you would say. I had expected or perhaps hoped, that you…" Realization dawned on his face. "It's that scoundrel, isn't it? You've fallen in love with him."

"Good Lord, Martin, now you're being…" Her breath caught. Hadn't she already suspected as much?

"I'm being what?"

"Far more perceptive than I would have thought." She shook her head. "You may be right."

"Of course, I'm right. It's not at all far-fetched that you would fall in love with the first man who—"

"That's enough, Martin," she said in a cold tone.

"I saw the way you looked at him, and that was not—"

"That is more than enough." She narrowed her eyes. "You have been my employer and, yes, my friend for eight years. If you wish either of those relationships to continue, you will not say another word."

He stared at her for a long moment. "I apologize." He sighed. "That was uncalled for. I suspect that's what jealousy does to a man. Because, you see, it should have been me."

She considered him thoughtfully. "It probably should have."

"There is, in most endeavors, an interval of time, usually finite, in which one might set forces in action to be of optimal benefit. A period of opportunity, if you will." His gaze met hers. "Has ours passed?"

"I'm afraid so." Odd to think of loving Martin with anything other than friendly affection.

"Regardless, I will warn you, India, now that I have at least realized what I want, I do not intend to give up." He considered her thoughtfully. "What do we do now?"

"Now?" She grimaced. "I have no idea."

What was there to do now? Oh, not about Martin, but now that she had accepted her feelings for Derek. Nothing had changed, not really. No matter what she'd said to Derek when they'd danced, she was no more suitable for him now than she had been when they first met. Was this what love did to you? Make you say things you didn't believe simply because you were in a man's arms.

Or did it make you believe that anything was possible, if only for the length of a dance?

Derek obviously had feelings for her. While she recognized that she had changed since they'd begun this quest for Heloise, she was not so foolish as to now believe love conquered all. Still, a man had never invaded her dreams before. Or her every waking thought. She'd never longed to be in a man's arms, or God help her, in his bed. Would it be so wrong to give into those desires? She'd never so much as considered being intimate with a man. But then she'd never had feelings like this before, either. If Paris was all they would ever have, shouldn't she seize whatever opportunity this adventure she'd stumbled into offered her? And really, was there a better place for seduction than Paris?

"You could marry me, you know," he said casually.

Her attention snapped back to Martin. "What?"

He squared his shoulders. "Marry me, India."

Surely he wasn't serious. "But I am in love with someone else."

"Someone entirely wrong for you."

"Is he?"

"Of course he is. You know that as well as I."

She was hard-pressed to deny it.

"Whereas I am perfect for you." Eagerness sounded in his voice. "You admit you have some affection for me, and I certainly care for you. I daresay any number of married couples don't have that between them. We could go on as we always have. Why, nothing needs to change at all."

"Come now, Martin—everything has changed."

"Nonsense. I refuse to accept that," he said in a firm manner. "However, I will let the matter rest for now."

"Good."

She had no desire to discuss Martin's ridiculous proposal although it would not have been quite so absurd a few weeks ago. If he'd asked her to be his wife before she'd left London, she probably would have accepted. Apparently this was something else love did to you. Once having tasted it, nothing else would suffice.

"Regarding Saunders." Martin's brow furrowed. "I hope your sensible nature and intelligence has not been dimmed by emotion."

She bristled. "I assure you it has not."

"You did not trust him when you left London."

"And now I do," she said firmly. "He has proven himself most trustworthy."

"And yet you have not found your cousin."

"No, but I am certain we will. Mr. Saunders is making every effort, but as I said, it is proving more difficult than we had hoped." She paused. "In addition, he has acknowledged his role in the Lady Travelers Society and has given me his word that he will set everything to rights." Or rather she was confident that he would, but Martin didn't need to know that.

"And you believe him?"

"Yes." She raised her chin. "I do."

"Well, as I am not in love with him, I do not. And I assure you, should I discover any proof as to his nefarious activities, I shall contact Inspector Cooper at once."

"I would expect you to do no less." She paused to find the right words. "And I think you're right—you do need a wife."

"Excellent." He beamed.

"But that will not be me." She shook her head. "We shall put finding you a suitable wife on our schedule when we return."

He considered her hopefully. "Then you will continue to be in my employ?"

"Only for as long as it takes to find my replacement."

"I see." He grimaced. "I've mucked this up terribly, haven't I?"

"I think we have both made errors in judgment."

Resignation washed across his face. "Mine in not seeing what was right in front of me."

The oddest sense of regret twisted her heart. He really was a dear man.

"At least we have a ball to look forward to." He smiled ruefully. "I haven't been to a ball in years."

"I know," she said in a brusque manner. "You think such things are silly and frivolous."

He chuckled. "Only because you think they are."

She stared at him for a long moment. "Have I really been that adamant about everything?"

"Yes. Always."

"Well, I daresay one can be efficient without being unyielding." She sighed. "I shall work on that, too."

"Too?"

"Martin." She took his arm and steered him toward

the stairs. "This trip has been a journey of revelation for me. Someday, I shall tell you all about it."

"Because we will always be friends?"

"Of course."

"You didn't say what your error in judgment was."

"Quite simply, I have never doubted that I was always right about everything, that there was no correct point of view other than my own." She heaved a resigned sigh. "I have now come to the realization that in that, I was terribly, horribly wrong."

CHAPTER TWENTY-THREE

*For the first-time lady traveler, the venture will
be filled with a number of never before experienced delights. A diary for recording sights and
impressions is highly recommended. Regardless
of age, one can never truly count on one's remembrances as one's memories fade with every
new adventure.*

—The Lady Travelers Society Guide

"Have you seen India yet?" Derek adjusted his cuffs
for perhaps the hundredth time. Where was the blasted
woman?

"One doesn't appear promptly at one's first ball."
Mother sipped a glass of champagne, her satisfied gaze
skimming over the impressively full ballroom. "One
waits to make an entrance."

Anyone of importance or anyone she deemed interesting, as well as a fair number of Her Majesty's citizens
in Paris for the exposition, had been invited. Mother had
mentioned more than once that there had been few re-
fusals to the invitation. But then who would turn down
an invitation to join the Marquess of Brookings and the
Marquess and Marchioness of Westvale?

Impatience pulled his brows together. "Did you tell
her that?"

"I might have mentioned it. Or perhaps I told Mrs.

Greer. Delightful woman and well aware of how to do things like this correctly." She paused. "Did you know that Professor Greer is escorting both his wife and India tonight?"

"I did." He smiled reluctantly. "Your doing no doubt."

"I understood Sir Martin wished to escort India, but as you had to join the rest of the family in greeting our guests, I thought it best if she accompanied the Greers. Estelle, dear woman, agreed with me."

"She doesn't like Sir Martin?"

"She feels about him as I do. He seems quite acceptable if a bit helpless, but then most men are."

"I had no idea." He chuckled.

"And my point is made." She smiled and waved at a guest. It seemed half of London society was here, as well as all the available flowers in Paris. There was scarcely a single spot in the ballroom that didn't host an urn of blossoms or an overflowing vase of blooms. Mother had certain standards when it came to her social events. "This is not a competition, you know."

"What is not a competition?" he said cautiously.

"Come now, dear—you know exactly what I'm talking about." Mother's gaze remained on the crowd. "I believe India made her choice when she refused to return to London with him. Now it's up to you."

"I see."

"I do hope so." She paused. "I assume you intend to marry her."

"That is my intention." He shook his head. "Convincing her will be another matter."

"As she has already refused to marry you once?"

"Not exactly, as I didn't actually ask her." Everyone in his family tended to overlook that particular fact. It was extremely annoying. "But she feels she is not an appropriate match for a future earl."

"And yet I like her far more than any of the appropriate matches you've paraded through our lives." She slanted him a pointed look. "As do you."

"Agreed." He nodded. "However, she is also convinced I am the mastermind—"

Mother's brow arched upward "Mastermind?"

"I know, I like it, too." He chuckled. "She is convinced I am behind the Lady Travelers Society."

"She doesn't know this was Guinevere and her friends' scheme?"

"No, she thinks I'm manipulating them."

"Goodness." Mother shuddered. "Don't ever let Guinevere know that." She hesitated. "You aren't, are you?"

"Yes, Mother." He rolled his gaze toward the ceiling. "I have been doing nothing but work for Uncle Edward for months now. However, as I am an acknowledged mastermind, I confess, in my free time, I have maneuvered three elderly women into serving as a facade for a fraudulent organization designed to steal the savings of other unsuspecting women while sending them unprepared into the adventure—or rather—the ordeal of travel."

"It sounds rather bad when you say it that way," Mother murmured.

"It is bad." He sighed. "I'm going to seek out additional legal advice when we return to London. I am hoping this can be resolved without anyone the wiser. I should like to avoid everyone ending up in prison."

"We shall hope for the best." She finished her champagne and signaled a server to take her glass. "On the bright side, India must think you're fairly clever."

"And she has taken it upon herself to reform me."

"She's turned you into a project?"

"So it would appear."

"That's a very good sign." Mother cast him a smug smile. "No woman wastes time improving a man if she doesn't wish to keep him. Even if she hasn't yet realized it."

He grinned. "Thank you, Mother."

"For pointing out the obvious?"

"For easing my nerves." He shook his head in disbelief. "I can't remember ever feeling this anxious over—"

"What time is it, dear?"

Derek pulled his watch out of his waistcoat pocket.

"Never mind, it's of no consequence. It is time for the dancing to begin." She put her hand on his arm and nodded toward the stairs. "And India is here."

The professor paused at the top of the stairs and surveyed the ballroom. Estelle stood on one side, India on the other.

Derek's breath caught. He was wrong.

She was beautiful.

More than beautiful, really. She was a vision, straight out of every dream he'd ever had. She wore some sort of pale green confection, a shade that reminded him of the translucent color of the curl of a wave of seawater. The gown floated around her as if in defiance of the laws of gravity and yet managed to caress her in all the appropriate places. Softly draped sleeves revealed tantalizing bare shoulders. The bodice dipped a bit low, too low, temptingly low. He'd always appreciated a revealing bodice on a woman's gown but not this gown on this woman. He couldn't recall ever having to fight the urge to throw his coat over a woman before. Her hair had been allowed further escape tonight, gently piled on top of her head, soft curls tumbling down one shoulder. A cascade of tiny pink roses drifted down her hair and across her bodice and scattered over her skirt.

"Thank you, Mother." He couldn't pull his gaze away from India. "Although, it really doesn't matter to me."

"I know that, dear. I didn't do it for you. Now—" she nodded toward India "—you should join her before someone else does."

He hurried across the room toward her, trying not to push people out of his way. The first dance was about to begin, and he had already claimed it. He reached the stairs just as she stepped onto the bottom step.

For a moment, he wasn't sure what to do next. In a perfect world, a world that existed only in dreams, he would sweep her into his arms, press his lips to hers and never let her go. In this world, however, a display of affection while surrounded by people eager for the next bit of gossip would only lead to rumor and gossip about Derek Saunders's latest indiscretion. He would prefer to avoid that.

He held out his hand. "You are late."

She placed her hand in his. Amusement flickered in her green eyes. "I am precisely on time, according to your mother."

"My mother wasn't counting the minutes until your arrival." He led her out onto the floor.

"And you were?"

"If I had had to wait another second for you, India—" his gaze met hers "—I would have gone to your room and fetched you myself."

"Would you?"

"I would, although it would have been a grave mistake."

"Oh?" A distinct challenge shone in her eyes.

He bent close and spoke softly into her ear. "We would never have left your room."

She sucked in the tiniest breath, then exhaled softly. "That is good to know."

Derek almost tripped over his own feet. What in the name of all that was holy did she mean by that? It was one thing for him to make flirtatious, slightly suggestive comments but quite another for her to do so. "Is it?"

She laughed. Which was no answer at all.

He turned to face her. "Are you flirting with me, Miss Prendergast?"

"You are the second man in as many days to accuse me of flirting."

"Not Sir Martin, I hope."

"No," she said firmly.

"Good."

The music began and she stepped into his arms. "Jealous, Mr. Saunders?"

"Yes."

"How delightful." She smiled, and he noticed the faintest dimple at the corner of her mouth. Charming and fairly begging to be kissed. How had he not noticed that before?

They moved together to the soft strains of an easy waltz, and he noted, as he had when they'd first danced together, how very right she felt in his arms. How smoothly they moved to the music as if they and the melody were one. As if they were meant to dance together. As if she was the perfect partner. *His* perfect partner. The thought was both exciting and terrifying. It struck him that all the other times he'd been in love, or fancied himself in love, there had never been so much as a moment of apprehension. Now, he realized he hadn't feared losing any of them. The idea of losing India knotted something inside him.

"Dare I ask what you are thinking? You seem very far away." She studied him curiously. "Your mind is certainly not on the here and now."

"On the contrary, India, my mind is entirely on the here and now. My thoughts are entirely on you." He maneuvered them around a couple that was moving far too slowly for even the sedate waltz.

"Now who is being flirtatious?"

"Not at all. Flirtation is a game of sorts, a teasing duel of words, and looks, and gestures, which may or may not lead to something more. Perhaps even something important. Flirtation can be nothing more than a distraction meant only for the moment." He gazed deep into her green eyes. "Or it can be a promise that will last forever."

"And is your flirtation a distraction or a promise?" Her tone was light but something—something wonderful—shone in her eyes. "Something for the moment or forever?"

"That may well be too important a question to answer in the middle of a crowd of relative strangers." He smiled and held his breath. "But I am willing to answer it if you are."

Her brow arched. "Turning the tables—are we, Mr. Saunders?"

"Whenever possible, Miss Prendergast." He chuckled and steered her through a perfectly executed turn. She followed his lead without so much as an instant of hesitation, as if she trusted him without question. "I must confess. When I envisioned looking up at the stairs and seeing you tonight I somehow imagined you wearing your gray dress, with your umbrella in one hand and your bag over your arm."

"I had considered it," she said thoughtfully. "But your mother went to great effort on my behalf, and she would be inconsolable if I were to appear in my gray dress. Indeed—" she grinned in a wicked manner "—I suspect she would be devastated should she ever even see my gray dress."

He laughed. "It is not up to her standards of fashion. But, I must confess, I rather miss it."

"You do not." She scoffed. "Although there is much to be said about a sensible, serviceable gray wool dress."

"There is indeed and as a gentleman, I shall refrain from saying it."

"How very thoughtful of you. And as you have confessed, I shall do so, as well." She hesitated. "I have never in my entire life had a dress this lovely and this perfect. The color alone, sea foam—"

"I thought it was green."

"*Sea foam*, Derek," she said firmly. "I never imagined wearing such a color. It's so…carefree. Your mother says it enhances the green in my eyes." She fluttered her lashes at him. "What you do think?"

"I think now you are fishing for compliments."

"I would never…" She paused. "Why yes, I believe I am. It's entirely unlike me but then I have never been to a ball or worn a—"

"Your eyes, India—" he pulled her a bit tighter against him "—rival the finest emeralds, whether you are wearing sea foam or gray wool. Your hair has the loveliest hints of burnished gold when it's allowed a bit of freedom and makes a man long to run his fingers through it. Your mouth is perfection itself and when you smile the most intoxicating dimple appears at the corner. Your lips beg to be kissed. And tonight, you are indescribable."

"Oh." A bemused expression crossed her face. "I was simply hoping for nice."

"*Nice* is not sufficient."

"I shall have to wear this dress all the time."

"It's not the dress, although it is lovely."

"Come now, Derek, I have always been the very definition of ordinary."

"In your eyes perhaps. Although I would imagine Sir Martin disagrees," he added in an offhand manner.

"Apparently." She sighed, and a troubled frown creased her forehead. "I shall have to find a new assistant for him and a new position for myself when we have found Heloise and return to London."

"You won't continue your employment with him?"

"I don't see how I possibly can after he...well, his actions, coming here and..." She shook her head. "It is both surprising and disappointing."

"Ah well, life is often unpredictable." Derek resisted the urge to grin with triumph.

"You're quite pleased with yourself, aren't you?"

"I have nothing to do with this." He adopted an innocent expression. "But, yes, I am."

The music faded and he led her to a graceful stop, releasing her with reluctance.

"Don't be smug—it's unbecoming."

"And yet you think it's charming."

"Perhaps a little." She bit her bottom lip—her delectable, luscious lip—to hold back a smile and his stomach tightened. "I believe my next dance is with the professor. Or perhaps it's promised to Martin. I should check my card."

She took his arm, and they walked off the floor.

"Try not to enjoy it."

She laughed, and the sound wrapped around his soul.

He vowed to himself never to take her laugh for granted and do whatever was needed to make certain he heard it every day, for the rest of his life.

"I have never danced with Martin so I can't say if I will enjoy it or not." Amusement twinkled in her eyes.

"I shall hope for the best. You do remember I claimed the last dance as well as the first?"

"I do."

"Although—" he took her gloved hand and raised it to his lips "—if I had my way, you would dance every dance with me." He met her gaze directly. "Always."

"You're trying to be charming again, aren't you?"

"Is it working?"

"Goodness, Derek, if I told you that it would only go to your head." She stared at him for a long moment. "But, if you must know...yes." A slow smile curved her lips. "Always."

INDIA DIDN'T HAVE a dance with Martin until midway through the second set. She had expected to dance with Lords Brookings and Westvale, as well as Professor Greer, but she did not anticipate dance after dance with strangers.

The first dance after Derek's, with a member of the House of Commons, was awkward. He was no more accomplished at idle chat than she. But with every new partner, she grew more confident—in both conversation and the dance. And every new partner was completely different from the last. Among those she had danced with thus far was a Scottish lord who had far more exuberance on the dance floor than skill, a well-known architect who was acquainted with Professor Greer and an American businessman who went on and on about the charms of Paris. A few weeks ago, India would have argued with him. Now…everything had changed.

Martin at last joined her for their dance, a hurt look on his face. "If I didn't know better, I would think you have been avoiding me. We have only one dance together. My dance card was given to me already filled."

"And wasn't that wonderfully convenient for both of us?" she said brightly. India had been surprised at finding her own dance card filled, but she was well aware Lady Westvale intended to fill Martin's with an eye toward partnering him with ladies who might share his intellectual interests.

"I have something to tell you," he said as he swept her into the dance. "But it seems I can't talk and dance at the same time." He was having a difficult time matching his steps to the music.

"We could just dance."

"This is important." He met her gaze firmly. "*Very* important."

At the next opportunity, he steered her through the columns to the gallery.

"Well?" She tried and failed to hide her impatience. "What is so important?"

"I heard Mr. Saunders confess to everything." A note of triumph sounded in his voice.

She narrowed her eyes. "Did you?"

"I did indeed." He smirked. She'd never seen him quite so self-satisfied before. It was most annoying.

She folded her arms over her chest. "Exactly what is *everything*?"

"Everything." Martin gestured wildly. "You know—all of it!"

"Exactly, if you please."

"Very well." He huffed. "I heard him admit that he

was the mastermind behind the Lady Travelers Society and that he was profiting from the desires of unsuspecting women who wish to travel. Or words to that effect."

"I see." Even though Derek would set things right, he should know better than to open his mouth about his misdeeds. What was the man thinking? "Who did he say this to?"

"His mother!" Victory rang in Martin's voice. "One does not lie to one's mother."

"And he used the word *mastermind*?" While Derek had seemed pleased at being called a mastermind, India doubted he would include such a title in any confession.

"He did indeed. And he said he wishes to avoid prison."

"Anyone with any sense wishes to avoid prison."

"Don't you see, India? I heard him confess." Martin fairly quivered with righteous excitement. "I can testify to that in court. We can have him arrested and tried and thrown in prison!"

"Goodness, Martin, I don't want him arrested."

Martin threw his hands up in frustration. "Because you love him. Really, India, you need to set that aside and consider the…the greater good, if you will."

"My feelings for him are beside the point. I have always been an excellent judge of character, and I now believe Mr. Saunders is a decent man who has simply wandered off the path of moral behavior. I have absolutely no doubt he will set everything to rights, which will be best for all concerned."

Disbelief shone in Martin's eyes. "Is that what you want?"

"Yes, it is."

"Very well." He shook his head. "But I am not happy about this, India."

"I didn't expect you to be." She paused. "Have you found a wife yet?"

"What?" He stared in disbelief. "Here? Now?"

"This is the perfect place to begin." She stepped to one side and directed his attention toward the gathering in the ballroom. "There are any number of eligible ladies here who are in Paris for the sole purpose of attending the exhibition. Ladies who are fascinated by progress and new ideas and the latest inventions. I daresay, some of these ladies—" she waved at the crowd in a grand gesture "—couldn't be more perfect for you than if we had ordered them from a catalogue."

"Don't be absurd." His gaze wandered over the guests. "Do you really think so?"

"I do." She nodded. "I asked Lady Westvale if there would be any possible matches for you here, and she made sure to put some she thought might be acceptable on your dance card."

He frowned. "This is rather quick, isn't it?"

"We did agree you needed a wife."

He stared at her, a forlorn look of resignation in his eyes. "You really aren't coming back to me, are you?"

"I thought that was understood," she said gently. "I think it's best." As long as Martin had her to manage his life, he would never find a life of his own. It wasn't fair to him or to her to remain in his employment. Odd that she had never realized that before. "But I will help you look for a new secretarial assistant, and we shall always be friends."

"That's that then, isn't it?" He managed a weak smile. "I came here to rescue you, you know. Save you from whatever dreadful fate might have befallen you.

This is not how I envisioned this ending." His expression darkened. "If it wasn't for Saunders, you would never leave me."

"Perhaps, but Martin." She placed her hand on his arm and gazed into his eyes. "If it wasn't for Mr. Saunders and Heloise's travels and Paris and all of it, you and I might have gone on as we always have for the rest of our days."

His gaze searched hers. "Would that have been so bad?"

"No." She shook her head. "But I see now it wouldn't have been enough, either."

He stared at her for a long moment. "Right again as always, India." He covered her hand with his. "As your friend, I should like to finish this dance with you."

She smiled. "I shall be delighted."

They stepped back on the floor and resumed their dance, mercifully nearing an end. In spite of his alleged acceptance of her decision, Martin had the distinct look of a lost puppy about him.

A few dances later, she found herself partnered with Lord Brookings, who seemed oddly preoccupied and not his usual self.

"Are you having a wonderful time tonight, Miss Prendergast?" Percival asked when they'd begun their dance together.

"I am indeed, my lord." She studied him closely. "But you aren't, are you?"

"I am. Or rather, I will. I simply ran into someone I did not expect to see."

She had noticed him dancing with a dark-haired woman a few minutes ago, an odd expression on his face. "Someone important?"

"Not anymore." He smiled down at her. "Have you met the American inventor Mother invited?"

"Not yet." She paused. "I gather this is your attempt to change the subject?"

He ignored her and continued. "The American's name escapes me for a moment but I do think…"

She smiled and surrendered.

Every now and then she would catch sight of Derek. He was not dancing as much as she, and it was rather satisfying. Sometimes, their gazes would meet, and her heart would race. Sometimes she would catch him unawares, in conversation or at the start of a dance, and she marveled at the odd turn her life had taken. All because Heloise wanted the adventure of travel. She wished her cousin was here now. Heloise probably would have liked this.

A sharp pang of concern or perhaps guilt stabbed her. She still had no idea where Heloise was, and India certainly shouldn't be having a wonderful time while the dear woman was missing. It had occurred to her more and more in recent days that perhaps Heloise was missing because she wished to be missing. Which made no sense at all, but then, the more India thought about it, the more Heloise's behavior before she'd left London struck her as unusual. If this was one of India's detective stories, there would be all sorts of clues. Regardless, they would pick up their search tomorrow and Heloise would never begrudge her this one night.

It truly was a remarkable evening. She scarcely recognized herself in the mirror and danced every dance, accompanied by often interesting conversation and a surprising amount of laughter. It was nothing short of magic.

In no time at all, the last dance was announced and once again she was in Derek's arms.

"Has your first ball been all you ever dreamed it would be?" He gazed down at her.

"Goodness, Derek, I have never dreamed of attending a ball," she said with a casual shrug. "However, I must say the evening fulfilled any expectations I might ever have had."

He chuckled. "I'm glad I was able to share it with you."

"As am I." She gazed up at him. "I wish…"

"A wish?" His brow rose. "From the woman who has nothing she would wish for?"

"Apparently, a great deal has changed since I said that." She paused. "I am not the same woman who started out on this quest."

"That's what quests are for. The journey is often more important than the destination."

"I feel I have changed a great deal."

"Oh, not entirely."

"No?" She stared up at him. "I would think you of all people would be pleased."

"I watched you this morning, helping my mother. You directed the arranging of furniture, of decorations, of flowers. You managed the kitchen staff and put the servers hired for tonight through their paces. You were a general deploying troops, the epitome of efficiency and organization. It was like watching a maestro conduct an orchestra." He shook his head, an admiring smile on his lips. "You had this house functioning like a fine Swiss watch."

"I am nothing if not efficient and well organized," she said primly.

"In that respect you haven't changed, nor should you. But you have emerged, I think. Like a butterfly from a cocoon." He studied her curiously. "You have allowed yourself to…to breathe, India."

"Yes, I believe I have at that." She thought for a moment. "It's quite, well, freeing to discover one doesn't have to always be right."

"I can imagine." He smiled and pulled her closer. "But you haven't told me your wish."

"It's my understanding that wishes don't come true if you tell them."

His gaze searched hers. "Will you tell me if it comes true?"

"Oh, I suspect you of all people will know." She smiled up at him and her heart swelled.

How strange to realize that all she'd never thought was possible, never cared about really, never concerned herself with might well be possible, after all. Even as a child, India knew better than to believe in fairy tales of princesses and dashing heroes and magic. Or silly stories of romance and true love and living happily together forever.

Tonight, for the first time in her life, she believed.

CHAPTER TWENTY-FOUR

WHEN INDIA PRENDERGAST was determined to do something, she would let nothing stand in her way. In that, at least, she had not changed. Even if the something in her way was her own trepidation and yes, cowardice.

At least she finally had a genuine use for the peach negligee and matching wrapper, a garment clearly designed for seduction and sin. One would think wearing a lace-trimmed weapon of carnal desire would give a woman set on seduction a fair amount of confidence, and indeed it did. Even if it was currently hidden under the bulky comforter she had wrapped around herself for the walk from her room to Derek's. Apparently, it took more than resolve and determination to completely change from proper, responsible spinster to harlot, even in Paris.

She squared her shoulders, drew a calming breath and knocked on Derek's door. And realized she had no idea how to properly seduce a man, although perhaps *properly* was not the right word.

After a few seconds—or an eternity—the door opened.

Clad in his red dressing gown thrown over striped silken pajamas, Derek stared in obvious confusion. She'd thought he had looked handsome and dashing and very nearly perfect earlier in his formal evening wear but now with his hair rumpled and the sash of his dressing gown loosely tied, he was improper and imperfect and nothing short of irresistible. Her heart raced.

He narrowed his gaze as if he couldn't quite believe his eyes. "India, is something wrong?"

"No, nothing at all." She shook her head.

"Then, why are you here?" he said slowly.

"Why?" She had rehearsed what she intended to say but apparently, when confronted with a man obviously fresh from his bed and knowing where this could—where she wanted this to lead, words failed her. "It's difficult to say exactly."

"What?" He shook his head in confusion.

Come now, India Prendergast, a firm voice in the back of her head said. *If this is what you want, and you do, tell the man.*

"Very well." She raised her chin. "I should like to… to be seduced. Or to seduce you, if you prefer. Although admittedly, I have no experience—"

"Good God, India." He grabbed her arm and yanked her into his room. "Get in here." Obviously, the man was eager to begin. "Unless you wish to announce your intentions to the entire house." Or not.

She nodded. "That might be best."

He shut the door behind him. "Surely, I didn't hear you correctly. What are you really doing here?" His gaze flicked over her. "And why are you wearing half the bed?"

"Derek." She braced herself. "Tonight I made a wish, and only you can make the wish come true."

"Bloody hell, India!" His eyes widened in sheer horror. "What did you wish for?"

"I wished for the night to never end."

He stared for an endless moment. She suspected it

would not be in the spirit of seduction to shift nervously from foot to foot yet it was terribly difficult not to do so.

"Oh no." He took a step backward. "This is some sort of trick, isn't it?"

"No, as I said—it's a seduction. Or an attempted seduction. Although it doesn't seem to be going very well." She pulled the coverlet tighter around her. "I did think with your reputation, you would understand and be, well, amenable to the idea." Her gaze drifted downward, and she cleared her throat. "Although I can see you're not unaffected by my arrival."

"Damnation." It was as much a groan as a word. Derek stalked across the room, grabbed a pillow and held it in front of him. "I'd have to be dead to be unaffected!"

"Precisely my intent. Well, not that you be dead, of course, but—"

"Your meaning was clear, and I congratulate you on your success. In spite of that thing you have wrapped around yourself, you are most…" His expression twisted as if he couldn't bear to say the words. "Provocative."

"Am I?"

"Yes, damn it all, India!" He uttered an odd sort of painful laugh. "With your hair…like that." He waved with his free hand. "All unrestrained and floating about your shoulders, and that tantalizing glimpse of lace, the flush on your cheeks, the sparkle in your eyes…" He glared. "A man can only take so much, you know!"

"Really?" She studied him thoughtfully. Odd that his discomfort eased her nerves. Perhaps this was one of those shoe-on-the-other-foot kind of things. After all, Derek had no doubt seduced a fair number of willing ladies. This might not be so difficult, after all. "You should know I have never done this before."

Obviously, she had stunned him into silence.

"Seduced a man, that is."

"Yes, I knew what you meant!"

"Or allowed a man to seduce me. Although I suppose it really doesn't matter, who seduces whom," she said thoughtfully. "At some point, I assume the seduction will be mutual."

"What?" The man could barely croak out the word.

"Carpe diem, remember? This is one of those unexpected opportunities, and I intend to seize it."

"If I recall, that was in reference to sightseeing. Not—" he waved at her "—whatever *this* is."

"Goodness, Derek." She heaved a frustrated sigh. "I believe I have explained *this* quite thoroughly. Or at least as thoroughly as was necessary. Indeed, I have been painfully obvious."

His eyes narrowed. "So you have never done this before, and yet here you are."

"Of course I have never done this. I am not a trollop. I had never kissed a man before you, either."

"Never?" He stared at her.

"No, never." She shrugged. "The opportunity never arose."

"And Sir Martin never—"

"Good Lord, no!"

"Then I'm the first man you ever kissed?"

"We've established that."

"Oh, well, hmm." He nodded thoughtfully. "That is interesting."

"I'm glad you think so." She summoned her courage and let the coverlet fall to the floor. "Shall we?"

His gaze traveled over her from the lace ruffles cascading down the front of the wrapper to the tips of her slippers. Only the fact that between the negligee and the robe there were two layers of the translucent fabric kept her from being completely exposed. But she'd studied herself in the mirror before leaving her room and knew full well there were peaks and shadows barely concealed by the gossamer material. Given the look in his eyes, and his tightened grip on the pillow, he had clearly noticed.

"So." She forced a light note to her voice and stepped toward him. "Should we…retire? To the bed?"

"That isn't—" He cleared his throat and stepped back. "That isn't how things like this are done. You don't simply go to a man's room in the middle of the night and say, 'Seduce me!'"

"I did offer to seduce you." She stepped closer. "I might need some assistance in that, but the offer remains."

He stared at her.

"Surely this is not the first time a woman has come to your room with an offer of this nature."

"No, it isn't. But that is entirely irrelevant. We're not talking about some woman. We're talking about you!" His brows drew together in a forbidding manner. "What did you think was going to happen here, India? Did you think you could simply waltz into my room, declare your intentions and I would throw you onto my bed and have my way with you?"

"That sounds like an excellent way to start." She nodded. "But you might wish to discard the pillow."

"I don't think so," he said, clutching the pillow tighter against him.

"I must say, I'm a bit surprised."

"*You're* surprised?"

She casually circled around him and sank down on the edge of the bed. "I never imagined this was going to be quite this difficult. I thought a man of your reputation would be more than amenable to a night of... amorous adventure."

"So *I'm* the trollop?"

She winced.

"Now see here, India Prendergast." Indignation rang in his voice. "Admittedly, I have had my share—perhaps more than my share—of *amorous adventures*. And while the offer is tempting—more than tempting—bloody hell, India, I love you! And you are not the kind of woman one dallies with—especially not on command! You are the type of woman one marries!"

She stared at him. "Does one?"

"It might very well depend." He stalked over to her, dropped his pillow, yanked her to her feet and into his arms. "Are you here because I am a means to an end? A way to make the night last forever? Or are you here because you want to be with me as much as I want to be with you? Because you cannot stand another minute without being in my arms? Because I have taken up residence in your heart and regardless of how ill suited we are for each other, we are as well inevitable?" His gaze bored into hers. "Because you love me?"

"Well..." Her breath caught. "Yes."

"That's settled then." He stared into her eyes but made no effort to let her go.

"I think you should kiss me now." She rested her hands on his chest, startled to note he had nothing on beneath the dressing gown beyond the pajama trousers. Just as startling was how exciting that was.

"Do you?" He swallowed.

"It seems like the thing to do."

"I believe I said the next time I kissed you it would be at a time and place of my choosing."

"And yet here we are." She slid her arms around his neck. "Seize the day, Derek." She tentatively touched her lips to his. "This is an unexpected opportunity."

He groaned and pulled her tighter to him. His arousal pressed against her through the layers of fabric, and the strangest feeling of need ached inside her.

"Kiss me, Derek," she murmured against his lips, shifting her hips to press closer. Any lingering apprehension vanished in the heat of his body next to hers.

"India." He moaned and pressed his lips to hers in a kiss firm but distinctly restrained. She could feel the tension in the hard muscles of his arms around her, as if he were holding himself in check. As if he were afraid. This would never do. He raised his head, released her and stepped back. "There. I have kissed you—now you should go."

"Derek," she said with a sigh. "I am a twenty-nine-year-old spinster, which did not bother me at all before I came to Paris. I usually wore gray or brown. I prided myself on my efficiency, and I considered myself quite ordinary. Now I find it rather sad and somewhat pathetic. I feel like an entirely different person. And it's your fault. You taught me to breathe, Derek, and now you have to suffer the consequences." She smiled in what she hoped was a sultry manner. "And I have no intention of leaving."

"And I have no intention of seducing you." His resolute tone was at complete odds with the sharp bulge beneath his dressing gown.

"Very well then. If you will not seduce me, I shall have to seduce you."

"Will you?" A distinct challenge shone in his eyes, and he shrugged. "Be my guest."

"You should know that novels of detection are not the only things I have read."

"Oh?" He smiled in a knowing manner. "Then by all means, proceed."

"You would be amazed at what one might learn through the joys of reading," she said under her breath. Although she really had no idea what to do now.

"I can imagine." He chuckled.

"You doubt me?"

He shrugged.

She studied him for a moment, then reached out and pulled the sash of his dressing gown free, letting it drop to the floor. The gown fell open, leaving the hard planes of his chest exposed. A smattering of hair covered his torso between his flattened nipples, then trailed down to disappear beneath the trousers. She moved closer and ran her hands over his chest. He shuddered beneath her touch, and his hands clenched into fists by his side, but he made no other movement. A sense of pure power washed through her. How long would it take for him to lose control?

She reached up and kissed the base of his throat, then ran light kisses down his chest. She felt his sharp intake of breath beneath her mouth and smiled to herself. Her hands pushed the gown off his broad shoulders, and it fell with a whisper to the floor. She reveled in the feel of his tensed muscles beneath her fingers, then slowly circled behind him, her hands never leaving his flesh. His back was as well defined as his chest. She stepped back and shrugged out of her wrapper, leaving her covered only by the nearly transparent material of the negligee. Odd that this wasn't the least bit embarrassing. No man had ever seen her so scantily clad, and yet there wasn't so much as a hint of apprehension. Instead it was all quite exciting.

She ran her hands over him, caressing his shoulders and tracing the ridges and valleys of his back with the tips of her nails. Her fingers drifted along the cleft of his spine, lower to the waist of his silk trousers, hanging low on his hips, and below to the curve of his buttocks. He tensed at her touch, and she savored the feel of his body and his response. She ran a finger along the edge of the fabric. His breath came a bit faster, as did hers. She moved closer to press against him and kissed the back of his neck. She wrapped her arms around him and reached for the drawstring of his pajamas, inadvertently brushing over his erection. He drew a deep, shuddering breath.

"India." The word was little more than a moan.

She tugged at the drawstring, and his hand caught hers.

"You realize there is no going back from this?" His voice was ragged with desire.

She swallowed hard. "I do."

He turned to face her, her hand still in his. "I have never taken a virgin to my bed."

"Then I shall be your first."

"No, you shall be my last." He pulled her to his lips. "Be forewarned, India Prendergast, I don't want a single night with you. This night is not all I want to last forever."

"Good." The word was little more than a sigh.

He kissed the palm of her hand, then her wrist. She shivered and a yearning ache spread low in her abdomen. He straightened, drew her into his arms and crushed his lips to hers. For a moment, panic surged through her. What had she done? It was quite exciting

when she was the one doing the seducing, when she was
in control. Now his mouth plundered hers, demanding
and insistent and…her mouth opened to his, and he
tasted vaguely of heat and brandy and spice. His arms
wrapped tighter around her and the beating of his heart
echoed her own. Something decadent and demanding—
desire no doubt throbbed deep within her.

His mouth trailed from her lips and along her jaw
to linger just below her ear. She caught her breath. His
lips ran kisses down the curve of her neck. He moved
the sleeves of her gown off her shoulders, his mouth
never leaving her flesh, heated beneath his touch. He
pushed the gown lower until it slid to the floor leaving
her naked in his arms. She shivered with the cool night
air and the feel of his body close to hers.

One hand caressed the small of her back and moved
lower to the curve of her bottom. He cupped her breast
and lowered his head to flick his tongue over the hardened nipple. She gasped, and her stomach tightened.
He sucked at her breast and the most astonishing sensations coursed through her. Without thinking, her body
pressed closer to his, his erection beneath the fabric of
his pajamas nudging between her legs. He shifted his
attention to her other breast, pulling the nipple into
his mouth, gently nipping and sucking until her knees
weakened and her nails dug into his shoulders for support.

He lowered her onto the bed and for a moment stared
down at her. "There is nothing ordinary about you, India
Prendergast. You are remarkable."

He ran his hands over her ankles and along the in-
sides of her legs, lightly caressing her knees and traveling ever higher to her inner thighs. Her legs fell open
of their own accord; she was conscious of nothing but

the astonishing feel of his hands on her skin—arousing and hypnotic. Flesh that had never seemed so alive. As if he had brought her to life.

His fingers slid between the soft folds at the meeting of her thighs and her breath hitched.

"Derek!"

"Carpe diem, Miss Prendergast," he murmured, sinking to his knees between her legs.

Surely he wasn't—she propped herself up on her elbows and stared at him. "Derek—you aren't? You wouldn't!" She stared. "Would you?"

"Oh, I will." He grinned, and his head disappeared between her legs.

Her back arched at the first touch of his mouth and she cried out. This was not at all what she'd expected. The girls at Miss Bicklesham's had shared a great deal of information but this had never… His tongue slid over her, and she moaned with the exquisite sensation. All thought of what she had expected vanished amid an onslaught of unimagined bliss. He toyed with her and teased her with his mouth and his tongue and his fingers. Her hands twisted in the sheets, and she moaned with the ever-increasing ecstasy. The strangest thing seemed to be happening within her. As if her body was growing tighter and tighter, nearing a point where she would surely die of pure pleasure or explode into a thousand pieces. It was quite the most incredible feeling. He slid a finger into her, and that too was different but not unpleasant. Then he slipped a second finger inside, and without warning she shattered. Sheer bliss and utter release thundered through her, and her body shook with the power of it.

A moment later Derek joined her on the bed and gathered her against him. Her mouth eagerly met his, and her hand slipped between them. She wanted to touch him, caress him, pleasure him as he had done her. But more—she wanted him inside her. Wanted to feel the hard length of him taking her, claiming her.

Aching desire again throbbed through her and she threw her leg over his. His erection nudged against her, and he groaned.

"India," he murmured against her skin, then shifted to position himself between her legs.

He stroked her for a moment until her breath came faster and his fingers were again slick with the evidence of her need. She arched upward to meet him and at last he slid into her, joining her, filling her. His movements were restrained and cautious, achingly slow and deliberate.

There was no more than a twinge of discomfort, awkward for a moment but then eclipsed by the most unique awareness. He seated himself fully within her then slowly moved, sliding out then sliding in, his pace measured and unhurried. With every movement, the strangeness of it all faded replaced by unexpected and amazing sensations. In the back of her mind she noted his thoughtful concern for her and was grateful but whatever demon of desire had been released within her demanded more. She wanted him harder and faster, and she clutched at his shoulders to urge him on. Pleasure, pure and intense, spiraled through her until that odd tension wound again tighter and tighter. He thrust faster in an ever increasing rhythm, her movements instinctively matching his. And when her body convulsed once more and stars obscured her vision and scattered through her blood, she felt him shudder hard against her and moan her name.

They lay entwined together for a minute or a lifetime.

She had no doubt lost the ability to move at all nor did she have any desire to do so. She could stay like this—her arms and legs entangled with his—forever. Not the least bit practical, of course, but there it was. Love coupled with passion was apparently a powerful force.

At last he withdrew, propped himself up on one elbow and studied her, a smile of contentment on his handsome face. A smile that no doubt matched her own.

"What are you thinking?" He kissed the tip of her nose.

"I suspect there's a great deal to be said for a man who knows what he is doing when it comes to seduction. Even when he is reluctant to do so." She giggled. Good Lord, she had never giggled in her life. What had this man done to her?

"That was an extremely practical observation, Miss Prendergast."

"I am an extremely practical woman."

"You realize you are mine now."

"What?" She laughed. "I belong to you?"

"Forever." He took her hand and laced his fingers with hers. "And you will marry me."

She struggled to sit up. "Will I?"

"I have ruined you, and there is no other option," he said firmly. "It's the only practical, sensible, rational thing to do."

She stared at him for a moment, then laughed. "You're being absurd. I am not a silly nineteen-year-old. I am nearly thirty years of age. You are under no obligation."

He rolled his gaze toward the ceiling. "Did you miss that part where I said I loved you?"

"Well, no but—"

"And the even more pertinent part where you said you loved me?" His eyes narrowed. "Didn't you mean it?"

"Of course I meant it." She sniffed. "I would never say something of that nature if I didn't mean it."

"I warned you there was no going back."

"I thought you meant, well." She gestured at the crumpled bedclothes around them. "This."

"I said I didn't want a single night with you."

"You did, but—"

"And furthermore you said you were wrong about the type of woman I should marry."

"I said I was possibly wrong."

"No, you said you were undeniably wrong."

"That was a momentary lapse…"

"I would never say anything of that nature if I didn't mean it," he mimicked her.

"I do not sound like that," she said loftily.

He scoffed.

"Perhaps the inflection might have been accurate."

He laughed, then sobered. "I have never asked a woman to marry me before." He shook his head. "Nor have I ever wanted to."

"I cannot do anything until Heloise is found," she warned.

"I can agree to that." He grinned. "Besides, you reformed me. The least you can do is make an honest man out of me."

"Have I reformed you?" Her gaze searched his.

"Without question." He nodded. "The moment we return to London I will do whatever is necessary to ensure the Lady Travelers Society is completely legitimate."

"Are you doing that for me or because it's the right thing to do?"

"Both."

"Good Lord, I really have reformed you." She

grinned with satisfaction. "I'm very good at this. Perhaps I shall become a reformer."

"The only one you may reform is me."

"There is much that needs to change in this world," she said thoughtfully. "I have never had the means to do anything about it."

"And think of all you could do if you were no longer employed. And eventually, as Lady Danby."

"There are a lot of women who have no choice as to their lot in life," she said. "Perhaps I could try to do something to help them."

"Excellent idea. But first." He pulled her back into his arms and rolled until she was beneath him, then nuzzled her neck. Once again that helpless, demanding feel of need washed through her. And with it a delicious sense of expectation.

Apparently, there was much to be said for being a harlot.

CHAPTER TWENTY-FIVE

*Travel expands one's horizons and broadens one's
mind and view of the world. If one is not open to
new experiences, if one is not willing to accept
broadening, one should stop reading this guide
immediately and stay home.*

—The Lady Travelers Society Guide

IT WAS NEARLY noon by the time Derek made his way
to the breakfast room. He had stood guard in the hall
while India made her way back to her room, comforter
and all. He didn't want so much as a whisper of gossip
to touch her. He grinned. She would hate being em-
broiled in scandal. He'd never given any consideration
to a woman's reputation, but then he'd never been with
a woman who had never been with another man before.

And he'd never been in love. Oh certainly he had
fancied himself in love any number of times. It had
always struck fast and hard and had vanished just as
quickly. Love, for him, had always been easy. Nothing
with India was easy. Why, he hadn't even particularly
liked her in the beginning. The feelings he had for her
had been slow to take root and slow to blossom. He'd
had to earn her friendship and her trust. Now—and she
could debate semantics all she wished—now she was
his. And he was hers. For today and for the rest of their
lives. This was right and this was real.

This was forever.

"Good day." He strode into the breakfast room with what he suspected was a silly grin on his face. He couldn't help himself. The rest of his life had begun in the wee hours of the morning and he couldn't wait for it to continue. He nodded to Val and the Greers, not the least bit surprised to see his mother had not yet made an appearance, and headed to the sideboard. "Estelle, you are looking even lovelier than usual today."

"Goodness, Derek, the things you say." She waved off his comment but beamed with pleasure nonetheless.

"I must say, Professor—" Derek poured a cup of Val's blend of coffee "—you seemed to be having an excellent time last night."

"I was indeed." The older man smiled. "There was a most interesting assortment of guests in attendance."

"And he does love to dance." Estelle patted her husband's hand.

The professor shot her a jaunty grin.

"You look in good spirits today," Val said.

"And you look dreadful." Derek took a seat next to his brother. "Why?"

"I did not sleep well." Val shrugged. "Oh, a telegram came for you this morning." He picked up an envelope beside his plate and handed it to Derek.

Derek opened the envelope and pulled out the message. "It's from Uncle Edward." He read the first line, looked up at the others and grinned. "Lady Heloise has been found safe and has returned to her home."

"Wonderful!" Estelle clapped her hands together.

"Excellent," the professor said with smile. "India will be extremely relieved."

"And now you can tell her everything," Val said. "Although you did say you would tell her after the ball."

"This will make that much easier," Derek said with a profound sense of relief. His uncle was apparently taking his role as mastermind behind the search to heart and had personally spoken with Lady Heloise. He resumed reading, and the momentary feeling of reprieve vanished. "Lady Heloise requests that while I may tell India she's home and well, she wishes to explain the rest of it herself."

"That takes it out of your hands then." Val shrugged.

"Indeed it does but…" He grimaced. "I hate keeping something like this from her."

"You didn't seem to have a great deal of difficulty keeping it from her before." Val studied him curiously.

"I don't like the idea of a lie between us." Derek's gaze returned to the telegram.

"It's not your lie," Val said.

"What lie?" the professor said in an aside to his wife.

"I don't know, dear," Estelle said quietly. "Now, hush."

"I am complicit in it." Derek blew a long breath. "And things are, well, different now."

"Now you're in love with her."

The Greers traded glances—Estelle's was distinctly smug, her husband's resigned.

"That does make a difference. But more important, she trusts me. I have no desire to betray that trust."

"Your reasons for not telling her everything are as valid now as they were before Lady Heloise's reappearance. The only difference is that now I agree with you." A firm note rang in Val's voice. "It is not your place to tell her this. This is no longer your decision."

"You're right, I suppose, but it feels wrong. It feels like a lie. But…" Derek shook his head. "It's not my story to tell. It's been taken out of my hands."

"What's been taken out of your hands?" India appeared in the doorway, cast him a brilliant smile—a smile full of shared secrets and promises—and nodded at the rest of the gathering, gesturing at the men to remain seated. "Lovely day, isn't it?" She headed for the sideboard. "Do forgive me. For some reason I am famished today." She took a plate and surveyed the offerings. "What isn't your story to tell, Derek?" she said over her shoulder.

Derek rose to his feet and glanced at Val. His brother was right—this was not his place. "I received a telegram this morning."

"Another from your uncle?" She selected several sausages. "I do so love these sausages. About business?"

"Not exactly." He braced himself. "India."

There must have been something in his voice. She set down her plate and turned around. "What is it? What's wrong?"

"Nothing is wrong," he said firmly. "In fact, I have wonderful news."

"Your cousin is home and safe in London," Estelle blurted, then winced. "Goodness, Derek, I do apologize but you were taking forever."

India stared at him. "Is this true?"

Derek smiled. "I believe the quest is over."

"Thank God." A sob broke from her, and she choked it back as her eyes filled with tears. "My apologies. I'm not an emotional sort—I certainly never cry. And I know given Heloise's nature that there was as good a chance that she had simply forgotten to write as there was that something dreadful had happened but…"

Derek moved close and wrapped his arms around her. Muffled sobs shuddered against his chest. "But she is home now, and all is well."

"It is, isn't it?" She sniffed then stilled. India raised her head and looked up at him. "What isn't your story to tell?"

"We should go," Professor Greer murmured to his wife.

"Absolutely not," Estelle whispered.

"Uh…" Derek had always considered himself fairly glib. Words came easily to him, especially when they were fashioned in the form of an excuse or an explanation. But now, staring down at India's expectant face, he realized there was nothing he could say. No one could make this right except Heloise. The only chance the older lady had of repairing whatever damage she may have done with her deceit was if she explained everything to India herself. God knows, Derek had no idea why she'd done what she'd done. No, he couldn't say anything even if he had any idea what to say. And absolutely nothing came to mind.

"Derek?" She stepped back, a frown furrowing her forehead. "What has been taken out of your hands?"

"I…" Even as he said the words he knew it was a mistake. But what choice did he have? "I really can't say."

She stared at him for a long moment, then held out her hand. "May I see the telegram?"

He hesitated.

"Bloody hell." Val jumped to his feet and grabbed the telegram out of Derek's hand. "Of course you can. He has nothing to hide." He passed the paper to India and glared at his brother. "Even if he's doing all he can to make you think he does."

"What does this mean?" India read the message. "Snuggs wishes Prendergast be told she is home. Requests nothing further be said." She shook her head. "I don't understand." Her gaze met his. "Do you?"

"No," Val said sharply.

"Yes," Derek said at the same time.

"Would you care to explain it to me?"

For a long moment their gazes locked. He ached to reveal everything. And while she might appreciate his candor, he knew he could cause irreparable damage by doing so. He couldn't risk her losing the only family she had.

"As I said," he said slowly, "it is not my story to tell."

Disappointment and hurt filled her green eyes. "But you do know this story, don't you?"

He nodded. "Some of it."

"And you have known for some time?"

"No." He shook his head firmly.

"But you knew before last night?"

"I did."

"I see."

I see? Never a good response but she was wrong. *I see* said a great deal. About trust and betrayal and disappointment.

He drew a deep breath. "You should go home, India," he said quietly. "You need to speak with Heloise."

"Indeed I do." Her tone was abruptly brisk and impersonal. "If you will excuse me, I must gather my things." She nodded at the group, turned and left.

Derek hesitated then followed her out of the room. "India."

"What?" She whirled toward him.

"Let me explain."

"Very well." She crossed her arms over her chest. "Explain."

"I only found out about this a few days ago."

"Then you had a few days to tell me about whatever this is and you chose not to."

As much as he wanted to, he couldn't deny it. "I

thought it was best, given Heloise had not yet been located."

"And now that she has—" her eyes narrowed "—it's not your story to tell?"

A horrible sinking sensation settled in his chest. "I'm afraid so."

"I see."

He winced.

"Then if you will excuse me." She nodded, turned and headed toward the stairs.

He wanted to run after her, confess everything but— regardless of whatever happened between them now— he would not be the one to destroy her relationship with the only family she had. Heloise's secrets were hers to tell. He could do nothing more than stand by India's side. If she would let him.

"What are you going to do?" Val asked beside him. Derek hadn't even heard him approach.

"Go with her," Derek said without thinking.

Val nodded. "I shall have a maid pack your bags. While we wait…" He took his brother's elbow and steered him toward the library. "I think a whisky is in order."

"It's too early in the day," he murmured.

"Good God, what has she done to you?"

"Nothing more than any avenging angel bent on reforming my wicked ways might do." He slanted his brother a halfhearted smile. "She has stolen my heart."

A SCANT QUARTER of an hour later, voices sounded outside the library door. Surely India couldn't be ready to leave so soon? Derek and Val exchanged glances and hurried into the hall.

India had changed into her gray dress and stood talking to the professor and Estelle, Luckthorne by her side. A subtle gleam of victory showed in the man's eyes. It did not bode well.

"Lord Brookings." India turned to Val with a polite smile. "I would like to thank you for your gracious hospitality. You have been most welcoming under awkward circumstances."

"It has been my pleasure, Miss Prendergast." Val took her hand and raised it to his lips, his gaze never leaving hers. "I hate to see you go."

"Are you leaving?" Mother's voice rang from the stairway and she hurried down the steps. "Surely not without saying goodbye?"

"I had intended to," India began, "but—"

"But we do need to be on our way if we are to be home at a reasonable hour," Luckthorne said firmly.

Mother shot him a curious look, then turned her attention back to India, stepped toward her and took her hands. "My dear child, I shall miss you terribly."

India paused then smiled. "I shall miss you, as well."

Mother glanced around. "Aren't you taking your new clothes with you?"

"I'm afraid I don't have anything to put them in. My trunk…" She shrugged. "Well, you know."

"I shall have them delivered to you in London." Mother nodded in that way she had of ending a subject, then leaned close to India and kissed her cheek.

"Thank you," India said quietly.

"I don't believe my bags are ready yet." Derek glanced at his brother. "Would you have my things sent on to me?"

Val nodded.

"Excellent." He turned to India. "As Sir Martin is so eager to be on our way, we should be off."

Luckthorne's eyes widened. "You're coming with us?"

"I am." Derek directed his words at Luckthorne but kept his gaze fixed on India. "I started this quest with Miss Prendergast. I intend to see it through to the end."

Luckthorne scowled. "I really don't think that's necessary."

"Regardless, I don't intend to be left behind." Derek shrugged in a casual manner as if this wasn't the least bit important.

"I see no reason why you should accompany us." Luckthorne stepped toward him in a challenging manner. *Good.* Perhaps Derek would get to thrash the man, after all.

"Might I speak privately with you for a moment, Mr. Saunders?" India stepped between the two men. "In the library perhaps?" She glanced at Val. "My lord?"

"Of course." Val nodded.

"Thank you—this won't take long." She walked into the library with a resolute step, Derek right behind.

"I shall hail a cab for—"

Derek closed the doors on Luckthorne's comment. He stepped toward her. "India."

"Derek." She held out a hand to stop him. "I am doing exactly what you said I should do. I am returning home to speak with Heloise."

"Let me go with you."

"No." She paused. "I am trying very hard to retain whatever semblance of my sensible nature that may still linger. I suspect it is the only way for me to proceed at this point. You have no place in that."

"But—"

"I cannot, at the moment, consider the repercussions of our actions last night or what was said."

"What was said was that I love you and you love me."

"I'm aware of that," she said, refusing to meet his eyes. "However..."

"However," he said slowly, "even now you cannot bring yourself to completely trust me."

"In that you're wrong," she said sharply, her gaze snapping to his. "The problem between us is that *you* don't trust *me*. You don't trust that I can face whatever this story that is not yours to tell entails. You don't trust that I have the strength or the courage or whatever is necessary. You don't trust that I will not fall apart at this revelation, whatever it may be. You may well be right but..." She drew a steadying breath. "I would hope, after all this time together, you had as much faith in me as I do in you."

"I do," he said staunchly.

"Furthermore, it appears I was right all along." She shook her head. "I am not the type of woman—no—I am not the woman you should marry."

He could deny it but it would do no good. "I don't know what to say."

She smiled a resigned sort of smile, and his heart twisted. "I think we've both said quite enough." She turned toward the door, then looked back at him. "I believe one of the Lady Travelers pamphlets says travel is an unexpected adventure. Thank you, Mr. Saunders, for the unexpected and the adventure." She nodded, opened the door, then closed it behind her.

For a long moment, he could do nothing more than stare, stunned by the finality of the faint thud of the door closing behind her. The woman he loved had just walked out of his life, and there was little he could do about it. Surely this awful aching sensation, this almost physical pain was heartbreak.

No, resolve coursed through him. She was wrong.

Again. He did have faith in her, in them. Why, the chances that they would ever meet in the first place let alone fall in love were slim. That they had found each other—the carefree scoundrel and the sensible spinster—was nothing short of a miracle. Or fate. And that was worth fighting for.

Trust had nothing to do with it. Letting Heloise tell her story was absolutely the right decision even if India didn't yet realize it. But she would and he would be there when she did. Once, he might have let her go. Resigned himself to the fact that he had lost her and go on with his life. But if he had learned nothing else from Uncle Edward in these months since his birthday it was that making the right decision was rarely easy. It took strength and courage and, yes, faith. Derek could be—he was—a better man than he had imagined. A man his father would be proud of.

India Prendergast was exactly the kind of woman—the only woman—he should marry. And he intended to do exactly that. Now he simply had to convince the stubborn, annoying creature who did not believe in love or romance that he was right and, once again, she was wrong.

He grinned. Another grand, romantic gesture was called for and he knew exactly what it should be.

The door opened and Val stepped into the library, followed closely by his mother.

Val stared. "Why on earth are you smiling? You do realize she's gone?"

"I do."

"She left this for you." Val handed him the souvenir medal he had given her on the Eiffel Tower. "She said she didn't need it."

"Well, I shall have to return it to her." Derek slipped it into his waistcoat pocket.

"Then you are going to go after her?" Mother said hopefully.

"Not quite yet."

"Why on earth not?" Mother's eyes widened. "She's accompanying Sir Martin, and I am certain he is going to use whatever has happened between you to try to engage her affections."

"Sir Martin has had years to engage India's affections." Derek chuckled. "I doubt that his efforts will be successful now."

"How can you possibly be sure of that?" Mother glared at him as if he had lost his mind.

"Faith, Mother." He shrugged. "It all comes down to faith."

Val studied him closely. "You have a plan, don't you?"

"More or less."

"Then you should be on your way to London." Mother waved in the general direction of England. "At once."

"Oh, I will but not quite yet. First—" he grinned "—I need to go to Prague."

CHAPTER TWENTY-SIX

"It is good to have you back, Miss." Denker, Heloise's butler, greeted India at the door.

"Thank you, Denker. It is good to be home." India heaved a weary sigh. It was far later than she had hoped, but then there were moments during the journey from Paris when it had seemed endless.

In the eight years she had worked for Martin, she could not remember ever thinking him irritating. Or ever wishing he would just stop talking, if only for a moment. But Martin went on and on about how Derek was not the right man for her and how he should probably be thrown in prison. It was pointless to argue, even if she'd had the strength to do so. Finally, she had told him she didn't wish to hear another word about Mr. Saunders and had said so in her coolest, no-nonsense manner.

The last thing she wanted to talk about was Derek. It was bad enough that she couldn't get him out of her thoughts. She had trusted him, but how could you trust a man who kept secrets from you? Even if those secrets were not his to tell. Which made no sense at all.

"Lady Heloise assumed you would be arriving today, although she was not certain when," Denker said. "She is in her rooms and asked that I awaken her when you arrived."

"Thank you, Denker." India paused. "How is she?"

"Frankly, Miss Prendergast, I don't believe she has ever been better."

India stared at him. "Do you really think so?"

"He thinks so, dear India, because it's true." Heloise sailed down the stairs and didn't so much as pause before throwing her arms around India in a warm embrace. "My darling girl, I am so sorry I worried you. That was the very last thing I wished to do."

Whether it was her concern over Heloise or the awful ache that had gripped her since leaving Derek, but something inside India shattered at Heloise's touch and she sobbed against the older woman.

"My poor child." Heloise rocked India and patted her head. "I don't believe I've ever seen you cry before. Not even when you were a girl."

"I don't cry." India sobbed. "I never cry."

"I know, dear. I've always found it most concerning."

India drew her head back and frowned. "Why?"

"Because it seems to me you have always held everything tightly inside you. As if you were afraid to let yourself feel too much. Or perhaps let others know that you did feel."

"Nonsense." India impatiently dashed the tears from her face and stepped back. "Where have you been? Why did you stop writing to me? What is it that you didn't want anyone else to tell me?"

"We do have a great deal to talk about. I have much to tell you, including one or two things I probably should have told you long ago." Heloise took India's arm and led her into the parlor. "You should sit down."

"I don't want to sit down," India said but sat on the sofa nonetheless. "What I want is answers."

"And you shall have them." Heloise settled on the sofa beside her. "But I daresay you won't like them."

"I don't expect to."

"Try not to judge too harshly, India." Heloise thought for a moment. "First, I never left England."

"What?" Of all the things India had been expecting— or perhaps feared—this was not among them. "But I received a number of letters from you."

"I did write the letters." She leaned forward in a confidential manner. "I found the Baedeker guides most helpful in that."

India stared. "They were very authentic."

"I thought so." Heloise nodded with satisfaction. "I wrote the letters and planned the itinerary with the help of the Lady Travelers Society—lovely women, I might add."

This made no sense at all. India nodded numbly.

"Then I sent Mademoiselle Marquette off on a tour of Europe with the letters in one hand and sufficient funds in the other." Heloise beamed as if she was quite proud of herself.

India wasn't sure she wished to hear more but, like a moth, this was a flame she could not resist. "And?"

"And that's where everything unraveled." Heloise heaved a heartfelt sigh. "Mademoiselle made it as far as Paris, decided to visit her family, somewhere close to Paris—I forget where—and then abandoned the entire plan, returning the remaining letters and most of the money I'd given her. This was extremely upsetting, and I would have discharged her at once had she not already submitted her resignation."

India could hardly believe her ears. All Heloise needed was a dead body and a fortune in stolen loot and she'd have all the makings for an excellent detective story.

India shook her head in confusion. "But why?"

"For you, dear."

"For me?"

"I didn't want you to worry."

"Well, it didn't quite go the way you wished," India said sharply. "I have been terribly worried."

"Precisely why I wish I could have discharged Mademoiselle Marquette myself." Heloise pressed her lips together. "She has proved most disappointing."

India stared. "I went to Paris to find you!"

"I know." A brilliant smile creased Heloise's lips. "I was so proud of you when I heard that. Was it wonderful?"

"Yes," she said without thinking, but it was true. In spite of everything, it had been wonderful.

"I must admit I am a wee bit jealous. I believe I shall have to go to Paris myself soon. I have always wanted to, you know."

"Heloise." India inhaled a calming breath. "Why did you arrange all this to make me think you were traveling when you say you never left England?"

"Yes, well." Heloise winced. "That is a bit awkward."

"*That* is the awkward part?" India snorted. "I can hardly wait to hear this."

"Sarcasm, India." Heloise cast her a chastising look. "Go on."

"Very well." Heloise folded her hands in her lap. "Some thirty-four years ago, when I was seventeen, I fell madly, passionately in love with a young man only a few years older than I. He was tall and dashing with dark hair and blue eyes. He had the most wonderful laugh and the wickedest smile I'd ever seen, as if he could see through to my very soul and my most secret desires." She smiled with the memory. "You're so sensible, I'm sure you can't imagine how easy it would be to fall in love with a man like that."

"On the contrary, Heloise," India said slowly. "I can understand it all too well."

"He was the son of a merchant. One of the reasons my father disapproved and forbid me to see him. I was far too timid to defy my father, which, in hindsight, was the greatest mistake of my life." She hesitated, no doubt lost in memories and regret.

"And," India said gently.

"And, a few months before I began my travels—"

"Your grand deception."

Heloise ignored her. "Quite by happenstance, I met him again. His hair is more gray than dark now and he is not as slender as he once was, but his eyes still sparkle with laughter and he still looks at me as if I were the loveliest, most wonderful woman in the world. He is a widow now, childless and quite wealthy."

At some point during Heloise's discourse, India's mouth had dropped open, and she now made a concerted effort to close it.

"We began seeing each other, and he wishes to marry me. But I felt—as it had been a very long time and we have both changed—that it would be wiser to become reacquainted with one another before taking such an irrevocable step. So, we have been at his country house for the last few months." Denker was right—she'd never looked happier.

"Why didn't you just tell me all of this? Why make me think you had left the country?"

"Because I knew you would disapprove," she said simply. "I didn't want to hear all the sensible, rational reasons why a man and woman—both past their fiftieth year—could not be together if they so desired. I

especially did not want to be lectured about impropriety nor did I wish to be convinced to abandon what you
would see as a foolish endeavor." She fixed India with
a firm eye. "It wasn't. James and I intend to marry as
soon as possible. But aside from everything else, I did
not want you to think less of me. I did not want you to
be disappointed."

India stared for a long moment. Heloise was no older
than Derek's mother, who was now on her third husband
and every bit as in love with him as she had been with
her first. India had never thought of Heloise as being
the sort of woman who had romantic dreams and desires. Apparently in that she was wrong. Terribly, horribly wrong. "You shouldn't have had to go to all this
trouble, spend all that money. You should have been
able to tell me."

"My dear girl, you are who, for the most part, I raised
you to be." She hesitated. "As for the money, well, I
haven't been entirely forthright with you about our finances, either."

"What do you mean?"

"I have a great deal of money, India. Far more than
you imagine. I have arranged for it all to be yours one
day, even after James and I marry. I have never spent it
freely because I have a dreadful fear of being old and
penniless and forced to rely on the kindness of relatives
so distant they scarcely know my name. Beyond that—"
she straightened her shoulders "—I've had money my
entire life, and it has brought me nothing save a modicum of financial security. I have no particular skills except for my art, an unreliable source of income under
the best of circumstances. Furthermore, I allowed my
father to run my life—admittedly out of fear of losing

my finances and in doing so, lost the love of my life. Aside from you, I am alone.

"When you came into my care, I realized I didn't like the way I had been brought up. To believe that a girl was of little purpose except to marry well. Because my finances are sound, I never needed courage or strength. I did not want you to become me."

India considered her cousin. This was a great deal to digest. She chose her words with care. "I was terribly worried about you, which makes it difficult to condone your deceptions—"

Heloise's expression crumpled.

"But that you found it necessary because of my un-yielding, unrelenting, always-right nature…" India met the older woman's gaze directly. This would have been an entirely different conversation before India went to Paris. "I am so, so sorry." She swallowed against the lump in her throat. "Can you ever forgive me?"

"My darling girl." Heloise sniffed back a tear. "There is nothing to forgive."

"And I do think, given that you concocted an elabo-rate scheme to make me think you were traveling, you underestimate your skills. It was all rather brilliant."

"Do you really think so?"

"I do." India laughed. "I truly do." She paused. "I am wondering, though."

"Yes."

"It doesn't matter really, nothing more than a point of curiosity but…" She studied her cousin, then smiled in a rueful manner. "How much money do you have?"

Heloise laughed with as much relief as amusement. The thought flashed through India's mind that Derek was right. This was not his story to tell.

And once again, she'd been wrong.

CHAPTER TWENTY-SEVEN

It is not enough to reach one's destination in a timely manner. The excitement of travel lies as much in the journey as it does the destination. Even the most disastrous of excursions brings unexpected adventure and gladdens the spirit. And we are the better for it.
                    —The Lady Travelers Society Guide

DEREK WAS FAR smarter than India had imagined. Certainly, the man would have to be shrewd to have come up with the Lady Travelers scheme in the first place, but that was only the beginning of the machinations of his clever mind.

He'd been absolutely right in refusing to say anything about what Heloise had done, although India wasn't entirely sure how much of her story he knew. Still, refusing to reveal the older woman's secrets had been both wise and gallant. One really couldn't fault him for that even if, at the time, India had.

She had thought, perhaps, he would immediately follow her to London. It was neither sensible nor rational, given the way they had parted, but then he was more prone to impulse and emotion than she. And the man had declared his love and his intention to marry her, after all.

But he did not appear on the first day after she returned, nor the second. On the third day she wondered if he was coming at all and asked Heloise to make discreet inquiries at the Lady Travelers Society. Heloise dutifully reported that, as far as Lady Blodgett knew, Derek had not yet returned to London. Why on earth not? What was keeping him in Paris? Unless, of course, he simply wished to stay as far away from her as possible. Which was silly. She was more than ready to acknowledge he was right and she was wrong. Again. Admittedly, he had no way of knowing that. By the time a full week had passed, India had to face the awful, obvious truth.

Whatever had happened between them in Paris, whatever feelings they might have had, whatever they might have shared or said was apparently relegated to Paris. Paris is where it had begun and Paris was where it had ended and Paris was where it would remain.

India had never imagined something like this could hurt quite so much. The deepest sort of unrelenting pain ached inside her. Regardless of what she did to keep her mind occupied, it was always there, hovering at the edge of perception, ready to sweep through her over and over again, and crush her heart. Pain made worse by knowing the blame could be squarely laid at her feet. Pity she had no idea what to do about it.

Still, the rest of the world continued without pause as if unaware of, or indifferent to, her utter despair. She met Heloise's intended—Mr. James Kirby—and they discussed plans for their upcoming nuptials, which the happy couple wanted without delay. India returned to work with Sir Martin but only until a suitable replacement could be found. She began that search at once.

On the eighth day after her return from Paris, India decided enough was more than enough. She had given him a full week. A long, endless week filled with dismay and grief and regret. Something needed to be done, and it was up to her to do it.

If Derek refused to seek her out, she would track him down to the ends of the earth if necessary. She did not intend to grovel but, at the very least, she owed him an apology. A sincere, heartfelt, admission of her error in judgment and an equally earnest request for forgiveness. Whether said apology also included a reinstatement of her feelings was yet to be determined, but she would certainly not rule it out. It was entirely possible Derek no longer shared her feelings, but that was a risk she would have to take.

India Prendergast had never been in love before and, at the moment, found it awkward and unpleasant and agonizing. But as brief as it had been, it had also been quite wonderful, fraught with enchantment and filled with hope and promise. And that alone was worth fighting for.

But first she had to find the blasted man. She stopped to send a telegram to Lord Brookings on her way to Sir Martin's house asking if his stepbrother was still in Paris and, if not, where was he? It was exactly ten words.

There were already several responses to the advertisements India had placed seeking a new secretarial assistant for Martin. She'd spent much of the day thus far considering the various applicants and preparing a detailed list of questions for individual interviews. She had no plans for her own future but she could not get on with her life until Martin was settled in his.

It was midafternoon when irate voices sounded in the foyer. Martin's butler—Kenton—perhaps the most serene creature in the entire world, never raised his voice.

"Miss Prendergast!" Lady Blodgett swept into Martin's library on a wave of indignation, Kenton a sputtering, outraged step behind. "A word, if you please."

"Lady Blodgett." India shot a quick look at Martin,

they both rose to their feet and she nodded to Kenton to take his leave. "Good day."

"It's not at all a good day. In point of fact, I would say it's a dreadful day." She pinned India with a hard look. "And you, Miss Prendergast, are to blame."

"Me? Exactly what have I done?" India asked cautiously.

"Now see here, Lady Blodgett," Martin began. The older lady shot him a venomous look, and the poor dear wilted. "What have you done, India?" he said weakly.

India shook her head. "I have no idea."

"My great-nephew, dear, dear Derek, returned to London this morning—" India's heart leaped "—only to be greeted very nearly the moment he stepped off the train by the authorities who dragged him off to Newgate!"

India gasped. "Good Lord!"

Lady Blodgett crossed her arms over her chest. "Do not feign innocence with me, Miss Prendergast. While I firmly believe Derek is not considerably worse than most men of his years and background, I am well aware that you think my dear, dear nephew is an unscrupulous scoundrel."

"I most certainly do not!" India huffed, then paused. "Well, not anymore. I admit I did when we first met but now..." She drew a deep breath. "Now, I think he's simply gone astray, but I believe he is truly a good man."

"Then why did you have him arrested?" Lady Blodgett shook her head in a chastising manner. "Not the least bit sporting of you, Miss Prendergast."

"I didn't have him arrested." Justified indignation colored her words. "He plans on atoning for his misdeeds, and that is more than sufficient. I do not want to see him in prison."

"Someone does," Lady Blodgett said darkly.

Martin cleared his throat. "I say, there might have been a bit of an, oh, misunderstanding."

At once India realized the truth. She stared at Martin. "What have you done?"

"Nothing, really." He tugged anxiously at his collar. "I might have mentioned in passing to Inspector Cooper that I had heard Mr. Saunders's confession with my own ears and I would be prepared, if necessary, to testify to that effect."

"Aha!" Lady Blodgett glared.

"And I might also, possibly—" Martin winced "—have suggested it would be wise to keep a close watch at the train stations as Mr. Saunders was likely to be returning from Paris at any time."

This was not at all like Martin, who, until he had decided to follow her to Paris, had been one of the least judgmental and disapproving people in the world. He would never have condoned illegalities but he was usually willing to give someone the benefit of the doubt. She had always found it most exasperating.

"How could you?"

"The man should be punished for his crimes," he said staunchly "There was a time when you agreed with me."

"Good Lord, Martin, life is not all black or white, good or bad. And people especially are not perfect. Nor should we expect them to be."

"*You* expect people to be perfect!"

"Yes, well…" She shrugged helplessly. "I was wrong."

"You may have been, but I was not." He drew himself up. "I thought it was for the best."

Lady Blodgett gave him a disgusted look. "My, you are a pompous ass, aren't you?"

"He really isn't," India said. "He's usually quite nice. I don't know what's happened to him."

"You've changed, India, and so have I. I told you I did not intend to give up." His gaze sought hers. "I thought if he was out of your life, you wouldn't have to leave mine."

"Oh dear, Martin." Her heart clenched. "I thought you understood."

"I did, until you and Saunders had that nasty falling-out and I thought—or hoped—things could go back to the way they had always been." He sighed. "But they can't, can they?"

"I'm afraid not." India turned to Lady Blodgett. "We need to free Derek at once. Regardless of what he has done, he is willing to set everything to rights and make amends for his less-than-ethical ways."

The older woman stared. "What are you talking about?"

"I'm talking about the fact that Derek is using the Lady Travelers Society as a way to defraud un-suspecting women out of their savings. You just said you knew I thought he was a scoundrel." India pulled her brows together. "What were you talking about?"

Lady Blodgett lowered her voice in a confidential manner. "I assumed you considered him a scoundrel because he has a decidedly colorful reputation."

"No." India shook her head. "Although that is not a mark in his favor."

"Nonetheless the fact remains, Mr. Saunders has been swindling helpless females who have succumbed to the questionable lure of travel." Martin glared at Lady Blodgett.

"He most certainly has not!" Lady Blodgett squared her shoulders. "I have."

India stared. "You have?"

"Not by myself, of course. Mrs. Higginbotham and Mrs. Fitzhew-Wellmore have been by my side every moment." She paused. "We really didn't see it as fraud, you know. Oh, we were aware that we had no idea how to plan or arrange for travel, but no one seemed to mind. None of our members complained about our lectures or our advice or our lack of actual travel experience, although admittedly, we might not have mentioned that. Regardless, we are a most convivial group all in all. Why, things were going along quite nicely until Derek took a distinctly different view of our activities, and dear Lady Heloise was lost, of course."

"Derek allowed me to believe this was his doing," India said slowly. "He was protecting you."

"And wasn't that noble of him?" Lady Blodgett fairly glowed with pride. "He's really a very thoughtful boy."

"So Derek has not been fleecing women out of their money?" As many times as she'd been wrong in recent weeks, this was her biggest mistake.

"Absolutely not."

Martin blew a resigned breath. "Perhaps I should pay a call on Inspector Cooper and arrange for Mr. Saunders's release."

"We shall all go," India said firmly. The least she could do was play a part in his rescue. Besides, he would probably be a little more inclined to accept her apology if she helped free him.

"You shall ride in my carriage with me, Miss Prendergast." Lady Blodgett started toward the door. "Sir Martin, you shall have to take a cab."

"But—"

Lady Blodgett's eyes narrowed.

"Yes, of course," Martin murmured. "A cab it is then."

A few minutes later, they were on their way. India could barely sit still. She tried and dismissed a dozen different ways of saying what had to be said. Perhaps it was best simply to blurt it all out. That she was wrong.

That she had gravely misjudged him. That she loved him. That she prayed he still loved her.

The carriage rolled to a stop, and Lady Blodgett turned toward her. "Before we go inside, I do need to clarify one point."

"Very well," India said cautiously.

The older lady studied her closely. "You harbor a certain affection for my nephew, do you not?"

India nodded.

"Dare I assume you are in love with him?"

"I'm afraid so."

"Excellent." Lady Blodgett beamed. "Then we should go in."

They stepped out of the carriage, and India realized this was wrong. Poor, dear Lady Blodgett's mind was perhaps not as sharp as it once was.

"Lady Blodgett." India took the older woman's arm and gently turned her back to the carriage. "We're going to Newgate, not the Explorers Club."

"You must have misunderstood, Miss Prendergast." Lady Blodgett shook off India's hand then took her elbow in a shockingly firm grip and steered her toward the door. "Effie is giving a lecture today on the perils of lost luggage."

"No one understands the importance of that particular topic more than I, but we do need to arrange for Derek's release."

"Oh, he's not in prison."

"But you said—"

"I believe what I said was that he had been taken to Newgate. I did not say he stayed."

"But you sent Sir Martin—"

"One makes mistakes when one is old and feeble, dear," she said in a lofty manner.

India stared. There was nothing feeble about Lady Blodgett.

The older woman led the way into the building. "Derek has, in fact, spent much of the day in the final arrangements of a business transaction." They stepped into the Lady Travelers lecture hall.

"Then where is he?"

"Hush." Lady Blodgett nodded toward the podium. Mrs. Higginbotham had already begun speaking. She was flanked on either side by large rectangular shapes covered with sheeting. Mrs. Fitzhew-Wellmore sat in a chair behind her. The room was impressively full. Lady Blodgett leaned close to India and spoke softly. "There doesn't seem to be an empty chair. Why don't you wait here while I join Effie and Poppy on the podium?"

India was not about to argue with an elderly woman in a room full of older ladies listening to how not to lose their luggage. At the moment she was entirely too restless to sit and much preferred to stand at the back of the room. Besides, she had yet to see Derek and obviously would get no further information from Lady Blodgett until Mrs. Higginbotham was finished.

"Here, we have a properly addressed and labeled trunk." Mrs. Higginbotham pulled off the sheet on the form to her right to reveal a new trunk covered in checked canvas with wood slats, leather bindings and brass accents. "This arrived only today from Paris."

"With your new clothes inside," a voice said quietly beside her. "Mother sent it."

"Derek!" Her pulse jumped.

"Quiet." His voice was little more than a whisper. "Aunt Guinevere does not like interruptions during the lectures."

"Yes, of course, but we have a great deal to talk about." It was all she could do to keep from throwing her arms around him.

"Shh." He nodded toward the podium. He certainly seemed to have no difficulty keeping himself in check. Her heart sank.

"And here we have a wretched example of what happens when luggage is not addressed properly." Mrs. Higginbotham aimed a chastising look at her audience, as if each and every one of them was complicit in the mislabeling of luggage. "While intended for shipment to Paris—" She pulled the cover off the second covered shape.

India gasped. "That's my trunk!"

"It instead traveled to Prague."

India stared. "Prague?"

"These things happen you know." Derek shrugged. "Prague, Paris, it's an easy mistake."

"No, it's not." India shook her head. "Prague and Paris are not at all alike save that they begin with *P*." She narrowed her eyes. "*You* filled out the luggage labels before we left London."

"Did I?" He smiled in an overly innocent manner. "I really can't recall. And it scarcely matters as you now have your trunk back."

"Derek—"

"Mr. Saunders." Mrs. Higginbotham's voice rang from the podium. "Might I suggest you take your discussion out of the room so that the attention of everyone here will be on today's topic of lost luggage rather than straining to hear what you and Miss Prendergast have to say to each other? Although I am certain it is fascinating."

"Quite right, Mrs. Higginbotham, it is fascinating. My apologies." Derek nodded to the rest of the group. "Ladies."

He grabbed India's hand and fairly dragged her out of the room. The moment the doors closed behind them, he turned to her.

"Derek, I—"

He pulled her into his arms and pressed his lips to hers, stealing her breath and searing her heart. At last he raised his head from hers and grinned down at her. "Good day, Miss Prendergast."

"Mr. Saunders." She stared up at him. Why was it with this man she rarely knew what to say? "You look…well."

He laughed. "Not bad for a man newly released from prison."

She winced. "I am sorry about that. Sir Martin thought—"

Derek's brow rose. "It was his doing?"

"I'm afraid so."

"Not yours?"

"No." She sighed. "Even before I found out the truth about the Lady Travelers Society and your great-aunt and her friends, I didn't want you incarcerated."

"I would prefer to stay out of prison."

"And keep Lady Blodgett and the others out of prison, as well."

He nodded. "I have made arrangements to ensure the society is completely aboveboard in the future."

"Oh?"

"Lord Westvale has a number of business interests and associates. One of them is something of a travel entrepreneur who thinks the idea of a travel society and agency aimed at women is brilliant. He is purchasing the assets of the society—mostly the membership rolls and the name—along with the services of Aunt Guinevere and her friends. They will receive a tidy initial sum as well as a quarterly stipend for their continued services. They will also remain the public face of the society, and will continue to give their lectures and their advice for as long as they wish to do so. They will not, however, arrange any travel. Ever."

She laughed. "Brilliant solution."

He grinned. "I thought so."

She studied him closely. "I haven't reformed you then, have I?"

"I'm afraid not."

"Because there was nothing to reform."

"Not when it comes to the Lady Travelers Society." He chuckled. "I am sorry you're disappointed, but I daresay I have any number of other wicked ways that you may turn your attention to."

"You intend to go on with your wicked ways?"

"Absolutely." He nuzzled the side of her neck. "As reforming me will keep you extremely busy."

"Good." She shivered beneath his touch and resisted the urge to melt into a small puddle at his feet. "Oh, as for my saying I was not the type of woman you should marry—"

"You were wrong."

She frowned. "Am I to spend the rest of my life being wrong about everything?"

"I do hope so." He grinned against her neck. "Think of the fun we will have."

The most tantalizing sense of anticipation filled her at the idea of exactly what that *fun* entailed. A feeling obviously attributable to the caress of his lips, which was indeed most delightful. She tried and failed to hide the breathless note in her voice. "I now see all those very legitimate reasons why we cannot wed are silly. Therefore, I am now willing to marry you."

He raised his head and stared down at her. "I don't believe I've asked."

"I am well aware of that." She huffed. "It is most annoying. Although you did state your intentions quite clearly."

"Regardless…" He shook his head regretfully. "I don't think a man can be held to anything he might say when he is not fully clothed."

"Very well then." She shrugged. "Don't marry me."

His brow furrowed. "Are you going to do this for the rest of my life?"

"Do what?"

"Drive me stark, raving mad."

She stifled the laughter bubbling up inside her. "I do hope so, Derek." She slid her arms around his neck and pulled his lips back to hers. What she'd found—what they'd found—certainly wasn't sensible or practical or rational. She doubted if anything connected to love would be at all efficient or organized. Odd that none of that mattered in the least compared to the sheer joy of being in his arms. Of him in her life. The carefree scoundrel and the sensible spinster.

For now, and for the rest of their days.

It made absolutely no sense at all.

THE DOOR TO the lecture hall quietly closed.

"Do you think they saw us?" Poppy's gaze slid from one friend to the next.

"Oh, I doubt it." Gwen waved off the question. "I suspect they wouldn't have cared anyway. And we only had the door open a crack. As it was, the three of us had to jostle for position."

"Poppy would barely let anyone else get a look." Effie glared at the other woman.

"There really wasn't much to see," Poppy murmured. "But it was quite lovely."

"Nor do we wish to intrude," Gwen said firmly. "We simply wanted to confirm our suspicions, and now we have."

"It's perfect." Poppy sighed, a wistful smile curving her lips. "Simply perfect."

"Another successful journey completed." Gwen nodded with satisfaction. "Thanks to us."

Effie frowned. "We didn't do anything."

"One could argue if we hadn't started the Lady Travelers Society in the first place," Poppy said slowly, "Derek wouldn't have had to try to find Lady Heloise and India wouldn't have insisted on accompanying him."

"We don't know exactly what transpired in Paris. They didn't find Lady Heloise, after all." Effie paused. "But it does appear to have worked out well."

"My dear friend, you know as well as I that the end of the road is never as important as the journey taken to get there. The grail is never as important as the quest. And as it is to our credit that my nephew and Miss Prendergast began the quest in the first place, we can legitimately take credit for the outcome."

"We certainly would have received the blame had it not gone well." Effie shuddered.

"Exactly." Gwen nodded with satisfaction. "I believe we can consider the Lady Travelers Society a most successful venture."

"I know I haven't had this much fun in years," Effie said with a thoughtful smile. "I never expected that."

"Neither did I." Poppy grinned. "And I must say I feel younger."

"An added benefit." Gwen laughed. "And who knows where the next road may lead." She cast an affectionate smile at these dear women who had been by her side for much of her journey through life and would be until they had all breathed their last.

"And I know I, for one, cannot wait."

* * * * *

The Proper Way to Stop a Wedding
(in Seven Days or Less)

The Beginning

Miss Celia Bromley refused to ruin her half sister Katherine's wedding.

Even if Celia did not especially like Katherine.

Even if Katherine detested Celia.

Even if Celia had fallen madly, irrevocably, hopelessly in love with Katherine's groom.

Day One

CHAPTER ONE

Danby Manor, May 1855

"ARE THERE ANY QUESTIONS?" Guinevere Blodgett beamed at her dearest friends in the world. Friends who had set aside everything in their own lives to come to Danby Manor at her request. But then wasn't that what friends were for?

Mrs. Ophelia Higginbotham and Mrs. Persephone Fitzhew-Wellmore—Effie and Poppy to those who knew them best—traded glances.

"Clarification more than questions," Effie began. "Apparently, you have sent for us so that we may help you in the preparations for the wedding that is to occur in one week's time. A wedding that really has nothing to do with you as it's the wedding of your niece's half sister to an earl's brother."

"And you have been, oh, lured into assisting," Poppy continued.

"Exactly." Gwen blew a long breath. "It wasn't by choice, believe me." She had arrived at Danby Manor two days ago and realized at once someone needed to take things in hand. And as the bride's father—and then the groom's brother upon her arrival—had asked her to do so, she couldn't bring herself to refuse. There was entirely too much at stake. "You are both well aware

that since my sister died, I have not been as close to
Celia as I would have liked."

"Because of that beast of a father of hers." Effie
sniffed. "And *that woman*."

"As much as I would like to blame them fully, much
of the fault lies with me." Gwen twisted her hands together and paced absently. "I should have taken steps
to ensure I saw Celia more frequently but they have
always lived in the country and my life is in London.
And Celia was usually away at school. But we do cor-
respond regularly..." Gwen cringed, well aware of how
feeble her excuse sounded. As indeed it was.

Gwen's sister, Viviane, had married Alfred, Viscount Bromley, a widower with two young daughters—
Katherine and Louise. Viviane had promptly given him
Celia but had unfortunately succumbed to influenza
some twelve years later, leaving the household in the
hands of Miss Frances Quince, Alfred's first wife's sister—also known as *that woman*. She had immediately
taken up residence, assumed the position of mistress of
the house and had sent all three girls away to school,
no doubt in the hope that should the legal prohibition to
marrying the sister of one's deceased wife someday be
abolished she would be in an excellent position. From
what Gwen had ascertained through the years, Miss
Quince was inordinately ambitious and wanted nothing
more than to be the next viscountess. The older girls
blamed their banishment on their half sister. Katherine and Louise had never considered Celia their true
sister. A belief no doubt encouraged by Miss Quince.

"You're not being at all fair to yourself," Poppy said
firmly. "We have watched you time and again try to see
Celia only to be rebuffed by her father and that woman.

And you did manage to visit with her when the family was in London a few months ago."

"Only twice. Even so, I should have tried harder." Gwen sighed then straightened her shoulders. "Regardless, I was asked by Alfred to come here to Danby to assist in Katherine's wedding. Apparently Miss Quince is not quite up to arranging a social event of this magnitude and is driving Alfred and his daughters mad."

"Not that they don't deserve it," Effie muttered.

"I could not agree more but—" Gwen fixed Effie with a firm look "—if this wedding does not go well, it will reflect upon the entire family. I want nothing more than to see Celia married to a good man and I think it's past time the three of us did something about that. And we shall start the moment we have put Katherine's wedding behind us."

"How delightful." Poppy grinned. "I've always enjoyed playing matchmaker."

"But Celia's cause will not be helped if this wedding is a shambles. The gossip would ruin any chances she might have at a good match. Reputation, as you know, is everything."

"Might I point out that Alfred's excessive gambling and loss of the family's fortunes to the point where none of his daughters had a season has already damaged that reputation beyond repair?" Effie said in a deceptively mild manner.

"Come now, half the gentry in England has exceptionally bad habits and lives on credit." Gwen waved off the comment. "The trick is not to acknowledge that publicly. Society runs on illusion. As Katherine is to marry the twin brother of the Earl of Danby, the guest list is extensive and socially prominent."

"No surprise there," Effie murmured.

"If this wedding is a disaster, I dare not think what the repercussions for Celia's future will be." Gwen shuddered. "The groom's mother died several years ago, so apparently I am the closest female relation on either side. Except for Miss Quince, of course, who does seem unable to manage this."

Gwen had realized very nearly the moment she arrived that the social events Miss Quince and Katherine had planned leading up to the wedding, as well as the nuptials themselves, were both extravagant and complex. But then the groom's brother was paying for it all. While Miss Quince had said no expense would be spared, Gwen suspected the earl was a bit less than thrilled at the expenditures even if he did seem to care too much for his brother to protest. At least thus far.

"Well, we are here now." Effie offered a feeble smile. "And it's not as if we had anything better to do."

A not uncommon occurrence, as the husbands of all three women were currently out of the country. Charles Blodgett and Malcomb Fitzhew-Wellmore were both engaged in pursuits of exploration, and Effie's husband, William, was a military officer currently in the Crimea. Gwen and Poppy considered it their duty as her friends to keep Effie's mind off the war as much as possible— a difficult task given the papers were full of reports of battles and men lost or wounded.

It was their husbands' penchant for wandering the world in the name of exploration or in service to Her Majesty that had led to the three women meeting in the first place, some ten or so years ago. They were of a similar age—all three now past their forty-fifth year—none of them had been blessed with children, nor did any of them have much in the way of family, and they became as close as sisters. Indeed, they thought of themselves as such.

"I for one am delighted to lend my assistance. I love weddings." Poppy nodded enthusiastically. "What exactly do you want us to do?"

"Unfortunately, there are any number of details still to be arranged. I'm certain, between the three of us, we shall overcome any difficulties, although this is a bit more complicated than one might expect." Gwen braced herself and favored her friends with a confident smile. "In addition to the wedding itself—which I understand is more restrained than the bride had originally wanted at the request of the groom—there is to be a rather grand pre-wedding ball."

Goodness, one would have thought Gwen had tossed a bucket of cold water over her friends' heads given the disbelieving looks on their faces. Perhaps it was best to continue before either Effie or Poppy or both called for a carriage for the lengthy ride back to the nearest train station.

"However—"

"Oh, good, there's a *however*," Effie said wryly. "I was afraid there wouldn't be."

"Aside from ourselves and family members, there are no other guests staying here at the manor, which will make things much easier," Gwen began.

"Will it?" Poppy asked faintly.

Gwen ignored her. "While the staff seems adequately trained, they appear to have taken a rather strong dislike to Miss Quince."

Effie snorted.

"Only the earl and his brother, Henry, inhabit the house and then only when they're not residing in London, which apparently they do most of the year," Gwen said. "This is a bachelor establishment, ladies. So it's obvious why our help is so desperately needed."

"To be expected really." Poppy shook her head. "Men are helpless when it comes to the more practical aspects of life."

"Hard to believe they can expertly undertake an expedition to the far corners of an unexplored jungle but they cannot manage to direct a cook to prepare toast for breakfast," Effie added.

Gwen nodded. "There's been no mistress at Danby since the earl's mother died a few years ago and the staff might be a bit lax."

"Then we had best get started." Effie drew a bracing breath. "What exactly do you want us to do first?"

"You have both been traveling today and I know how wearing that is, so, for the moment, I want you to do nothing more than rest," Gwen said firmly.

"To gather our strength, no doubt." Effie's brow furrowed. "As we shall obviously need it."

"I have made lists of all that must be accomplished as well as charts delegating who should do what on which day and so on and so forth. I shall distribute those at tea and we can discuss all the details then."

"Will Miss Quince be assisting us?" Poppy asked.

"She has taken to her bed with a sick headache." Gwen shook her head in a mournful manner and summoned up her most sympathetic expression. "Poor dear."

"Poor dear, indeed." Effie tried and failed to look appropriately concerned but then Effie, and Poppy as well, held Miss Quince only slightly less responsible for keeping Gwen from her niece than they did Celia's father.

"One more thing." Gwen hesitated. She wasn't at all sure if she was right but something odd had struck her the first night at dinner and then again last night.

It was subtle and she could very easily be wrong. "You are both intelligent women and have been known to be quite observant. Do let me know if you notice anything…unexpected."

Once again her friends traded looks.

"What do you mean by 'unexpected'?" Caution sounded in Effie's voice.

"Goodness, Effie." Gwen huffed. "If I could tell you that, it wouldn't be at all unexpected but rather extremely expected. Don't you think?"

Effie's eyes narrowed.

"Besides, I want your unbiased, completely dispassionate opinion." Gwen chewed on her bottom lip thoughtfully. "Suffice it to say, I'm not sure all is as it appears. Or perhaps as it should be. I might well be wrong. However, if I'm right…"

Effie grinned. "I do love your howevers."

"If I'm right…" Gwen settled her gaze first on Poppy then shifted to Effie. "We shall have to take it upon ourselves to do something about it."

CHAPTER TWO

"MRS. BLODGETT, MRS. HIGGINBOTHAM and Mrs. Fitzhew-Wellmore—" Edward, the Earl of Danby, stood at the head of the dinner table and raised his glass in a toast "—welcome to Danby Manor. I cannot remember the last time so many lovely guests were gathered around this table. Thank you for improving the conversation—" he grinned "—and the view."

"Allow me to add my thanks, as well." Henry Saunders favored the newcomers with a welcoming smile then retook his seat.

It was indeed unusual to have any guests at all at the country house and rarer still to have ladies in residence. But between Katherine, her sisters Louise and Celia, Celia's aunt and her aunt's friends, the men in residence were outnumbered two to one. More, really, if one included Miss Quince, who was indisposed tonight and not at dinner. Apparently it took a flock of women to arrange a week of prenuptial events culminating in the extravaganza that would mark the joining in marriage of a man and a woman. Henry believed he might have heard doves mentioned but he preferred not to think about it. If he had his way, the ceremony would be simple and the celebration restrained.

His gaze caught his fiancée's. Katherine was seated beside Edward at the head of the table; her sister Louise sat on his left, devoting all of her attention to Edward.

Hoping to ensnare another Saunders brother, no doubt. Katherine cast him a brilliant, perfect smile and a wave of shame washed through him. Even if his thoughts about Louise were true, they were unkind. After all, she would be his sister-in-law when he married the incomparable Katherine.

Katherine Bromley might well have been the most beautiful woman Henry Saunders had ever seen. He was realistic enough about himself to understand that was why he was originally attracted to her. With her dark hair, vivid green eyes and delectable figure, she was the center of attention anywhere. When he met her, a scant three months ago, he had been most grateful none of the Bromley daughters had had an official season. Katherine would have been snatched up immediately, in spite of the family's financial difficulties. As it was, she had reached the advanced age of twenty-four without having wed. Henry had fallen head over heels for her very nearly at first sight.

It was not at all like him. While Edward—Ned to his brother—was the older of the twin brothers, and as such the one who had inherited the title of Earl of Danby from their father, Henry was the more sensible and responsible of the two. Ned often said it was a pity he was born a few minutes sooner as Henry had the temperament and the nature to be an excellent earl. Admittedly, Ned had spent the first few years after Father's death continuing his wild ways with little regard to the duties that had been thrust upon him, and Henry had been the one to make certain the needs of the estates and the family's business interests were met. It wasn't until their mother had died three years ago that Ned had finally accepted his fate. As if Mother's death had brought home to him the full responsibilities of his position. It had come as a shock to Henry when he realized his devil-may-care brother had become—for lack of a better word—an adult. Now the brothers worked together in a congenial and productive manner that served them both well.

In spite of being twins, their appearance was as individual as their natures. In their youth, they had often bemoaned the unfairness of not being identical and able to pass for each other. While they shared similar dark hair and brown eyes, and did indeed look like brothers, Henry was a few inches taller than Ned with a slighter build, whereas the earl's shoulders were broader, his form more solid. Both were considered above average in appearance, although Ned had always been rather dashing and exuberant, while Henry was far quieter and inclined toward pursuits of a scholarly nature.

Now, at the age of twenty-seven, both men were viewed as extremely eligible bachelors. While Henry had a significant fortune in his own right, Ned, of course, was a better catch and was hotly pursued by young ladies eager to be a countess and their equally eager mothers hoping to snag a title for their family. It was another mark of the disparity between the brothers that if anyone was asked which of the two was more likely to lose his head over a beautiful woman, Ned was the brother who came to mind, as he had indeed done so any number of times in the past.

Of course, he'd never been so stupid as to ask for their hand in marriage.

"You are a lucky man, Henry."

"Lucky?" His attention jerked to the lady seated beside him. Mrs. Blodgett was somewhere in her forties and was quite lovely for her age. As were her friends.

"Indeed." She nodded in Katherine's direction. "Katherine will make a beautiful bride."

"Oh, yes, Katherine." He smiled. "I am most fortunate."

It had all happened so fast. In hindsight, Henry wasn't sure how it had happened at all. Katherine was in many ways perfect—every man's dream come to life. And from the beginning, *she* was interested in *him*. That alone made her almost irresistible. Henry was used to being second to his brother, especially when it came to women, and he had never especially cared. But Katherine had eyes only for him.

He had been enamored of her in a lost-puppy sort of way from the moment they'd met. She had quite frankly swept him off his feet. It was as if he had been sucked into a whirlpool, an unrelenting force of nature. One moment she was gazing into his eyes and the next he'd been engaged. He had no idea what he had said but it had been heartfelt. Katherine had thought it important to wed as soon as possible, saying now that they had found each other, it would be foolish to put off starting their lives together. It had been terribly romantic and he had agreed wholeheartedly. Now it seemed absurd and ill-advised and rather stupid. He couldn't help but wonder if she had feared he might change his mind. Indeed, by the time he'd realized what a huge mistake this was, he was well on his way to the altar.

The enormity of his error in judgment loomed over him like a forbidding cloud, made all the darker for its unfamiliarity. Henry did not make mistakes. Nor was he ever the brother in the midst of a storm.

No, Henry Saunders was the responsible one. The one who should have been born first. He'd wondered on occasion why he hadn't as his nature was far more suited to the duties of the position of earl than his brother. But for all his acceptance of responsibility, he'd never had any desire for the title and everything it entailed. Indeed, his life was quite pleasant. He had the financial means to do as he wanted, the time to spend as he wished, satisfying work to fill his days and a staff that was as much family as employees. Someday, he expected to find a wife that would fit nicely into that life. He had certainly been with women, although he was not as accomplished in that respect as his brother. But he had only once before thought himself in love. He certainly never expected to fall in love again very nearly at first sight.

Or to fall out of love just as quickly.

"I'm afraid I don't know her well." Mrs. Blodgett studied Katherine. "Although she seems quite pleasant."

"Doesn't she, though?" Henry said without thinking then winced to himself. His comment was more telling than he had planned. Unfortunately, the more he grew to know Katherine, the less he wished to spend the rest of his life with her. He'd never been engaged before but he was fairly certain one should not think of one's future wife as shallow, vain and selfish. Worse, while she had seemed to adore him initially, now her feelings struck him as more rehearsed than genuine.

The fact of the matter was that he and Katherine shared no common ground. There was nothing Henry enjoyed more than immersing himself in a good book. Katherine disdained literature, preferring ladies' magazines, more for the fashion than any literary offerings. Henry preferred a quiet life with no more than a moderate number of social functions, whereas much of Katherine's talk of the future centered around the parties and soirees and balls they would attend after their marriage. Henry enjoyed museums and galleries and was intrigued by new artists. Katherine thought history was best left in the past and her idea of fine art was something created by a prestigious artist that looked nice on a wall. Aside from preparations for the wedding, much of her time was spent with her aunt and sister Louise planning how to decorate his house in London and discussions of what kind of grand house she wished him to build in the country. Henry had never particularly thought about money—although it was nice to have—and while he'd never been especially frugal, neither did he spend with wild abandon. Katherine was freely spending his family's money for the week's festivities. Admittedly, it was understandable given her own family's finances, and while Henry did not begrudge her that, he did hope this was just a momentary indulgence on her part. He feared he was wrong.

"My apologies, Mrs. Blodgett, but I'm afraid I'm confused. I would have assumed you knew Katherine, as well as the rest of the family, quite well."

"One would assume that." Mrs. Blodgett studied Celia sitting across the table from them, talking in an animated manner to Mrs. Higginbotham. "My sister was Celia's mother. Unfortunately, after her death, I was not able to see my niece as often as I would have liked."

"I gather you regret that."

A wry smile curved her lips. "You are remarkably perceptive, Henry."

"Some things are obvious, Mrs. Blodgett." He smiled, his gaze following hers. "At least to me."

Try as he might, he could not keep his thoughts off Katherine's youngest sister. Fair-haired and petite in stature, Celia wasn't as stunning as Katherine, but simply quite lovely in a quiet sort of way. There was something about Celia Bromley that was almost irresistible. Henry couldn't truly describe it and was afraid to try. From the moment he'd met her, quite by accident at one of his favorite booksellers', the moment he'd looked into her blue eyes, something inside of him had clicked like the turn of a key in a lock, as if all the puzzle pieces of his life had abruptly snapped into place. He'd had the strangest sense of recognition somewhere deep in his soul, as if they'd been destined to meet or had met before or had known each other always. The French called it *coup de foudre*, a bolt of lightning. Love at first sight. It was absurd of course. Only the French would give credence to such a thing. Silly, spontaneous feelings that struck without warning were certainly not to be trusted, not by a rational, sensible man.

Regardless, he'd found himself returning to the bookseller's more frequently than was his habit in hopes of meeting her again. It was hopeless, really—he didn't even know her name. Henry put any thought of her out of his mind and managed to convince himself whatever he had experienced was due no doubt to the onset of a cold or something he'd eaten that had disagreed with him, or simply dwelling on the incident gave it more importance than it warranted. Then he met Katherine and his life changed irrevocably. It wasn't until he'd already asked for her hand that he was introduced to her sisters and realized the awful, glaring truth. His brief encounter was his new fiancée's younger half sister. He couldn't help but wonder if he'd been so susceptible to Katherine's charms because somewhere deep inside he was mourning the loss of something he'd never had.

Neither of them acknowledged their previous encounter, at least not aloud. What difference did it make anyway? It was too late. He was to marry her sister and no matter what feelings Celia Bromley might stir inside him, there could be nothing between them. Still, in spite of his best efforts, he couldn't keep his gaze from wandering in her direction. Couldn't stop the odd twisting of his heart when she was near. Couldn't prevent thoughts of her that lingered in his mind and invaded his dreams. Without warning, Celia turned her head and her gaze met his. For a moment, it was as if all the air had rushed out of the room. As always, the look in her eyes was a reflection of his own—a mix of caution and longing and resignation. Not that either of them had ever admitted such a thing. Nor would they.

"Indeed, Henry, some things are more than obvious."

His gaze snapped back to Mrs. Blodgett and at once he realized his mistake. A truly innocent man would not have taken her casual comment as an indictment. But Mrs. Blodgett simply smiled in an innocuous manner and promptly changed the subject. "Your brother says you are quite interested in antiquities and all things ancient."

"Yes." He cleared his throat. "Indeed I am."

"My husband and some of his associates have been discussing an expedition to find the lost city of Troy."

"Really?" Henry stared. "What an extraordinary adventure that would be."

"Charles is a most adventurous sort and the more extraordinary the better." She smiled in an affectionate manner.

"You must miss him when he's away on his extraordinary adventures."

"Indeed I do but someday I shall wear down his resistance and he shall take me with him."

"But you're a woman."

"How clever of you to notice, Henry."

"My apologies, I didn't mean—"

"No apology needed." She waved off his comment. "Even in these modern times, the idea of a woman traveling anywhere not considered completely civilized is unthinkable. I do hope that will change one day but I am not overly optimistic. It is universally accepted that a woman's place is to be safely left behind to tend to house and home."

"And you disagree with that?" Caution edged his voice.

"Not entirely but even the most content among us can occasionally long for something a little more exciting. For now, I suppose we need to console ourselves with adventures of a less extraordinary nature." She smiled. "Walking down the path of life hand in hand with the right person is something of an adventure in and of itself. When one's heart is engaged—" she glanced down the table at Katherine "—it can be the most extraordinary adventure of all."

"No doubt," Henry said faintly.

It was bad enough to realize one wasn't in love with the woman one was committed to marry, but to accept the awful growing conviction that one didn't especially like her was much worse. But even that paled in the face of the horrible truth of the matter.

Henry Saunders had indeed found the love of his life and there was nothing he could do about it.

CHAPTER THREE

WHAT AN ABSURD SITUATION. What a ridiculous thing to have happened.

Celia Bromley paced the width of the room allotted her in Danby Manor. She wasn't sure how it had happened—it certainly wasn't intentional. Fate was no doubt to blame. Of course, if one believed in fate, then this was even worse as—

A knock sounded at her door.

"Come in," she said with relief. A distraction from her own thoughts would be most welcome.

The door opened and Aunt Guinevere popped her head in. "Are you busy, Celia? Might I join you for a chat?"

"Of course, Aunt Guinevere." She could think of nothing better to take her mind off Henry Saunders's brown eyes and engaging smile. "Please come in."

Aunt Guinevere stepped into the room, closed the door behind her and looked around. "My, this is lovely."

"Isn't it, though?" Celia smiled.

She'd never in her life had a bedchamber this nice. Of course, she'd never had one quite so large, either. No, the rooms at home at Bromwick Abbey were neither as gracious nor as beautifully appointed as those here. Danby Manor was most impressive and the abbey had seen better days. But then that was the price one paid when one's home was more than five hundred years old, had started life as a humble monastery and had never had an owner interested in more than a modest expansion.

"No wonder Katherine and Miss Quince had insisted on arriving well in advance of the wedding," Aunt Guinevere said, still surveying the room.

Katherine and Aunt Frances had thought it best to take up residence at Danby a full month before the wedding with the excuse that there was a great deal to be done. There was indeed, but Celia was certain the lure of elegance and comfort to be found at the manor was ultimately responsible for the family's lengthy stay.

It would have been much better for all concerned if they just sent the bride and her aunt. But of course that would never do. There were questions of propriety about two unmarried women residing in the same house with two unmarried gentlemen—no matter how grand the house. Regardless of his other failings, Father was a stickler for propriety when it came to the reputations of his daughters. Pity he hadn't been a bit more concerned about his own reputation—especially when it came to matters of finance. But Father had never quite grasped the idea that once his inherited funds were expended, there would be no more without some sort of effort on his part. Nor did he seem to understand gambling was perhaps not the best method for acquiring an income—especially if one was not particularly skilled or lucky. Fortunately, her grandfather had recognized this flaw in his heir and had set aside funding—managed by inflexible solicitors—to provide for schooling and minimal dowries for his granddaughters as well as a small, untouchable trust that provided an extremely modest yearly income. Not large enough to claim their place in society but sufficient to keep a roof over their heads.

"I am sorry I didn't see more of you when you were in London." Aunt Guinevere settled in one of two matching lady's chairs positioned by the window that overlooked the back garden.

"As am I but it couldn't be helped," Celia said with a smile. "We were only in London for a few months and we did manage to see each other twice." Even that had been difficult to arrange. Neither Father nor Aunt Frances had ever liked Aunt Guinevere but then Celia was fairly certain the feelings were mutual. But she and Aunt Guinevere wrote frequently and that was nearly as good as seeing one another in person.

"And did you enjoy your stay?"

"Oh, Aunt Guinevere, it was truly wonderful." Celia leaned toward the older woman. "I went to the Tower and the Zoological Gardens, and the Society of Antiquaries museum, and Madame Tussaud's, and Soane's Museum and, well, everywhere. I spent a great deal of time at the National Gallery and the British Museum."

The older woman bit back a smile. "I believe you mentioned some of that when we met in London."

"Probably, but it's worth repeating." Celia grinned. "I think I could quite happily spend every day for the rest of my life going back and forth between the National Gallery and the British Museum."

"There are worse ways to spend your life." Aunt Guinevere smiled. "The British Museum is where I met your uncle Charles, you know. We were both attending a lecture on Etruscan artifacts."

"I intend to live in London one day," Celia said firmly.

That she had managed to visit London at all was something of a miracle and due entirely to Aunt Frances. Unbeknownst to anyone else in the family, Aunt

Frances had received a small inheritance. She had wisely kept her windfall to herself as Father would have insisted she contribute to the family coffers given he provided a home for her. Regardless, at the beginning of the new year, Aunt Frances had decreed they would reside in London for several months in an effort to find a wealthy, well-connected husband for Katherine—who was not getting any younger—and hopefully Louise and Celia as well before all three girls became spinsters and remained their father's responsibility for the rest of their lives. Father agreed without hesitation. The idea of three less people demanding he give up his foolish ways and do something of worth with his life was irresistible to him. And, as Frances had the money to pay for letting a London residence, it seemed an excellent plan.

Unfortunately, London society was not overly interested in sisters aged twenty-four, twenty-three and nineteen no matter how lovely or accomplished they were. Still, Aunt Frances was determined to see at least one—if not all three girls—wed and did manage a few invitations, mostly for Katherine and Louise. Katherine had done her part by meeting and enchanting the brother of an earl, who reportedly had a significant income, even if he was not her first choice. Celia had no illusions about her older sister. Katherine was almost as clever as she was mercenary. She immediately realized she did not appeal to the earl and set her sights on his brother.

"I know I would never want to live anywhere else." Aunt Guinevere paused. "Will Katherine and Henry be living in London after they're wed?"

"I believe so. Henry and his brother manage the family business interests and Henry has a lovely house in Mayfair."

It was at Henry's house that Celia had discovered the gentleman she'd had a chance conversation with at a bookstore, the man she couldn't get out of her head, was soon to be her brother-in-law. He had already asked for Katherine's hand and had invited the rest of the family and his brother to join him for dinner. It was an evening of revelation in any number of ways.

For one thing—Henry Saunders wasn't at all the type one would have thought would appeal to Katherine. He was handsome in a quiet sort of way but not the kind of man one read about in novels of romance or adventure. One did not swoon with immediate passion when meeting the calm, self-possessed Mr. Henry Saunders. He was obviously intelligent and scholarly and somewhat restrained, in contrast to his brother, who was brash and amusing and worldly.

Indeed, upon one's first meeting one might have thought Henry entirely too somber, even cold in nature. Until one gazed into his brown eyes and saw compassion and intelligence and all manner of wicked amusement. And the oddest sort of recognition. As if he saw something in her no one else had ever seen. The moment he touched her hand, the strangest sense of awareness shot through her as if she had just met her fate. It was at once terrifying and exciting and utterly hopeless.

"He seems quite pleasant."

Celia's gaze shot to her aunt's. "Who?"

"Why, Henry of course. Mr. Saunders." Aunt Guinevere's brow arched upward. "Were we speaking of someone else?"

"No, of course not. Sorry, my mind must have wandered." Precisely as it had done since the moment she'd met Henry. She drew a deep breath in hopes of regaining some semblance of composure. "Henry is very nice and very clever and a man of honor."

"Not the kind of man to go back on his word, then?"

Celia shook her head. "Good Lord, no."

No, she thought sadly, Henry Saunders was not the type to rescind an offer of marriage even if he discovered his fiancée was petty and greedy and not an especially nice person. Even if he realized he was making a horrendous mistake.

Even if the look in his eyes when his gaze met his fiancée's younger sister's matched the feelings in that sister's heart.

Henry was as fine a man as Celia had ever met and deserved better than Katherine. But, although Katherine, and Louise as well, had never considered Celia anything other than a mistake on their father's part, Celia could not bring herself to tell Henry that Katherine's interest was more in his family's position and his fortune than it was in him. Family, after all, deserved one's loyalty even if members of that family had done nothing to warrant it.

"One might say a moment of dishonor," her aunt said slowly, "might be worth avoiding a lifetime of misery."

Celia frowned. "What do you mean?"

Aunt Guinevere reached out and took Celia's hand. "What I mean, my dear child, is that Henry Saunders gives every appearance of a man in love."

"Not surprising." Celia's stomach lurched. "He is, after all, to be married in a week."

"Celia dear—" Aunt Guinevere paused to gather her thoughts "—I have been married for more than twenty-three years and in love for longer than that. I have learned to recognize that feeling in other people. It's really not hard if one pays attention. But few people do. Especially not in this house. Except perhaps for the earl."

"I have no idea what you're talking about," Celia lied.

"I'm talking about the way Henry looks at you and the way you look at him."

"Oh, well, that's really not..."

"Even Poppy and Effie noticed. We discussed it right before I came to speak to you."

Celia started to deny it but her aunt would never believe her. "It scarcely matters." She drew a deep breath. "Regardless of how I feel about him, of how he might feel about me...it's pointless. Surely you see that?"

"What I see is a man about to plunge into a lifetime with a woman I suspect he doesn't even like." Her brows drew together. "Has Katherine always been this— Oh, I don't know what the word is. So many come to mind."

Celia bit back a smile. "I'm afraid so."

"And does she usually look at you as if there was something quite vile about you?"

Celia laughed. "It's not that bad."

Aunt Guinevere stared as if she'd just realized— or perhaps accepted—something quite awful. "I have done you a terrible disservice." She shook her head. "I should have rescued you from that household years ago. Between those dreadful half sisters of yours and the frightful Miss Quince—can you ever forgive me?"

"There's nothing to forgive." Celia shrugged. "I was away at school most of the time. I've only resided at the abbey since I graduated. And Father isn't so bad. Although it's not especially gratifying to realize your father is not the cleverest man in the world."

Aunt Guinevere choked back a laugh.

"Neither Katherine nor Louise has ever liked me, which bothered me a great deal when I was young but I had Mother then." Celia paused. It had been seven years since her mother had died but there were moments when the grief was as fresh as if it had been yesterday. "After she died, I realized it was silly to continue to try to earn their affection, and besides, I didn't like them, either. Aunt Frances, on the other hand, was never of any concern as she has always disliked everyone equally." Celia grinned. "Except Father of course."

"Even so—"

"Come now, Aunt Guinevere." Celia pinned her with a firm look. "I am not ill-treated. I am not the heroine of some sad little fairy story. There is no need for you to feel the least bit sorry."

"Very well, then, I won't." Her aunt paused. "But after the wedding, I want you to come live with me and Charles in London."

"Live in London?" Celia's breath caught.

"You did say you wished to live in London."

"Someday perhaps but…" But why not now? "Very well." She grinned. "There is nothing I would rather do."

"Excellent." Aunt Guinevere beamed. "Although I should warn you, it will frequently be just the two of us as Charles is always off on one exploration or another."

"I know." Celia considered the older woman. "I must say, I have always admired your independence."

"I assure you, it often looks better from afar," Aunt Guinevere said wryly. "And as much as I would miss the kind of freedom I have, I would sacrifice it without a moment's hesitation to see more of my husband."

"But you do so well alone."

"I have friends, Celia. There is nothing better than friends. Unless of course it's family." She frowned.

"Should I tell your father you're coming to London or do you wish to?"

"Goodness, Aunt Guinevere, I'm nineteen years old, an adult fully capable of making my own decisions. I shall tell him. I daresay Father will be delighted at having one less female around."

"Then that's settled," Aunt Guinevere said firmly. "Now then, we need to determine a way to stop this wedding."

"Stop the wedding?" Celia stared.

"Of course." The older woman nodded. "You are in love with him, aren't you?"

"I…" Celia considered the question. She'd never been in love before but surely that was what this was. "Have you ever met someone and the very moment you looked into his eyes you knew that he was the one person in all the world for you? Knew without doubt or question as you had never known anything in your life before?"

"Once."

"Then yes." Celia shrugged helplessly. "Much to my dismay, I am in love with him."

"And I would wager a great deal he is in love with you, as well. Which means we can't possibly let poor, dear Henry marry Katherine. He'll be miserable for the rest of his life and she will probably be fairly unhappy, as well. No, it's best for all concerned that we find a way to stop this wedding."

"Absolutely not." Celia jumped to her feet, spurred as much by guilt as shock. Hadn't the same thought occurred to her? "That would be wrong." She paced. What was her aunt thinking? She swiveled toward the other woman. "The scandal would cast a shadow on everyone's lives, including Henry's and his brother's." She resumed pacing. "Regardless of how we feel about one another, Katherine is still my sister. I would hate to ruin her wedding, not to mention her life."

"From what I've observed it's fairly obvious her life, as well as his, will be ruined if they do marry. Barring death, marriage, my dear girl, is forever."

"Henry will never go back on his word. It's just not in his nature to do something like that. He's far too honorable and kind and..." Her aunt was right. Henry and Katherine certainly weren't in love. A bit of scandal versus an entire lifetime of unhappiness, well, it was something to consider. One might say it would be a favor to both of them to stop the wedding. Of course, Katherine would never see it that way. Still, wasn't it Celia's duty really to help her sister avoid spending the rest of her days in a loveless, ill-fated union? She paused in midstep. "How?"

"How?"

"How would you stop the wedding? Not that I think you should," Celia added quickly. "I am simply curious."

"I don't exactly know how. Yet." Aunt Guinevere's brows drew together thoughtfully. "It would have to be subtle."

"I will have no part of it," Celia warned.

"Extremely discreet," Aunt Guinevere murmured, obviously already working on an idea.

Celia stared. The woman was as diabolical as she was independent. There would be no stopping her now.

"Nor do I want to know any of the details."

"Absolutely right, my dear." Aunt Guinevere nodded firmly. "Your hand should be nowhere near this. We'll come up with a plan. Something clever and subtle and perfect."

Celia groaned. "Good Lord, Aunt Guinevere. You sound positively wicked."

"Nonsense, Celia, I'm not at all wicked." Aunt Guinevere grinned. "But I do try."

Day Two

CHAPTER FOUR

"I TELL YOU he's losing interest in me." Katherine's voice sounded faintly from Miss Quince's room. "He's not nearly as enthralled as he was."

Gwen caught herself, her hand a scant inch away from knocking on Miss Quince's door. The door stood the tiniest bit ajar, cracked open so slightly Gwen doubted the inhabitants of the room were aware of it. In spite of her best intentions and the certain knowledge that no one ever heard anything good when one eavesdropped, Gwen leaned closer to the door.

"Good Lord, Katherine." Miss Quince huffed. "I would think you of all people would be able to keep a man's attention."

Gwen winced. She could well imagine the look on Katherine's face.

"How was I to know it would even be necessary?" Katherine snapped. "It never occurred to me his attention would lag."

"Perhaps if you were more the loving and attentive fiancée—"

"Loving and attentive?" Katherine scoffed. "*He* is lucky to have *me*. I am not the kind of woman who happens along every day. Especially not for someone as ordinary as Henry. Men like Henry rarely have women like me on their arm." She sniffed. "He should be grateful."

Gwen's jaw clenched.

"Gratitude may not get you to the altar," Frances warned.

"I realize that!" Katherine's voice faded in and out as she apparently paced the room. "While Henry is not the most exciting man in the world, he has unquestioned honor. A man of his word, that sort of thing. He would never renege on his promise to marry me."

Gwen resisted the urge to scoff aloud.

"Then you have nothing to worry about," Miss Quince said in a placating tone.

"You are not listening to me," Katherine said impatiently. "Something has changed. And I do worry. I worry when the look in his eye is not one of adoration but speculation. When he no longer seems eager to spend time with me. When he stops asking if I would like to go for a stroll to see the gardens or the fountains or whatever else there is to see here."

"I thought you told him you are not fond of the out-of-doors?"

"That's beside the point. He's not particularly keen to be indoors with me, either. Not anymore."

"What are we going to do?"

"I don't know." Katherine blew an annoyed breath. "I don't wish to wager my future on a man's sense of honor. Even Henry's. What if he decides breaking his word is less objectionable than marriage to me?"

"That's a possibility, I suppose." Worry sounded in Miss Quince's voice.

"I have passed my twenty-fourth birthday. Henry is my last chance at an excellent match. The last possibility for a title and fortune and everything I—we've—always wanted. We have to do something."

"One would think there would be some way to guarantee he keeps his word and marries you."

"Yes, well, unfortunately, nothing comes to mind. If his word alone is not enough to ensure our marriage, I can't imagine what else might make a man enter into a marriage he didn't want."

"What else…" Miss Quince sucked in a short breath and her tone brightened. "Henry wouldn't have a choice if—" triumph sounded in her voice "—he ruined you."

Silence fell in the room and Gwen strained to hear. Surely even Katherine wouldn't consent to such a thing?

"Ruined me?" Katherine said thoughtfully. "You mean actual indiscretion or simply the appearance of improper behavior?"

"Given all there is to gain, it seems a small enough sacrifice."

Gwen stifled an indignant gasp.

"That does seem to be the only answer." Katherine sighed. "Then I shall have to join Henry in his bed tonight. Or perhaps I should already be there when he…"

Gwen carefully stepped away from the door. It wouldn't do for Katherine or Miss Quince to know they had been overheard. Forewarned was forearmed, after all.

Any reservations she might have had about stopping Katherine's wedding had vanished with the younger woman's words. Determination swept through Gwen. No man deserved to be tricked into marriage. This wedding would absolutely not take place. Henry's future, as well as Celia's, was at stake.

A scant half an hour later, she and her friends were gathered in the small sitting room off her new bedroom.

"My mother always said listening in on a private conversation is ill-mannered." Poppy crossed her arms in a show of moral indignation. It really didn't suit her. "I am shocked by your behavior, Gwen. Simply shocked."

"That's what you find shocking about all this?" Effie scoffed. "Gwen's behavior?"

"I expected better of her, that's all." Poppy paused. "Of course, the rest of it is shocking, as well."

"And Poppy is right when one *deliberately* sets out to eavesdrop. That would be most improper," Gwen said quickly. "However, in this particular instance, it was completely accidental on my part and therefore can be forgiven. I simply went to Miss Quince's room after breakfast to discuss the arrangements for this week's festivities. I had no idea she and Katherine would be in the midst of plotting to make certain Henry has no possible way to avoid this marriage."

"And you actually heard them say if Katherine could find a way into Henry's bed, he'd be trapped?" Effie asked.

"I heard it all." Gwen shook her head. "And I do believe this casts things in an entirely different light."

"Without question." Poppy frowned. "Why, when you first said we needed to stop the wedding because Henry and Katherine aren't in love and that Henry is actually in love with Celia, I felt my conscience twinge just the tiniest bit. Although I will always be on the side of love."

"As will we all." Gwen nodded. Poppy was a genuine romantic and even Effie—who did tend to be considerably less starry-eyed than Poppy—was a staunch believer in true love.

"But now that we know how truly despicable the bride is…" Poppy squared her shoulders. "Why, it seems to me we have no choice but to rescue poor Henry."

"So, just to make certain I fully understand, our *mission,* if you will, is to—" Effie counted the points off on her fingers "—plan and coordinate the various events leading up to this wedding—now a mere six days away—"

"Goodness, Effie, while Miss Quince is somewhat overwhelmed, she did provide us with a framework of sorts." Gwen adopted her most confident smile. "The invitations have gone out."

"That's something, I suppose." Effie cast her a skeptical look. "Then aside from the invitations, we have the wedding and accompanying events to organize all while keeping the bride out of the groom's bed—"

"Not just his bed." Gwen narrowed her eyes. "There are all sorts of places in a house like this for an assignation."

"There is that," Poppy said under her breath, obviously reflecting on her own memories of amorous encounters.

"Very well, then," Effie continued, "keeping the bride and the groom apart—"

Gwen nodded.

"—as well as devising a plan to stop the wedding altogether." Effie studied her friend. "Is that all?"

"Isn't it enough?" Gwen grinned.

"Oh, this does sound like fun." Poppy's eyes sparkled.

"Do you have a plan?" Effie asked. "For any of this?"

"Well, as you can see, I now occupy a different bedroom. I spoke to the butler and he has arranged different rooms for you both, as well. Your things are being moved even as we speak." Gwen smirked. "Henry's room is across the hall from this one, Effie's room will be on one side of Henry's and Poppy's on the other."

"We are surrounding the poor man," Effie murmured.

"For his own good," Gwen pointed out. "The greatest potential for scandalous behavior is under cover of night. Therefore, we shall have to make certain he stays in his room and does not have any unexpected guests."

"What do you suggest we do?" Effie's brow arched. "Stand guard outside his room?"

"Excellent idea." Gwen beamed. "I was thinking the very same thing myself. We will take turns and watch his room all night."

"Although I think it would be best if we sat rather than stood," Poppy said thoughtfully.

Effie's eyes widened in disbelief. "Whether we sit or stand, how are we going to explain ourselves?"

Gwen dismissed the question with a wave of her hand. "Oh, we'll think of something. Daytime is a different problem entirely, although Henry does not strike me as the type of man who could be easily seduced during the daylight hours."

"Pity," Poppy murmured.

"Even so, Katherine is a powerful temptation," Effie said. "And she did manage to get him to propose."

"No man is truly safe when it comes to a beautiful woman." Gwen thought for a moment. "However, Katherine is the bride and therefore should be the center of attention this week. The center of *our* attention. As we are now the ones putting all the arrangements together, it makes perfect sense that one of us will be with her every minute."

Effie stared. "Sometimes I find you positively frightening, Guinevere Blodgett."

"Thank you." Gwen tried and failed to keep a grin off her face.

"Still…" Poppy's forehead furrowed. "That's only half of it. While we do seem to have an acceptable plan to keep Katherine from ensuring that Henry *has* to marry her, we still have no way to stop the wedding from happening at all."

"It's obvious that Henry Saunders is not the type of man to go back on his word. He has said he would marry her and marry her he will." Effie shook her head. "In spite of Katherine's fears—as much as he might want to—I suspect he'll never break it off with her."

Gwen sighed. "No, I'm afraid not."

"It has always struck me as much more civilized and, well, *proper* when the bride is the one to call off a wedding. One does tend to think a bride has legitimate reasons, whereas when a groom begs off, it's attributed to cowardice. Or something of a sordid nature. It's a pity we can't get her to break it off with him," Poppy said with a sigh.

Gwen and Effie traded glances.

Effie grinned. "That's rather brilliant, Poppy."

"It is?" Poppy's eyes widened.

"Oh, it is indeed. Henry may be too honorable to beg off from this wedding, but Katherine has no such scruples. She'll abandon him in a moment under the right conditions." Gwen smiled slowly. "And I know exactly what those conditions will be."

CHAPTER FIVE

HENRY SAUNDERS HAD never considered himself irrational, weak or stupid. Apparently he was wrong.

The moment he spotted Celia descending the terrace steps into the gardens, he should have turned around, walked back into the house and as far away as possible. Instead, he found himself hurrying after her, ignoring the voice in his head that fairly screamed he shouldn't follow her. That insisted this was a dreadful mistake. That no good could come of being alone with Celia Bromley. He'd heeded that voice for the three weeks since her arrival at his family's country home—three endless, torturous weeks of indecision and doubt and longing. Now he ignored it. A man could only take so much.

He crossed the terrace and started down the stairs. Perhaps if they spent a few minutes together he could get her out of his head. That she was here at Danby in the first place was absurd, really, when one thought about it. They'd shared no more than a chance encounter at a bookstore. Nothing more than a moment in which two people reached for the same volume and their hands brushed, followed by a bit of amusing conversation. Admittedly, that conversation had lasted much of the afternoon, but it was a casual flirtation, nothing more significant than that. Or at least it shouldn't have been. But in that second when his hand had touched hers, her gaze had met his, there had been an instant of perfect clarity, of shocking awareness. It was absurd of course. Henry didn't believe in such foolish romantic nonsense.

And yet his blood raced in her presence. His heart thudded hard in his chest when her gaze met his. And something inside of him ached with an odd emptiness when he thought of what he had missed. Perhaps if he could just talk to her alone, he might break the spell he'd been under since they first met.

Or he'd be doomed forever. Still, it was a chance worth taking. It was damned difficult to remember he was expected to marry one sister with another constantly in his thoughts.

He reached the bottom of the stairs and considered his choices. Celia was nowhere to be seen. In front of him, centered between the two curved stairways that flanked the terrace and led into the garden, was a large circular pool. Frolicking water nymphs and dolphins carved of stone spouted water in the middle. The fountain and pool had been designed by an ancestor a hundred or so years ago, and while Henry was not at all drawn to whimsy, he had loved this spot in the garden all of his life. It was nothing short of magical.

The pool was bounded by a semicircular beech hedge with arched openings leading into the gardens beyond. The one farthest from the house led to the tennis courts and he was fairly certain she would not have gone in that direction. The rose garden and formal plantings, designed at the beginning of the century to reflect a continental style, could be reached through the archway on the right. The arch on the left was the entry to a world of extravagant topiaries, fanciful silhouettes, unexpected figures and fantastic forms all carved and shaped out of living trees. This was the oldest garden on the grounds, originally planted nearly two hundred years ago. He and Ned had played here as boys and, regardless of how fashion and taste might change with the years, they had promised the topiary garden would always be a part of Danby Manor.

He had no idea which archway Celia had selected but perhaps her choice might be taken as a sign. If she chose the formal gardens, then obviously they were not meant to be and he could renew his efforts to vanquish her from his thoughts. If she picked the topiaries, well, he'd cross that road if and when he came to it.

He strode toward the left-hand arch, stepped under the wide shaped branches and into the topiary garden. As he had since childhood, he paused and for a moment was a Lilliputian staring up at giant Gullivers.

"Are you following me?" an amused voice off to one side asked. His heart leaped.

"No, of course not." He kept his gaze on the carved giants in front of him. He didn't need to turn to know Celia was sitting on one of the stone benches that flanked either side of the archway.

"Really? I could have sworn you were." A teasing note sounded in her voice.

"And if I admitted I was?" His tone matched hers but there was an undercurrent of truth he couldn't quite hide.

"Oh." She paused. "I see."

Something inside him snapped and he turned toward her. "Do you?"

Her eyes widened and she rose to her feet. "No, not really. Not at all."

He stepped toward her. "Celia—"

"No." She held out her hand to stop him. "Don't come any closer. Please."

The look in her eyes clutched at his heart. "Are you afraid of me?"

Her brows drew together. "Why on earth would I be afraid of you?"

"I don't know." He ran a hand through his hair in frustration. "I just thought…the way you looked at me… It seemed… I don't know."

She stared at him for a moment then laughed. "Good Lord, Henry, I would never be afraid of you."

"Good." He nodded. This woman made no sense whatsoever. It was…delightful. "Although you did look rather afraid."

"Well, I am."

He frowned. "You're very confusing."

"Do you think so?" She considered his words. "Most people don't think I'm the least bit confusing. I rather like that you think I am." Her blue eyes twinkled with amusement.

"I'm glad you're happy," he said wryly.

"Oh, I'm not at all happy. I'm really quite distraught. And I am afraid, but not of you." She drew a deep breath. "Of us."

His blood pounded in his ears. "Us?"

"It's no doubt quite impertinent of me and most presumptuous. Why, you might not feel at all the same, but—"

"I do."

She stared. "You do what?"

"Feel the same."

"Do you?"

He nodded. "I'm afraid so."

"Oh dear." She twisted her hands together. "That is awkward. Delightful," she added then grimaced. "But awkward."

"Because I am to marry your sister?"

"Of course. I can't think of any other reason why it would be awkward. Unless you were supposed to marry someone other than my sister, then I suppose that would be awkward, as well."

He grinned in spite of himself. "Yes, well, I imagine that would be."

"You're not, though, are you?" Her eyes narrowed. "You don't have another fiancée, do you? In addition to Katherine, I mean."

"No, I don't." He laughed. "But you're right. An additional fiancée would be awkward." He sobered. "Tell me why you're afraid of us."

She studied him for a long moment, absently chewing on her lower lip. The most insane desire to taste that lip rushed though him. He ignored it.

"I barely know you, Henry, yet it doesn't seem to matter." Her gaze wandered past him, as if she was working something out in her own mind. Looking for an answer that was not easily seen. "Since the moment I met you at the bookseller's, I have thought of you constantly. I even went back several times in hopes of seeing you."

He resisted the urge to grin with satisfaction.

Her gaze shifted back to his. "You can imagine my shock when I met you again only to discover you were the man my sister intended to marry."

"I can indeed. Believe me, you were not alone in your surprise."

"There is nothing that can be done about it." She shook her head. "You are an honorable man. I am certain of it. I know we've barely spoken but I admit I have observed you during my stay here."

"Yet we've not had so much as a moment alone together."

"I am well aware of that." She raised her chin. "Quite honestly I have been avoiding you. And I suspect you've been avoiding me, as well."

He shrugged. "It seemed best."

"And yet now, here—" she waved absently at their surroundings "—you sought me out."

"I couldn't bear it anymore, Celia." His gaze caught hers directly. "To have you so close and yet…"

"So far away?"

"And out of reach." He blew a frustrated breath. "I don't know what to do. I have never had feelings like this and yet the circumstances…" He shook his head. "I thought perhaps if we talked, then whatever this is between would be laid to rest."

"Because we shared no more than an afternoon. And what seemed extraordinary and magical in hindsight would vanish in the here and now. And we could both put it behind us and go on with our lives."

"I fear it hasn't worked." He cast her a wry smile.

"These brief moments have only served to make me want more. Another hour, another afternoon, a day, a week…forever."

"My dear Henry." She smiled and the sadness in her eyes twisted his heart. "We have made a dreadful mess of this."

"I have," he said staunchly. "I should have tried harder to find you. I should never have given up. I allowed myself to be sensible and rational and to decide those few hours with a lovely woman in a bookstore were nothing of true significance. I should have known better. My heart should have known better."

"Hearts are notoriously incompetent when it comes

to good judgment. Pity we must live with the consequences." Her voice softened. "You're a good man, Henry. The kind of man who honors his obligations. I don't think I would feel about you the way I do if you weren't. I don't think I could."

There was nothing he could say. She was right. His word was his bond.

Her gaze meshed with his. "I have never in my life wanted to throw myself into a man's arms and yet with you, I can barely keep myself from doing so. However…"

"However." His gaze searched hers. "It doesn't matter, does it?"

"Do you believe in fate?"

"I never have but that was before I met you."

"I do. I always have." She paused, obviously to consider her words. Henry feared they would not be what he longed to hear. "It seems to me if fate truly meant for you and I to be together, we would have met again before…" She shook her head. "As it is, I fear fate sadly intended us to be star-crossed, as it were. Nothing more than friends perhaps."

"I'm not sure I can be your friend." His gaze bored into hers and he knew the regret in her eyes mirrored his own.

"Then we can have nothing at all." She looked as if she were about to say something else and instead nodded. "I'm not sure this has been of any benefit to either of us." She smiled. "But it was nice to speak with you again. It's probably wise for us to continue to avoid encounters like this. Good day, Henry." She started off.

"Wait." He had to stop her even if he had no legitimate reason for doing so. But it did seem that she had just said goodbye and he wasn't sure he could bear that.

She turned back toward him. "Yes?"

He said the first thing that popped into his head. "I know there can never be anything between us and I accept that. But you will dance with me, won't you? At the ball?" Perhaps if he could hold her in his arms, just once, he could let her go forever.

"I don't think—"

"One dance, Celia, nothing more than that. And then we will go our separate ways as if nothing had ever happened between us. Grant me that much."

She studied him for an endless, silent moment then favored him with a polite, impersonal smile. His stomach plunged. "Of course, Henry, it would be quite rude to refuse you a dance. You are marrying my sister, after all." She nodded and took her leave.

He stared after her for a long moment and accepted the truth.

This was the woman he should be marrying. This was the woman who had claimed his heart. And for the rest of his days, this was the woman who would own it.

Even if it was broken.

CHAPTER SIX

CELIA STEPPED THROUGH the verdant archway and started toward the house trying to maintain a sedate pace even though everything inside her urged her to run. To flee as fast as she could. She kept her chin tucked, her gaze on the ground in front of her and her fists clenched in an effort to keep from crying. How utterly ridiculous. Tears never helped anyone.

This wasn't the least bit fair but then Celia had realized long ago that life wasn't particularly fair. It wasn't fair that her mother had died. That her father was an idiot. That her sisters did not treat her as one should treat a sister. And most unfair of all—that her oldest sister was marrying the man Celia loved.

And there was nothing to be done about it. Regardless of whatever plan Aunt Guinevere and her companions devised, Katherine would never let Henry go. And Henry would never go back on his word.

"I say, Celia, are you all right?"

Celia jerked her head up and stopped short, nearly colliding with the earl. "I beg your pardon, my lord. I didn't see you."

"No, you are most definitely preoccupied." He studied her curiously. His eyes were the same dark brown as Henry's and it was obvious they were brothers but no one would have ever suspected they were twins. "Is something wrong?"

Yes, everything is wrong! "Nothing of significance."
She forced a pleasant smile. "My mind was elsewhere,
I'm afraid."

"Someplace more interesting than this, I would
hope."

"Not at all," she said firmly. "I think Danby is most
interesting. And the history of the manor is fascinating."

His brow rose. "You enjoy history, do you?"

"I always have. Particularly in a place like this." She
glanced around. "You can feel history all around you
here, like a living, breathing thing. The mark of those
who have come before is evident everywhere you look."

He leaned closer and lowered his voice in a confidential manner. "Have you met the ghosts, then?"

Delight widened her eyes. "You have ghosts?"

"I can't imagine any self-respecting estate anywhere
in England that doesn't have at least one. But alas—" he
heaved an overly dramatic sigh "—in spite of all sorts
of stories passed down through the years and my best
efforts, starting in my youth, I have yet to meet one."

"That is a shame."

"Indeed." He shook his head mournfully then brightened. "I know, Celia, you and I could hunt for ghosts.
Perhaps tonight?" He smiled in a wicked manner. "After
dark?"

She stared. "Are you flirting with me, Edward?"

"I am trying."

"And I am flattered." She returned his smile. "But
I'm not sure hunting ghosts with you in the dark is a
good idea."

"And I thought it was an excellent idea." He wagged
his brows in a wicked manner.

She laughed.

He grinned. "So you like my family's ancestral home, then?"

"I can't imagine anyone not liking it. The manor itself is magnificent, and on a beautiful day like today, the gardens are irresistible. Your gardeners are to be commended."

"Actually, this is largely to my brother's credit." He glanced around, pride shining in his eyes. "When I was paying no particular attention to my responsibilities, Henry was. He is the one who made certain this estate, and everything else, was attended to as it should be." He paused. "Henry is a good man. Perhaps the best I know."

"My sister is a fortunate woman." Without warning, tears welled in her eyes and she blinked rapidly.

"Are you sure you're all right?" Concern sounded in his voice.

"Quite, thank you." She waved her hand in front of her eyes, wishing she'd remembered her fan, but she hadn't planned to come outside at all. She had indeed been lured out-of-doors by the beauty of the landscape. "A bit of dust in my eye. It will be fine in a moment."

"I was looking for Henry but perhaps I should escort you back to the house instead."

"That's most kind of you, my lord, but not at all necessary. I encountered your brother in the topiary garden a few minutes ago. I suspect he's still there."

"If you're certain." His gaze strayed to the entry to the garden. "There was something I wished to speak to him about."

"Then I would feel quite badly if you abandoned your purpose simply because there is a speck of dust in my eye. Or rather, there was." She cast him her brightest smile. "I told you it would be fine and it is." She waved toward the garden. "Now do go and find your brother. I have all sorts of things I need to attend to, so I shall be on my way."

"Very well, Celia." He smiled. "I will see you at dinner, then?"

"I would never miss dinner." She grinned. "Your cook is very nearly as remarkable as your gardens."

"She will take that as a great compliment." He laughed. "Good day, Celia."

"Good day, my lord." She turned and started back toward the manor. Edward was a charming man, most amusing and quite dashing. But he wasn't Henry.

Celia never would have thought it was possible to love someone with no more between them than an afternoon's conversation and a slight brush of the hand. It was far-fetched and absurd and completely ridiculous. And yet, she'd never been so certain of anything in her life.

Was it at all possible that Aunt Guinevere and her friends could truly come up with a way to stop this wedding? If anyone could save Henry, surely it would be those three.

Realization struck her like a physical blow and stopped her in midstep.

If Henry was worth having, he was certainly worth fighting for. Celia hadn't wanted to be involved in whatever scheme her aunt concocted—out of misplaced family loyalty, no doubt. But that was no way to save the man one loved.

Resolve washed through her. She would speak to Aunt Guinevere at once.

Perhaps Celia and Henry were indeed star-crossed. Perhaps they weren't meant to be together but he deserved better than to spend the rest of his days with Katherine. And as the woman who loved him, it was up to Celia to do all she could to make certain of it.

CHAPTER SEVEN

HOW WAS HE going to extricate himself from this mess?

Henry sat on the stone bench, elbows on his knees, chin propped in his hands and stared at the topiaries carved to replicate the figures in the fountain, stylized nymphs and dolphins, caught forever in a carefree romp. No worries, no problems, nothing to mar their leafy exuberance. He quite envied them even if it was pointless. They were trees, after all.

Try as he might he could not think of a way to escape marrying Katherine. It was not as if she had deceived him in any way, although it was painfully clear to him now that his appeal for her lay only in his fortune and family name.

And then there was the problem of Celia. How could he spend the rest of his life with Katherine when Celia was the woman he loved? Regardless, there was nothing to be done about it. He would dance with her once and that would be that. A voice in the back of his head noted the lie. He ignored it.

"There you are." Ned strode into the garden. "I was looking for you."

"Were you?" Henry said absently.

"I met Miss Bromley, Celia, on the way here." Ned settled on the bench beside him. "Lovely woman."

"Yes, she is." It was oddly fortunate that Katherine was not fond of her youngest sister.

"Clever, too."

"She does seem clever, yes." Why, after their marriage he and Katherine would probably rarely see Celia at all.

"I've quite grown to like her in these past weeks."

"There's nothing not to like." Yes, that would be best for all concerned, really. Besides, he and Katherine would live most of the time in London and Celia would be at Bromwick Abbey.

"No." Ned chuckled. "Not one little thing, at least so far as I can tell. She's intelligent, and not afraid to show it. It's unusual and I like that. She's witty and amusing, and really quite pretty." He paused. "Although, Katherine is the true beauty of the family."

"Katherine is beautiful." Henry nodded. He would have one dance with Celia and that would be the end of it.

"But Celia, well, there's something about Celia," Ned mused. "That fair hair and those blue eyes. A fetching figure on her, as well. I find her very nearly irresistible."

What an idiot he was. One dance would never be enough.

"I believe I shall have to do something about that. I've only hesitated thus far because I wasn't sure what the rules were about pursuing the sister of one's future sister-in-law. Although I've never been fond of rules." Ned paused. "The ball will be the perfect setting to begin my efforts. Yes, indeed, a beautiful summer night with romance in the air. I always look especially dashing in formal attire. It will be perfect." He chuckled. "We'll share a dance or two. She will have my undivided attention—no woman can resist that. I'll murmur a few compliments in her ear. Something about how she looks like a goddess descended to earth to enchant unsuspecting mortals. Women adore that sort of thing. I'll suggest a turn on the terrace and perhaps a walk in the gardens, under the moon or the stars, whichever is appropriate. And then, when she is very nearly swooning with the romance of it all, I'll take her in my arms and—"

"What?" Henry's attention jerked to his brother. "What are you talking about?"

"I knew you were off somewhere." Ned smirked. "You haven't heard a word I've said."

"No, I have other things on my mind." Henry narrowed his eyes. "You were talking about seducing some…" He sucked in a hard breath. "You were talking about seducing Celia!"

"I was not." Ned scoffed. "I was talking about charming and enchanting her." He grinned. "Seduction would come later."

"Absolutely not!" Henry glared. "I won't have it. I don't want you going near her."

"I don't see why not." Ned shrugged. "She's not a child. She's certainly available. And she is quite, oh, what is the word? Delicious? Oh, yes, that's good."

Henry gasped.

"Delectable, really." Ned cast his brother a wicked grin. "A truly tasty morsel and I do believe—"

"That's enough, Ned. I will not have you leering over Celia in that manner. You will leave her alone. Do you understand?"

"Why should I?"

"Because…"

"If you don't have a better reason than that—"

"Because…"

"Because she deserves better than me?"

"Yes!"

"Because she deserves someone who will love and cherish her?"

"Yes!"

"Because you already love her?"

"I…"

"Come now, Henry, I have been in love often enough to know the signs."

"Yes!" Henry huffed. "Yes, Ned, damn it all, I love her."

"Ah-ha!" Ned jumped to his feet and aimed an accusing finger at his brother. "I knew it. I've known it from the beginning. That first night, when we met the rest of Katherine's family, I knew you had met Celia before."

Henry sighed. "We met at a bookstore. Only once but…"

"But it was enough?"

"Yes." Henry shook his head. "I haven't been able to think of anything but her since then."

"This was before you met Katherine?" Ned sat back down on the bench.

"Yes, but—" he struggled to find the right words "—I didn't have her name. I went back in hopes of seeing her again but I didn't. So I decided it was foolish to continue to pine over a woman I spent no more than a few hours with. And then I met Katherine and you know the rest."

"I've been watching the two of you—you and Celia, that is. There's a tense sort of longing between you when you look at each other. I can't believe no one else has noticed, although you have both been discreet, I'll give you that."

"We have been more than discreet—we've avoided each other." He paused. "Until today."

"You mean just now?" Caution sounded in Ned's voice. "What happened?"

"I thought if I could talk to her, perhaps…" Henry ran his hand through his hair.

"Perhaps it would be enough?"

Henry nodded.

"But it wasn't?"

"No, and it doesn't matter. I am to marry Katherine and there's nothing to be done about it." Henry blew a long breath. "The worst part about all of this is that I don't especially like Katherine."

"*That's* the worst part?"

"Well, yes. If I liked her, I could imagine the rest of our lives together. And it would be easier to put Celia out of my head."

"I doubt that."

"Oh, I was infatuated with Katherine in the beginning but the more I'm with her, the more I know her—"

"Exactly." Ned shuddered. "She's rather frightening."

"Isn't she, though?" Henry heaved a resigned sigh. "First I meet the woman who may well be the love of my life and I lose her—or rather I can't find her again. Then I fancy myself in love with a beautiful creature who now appears to want me more for my fortune than anything else." He glanced at his brother. "I don't think Katherine is all that fond of me, either."

"I don't think she's fond of anyone."

"I've been something of an idiot, haven't I?"

"In the scheme of things, it's probably your turn." Ned grinned then sobered. "You'll have to call off your wedding, you know."

"I can't." Resignation swept through him. "I gave my word."

"You will be a cad but that's far better than marrying the wrong woman."

"No, it's not." He distinctly remembered Father telling him that doing what was easy didn't make a man but rather it was doing what was right, no matter how difficult it might be. Owning up to one's mistakes was what gave a man strength and fortitude and character. And made a father proud. "I can't go back on my word. It would be wrong and I could never forgive myself."

For a long moment, they sat in silence, the only sounds the tinkling of water from the annoyingly joyous nymphs and dolphins on the other side of the hedge.

"It's hard to be the good brother, isn't it?" Ned said with a wry smile.

Henry scoffed. "You have no idea."

"Never fear, old man." Ned patted his brother's back. "I'll come up with something."

"Will you?" It was an interesting thought but Henry doubted even Ned—who had vast experience in extricating himself from all kinds of awkward situations through the years—could save him from this.

"Of course I will. I don't have any ideas yet, but there are still four days until the wedding. Plenty of time."

"There's nothing you can do."

"Come now, Henry. I'll think of something. I always do. Besides—" Ned grinned "—what's the good of being the earl if you can't save your twin brother from ruining his life?"

Day Three

CHAPTER EIGHT

"Thank you for joining me, Mrs. Blodgett." The Earl of Danby shifted in his chair, obviously a bit ill at ease. Gwen suspected his discomfort had nothing to do with the chair.

"Well, when an earl, and one's host, invites you to join him privately in his library for tea, one does not turn down the invitation as it obviously means one of two things." Gwen smiled pleasantly.

"Oh?"

"Either he has a matter of importance to discuss or he is interested in something of a more personal nature, in which case he should be set straight immediately." She paused. "As I am old enough to be your mother, I am assuming the former."

"Regardless of age, you are an extremely attractive woman, Mrs. Blodgett."

"I am an extremely married woman, my lord."

"And I would never…" He grinned. "Well, I would and I have but I won't."

She laughed. "Imagine my relief, my lord."

"Edward, please."

"Guinevere, or my friends call me Gwen if you prefer."

"Gwen it is, then." He considered her for a moment. "I shall be blunt. I think this marriage between my brother and Katherine Bromley is a dreadful mistake."

"Do you?" She calmly sipped her tea.

"Don't you?"

Gwen chose her words with care. "I fear the reasons Katherine wishes to marry Henry are more of a mercenary nature than anything having to do with true affection."

"You see it, too, then."

"It's painfully obvious to me."

He nodded. "For that reason alone I would want to stop this wedding." He thought for a moment. "You must understand, for all that Henry seems the more sensible and intelligent of the two of us, he is not as— Oh, what's the word? Wise, I suppose, as I am when it comes to the more unscrupulous tendencies of the fairer sex. I have been pursued by women seeking my title and fortune from the time I was old enough to be considered of marriageable age." He grinned. "It has not been entirely unpleasant."

"No, I would imagine it hasn't." Gwen bit back a grin. The man was incorrigible.

"But I am far more intelligent than most people assume. I am not one to be swept off my feet by a pretty face more interested in what I am and what I have than who I am. But that comes from experience and I will admit it was a difficult lesson to learn." He grimaced. "My brother's experiences with women have been entirely different than my own and he is far more trusting than I am. When it comes to this particular area, Henry is, or rather was, a bit naive."

"Was?"

"He, too, has now learned his lesson." Edward blew a resigned breath.

"He doesn't have to go through with the wedding."

Gwen shrugged. "He can beg off. Certainly, it will create a bit of scandal but surely that's better than being trapped in a marriage he doesn't want."

"My thoughts exactly." The earl nodded. "However, my brother is a better man than I am. His sense of honor will not permit him to go back on his word. I have no such scruples." He leaned forward. "I am hoping you will help me find a way to get him out of this, to stop this wedding and save my brother from a lifetime of misery."

"That's quite a request, Edward," she said mildly, resisting the urge to crow with delight. With the earl's assistance, their plan would be far more likely to succeed. Still… "You said 'for that alone' a minute ago—am I to gather there are reasons aside from Katherine's less-than-noble motives why you wish to stop this wedding?"

He chuckled. "You are a clever creature, Gwen."

She grinned. "Thank you, Edward."

"My brother is in love with your niece."

"Excellent, as my niece is in love with your brother."

"Any idiot can see it. I can't believe no one else has noticed. I've watched the two of them try not to look at each other since Celia and her family arrived at the manor. It's best, really, because when they do…" He smiled in an oddly wistful way. If one could feel sorry for a handsome, dashing man with power and position and wealth, one would feel sorry given that smile alone. "Well, I have to admit I am extremely envious. I hope someone will look at me that way someday."

"I think the rest of the family is too busy counting their chickens, as it were, to see what's right under their noses. But I noticed, as did my friends."

"Speaking of your friends…" He frowned. "Are your rooms to your liking? My butler said you and the other ladies requested different rooms and I understand Mrs. Higginbotham sat reading in the hall outside her room all night. She told a footman that she heard rats in the walls. He offered to find her a different room but she refused."

Gwen hesitated. If they were going to join forces, she should probably be honest with the man. "The rats may not be in the wall, Edward. I believe Katherine may wish to guarantee the wedding proceeds as planned by means of a, oh, scandalous nature."

"A scandalous nature?" Edward frowned in confusion. "I don't—" Understanding dawned on his face. "My brother's room is next to Mrs. Higginbotham's new room."

"And next to Mrs. Fitzhew-Wellmore's and directly across the hall from mine." Gwen cast him a satisfied smile.

The earl stared for a long moment. "You are somewhat devious as well as clever, aren't you?"

"I do try, Edward."

"I think I'm very lucky you're married." Admiration sounded in his voice.

She laughed.

"I can't have you and your friends guarding Henry's room all night." Edward's brow furrowed. "I could change rooms with my brother."

"Then you might be the one trapped into marriage."

"I assure you, better women than Katherine have tried." He shook his head. "However, whereas scandal has never especially bothered me, I must admit I do find myself more and more inclined to avoid it. Upholding the family name and all. Regardless, I cannot permit you and the other ladies to continue to lose sleep. I shall post a footman at Henry's door beginning tonight."

"Oh, and that wouldn't cause gossip among the servants, would it?" Gwen shook her head. "Far better for them to think that the earl's guests are a bit odd rather than to so much as suspect the truth. Besides, Mrs. Higginbotham wasn't there all night. I took a few hours, as did Mrs. Fitzhew-Wellmore." She leaned toward him in a confidential manner. "I believe Poppy considers it something of an adventure in pursuit of a worthy cause. I am not inclined to spoil her fun."

"Very well, then, if you insist. I shall do my part by maintaining a close watch on my brother during the day." He considered her cautiously. "Aside from keeping Henry out of a situation where he would have no hope at all, I don't suppose you have any other ideas."

"One or two, perhaps."

"I hoped you would." He grinned. "Please, go on."

"Well, it seems to me Henry's sense of honor will never allow him to be the one to beg off from this wedding."

Edward nodded. "We've established that."

"So Katherine must be the one to call it off."

Edward snorted. "She'd never do that."

"Come now, Edward." Gwen took a serene sip of tea. "Why does Katherine wish to marry Henry in the first place?"

"Social position," he said promptly. "And his money."

"Which of the two do you think is more important to her?"

He scoffed. "Money of course."

"And if she were somehow to become convinced he doesn't have any?"

"She'd…" He stared at her, a slow smile spreading across his face. "Remind me never to cross you, Mrs. Blodgett."

"Goodness, my lord." Gwen smiled in her most wicked manner. "Wouldn't that be fun."

CHAPTER NINE

"I DON'T KNOW why we have to continue to bother with this." Katherine glowered at the others reflected in the mirror. She stood on an ottoman in the center of a ladies' parlor that had been given over for their use—although it hadn't been given so much as it was overtaken. Celia's family had swept into Danby Manor like an invading army. "I think the dress is quite perfect."

Katherine's gaze returned to her reflection and the dress she would wear to marry Henry. It was a beautiful ivory color with tiers of lace-edged satin cascading down the skirt and delicate lace dripping from the sleeves. It was indeed perfect. Aunt Frances was determined to see her oldest niece wed and wed properly. She had managed to find a seamstress in London who could create something exquisite in a matter of days, as no less than exquisite would do for Katherine. It had struck Celia as something of a miracle, but then Louise had confided to Celia that the gown had originally been made for another bride who no longer needed it, which did explain how Aunt Frances had been able to procure a dress of such excellent quality and fine detail so quickly. It was apparently something of a bargain, as well. Still, it was far nicer than anything any of them had ever had.

Katherine knew nothing of this and was vain enough not to realize there was a reason why the fit needed adjusting. Aunt Frances had been fussing with it ever since they arrived at Danby and had quite happily turned the entire matter over to Mrs. Fitzhew-Wellmore and Mrs. Higginbotham, who were both quite skilled with a needle. Which worked out rather well as Aunt Guinevere had told Celia that Katherine was not to be out of sight for so much as a moment. She hadn't explained why but it was apparently part of the ladies' plan to rescue Henry. In spite of Celia's newfound resolve to assist in whatever they had in mind, Aunt Guinevere had said that, on further consideration, it might be best if Celia didn't know the details of their plan. When they had one, she'd added, which was not at all encouraging.

Katherine smiled smugly. "And I look quite perfect in it."

Mrs. Fitzhew-Wellmore and Mrs. Higginbotham exchanged glances but then they were not as used to Katherine as Celia, Louise and Aunt Frances were. Aunt Frances studied her niece with a worried expression while Louise lounged in a chaise paging through a lady's magazine.

"Perhaps," Aunt Frances said. "But I'm not entirely certain."

"I think it still needs work," Mrs. Fitzhew-Wellmore said firmly. She knelt on the floor adjusting the hem of the dress. "The fit and the length are not yet right."

"I think the fit is just fine." Katherine huffed.

"You do look wonderful, Katherine," Celia said helpfully.

"No one asked for your opinion, nor does anyone want it," Katherine snapped. "And I'm tired of standing here."

"You do want to look your best, Katherine," Aunt Frances said. "One must make sacrifices."

"Indeed one must." Mrs. Higginbotham fiddled with the waist of the dress. "Why, I can see where it needs just a bit more taking in. You have such a lovely figure, it would be a shame not to show it off to best advantage."

Katherine preened.

"Yes, I see a problem right here." Mrs. Higginbotham pinched a bit of the fabric on the seam joining the skirt and the bodice.

"Ouch." Katherine glared. "You pinched me!"

Louise coughed back a laugh. One thing Celia could say about Louise was that while she had never particularly liked Celia, she didn't seem overly fond of Katherine, either.

Mrs. Higginbotham ignored her. "Hand me a pin, Poppy."

"Now you're going to stick me!" Katherine cried.

"Not unless you move," Mrs. Higginbotham muttered. "I cannot be responsible if you move."

"Well, it's hard to stand here and not move when you insist on poking me and tugging me and— Ouch!" Katherine glared at Mrs. Higginbotham. "You did that on purpose!"

"I told you not to move." Mrs. Higginbotham glared back but the tiniest gleam of satisfaction shone in her eyes. Celia would have wagered she did indeed stab Katherine deliberately.

"Now, now, Katherine," Aunt Frances said in a consoling manner. "I'm certain it was nothing more than an accident. Why, Mrs. Higginbotham and Mrs. Fitzhew-Wellmore have been most generous with their time and skill and we are extremely grateful."

Katherine shrugged.

"I would imagine the sister-in-law of an earl would

be gracious, as well," Louise said under her breath and turned a page of her magazine.

One could almost see Katherine transform at her sister's comment. For a moment, she was every bit as beautiful as she thought she was. She cast Mrs. Higginbotham her most charming, and well-rehearsed, smile. "My apologies, Mrs. Higginbotham, and to you as well, Mrs. Fitzhew-Wellmore. I am terribly sorry for my behavior. I fear I grow a little on edge as the wedding approaches." She heaved an overly dramatic sigh. "It's all so overwhelming, being the bride and the center of attention."

"Understandable, dear," Mrs. Fitzhew-Wellmore said in a brisk manner. "One is always a bit apprehensive when one is about to plight one's troth with the man of one's dreams."

Katherine cast her a quizzical look.

"Mr. Saunders?" Mrs. Higginbotham said pointedly.

"Henry," Celia prompted.

Katherine shot her a hard look. "Yes, I know. Dear, dear Henry."

"There are few things more nerve-racking than to be about to shackle one's life to a man's for the rest of one's days. It's such an enormous, irrevocable step," Mrs. Higginbotham said. "After all, marriage is forever."

Katherine smiled weakly.

"There are few things I like better than seeing two people in love vow to be together until death. It's so terribly romantic." Mrs. Fitzhew-Wellmore released a heartfelt sigh. "They say one can't live on love alone but I'm certain you'll manage." She slanted a sly look at Mrs. Higginbotham.

"Yes, indeed." Mrs. Higginbotham nodded. "There is nothing more admirable than two people who cast aside all thoughts of practicality, especially when it comes to finances, and marry for nothing more than affection."

"Well, yes, but Henry does have a substantial fortune," Katherine said smugly. "And he is his brother's heir."

"Yes, of course." Mrs. Higginbotham shrugged. "I had simply heard that Mr. Saunders—"

"Effie!" Mrs. Fitzhew-Wellmore snapped. "That's nothing more than gossip and I thought we agreed it would be best to keep it to ourselves."

"What kind of gossip?" Katherine's brow furrowed.

"Nothing to worry yourself about," Mrs. Fitzhew-Wellmore said in an offhand manner. "I doubt that any of it is true." She paused. "Probably."

"Really, Mrs. Fitzhew-Wellmore," Aunt Frances began, "if you have heard something about Mr. Saunders, I think we should know what it is."

"Oh, yes, do tell," Louise said.

What on earth was this about? Celia glanced from one of her aunt's friends to the other. It was Celia's understanding—as well as that of her family—that Henry and his brother were both quite well situated financially. It didn't matter to Celia if Henry had money or not but it would certainly matter a great deal to everyone else.

"Absolutely not," Mrs. Higginbotham said firmly. "Poppy is right. It's not our place to say anything and who knows if the rumors are true."

"Besides," Mrs. Fitzhew-Wellmore added, "tittle-tattle about bad investments or massive debt or ill-advised speculation or insolvency really must be taken with a grain of salt."

Katherine's eyes widened. "Insolvency?"

"Not everyone is good at managing money." Mrs. Higginbotham pinched another bit of fabric. Katherine didn't so much as flinch. "Oh dear, I am sorry. Did I pinch you again?"

Katherine ignored her. "What did you mean about bad investments and massive debt?"

"Nothing to worry about, I'm sure." Mrs. Fitzhew-Wellmore looked up at her with a pleasant smile. "And you do have a dowry, don't you?"

"Yes, but—"

"Rather meager, really," Louise murmured, turning another page. "For the sister-in-law of an earl."

Mrs. Higginbotham frowned. "It's not significant, then?"

"It's, oh, modest," Celia said. "Our grandfather had it set aside for us."

"I'm certain any financial difficulties Mr. Saunders may be experiencing would be alleviated by the earl," Aunt Frances said staunchly.

"Ah, yes, the earl." Mrs. Fitzhew-Wellmore exchanged knowing glances with her friend.

Katherine's gaze shifted from one lady to the other. "What do you mean—'ah, yes, the earl'?"

"If you don't stay still, I shall stick you again." The threat rang in Mrs. Higginbotham's voice.

"I demand to know what the two of you have heard." Katherine glared. "I have the right to know. I am marrying into the family, after all."

"And I refuse to spread idle rumors that probably aren't true." Mrs. Fitzhew-Wellmore rose to her feet.

"Do you really think so?" Celia asked. If indeed Henry didn't have a fortune and his brother had financial problems, Katherine might well decide not to marry him. Henry would no doubt be fine without money—he was competent and intelligent and could certainly make his own way in the world—but Edward wouldn't do at all well. Charming and handsome were not really marketable qualities. Poor man.

"Goodness, dear, there's always a grain of truth in any rumor but I certainly wouldn't worry about your sister's future." Mrs. Fitzhew-Wellmore smiled at Katherine. "She is about to marry the man she loves, after all. Money is insignificant in comparison to that."

"Still, it is nice…" Katherine said more to herself than the others.

"Nice but not nearly as important as affection," Mrs. Higginbotham said. "Even a substantial fortune will not keep you warm at night."

Aunt Frances gasped. "Mrs. Higginbotham! I'll thank you to keep a civil tongue in your head."

"Miss Quince." Mrs. Higginbotham's eyes narrowed.

Celia winced. Louise looked up from her magazine. Katherine continued to study herself in the mirror, her brow furrowed in thought.

"If you have concerns about anything I might say," Mrs. Higginbotham began, "perhaps it would be best if I took my leave and left you to finish the difficult task of attempting to fit a dress obviously made for someone else to your niece's specific measurements."

Aunt Frances paled.

"What do you mean—not made for my measurements?" Katherine asked, her frown deepening.

"Nothing, dear," Aunt Frances said quickly. "The seamstress was…um…um… French, I believe. Which is why there are a few problems with the gown." She lowered her voice in a confidential manner. "Her grasp of the English language was not as good as one would hope it would be."

Celia stared. Aunt Frances was far quicker and much more clever than Celia had ever realized. If Aunt Guine-

vere and her friends were going to stop this wedding,
Katherine might not be their biggest obstacle.

"Furthermore," Mrs. Higginbotham continued, "if
your nieces are not aware of the more intimate aspects
of marriage—"

"Effie," Mrs. Fitzhew-Wellmore warned.

"—then you have obviously failed in your duties,"
Mrs. Higginbotham finished in a lofty manner.

Aunt Frances clasped her hands together. "My nieces
know everything it is appropriate for them to know as
properly bred young ladies."

"Then I would say it's going to be a most interesting wedding night," Mrs. Higginbotham said under her
breath.

Mrs. Fitzhew-Wellmore groaned. Louise snorted
back a laugh.

"Mrs. Higginbotham!" Aunt Frances snapped.

"Yes, Miss Quince?" Mrs. Higginbotham asked.

Aunt Frances stared at her then drew in a deep
breath. "While your candid manner of speech is not entirely my preference, your sewing skills are exceptional.
This gown is far beyond my own meager abilities. I
would be grateful if you—and Mrs. Fitzhew-Wellmore
of course—would continue to work your...*magic* to
make Katherine's dress as perfect as it can possibly
be." She summoned a tight smile. It obviously wasn't
easy for her. "Most grateful."

"Why, I can't think of anything we'd rather do than
to help make Katherine's wedding everything she's ever
wanted." Mrs. Higginbotham smiled in an overly pleasant manner. "And all that she deserves."

Day Four

CHAPTER TEN

"You want me to do what?" Gwen stared at the earl.

Edward chuckled. "You needn't look at me as if I've lost my mind."

"You're asking me to hide in a cupboard." What was the man thinking? "Rational people do not usually ask others to hide in a cupboard. Besides, I am already dressed for the ball—"

"And might I say you look lovely tonight."

She ignored him. "Guests will soon be arriving and I still have a few things to take care of. Miss Quince has decided her participation is no longer necessary, so everything has fallen to me and my dear friends, who may never forgive me. Organizing balls and weddings in a grand house with a staff of dozens is not something we do routinely, you know. It has been an exceptionally long and busy day. Myriad details still need to be attended to and I don't have time for nonsense."

"It's not nonsense and I'm not asking you to hide in a cupboard," Edward said patiently. "You're absolutely right, that would be mad."

Gwen narrowed her eyes. "Then what are you asking?"

"I have not explained this well." Edward strode across the library to the door concealed in the paneling he had indicated a moment ago. He pulled it open with a flourish. "As you can see, it's not a cupboard.

This is my private office and it is substantially bigger than a cupboard."

She peered around him. It was not as large as the library but was a good-sized room. A door on the far wall probably led to the hall or another room.

"Very well, it's not a cupboard." She crossed her arms over her chest. "And you're right, you have not explained this at all well."

"My apologies." He grinned. "It's not often I participate in subterfuge and clandestine endeavors. I find it rather exciting." He grimaced. "Which means my life has become extraordinarily dull of late."

"Would you please tell me what you are talking about?" Gwen hadn't stamped her foot in frustration since her girlhood but it was hard to resist doing so now.

"All I'm suggesting is that you stand in the office, on the other side of the door, which we will leave open a crack, so that you may hear what transpires."

"What is going to transpire and why do you want me to hear it?"

"Because it's your brilliant idea." He beamed.

"Which brilliant idea is that?" The day had been filled with countless minor difficulties. And each and every one did seem to require a solution that was at least clever if not brilliant.

"Why, convincing Katherine that Henry and I are on the brink of destitution so that she will call off the wedding of course."

"Oh, that brilliant idea." Gwen couldn't resist a smug smile. It was rather brilliant at that.

Effie and Poppy had begun what Effie insisted on calling a campaign yesterday by subtly mentioning gossip about Edward and Henry's financial instability. Today, as they decorated the ballroom, continued to fit

Katherine's wedding dress, discussed the menu for the wedding breakfast with the cook, arranged flowers and dealt with endless tiny details, all three ladies refused to speak further of rumors or gossip or innuendo. That in spite of pleas from Miss Quince and Katherine. Gwen thought it best not to tell Celia the truth about the alleged gossip. For one thing, she wasn't sure her niece was devious enough to carry on the charade. And for another, if Celia truly loved Henry, his fortune—or lack of it—would make no difference. Or at least it shouldn't. Far better to find out now if it did.

It was really quite amazing how very much could be said by saying hardly anything at all. And Gwen, Effie and Poppy's efforts were beginning to bear fruit. Miss Quince had a decidedly pinched look of worry about her and Katherine seemed at once preoccupied, concerned and annoyed. Which no doubt explained her fouler than usual mood and tendency to bite the head off all who came near her. Of course, Gwen and her friends were becoming a bit testy themselves. Spending part of every night in a chair in a corridor apparently did that to a person.

"And I am about to do my part. As I do think it will be a riveting performance—" he ushered her into the office "—I should like an audience of at least one. The play's the thing, you know, Gwen."

"I wouldn't quote Hamlet, Edward. He did not end well." She stepped over the threshold and into the office. "Do you really think this is necessary?"

"My dear Gwen, it's not only necessary." He cast her a wicked grin. "It's going to be fun."

"Oh, well, as long as it's going to be fun." She bit back a smile.

"You may sound chastising all you wish, but I would wager you are going to enjoy it."

"I'll enjoy it more if it works." She turned toward him. "Do you care to tell me exactly what you are planning?"

"Absolutely not. I think it would be best if you were surprised." He pulled the door closed, leaving it open no more than a crack. "And impressed."

She heard him move away from the door and settle in the chair behind his desk that creaked when he sat down. She waited for what was surely an hour but perhaps was less than a minute.

"When do you expect whatever this is to occur?" she called.

"Anytime now," he said in a normal tone.

She paused. "You're right. I can hear very well in here."

"I know."

"How do you know?"

He cleared his throat. "You're not the first person to have hidden there."

"I see." And wasn't that an interesting story? She waited another eternity then called again, "I should warn you, I intend to spread rumors about your finances at the ball tonight."

"Really? How delightful."

"Delightful?"

"In the past, rumors about me have been of a far more scandalous nature." She could hear the grin in his voice. "This will be mild in comparison."

A knock sounded at the library doors.

"Quiet," Edward said. "The curtain rises."

A frisson of excitement skated up Gwen's spine. Her life was extraordinarily dull, as well.

Gwen heard the door open.

"I beg your pardon, my lord," Edward's butler said. "Miss Bromley is here. She says you requested to speak with her."

"Indeed I did." The chair scraped against the floor as he rose to greet his guest. Katherine perhaps? "Please send her in, Jervis."

"Yes, my lord."

"And when my estate manager arrives, please show him in at once. He has papers I need to sign."

"Yes, my lord." Jervis hesitated. "This is entirely inappropriate, sir, but might I say something?"

"You've been with this family since my father was alive, Jervis, and I value your opinion. Please go on."

The butler's tone took on a confidential tenor but he lowered his voice only slightly. Gwen could hear him quite clearly, as could anyone standing behind him.

"I just wished to ask you if you're certain you need to take this step. Selling off much of the estate property strikes me as a drastic measure."

"I have given this a great deal of thought, Jervis." Edward heaved an overly dramatic sigh. "And it is a drastic step but one that cannot be helped, I'm afraid. Unfortunately, I fear it's just the beginning. We shall soon have to decide which of the staff we will be letting go but that can wait until after the wedding. These are desperate times."

Desperate times? Gwen stifled a laugh.

"I understand, sir." Jervis paused. "Should I show Miss Bromley in?"

"Yes, of course. Thank you, Jervis."

Gwen did wish she could see Edward's face but the angle of the nearly closed door did not permit it. A moment later she heard Katherine enter the room.

"Katherine, my dear, you have outdone yourself. I daresay I have never seen a creature as dazzling as you are tonight. My brother is a lucky man."

"Thank you, Edward." Caution sounded in Katherine's voice. "Your butler said you wished to speak to me on a matter of some importance."

"Yes, I do. Please sit down."

The rustle of skirts indicated Katherine settled in one of the chairs positioned before Edward's desk. Edward resumed his seat. He really should get that chair oiled.

"I should be speaking to your father about this but as you are soon to be a member of the family, I thought it best to discuss this with you directly."

"Is something amiss?" Katherine asked lightly.

"Oh, no, not really." Edward paused for a long moment. "I find it distasteful to discuss such matters. I have no wish to cast a shadow over the happiness of this week's wedding festivities. I'm not sure how to say this."

"Good Lord, Edward. Simply say what you have to say." Katherine's tone was a bit sharper than she had perhaps intended.

"Very well, then." Edward drew a deep breath. "When Henry said you and he were to be married, in spite of your father's financial difficulties, we both expected your dowry would be substantial. We understood dowries had been set aside for you and your sisters by your grandfather."

"It was most thoughtful of him."

"Indeed it was. Regrettably, the amount of your dowry is far less than we had hoped."

"It is somewhat modest," Katherine said slowly.

"Still, it may well cover the expenses incurred this

week for the ball and the wedding itself. Which is something to be grateful for at least."

"Is it?"

"Keeps the creditors away for another day." Edward uttered a harsh laugh. The man was a far better actor than Gwen had imagined. "After the wedding, however…"

"After the wedding?"

"After the wedding is a different story, I'm afraid." Edward blew a long breath. "You should be aware that Henry's fortune is, and always has been, tied inexorably to mine. And mine is…"

"Yes?"

"It's difficult for a man to admit his investments have not turned out as he hoped or that his debts are exceeding his assets."

"Bad investments, massive debt and insolvency," Katherine murmured.

"It's not quite to that point yet. Well, insolvency anyway. And I am taking steps to prevent bankruptcy," Edward added quickly. For a moment, Gwen almost believed him herself. "Selling off property, economizing, that sort of thing."

"Yes, I am familiar with that sort of thing," she said weakly.

"Excellent." Edward exhaled a sigh of relief. "I cannot tell you how pleased I am that Henry has found a bride well used to the modest circumstances we will soon find ourselves in. I say." His tone brightened. "Do you know how to cook?"

"Good Lord, no." Horror sounded in Katherine's voice. "We have always employed a cook."

Gwen pinched the skin between her thumb and first finger to keep from laughing.

"I shall have to ask your father how he manages it. After the wedding of course. No need to sully this festive occasion with practical matters like finance and impoverishment."

"No need at all," Katherine said faintly.

"I hear there's a woman in the village who can come in to cook once or twice a week. And I'm sure the three of us will manage quite nicely until our circumstances turn around. Which I am confident they will do. Eventually."

"But Henry and I will be living in Henry's house in London."

"I'm afraid London is out of the question."

"What do you mean?" A definite hint of panic edged Katherine's words.

"Oh, well, this is awkward."

"What's awkward?" Katherine's voice rose.

"Henry hasn't told you, then?"

"Told me what?"

"His house in London is not as much his as it is his family's." Edward sighed deeply. "That house, you see, along with my residence in London, as well as nearly everything else, will have to go. However—" his tone brightened "—we should be able to keep Danby Manor. For a while anyway. So good news, there."

"That is…good."

The chair groaned as Edward obviously got to his feet.

"I do hope I haven't upset you but I thought it best if everything was out in the open." He chuckled. "Wouldn't want any unexpected surprises after the wedding day."

"No, of course not…"

"Fortunately, as you and Henry are a love match, our

reduced financial circumstances will be nothing more than a bump in the road of your life together."

"A bump in the road," Katherine echoed then cleared her throat. "I believe our guests will be arriving shortly, so if that is all…" Her skirts rustled.

"I can't think of anything else. I must say, I'm glad you've taken this so well. Not everyone would, you know. And I can't tell you how delighted I am that my dear brother will have someone like you by his side throughout the difficult times ahead. For the rest of your days. Until you both breathe your last."

Goodness, that was a bit much. But Edward was right. This was fun.

"Perhaps you should retire until the guests arrive, Katherine. You're looking a bit pale."

"I believe I shall."

Gwen heard the library door open and close.

"You can come out now."

Gwen pushed open the door and stepped into the room. Edward stood by an open cabinet, disguised in the same manner as the door to his office, pouring two glasses of what looked like good Scottish whisky.

"A splendid performance, Edward, simply splendid." Gwen crossed the room and accepted a glass. "I'm assuming it was all an act."

"I assure you, Gwen, our finances are as sound as the Bank of England itself." He grinned. "I was good, wasn't I?"

"You were indeed. As was your butler." Gwen sipped her whisky and savored the intensity of the drink. It was an excellent quality. "Did you tell him what this was about?"

"I did need his cooperation and I do trust Jervis implicitly. Besides, as it turns out, Katherine has not endeared herself to the staff."

"Imagine my surprise." Gwen grinned. "My congratulations, Edward. Why, I almost believed you myself."

"That's good to know and I do thank you. But the more important question is—" he raised his glass "—did she?"

CHAPTER ELEVEN

IT WASN'T AS if this was her first ball. Celia had been to any number of balls before. Specifically, four such social events, which probably did not qualify as "any number." One was even in London, although admittedly the rest were country affairs, as was the ball tonight. But this was given by an earl. Certainly Father was a viscount but there was a vast difference between a nearly impoverished viscount and a wealthy earl. In this ballroom, liveried footmen carried trays of champagne, and a constantly replenished refreshment table offered bowls of fresh berries and platters of cakes and all manner of sweets and savories. And it did seem most of the people here were Lord So-and-So and Lady Such-and-Such and Sir Whateverhisnamewas. It was a most imposing gathering.

Aunt Guinevere, Mrs. Higginbotham and Mrs. Fitzhew-Wellmore knew a startling number of people and were apparently quite well connected. Between introductions from the ladies and those made by Edward, Celia must have met nearly everyone at the gathering.

Still, it was not as enjoyable as it might have been under other circumstances. The underlying purpose of the evening, after all, was to celebrate the upcoming nuptials of Henry and Katherine.

And then there were the rumors Celia overheard in passing. The offhand remarks she caught all evening about Henry and Edward's financial problems. She wondered if this was part of her aunt's plan to stop the wedding but when Celia mentioned it, Aunt Guinevere said she had more pressing matters to attend to than gossip. Which did seem to indicate Aunt Guinevere had something else in mind and the talk might well be true. Poor Edward. He really did need a nice, rich heiress. Perhaps Aunt Guinevere and her friends could find him one.

Celia's dance card had been given to her already filled with eligible men, as was Louise's. As the bride, Katherine's card was filled as well, mostly with older gentlemen, friends of Henry's family and the like. Katherine did not look pleased. Indeed, she appeared less and less the blushing bride and more and more vexed as the night wore on. Perhaps she, too, was hearing the rumors. Regardless, she kept a perfect smile plastered on her face. No one who did not know her well would have suspected she was anything but blissfully happy.

"I believe this is my dance," Henry said behind her.

Celia braced herself. She had noted Henry's name on her dance card and had protested to Aunt Guinevere. In spite of agreeing to one dance with him, upon further consideration, she thought it would be best not to tempt fate. It was increasingly difficult to spend any time with him at all without wanting more. But her aunt had said it would be extremely odd if the bride's sisters did not share a dance with the groom. Still, it did not strike Celia as a wise idea, although it did seem there was no choice. She adopted a polite expression and turned toward him.

Her smile faltered at the intense look in his eyes.

Henry nodded a bow. "You look lovely tonight, Celia."

"Thank you, Henry." Pleasure coursed through

her. The pale blue gown—flounced satin with lace-trimmed bodice and short, puffed sleeves that revealed her shoulders—was her very best and she did look well in it. Still, it was lovely to hear. Especially from him.

"I was afraid you intended to avoid me." He offered his arm.

She laid her hand lightly on his sleeve—steeling herself to the feel of his arm beneath her touch—and accompanied him onto the dance floor. "I did, but my aunt pointed out how curious it would appear if I did not share a dance with the man who will soon be my brother-in-law. I assume you are dancing with Louise, as well."

"I already have. It was quite…enlightening."

"Oh?"

"Apparently Louise is somewhat concerned as to my finances." He took her right hand in his left; his other hand rested on the small of her back. A shiver ran through her. She swallowed hard and carefully placed her left hand on his shoulder.

"Should she be?" she said absently, amazed that she could manage to say anything at all.

"No." Irritation sounded in his voice. "She mentioned hearing some sort of rumor."

There was something so horribly right about being in his embrace. As if she were made to fit perfectly against him. As if his arms should always be around her. She wondered that she didn't swoon at the feel of his body close to hers. Her heart fluttered hard in her chest.

"Have you heard anything?"

"What?" She stared up at him. "I am sorry. I'm obviously somewhat distracted and…well…"

"No, I'm the one who should apologize." His expression softened. "I shouldn't be talking about this. I daresay it's probably of no real significance."

"Goodness, Henry." She forced a lighthearted note into her voice. "If we are to have only one dance together, I should hate to ruin it with talk of gossip."

"You're right of course."

The music started and he gathered her a bit closer. Not so close as to violate the bounds of propriety but close enough that she could feel the heat of his body. See the rise and fall of his chest with every breath, smell the faint spicy scent of him. She'd never quite realized how terribly personal the simple act of sharing a waltz really was. This might be why it was once considered quite scandalous. Understandable, really, although the intimacy of it might well depend on with whom you were sharing that waltz.

Perhaps it was the strain of all that stretched between them, the weight of everything they would never say to each other. Everything they would never do. Perhaps it was the acknowledgment that this dance would be their first and their last. Or perhaps he was as afraid as she to say anything at all, afraid of what either of them might confess in an unguarded moment, but they danced together in silence. Silence heavy and fraught with longing and resignation. Apparently, if they weren't going to talk about gossip or financial problems, they weren't going to talk about anything at all.

"I am not an especially proficient dancer," Henry said finally.

"I think you're doing quite well."

"Edward is much better. You should dance with him."

"I believe his name is on my dance card," she said and again silence fell between them. This was far worse than anything she could have imagined. And it was absurd.

"I really don't think—" she began.

"This wasn't at all—" he said at the same time.

Her gaze locked with his and for a long moment they stared into each other's eyes. At last he grinned and she laughed.

"The last thing I expected was that this would be awkward." Henry shook his head.

"As did I." She paused. "Dare I ask what you did expect?"

"I don't know, really. Perhaps I thought…" He sighed. "I thought if I danced with you once, it would be enough to sustain me. I would not have the need to dance with you again. Or hold you again in my arms or—"

"Henry." She kept her voice light but her tone was firm. "This discussion does neither of us any good." Still… "And were you right?"

"Apparently not."

"Which only adds to the awkwardness," she murmured. For the briefest of moments, the thought flashed through her mind that perhaps Aunt Guinevere was right. Perhaps the sanctity of one's word could be sacrificed for the happiness of one's future. But it did seem to Celia that was a decision one had to make for oneself, no matter how much someone else longed to do so. She drew a steadying breath. "Come now, Henry, we are made of sterner stuff than to moan about those things that cannot be changed. We have accepted our fate and that is the end of it."

He studied her with amusement. "I suspect you would be a very good influence on me, Celia Bromley."

"And I suspect you are the last person who needs a good influence."

"I have been giving this, giving us—"

"There is no us."

"I realize that. Nonetheless, even you have to admit there is something—"

"Henry—"

"Please, Celia, allow me to continue. As I was saying, I have given our circumstances a great deal of thought. Indeed, I've thought of little else." He paused. "I think in the future it would be best if we avoided each other altogether, at least until whatever feelings we share have faded."

And wasn't that the saddest thing she'd ever heard? "I agree, although I should like to point out I was not the one who asked to dance with you."

A corner of his mouth quirked upward in a wry half smile. "It appears I am not as strong as I would wish when it comes to you."

The oddest lump formed in her throat.

"It shouldn't be difficult, really," he continued. "Katherine and I will either be in London or here at Danby Manor, whereas I imagine you will return to Bromwick Abbey."

"Actually, I won't be returning to the abbey. My aunt has invited me to come live with her in London and I think it's time—past time, really—that I moved beyond the borders of my very narrow life to see what the rest of the world entails."

His brow furrowed. "I see."

"As Katherine and I have never been especially fond of each other, I daresay I won't be invited to dinner regularly, if at all. And London is a very big place. I can't imagine we will stumble upon one another unexpectedly. I do, however, intend to find a new bookstore to frequent," she added quickly.

"That's probably for the best." He led her through an easy turn.

"I wish you would stop saying that," she said without thinking.

"Saying what?"

"That it's for the best." Her tone rang sharper than she had intended. "I have done what's for the best my entire life. But none of this feels *for the best*. In fact, it feels quite horrible."

His hand tightened around hers. "And yet, we agree, we have no choice."

"On the contrary, we have choices." She blew a frustrated breath. "They are simply very bad choices. The kind of choices neither of us would be able to live with. The kind that would surely, eventually, destroy us."

"As I said—" he smiled, a sad, wistful sort of smile "—we have no choice."

They continued on in silence, moving to the music without conscious effort, in perfect step with each other. As if they had danced together always. As if whatever wicked gods ruled this sort of thing were pointing out just how much they were losing. And no doubt laughing. Would this dance never end?

"I find the silence between us to be worse than when we are saying things that we shouldn't," she said at last and summoned a brilliant smile. "The weather is delightful for this time of year. Don't you agree?"

"I do indeed." He chuckled. "But I daresay we can find something fairly innocent to talk about besides weather." He paused. "Your aunt mentioned that your uncle is given to the pursuit of extraordinary adventures. If, as you said, you are to move beyond the borders of your life, do you foresee following your uncle's example and having extraordinary adventures?"

"Now you're teasing me."

Henry gasped in feigned indignation. "Me? Never!"

She ignored him. "No, of course I can't have extraordinary adventures like Uncle Charles. I am a woman, after all. I don't imagine I shall be exploring the jungles of Africa or searching for the remains of lost civilizations." She thought for a moment. "But I suspect if one seizes opportunities when they are presented, life itself can be an extraordinary adventure."

"Your aunt also said going down the road of life hand in hand with the one you love is an extraordinary adventure."

Celia stared up into his dark eyes. No matter how innocuous their conversations began, they always drifted into dangerous waters. "I imagine it is, Henry, I imagine it is."

Mercifully, the music finally drew to a close. She wanted—no, needed—to put distance between them. She stepped out of his arms at once, ignoring how incredibly difficult it was to do so. And ignoring as well the aching sense of loss sweeping through her.

"Celia." Her name was a plea on his lips. Or a prayer. A desperate sort of resignation shone in his eyes.

Her throat tightened. "I believe I see my next partner," she lied, peering around him. She clenched her fists and dug her nails into her palms. Any minute now, she would lose whatever self-control she still managed to cling to and dissolve into a whimpering puddle of sorrow right here in the middle of the ballroom. She summoned a bright smile. "If you will excuse me, Henry."

She nodded and started off, feeling his gaze following her every step. Hopefully, she would soon lose him in the crowd and the mild chaos that blossomed between every dance with couples either stepping off the floor or taking up new positions. Celia had no idea who her next partner was nor did she care. She had no desire to dance at the moment. She needed a few minutes of respite to compose herself.

And she needed air. She snapped open the fan that hung at her wrist. It was pointless. The room was overly hot and far too crowded and a feeble fan was of no good at all. Her blasted corset was probably too tight as well but then it always was. She made her way toward the terrace doors, propped open as a futile invitation to the fresh air outside.

She paused and looked back at the gathering. She didn't see Henry, which hopefully meant he didn't see her. She didn't want him following her onto a darkened terrace. No, all she wanted was a moment to breathe. A moment alone to come to grips with the deep wrenching feel of sorrow and loss that wrapped around her very soul.

And shattered her heart.

CHAPTER TWELVE

EVEN AS CELIA disappeared into the milling crowd, Henry's heart cracked with a pain that was almost physical. How could he let her walk away?

How could he do anything else?

He turned and wandered aimlessly through the crowd. He couldn't go back on his word but perhaps there was another way out of this marriage. Maybe he should simply be honest with Katherine. They'd barely talked at all since her arrival at Danby, at least not privately. She and her aunt had been far too busy with preparations for the wedding and he'd been too busy realizing what a fool he'd been. But wasn't it entirely possible that she, too, now understood what a mistake their marriage would be?

Henry spotted her about to dance with Mr. Jennings. Jennings owned a nearby estate and Henry had known the family all of his life. He made his way toward them.

"I beg your pardon, sir." Henry smiled. "But I have not danced with my fiancée all night, so I was hoping—"

"Quite right, my boy." The older man chuckled. "I am disappointed of course, but I know the way these things are."

"I, too, am disappointed." Katherine cast him a brilliant smile. "Another time perhaps."

"I shall look forward to it. She is all yours, Henry.

Miss Bromley." Jennings nodded a bow to Katherine and took his leave.

"Thank God," Katherine said with a sigh of relief. She stepped into his arms and they started into the dance. "I'm not sure I could take one more minute with yet another old letch who fancies himself a gift to women."

"Mr. Jennings was a very good friend of my father's," Henry said mildly.

"Regardless, I found him—I find all of them—to be dreadfully unappealing." She frowned and glanced around the ballroom. "There are a fair number of young suitable gentlemen here. Why is my dance card not filled with their names?"

"I have no idea, Katherine. I did not fill out your dance card, but perhaps it's because you are to be a bride in a few days and their dances are reserved for the more eligible ladies."

"I suppose." She huffed.

"Katherine," he began, "I've been wanting to talk to you."

"About what, Henry?" she said absently, her gaze still scanning the ballroom.

"I think everything has happened too quickly." He braced himself. "I think we should postpone the wedding."

Her gaze snapped to his. "What?"

"I wish to be perfectly honest with you."

Her eyes narrowed. "Go on."

"We barely know each other. And frankly, the more we are around one another, the more apparent it is that we do not suit."

She frowned. "Don't be absurd."

"I think our marriage is a mistake."

"Because we don't know each other well?" She scoffed. "Good Lord, Henry. Getting to know each other is what marriage is all about. Why, most people scarcely know more than each other's names when they marry."

"Regardless, I think two people who are about to be wed should have something in common. And I get the distinct feeling you don't particularly like me."

"Nonsense, Henry, of course I like you." She fluttered her lashes in a practiced manner. "Don't you like me?"

"I don't really know you."

"We're back to that again, are we?" She shrugged, managing to do so without so much as a tiny misstep. "I shall make you an excellent wife. You really don't need to know more than that."

"Even so—"

"You are everything I have ever wanted in a husband, Henry. Your family's name and reputation are impeccable. Oh, certainly, Edward had a bit of fun in his youth but nothing society hasn't already forgiven. Excellent breeding—quality—always shows. I couldn't hope for more. Best of all, your brother is an earl and at the moment you are his only heir."

Henry stared. "I do anticipate Edward will marry one day."

"Until then, you are next in line to be the Earl of Danby. And who knows what might happen in the future. If anything were to happen to—"

"Katherine!"

"God forbid." She sighed. "But the fact remains that you are next in line to be the earl. And if Edward doesn't marry and have an heir, our son would be the next earl. I should like to be a countess—that should come as no surprise to you. Barring that, I wouldn't at all mind being the mother of an earl."

Shock held his tongue. He had no idea what to say.

"In addition, you are rather handsome." She smiled pleasantly. "That will suffice for now. It is unfortunate about your finances—"

Henry frowned. "Have you been listening to gossip?"

She hesitated. "I have heard the rumors, of course."

"I assure you, nothing you've heard is even remotely accurate."

"Come now, Henry." She cast him a pitying look. "I spoke to Edward. He told me everything."

"Did he?" Henry said slowly. What was his brother up to? "What do you mean by 'everything'?"

She studied him closely for a moment. Her eyes widened with understanding. "You don't know everything, do you?" She shook her head. "Poor Henry. I never realized how difficult it must be to be the spare heir."

He ignored her. "I do not intend to discuss matters of finance with you in the middle of a dance floor or ever. Even as my wife, my finances, and my family's, are none of your concern."

"Very well." Her expression hardened. "But you did say you wished to be perfectly honest with me."

He nodded.

"In the interest of perfect honesty, then, on my part anyway, let me say this." A determined gleam shone in her green eyes. "Postponing this wedding is the first step toward canceling it altogether. I will not permit that. I much prefer to be the sister-in-law of an earl whose fortunes will surely reverse at some point than the daughter of a penniless viscount with no prospects whatsoever. If you are having second thoughts now, I would suggest it's not uncommon for a groom as his wedding day approaches and indeed is to be expected."

"I think this is a mistake."

"Then it is one we shall live with," she said sharply. "You asked my father for my hand, you asked me to marry you. I accepted you in all good faith. And I expect you to abide by your word."

He stared down at her. "Don't you want to be happy, Katherine?"

"My dear Henry." She smiled up at him, a wicked, nasty sort of smile, and his stomach turned. "I fully intend to be."

CHAPTER THIRTEEN

KATHERINE HAD AT least been perfectly honest.

Henry leaned against one of the gallery columns, a glass of whisky in his hand, and gazed unseeing at the crowd of friends and acquaintances. Everyone seemed to be having an excellent time. He doubted that aside from Ned and Celia, a single person here knew how very much the groom wished to cancel the wedding and how very determined the bride was to go through with it.

Henry now knew exactly where he stood with his bride-to-be. She had not only confirmed his suspicions but strengthened his desire not to marry her. Even if he'd never met Celia, this was a dreadful, horrible, irrevocable error in judgment. Something very much akin to panic simmered inside him.

Perhaps he and Celia should run off together. Go somewhere far away. Why not America? It did seem to offer considerable opportunity. Or anyplace where they could leave the past behind. But he would know he had broken his promise, and worse, *she* would know and she was right. Doing what they knew was wrong would eventually destroy them.

How could he possibly marry that woman?

How could he not?

Going back on his word went against everything he believed, everything he thought himself to be. Everything his father expected him to be. Ned was right. It was hard to be the good brother.

Had Ned heard the gossip about their finances? His brother really should be aware of that. And what on earth had he said to Katherine? Henry scanned the crowd but Ned was nowhere in sight. He signaled a passing footman.

"Have you seen his lordship, John?"

"Not recently, sir."

"Then where did you last see him?"

"He was stepping out onto the terrace." The young man paused. "But he was not alone."

"Of course not." Henry sighed and handed the footman his nearly empty glass. While Ned had accepted his responsibilities in recent years and put most of his scandalous ways behind him, he still could not resist an assignation with a lovely woman.

"It has been some time since then, sir," John added.

Henry nodded and started toward the open doors. A voice in the back of his head noted he had not seen Celia since their dance. He glanced around the ballroom but couldn't spot her pale blue gown. Perhaps she was simply out of sight. Or perhaps she had decided to retire for the night.

Or perhaps she was on the terrace with his brother?

Something vile and hard washed through him and his step quickened. How could Ned do this to him? Ned knew how Henry felt about Celia. Even if there was nothing Henry could do about it. Even if she was certainly free to be with someone else. Even if…

No, regardless of the circumstances, his brother would never attempt to seduce a woman Henry loved. His ire faded. Henry may well be the good brother but Ned was certainly not bad. A bit wayward perhaps. He'd always savored a good time and had never hesitated to break the rules of proper behavior. For the most part, that was in the past. Besides, if Henry trusted no one else in his life, he trusted his brother.

Of course, if Ned had encountered Celia and she was upset over her exchange with Henry, it was entirely possible Ned had tried to comfort her. Wrapped his arms around her as one might do to a friend in need. And if she then lifted her face to his, Ned might look into her remarkable blue eyes and forget—just for a moment—that Henry was in love with her. And he might lose himself in those eyes and press his lips to hers...

Absolutely not!

Ned was not so weak as that. Nor was he so thoughtless.

Henry stepped out onto the terrace and glanced around. There were several figures at the far end to his right. To his left, a flash of silk caught the starlight. Partially in the shadows, a female figure gazed out at the gardens. It might not be Celia but the closer he neared, the more certain he was that it was her.

"Celia?"

"Henry! What are you doing here?"

"Looking for you." He paused. "You're alone, then."

"Of course I'm alone. Although you would be surprised at how many people wander out on this terrace who are not alone and are obviously looking for more than just a breath of—"

Before he could stop himself, before he even realized what he was doing, he reached out, pulled her into his arms and pressed his lips to hers. She braced her hands on his chest and he thought she meant to push him away. Instead, her hands fisted in the fabric of his coat and she pulled him tighter against her.

For a long moment he savored the feel of her mouth, soft and yielding beneath his. He relished in the taste of her, of strawberries and champagne and sunshine. She clung to him and he lost himself in a haze of sensation and need. Surely this was how a man must feel when he was drowning, buffeted by forces beyond his control, helpless yet welcoming the oblivion.

He knew the moment she came to her senses. Her lips against his stilled and she pushed out of his arms.

"Good Lord, Henry, what are you thinking?"

"I don't know." He ran his hand through his hair. "I haven't been thinking since the moment I met you."

"Apparently not, as you asked my sister to marry you."

"True, but if I hadn't I never would have found you again." And wasn't that a point in his favor?

"And a lot of good that does us." Apparently not.

"I am well aware of that."

"You kissed me, Henry." She scowled at him as if he had done something truly horrible. When in fact it had been quite the most wonderful kiss of his entire life.

"I am aware of that, as well." He paused. "Might I point out you kissed me back?"

"No, you may not!"

"And I would wager you enjoyed it every bit as much as I did."

"That is beside the point." She blew a frustrated breath. "Apparently, I wasn't thinking, either."

"I do apologize." Although while he felt it necessary to apologize, he wasn't truly sorry. The memory of that kiss would have to last a lifetime. "I don't know what came over me." He shook his head. "I am not usually so impulsive, or impulsive at all, but I thought you were out here with Edward—"

"Edward?" She glared. "Why on earth would I be out here with Edward?"

"You wouldn't be the first," he said without thinking and immediately wished the words back.

She sucked in a sharp breath. "You thought I might be here with Edward for, well, the sorts of things everyone else seems to come out here for?"

"I didn't mean that the way it sounded."

"With your brother?" Her voice rose.

"No." He scoffed. "Of course not. Well, not really."

"I should hope not. I can assure you that if I was here with Edward, it would be for no other purpose than to indulge in a few moments of private conversation."

"I realize that." He hated the note of desperation in his voice but he couldn't seem to vanquish it. "It's just that Edward had said how wonderful you were and had mentioned that he might well be interested—"

"Good Lord!" Disbelief rang in her voice. "Are you both mad?"

"I don't know. It's possible, I suppose, but I doubt it." Although at the moment, madness was not a bad excuse. "He only said what he did to entice me into admitting how I felt about you."

"So you were jealous?"

He shrugged in a helpless manner.

"I see." She paused. "Was it like the dance, Henry? If you kissed me just once, it would be enough?"

"No, I—"

"It isn't, is it?"

"No."

"If anything, you've made it worse." She shook her head. "We cannot continue to say we aren't going to see each other and then do so whenever the opportunity presents itself."

"You're right, of course."

She drew a deep breath. "There cannot be a repeat of this."

He nodded. "I know."

"I want your word. Promise me this will not happen again."

He stared at her for a long moment. "I can't."

"And I cannot guarantee that I am able to keep my own feelings at bay." Her voice softened. "I never imagined something so very wrong would feel so very right."

"Celia, I—"

"But I cannot—I will not—allow this to happen again." Even in the faint starlight he could see determination in the set of her chin. "The only way to truly deal with temptation is to remove it entirely."

"What do you mean?" Fear clutched at his heart.

"As neither of us apparently has the strength of character necessary to manage our circumstances—" she heaved a resigned sigh "—as soon as possible, even before the wedding if it can be arranged, I intend to leave Danby to take up residence in London with my aunt. And…"

His breath caught. "And?"

"And I never want to see you again, Henry. I can't." She stepped toward the terrace door then paused. "It's for the best." She nodded and continued on her way, out of his life. Forever.

He stared after her. She was right, one dance, one kiss would never be enough with Celia. He was an idiot to have believed that for so much as an instant.

But then stupidity seemed to have become part of his nature of late. Since he'd met Celia, since he'd met Katherine, he'd done one ill-advised thing after another.

But the most insane act of all still lay ahead. And that he could do something about.

Resolve swept through him and he started toward the ballroom. If Ned hadn't yet come up with an idea to save Henry from this wedding, Henry would have to beg off. He was not going to sacrifice the rest of his life to a stupid mistake. After tonight, after everything Katherine had revealed, going through with the wedding would be absurd. Living with himself after going back on his word wouldn't be nearly as hard as living with Katherine. Celia might never understand but then he suspected he had already lost her. He would be miserable enough spending the rest of his life without her; he'd prefer not to compound that with a wife he couldn't abide. Father would have understood—once he met Katherine. Besides, his father never would have encouraged him to keep his commitment to a woman who was only interested in his family connections and his fortune. Father had a name for women like that.

Henry found Ned engaged in a lighthearted flirtation with a pretty red-haired lady. He caught his brother's gaze and indicated he needed to speak to him. A few minutes later Ned joined him in the library.

"What did you say to Katherine?" Henry asked without preamble, handing his brother a freshly poured glass of whisky.

Ned studied him coolly. "Are you certain you want to know?"

"Yes."

"You won't like it. It involves a certain amount of deceit and deception and outright lies."

"I am a desperate man, Ned. I am willing to accept anything that will save me."

"It might jeopardize your standing as the good brother."

"It's a risk I will take," Henry said wryly and sipped his whisky.

"So the good brother isn't quite as good as one might think." Ned grinned.

"Desperate times, Ned. Now, what have you done?"

"As we agree that one of the qualities your bride seems to appreciate most in you is the size of your banking accounts—"

Henry grimaced.

"—one can assume if you'd lost your fortune she would call off the wedding. So I simply led her to believe you were broke." Ned took a sip of whisky. "I told her we both were."

"Do you realize there are rampant rumors about that very thing?"

"Excellent." Ned grinned. "You can thank Mrs. Blodgett and her friends for that. It was their idea."

"Was it?"

"And a brilliant one at that." Ned chuckled.

"But it's a lie." Henry stared at his brother. "Unless there is something you're not telling me."

"I suspect there are all sorts of things I haven't told you." He flashed his brother an unrepentant grin. "Did you meet that lovely widow I was—"

"Ned!"

"Yes, I suppose that can wait. Although she's American and quite engaging… Not that it matters at the moment of course." He paused. "I realize you do not condone deceit, Henry. And for offending your overly honest sensibilities, I do apologize. However—" he raised his glass "—it was done in your best interest and regardless of what you might think, I will not tell

Katherine the truth. If this saves you from an unwanted marriage to that scheming witch—"

"It won't." Henry shook his head. "I spoke with Katherine earlier, hoping that she had realized what a mistake our marriage would be. It seems she is confident in your abilities to recover the family fortunes."

"Surely not." Ned stared in disbelief.

"Oh, yes. Furthermore, she doesn't seem to think that you will ever marry, which means eventually I, or my future son, will be the earl." Henry blew a long breath. "Apparently, she wants the position more than the money."

"Well, this is certainly an unexpected twist in the game." Ned thought for a moment. "We'll simply have to come up with something else."

"No, Ned." Henry shook his head. "I'm going to beg off. I can't marry her."

"You've never gone back on your word."

"Then this will be a first."

"I can't allow that." Ned shook his head. "For one thing—you'd never forgive yourself. For another—it takes a great deal of pressure off of me for you to be the good, honorable brother. I would hate to give that up."

"But—"

"I'll talk to Mrs. Blodgett." Ned's forehead furrowed in thought. "She's shockingly devious and somewhat diabolical. I find her delightful. Between the two of us, we'll come up with a new plan."

"I would much prefer Katherine be the one to end it." Henry considered his brother then nodded. "Very well. I'll give you until the day before the wedding, the day after tomorrow. But if you haven't thought of something by then, I'll break it off with Katherine. I won't add insult to injury by leaving her at the altar."

"Leave it to me, Henry. With Mrs. Blodgett's help, I'm certain we can think of something brilliant." He cast an affectionate smile at his brother. "And then you can be with Celia."

"Yes, well, I'm afraid I've mucked that up beyond repair."

"But I saw you dancing with her."

"I thought just one dance, one kiss, and we could go on with our lives as expected."

Ned's eyes widened. "You kissed her?"

"It was a stupid thing to do." Henry shrugged. "She never wants to see me again."

"She'll change her mind when you are a free man." Confidence rang in Ned's voice.

"Do you really think so?"

"Without question," Ned said firmly. "Refusing to see you again is what Celia believes to be the right thing to do. And at the moment it probably is. But she is an intelligent woman. Once you are no longer engaged to Katherine, Celia will realize that the reasons you can't be together no longer exist."

"Are you sure?" For the first time tonight, the smallest spark of hope flickered inside him.

"One can never be completely sure with women. They are odd, curious creatures who cannot be fully understood or predicted. Especially when they are in love. But with a bit of persistence and determination, I do think there's a very good chance that you can win her back." He met his brother's gaze directly. "I know you, Henry. You may well be able to eventually accept going back on your word but you'll never forgive yourself for not fighting for the woman you love."

Day Five

CHAPTER FOURTEEN

"I NEVER WOULD have imagined that we had it wrong." Gwen paced the width of the library, doing her best to avoid Edward, who paced the length.

"I must say, I don't like being wrong," Edward muttered. "It's not the first time of course, but I don't like it. My father never made mistakes. He was, well, infallible. The perfect earl, if you will."

Whose shoes were no doubt incredibly difficult to fill.

"Perfect or not, I daresay even an infallible earl would fail to suspect an ambitious female would be more interested in social position than in wealth." Gwen still found it difficult to believe that Katherine would choose social position over money.

"There has to be a way to maneuver the woman into throwing Henry over."

"But Katherine wants something that isn't entirely within her reach." Gwen pulled up short. "Good Lord, she is as much a gambler as her father. She's betting you will not have an heir other than Henry."

"Or she's wagering I'll die." He shuddered. "And sooner rather than later, I suspect."

"Perhaps we should be sitting outside your room at night?"

"Oh, would you, Gwen?" He cast her a wicked smile.

"Stop that, Edward." She choked back a laugh. "This is serious."

"I am serious."

"No wonder you have a less-than-spotless reputation."

"*Had* a less-than-spotless reputation," he said firmly. "I have reformed a great deal in recent years. Responsibilities of the position and all."

"Regardless, I have never met anyone as flirtatious as you."

"Thank you," he said in a most immodest manner. "It's a gift."

"Pity you haven't put that gift to better use. If you had found a wife, you might already have a son and heir, and Katherine would have no reason at all to marry Henry."

Edward stared. "That's it!"

"What's it?"

"If there was another heir, Katherine's hopes would be dashed."

"Yes, well, as clever as that is—" she rolled her gaze toward the ceiling "—you don't have a son and I doubt that you can come up with one by tomorrow."

"But when a man has the kind of reputation I had, it's not at all uncommon for a previously unknown heir to pop up."

"Edward—" she chose her words with care "—it's one thing to spread a few rumors about the state of your finances. Those will easily disperse when it's obvious your fortune is sound. But gossip about an heir will cling to you forever and cast doubts about your right to the title." She shook her head. "I don't think that's the least bit wise."

"Probably not." He thought for a moment. "Unless…"

"Dear Lord, I know I am going to regret asking." She braced herself. "Unless what?"

"Unless it's not my heir." A slow, satisfied grin spread across his face. "It's brilliant and it will work. I'm certain of it." He narrowed his eyes. "Katherine doesn't know anything at all about my family, does she?"

"I have no idea, although I suspect the only inquiries she might have made would have been about the size of your income." She drew her brows together. "I haven't noticed her taking any particular interest in Danby itself or asking about any of those endless portraits of ancestors you have hanging on the wall."

"Excellent." He beamed.

"Why?"

"You shall see. Just remember—" he chuckled "—the play's the thing."

The annoying man was certainly enjoying himself.

"Very well, Edward, as long as you remember, at the end of *Hamlet*—" she crossed her arms over her chest and met his gaze directly "—all the principal characters are dead."

Day Six

CHAPTER FIFTEEN

"HAS YOUR BROTHER told you what this is all about?" Mrs. Blodgett said quietly to Henry. Once again, she was seated beside him for luncheon.

"I'm afraid not." What was his brother up to now? "I would imagine this is all part of his plan."

A table had been set up out-of-doors under a billowing canopy some distance from the front drive. An unfamiliar carriage waited near the front entry.

"As no doubt is his insistence on having luncheon here." Her brow furrowed. "But why on the front lawns rather than the terrace? Although, with Danby in the background, it is rather scenic."

"All he said to me was that the day before my wedding was a special occasion. It should be spent under blue skies in front of our ancestral home."

"That's rather poetic of him."

"I know. I find it highly suspicious." Henry shook his head. "Ned instructed me to behave as normally as possible but also said I should keep my mouth shut, no matter what happened. That I should not question, deny or confirm. I should act as if I know absolutely nothing, which shouldn't be difficult as I know absolutely nothing."

"Oh, that doesn't bode well."

"Apparently, my brother doesn't think I'm particularly good at deceit."

Mrs. Blodgett cast him a worried look. "I do hope Edward is as clever as he thinks he is."

"My dear Mrs. Blodgett," Henry said drily. "Nobody could possibly be."

"He wouldn't give me any details but he is shockingly smug about whatever he has in mind. He did ask me to make certain everyone was in attendance." Mrs. Blodgett glanced down the long table. All those staying at Danby were here including Celia. "And he said I would know what to do when the time came."

"And will you?"

"I have no idea. I hope so." She frowned. "He does tend to be a bit theatrical but I do wish I knew exactly what he was planning. One does like to be prepared."

"Apparently, my brother has a great deal of confidence in you." He chuckled. "He describes you as diabolical, you know."

"Does he really?" She grinned. "How perfectly lovely of him. I quite like that." Her smile faded. "Edward also told me that if his plan doesn't work, you were prepared to do what was necessary."

He tightened his jaw. "I will."

"You know, Henry—" she laid a hand on his arm and looked into his eyes "—it's not dishonorable to go back on your word when abiding by it would cause more harm than good."

"Thank you, Mrs. Blodgett." He shrugged. "I keep telling myself that."

His gaze wandered to Celia. She had not once looked in his direction. When this was all over, when he was free…

"Who do you think that is?" Mrs. Higginbotham said from across the table. She peered around Henry for a better view of the house.

Everyone at the table turned and stared.

Ned stood on the front steps accompanied by a red-haired woman and a young boy. Was it the same woman his brother had met at the ball? The American? Henry clenched his teeth. This was not the most appropriate day for Ned to be engaged in a new flirtation. But why on earth would the woman have a child with her? Ned escorted them to the carriage and they exchanged a few words. At this distance it was impossible to tell if their conversation was amicable or merely polite.

Ned handed the woman and the boy into the carriage. He clasped his hands behind his back and watched as it drove away. Even from here, there looked to be a distinct edge of defeat about him.

"What is he doing?" Miss Quince asked.

"Well, he's watching the carriage drive off, obviously." Mrs. Higginbotham scoffed.

"He doesn't look at all happy," Mrs. Fitzhew-Wellmore said.

"No, he doesn't, does he?" Mrs. Blodgett cast Henry a pointed look.

Ned strode toward them looking remarkably ill at ease. Even distraught.

Henry got to his feet. "What is it, Ned?"

"I've just had some, well, disturbing news." Ned shook his head in a mournful manner.

Viscount Bromley stood up. "Would you prefer to be alone, Danby?"

"No, no, we're all to be family soon enough. You should hear this as it affects all of us." Ned heaved an overly dramatic sigh.

"What is this about, Edward?" A hard note edged Katherine's words.

"It's about…" Ned paused in the manner of a master storyteller. His gaze flicked to Henry's. "Charles."

"Charles?" Henry said without thinking.

Mrs. Fitzhew-Wellmore gasped. "Not your Charles, Gwen?"

"No, no, of course not." Mrs. Blodgett looked at Ned. "It isn't my Charles, is it?"

Ned stared. "You have a Charles?"

"Yes." Mrs. Blodgett huffed. "My husband's name is Charles."

"Oh. Sorry." Ned shook his head. "It's not that Charles."

"Then which Charles is it?" Louise asked.

"How many Charleses are there?" Mrs. Fitzhew-Wellmore's gaze skipped around the gathering as if she expected Charleses to come out from every corner.

"Apparently at least two. But the Charles I'm referring to is—" he slanted a quick look at Henry and sighed again "—our older brother."

Shocked gasps swept through the gathering except for Mrs. Blodgett, who—while looking as somber as possible—could not quite hide the twinkle of amusement in her eyes. Ned was right—she would know what to do when the time came.

"Ah, yes." Henry shook his head woefully, assuming that was the right thing to do. He might be the good brother but he was no less clever than his twin. Unless he was sadly mistaken, he had a fair idea of what Ned was doing. "Poor Charles."

"What older brother?" Katherine jumped to her feet. "You don't have an older brother."

"Not anymore." Ned sniffed back a tear.

Mrs. Blodgett choked then wiped her eye. Her dramatic bent was as pronounced as his brother's.

"Charles was five—'

Mrs. Blodgett cleared her throat. Ned was terrible at mathematics.

"—fifteen years our senior and left home more than a decade ago. He and father had a dreadful falling out. Father disowned him—or threatened to anyway. And Charles left, went to America. A few years later we heard he was dead."

"And was he?" Celia stared, fascinated.

Ned looked appropriately startled. "Well, yes."

"So who was that woman?" Louise looked every bit as fascinated as Celia.

"It appears..." Again Ned paused. He was getting very good at this. "That woman was Charles's wife."

Miss Quince clapped a hand to her cheek. "Surely not."

Ned shrugged. "I'm afraid so. She has all the appropriate documentation."

Katherine's face paled. "Then you're not—"

"The earl?" Ned shook his head. "Apparently it's the boy. That was—" he hesitated in the manner of an overly dramatic storyteller about to reveal a point of great importance "—Charles's son."

A sharp intake of breath sounded from nearly everyone at the table. Celia's gaze met Henry's, her eyes wide with shock.

"I don't believe you," Katherine said staunchly. "I've never heard of any brother."

"Come now, Katherine. It's understandable that they don't talk about him. He left under difficult circumstances," Mrs. Blodgett said coolly. "And he's dead."

"But..." Katherine's gaze darted from Ned to Henry and back. "But I saw you talking to that woman at the ball. You certainly didn't look like she was telling you anything of importance at all. In fact, it looked a great deal like you were engaged in a serious flirtation."

"And I was." He shook his head. "I found her most delightful. But I had no idea who she was. She didn't reveal her true identity until she arrived here today. With Charles's son." He swallowed hard. "The Earl of Danby."

For a long moment no one said a word.

"This is absurd and I have had quite enough." Katherine glared at Ned. "Edward, you are an idiot."

Ned stared. "I beg your pardon?"

"Katherine," Henry snapped. She was still his fiancée, after all. "I will not have you speaking to my brother in that manner."

She ignored him, directing her comments to Ned. "First, you lose all your money and now you've lost your title."

"Apparently he never really had it," Mrs. Higginbotham said in an aside to Mrs. Fitzhew-Wellmore.

"I want no part of any of this." Katherine turned to Henry. "Very well, Henry, you are pleasant enough, I suppose, but you're right. We do not suit. I was certainly willing to overlook that in light of your other excellent qualities but as those excellent qualities no longer exist— I agree. This marriage is a mistake. Furthermore, I have no desire to ever set eyes on you again. I assume you are agreeable to that and there shall be no overt fuss about this?"

"We shall put out that this was a mutual decision," Henry said. "There shall be no blame placed on either side."

"That's something, at any rate." She glanced at the viscount. "Father?"

"Yes, of course." The viscount hurried to his daughter's side and offered her his arm. He glanced at Ned. "We'll be leaving Danby as soon as possible."

Ned shrugged apologetically. "I think that's wise."

His lordship nodded. He and his oldest daughter started toward the house, Miss Quince, Louise and Celia trailing behind. Celia tossed a quick look over her shoulder at her aunt but Henry couldn't see her face. He had no idea what she was thinking.

They were almost to the door before anyone said a word.

"I should go after her, shouldn't I?" Henry said.

"What a lovely romantic impulse, Henry, but no." Mrs. Blodgett shook her head. "You should not. Give her some time to grasp all that's happened." She paused. "You do realize she doesn't know the truth about your finances or your—" she cleared her throat "—brother."

"Nor does she need to."

She shot him a hard look. "Don't make this a test, Henry. That sort of thing is prone to misinterpretation and never turns out well."

Heat rushed up his face. "No, of course not."

Mrs. Blodgett favored him with a sympathetic smile. "Well, no one expects you to be thinking clearly at the moment."

"I beg your pardon, my lord." Mrs. Fitzhew-Wellmore waved at Ned. "But Effie and I are a bit confused."

"There is no older brother Charles, is there?" Mrs. Higginbotham asked.

Ned grinned. "Not that I know of."

"I must congratulate you, Edward." Mrs. Blodgett smiled. "That was a brilliant performance."

"Thank you, Gwen. Although I must admit, it does seem rather a great pity." Ned grinned in an overly satisfied manner. "I would have made one hell of an actor."

CHAPTER SIXTEEN

"ALL THINGS CONSIDERED, my lord, this is probably for the best," Father said to Edward.

A scant half an hour after the revelation of a previously unknown heir, Celia, Henry and his brother, Aunt Guinevere and her friends gathered in the front entry to bid farewell to Celia's family. Katherine and Aunt Frances were already waiting in the carriage, obviously having no interest in further conversation. It was indeed for the best.

Louise leaned toward Celia and spoke quietly, for Celia's ears alone. "You're not dressed for traveling."

"No." She met her half sister's gaze firmly. "I'm not."

"How very interesting." Louise studied her thoughtfully.

"I am sorry this turned out as it did but it can't be helped, I suppose." Father cast Edward a sympathetic look. "Believe me, I understand how awkward this sort of thing can be. Although I have been fortunate enough not to have lost my title along with my fortune."

"Oh, I'll come up with something." Edward adopted a hopeful expression. "I always have."

"Good luck to you, then." Father glanced at his two younger daughters. "If the two of you are ready, we should be off."

Celia braced herself. "I am sorry, Father, but I'm not

going with you. I've decided to return to London to live with Aunt Guinevere."

Father snorted. "You'll do no such thing."

"I am an adult, Father. I can do as I please."

"You are still my daughter and as your father you will do as I say."

"On the contrary, Alfred." Aunt Guinevere stepped forward. "According to my solicitor, if Celia does not reside where I think is best, a family trust—my family's trust—that she will get a portion of at a specific age will not be allotted to her. I think her financial future is much more important than your obviously heartfelt desire to keep her at home."

"I've never heard anything about a family trust." Suspicion drew his brows together.

"Really?" Aunt Guinevere adopted an innocent expression. "I can't imagine my sister wasn't aware of it."

"She never said anything to me about a trust." His eyes narrowed. "Why is it up to you to decide where Celia lives?"

Aunt Guinevere shrugged as if the answer was obvious. "I am the oldest surviving daughter."

Father glared. "And if Celia doesn't live where you wish, she won't get her share?"

"I believe that's what I just said." Aunt Guinevere smiled pleasantly.

"Very well, apparently I have no choice," he said sharply. "And I suppose it's one less female underfoot. Celia." He turned to his daughter. "I hope you know I have always cared for you. I'm simply inept when it comes to any number of relatively important matters. I do apologize for that."

Celia's throat tightened. "There's nothing to apologize for."

"Thank you, my dear. I shall try to get to London to visit you on occasion and you will always have a place at the abbey." Father cast her an affectionate smile. "And I do expect you to write."

"I will." Celia nodded.

Father turned to Louise. "Come along, then. We should be off."

Louise favored Celia with a surprisingly genuine smile and started out the door.

Father followed after Louise, pausing as he passed Aunt Guinevere. "I don't trust you for a moment, you bloody witch. Take care of my girl." He nodded at Celia then took his leave, Henry and Edward escorting him out the door.

Celia stared at the open doorway and blinked away what might possibly have been a tear. What on earth was happening to her? This was at least the second time this week that tears had filled her eyes.

She inclined her head to the side and lowered her voice. "There is no family trust, is there, Aunt Guinevere?"

"Oh, if only there was, dear." She paused. "I'm quite proud of you, you know."

"I'm rather proud of myself," Celia said with a shaky smile. "That was far more difficult than I had imagined."

"That, my dear girl, was easy compared to this." Her aunt nodded toward Henry and Edward coming back into the house. A footman closed the doors behind them. "Men are not as intelligent as we allow them to think they are. However, the right man is worth a great deal of trouble."

"I told him I never wanted to see him again." *Right after he kissed me. Right after I kissed him back. Right after I knew I would never be the same again.* "I was quite adamant about it."

"You thought you were doing the right thing—the noble thing. No one can fault you for that. I daresay men change their minds as much if not more than we do. But one of the benefits of being female is that, as a woman, you are practically expected to change your mind." Aunt Guinevere glanced at Henry. "After a proper amount of heartfelt persuasion, of course."

"Celia." Henry stepped toward her. Her heart sped up. "Might I have a moment?"

Celia hesitated. She had no idea what to say to him. "Henry, I—"

"As much as I hate to interrupt," Edward said, "you should know, none of this was Henry's idea. He had nothing to do with any of it."

It occurred to Celia to ask "Any of what?" but at the moment she didn't care. She met Henry's gaze. "Go on."

"It appears I am not to be married to Katherine, after all." His gaze bored into hers, intense and determined, and something very much like joy swept through her.

"It does appear that way." She was almost afraid to breathe.

"So it strikes me that I now have the opportunity for an extraordinary adventure." He held out his hand to her. "Will you join me?"

"For an extraordinary adventure?" She placed her hand in his. "I would be a fool to miss it."

"For God's sake, Henry." Edward groaned. "Kiss the girl."

Henry grinned, pulled her into his arms and pressed his lips to hers. And any doubt, any misgivings, any hesitation was dashed aside by the warmth of his lips on hers and the delight of his arms around her and the bliss of knowing she was where she belonged. This was right and perfect and exactly as it should be.

Celia barely noticed Aunt Guinevere's voice. "I think this ended well."

"And I must say I enjoyed it," Mrs. Higginbotham added. "It's very nearly as much fun to separate a couple that shouldn't be together as it is to match a couple that should."

"We should keep that in mind," Mrs. Fitzhew-Wellmore said.

"Should we ever find ourselves in this sort of situation again. Not that we would…"

Dimly, in what sounded like a vast distance away, she heard her aunt and the other ladies agree Celia and Henry should head for Scotland immediately, where they could marry without delay. And she heard Edward say something that sounded like he was coming as well and it was mentioned that there were guests expecting a wedding tomorrow to be dealt with…

And none of it mattered.

This was just the beginning of the adventure of walking a road together hand in hand.

And it would indeed be extraordinary.

The End

Get 2 Free Books,
<u>Plus</u> 2 Free Gifts -
just for trying the *Reader Service!*

STRS17R